MISSING YOU

Book 3 of the Revd. Anna Maybury Series

Kirsty A. Wilmott

BEAR PRESS

© Kirsty A. Wilmott 2023

All rights reserved

Kirsty A. Wilmott has asserted her moral right
to be identified as the author of this work

ISBN
Hardback: 978-1739-636722
Softcover: 978-1739-636739
eBook: 978-1739-636746

A CIP record for this book is available
from the British Library

For Bear Press
Development: Jutta Mackwell
Editor: Bridget Scrannage
Editor: Ann Peacocke
Art Director: Sarah Joy

Cover Image
Kilcobben Cove
© Geoff Squibb 2023

Set in 11/15pt PT Serif

1v01

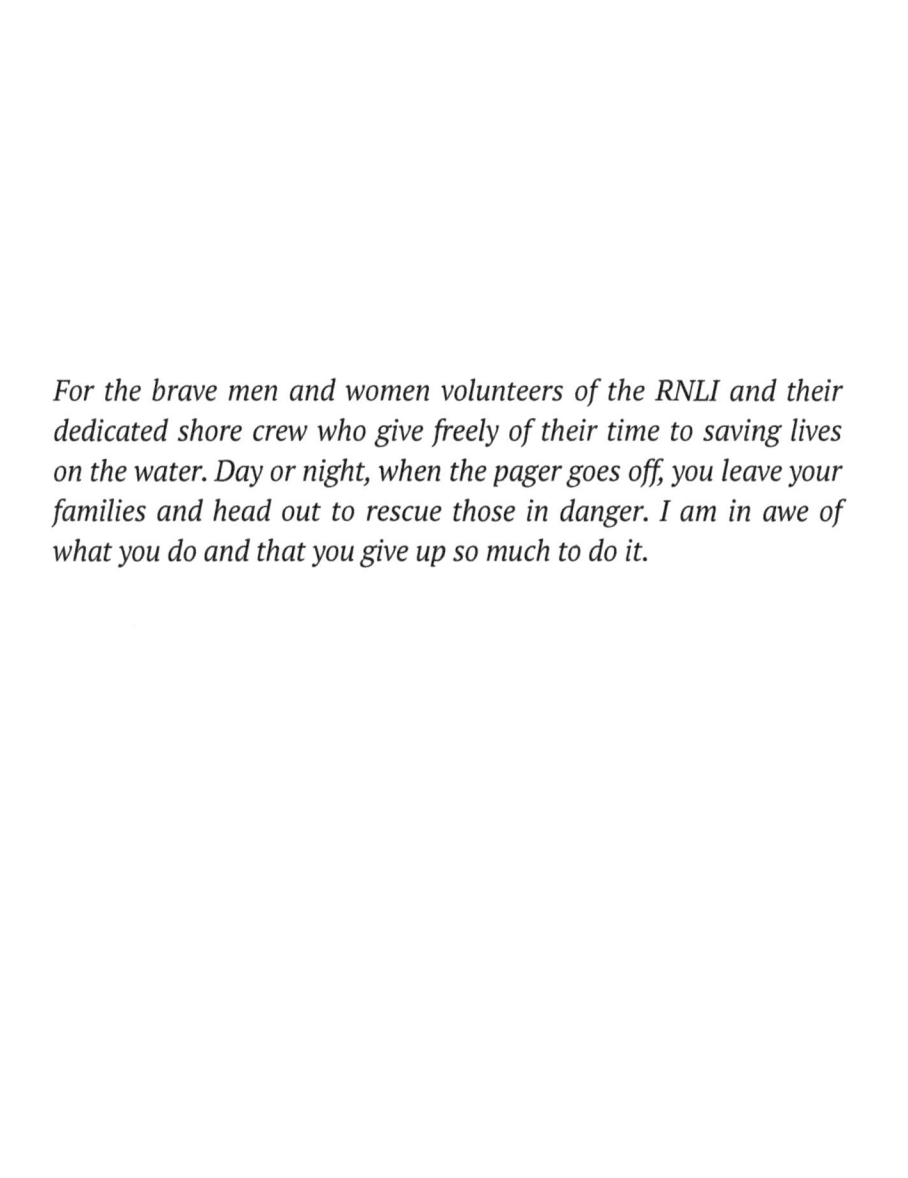

For the brave men and women volunteers of the RNLI and their dedicated shore crew who give freely of their time to saving lives on the water. Day or night, when the pager goes off, you leave your families and head out to rescue those in danger. I am in awe of what you do and that you give up so much to do it.

The Lizard, Cornwall

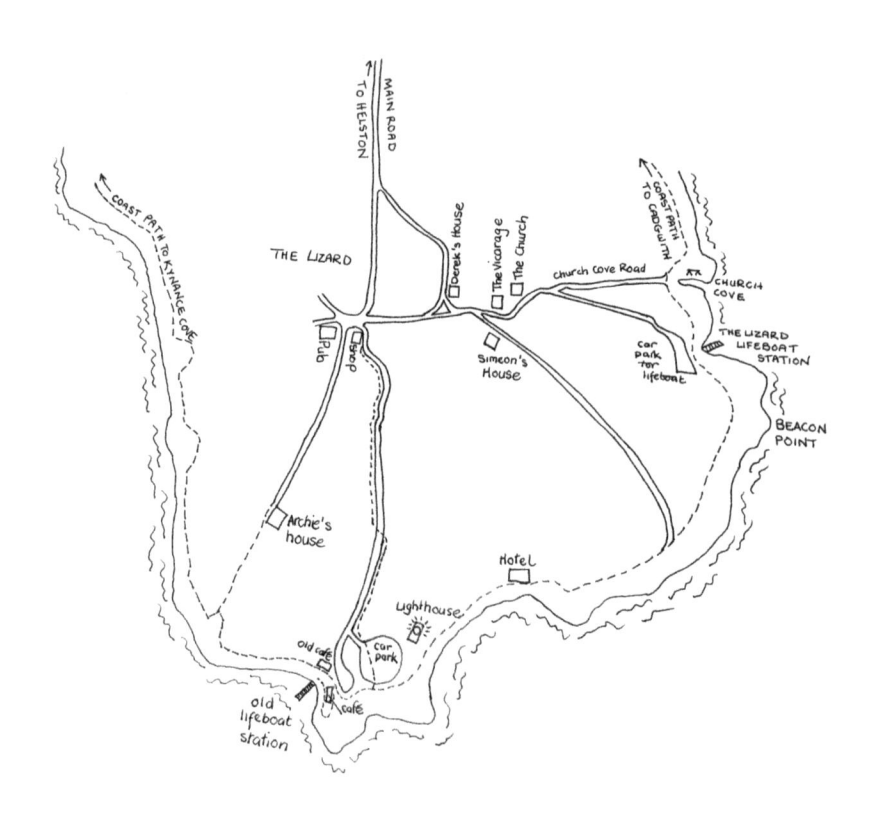

Characters

Reverend Anna Maybury – Vicar of The Lizard Village.

Archie Wainwright – Churchwarden; retired Navy.

Caroline (Caz) Denbigh – Lifeboat volunteer.

Catherine Edwards – DI Tom Edwards' Mum; recently moved to the village.

Derek Harris – Retired architect; partner to Harriet.

Genni Rowe – Lifeboat volunteer; primary school teacher; lives in Mullion.

Georgie Harbrook – Youth worker in Exeter.

Gerald Denbigh – Caz's dad; retired Met Officer.

Harriet Williams – Derek's partner; helps out with the church retreats.

Jean Roebuck – A parishioner; runs the local shop.

Jim Andrews – Lifeboat coxswain; works at the local garage.

Margery Andrews – Wife of Jim; works in Helston.

Phil Mattock – Landlord of the local pub.

Simeon Tyler – A parishioner; adopted a dog called Belle.

Toby Andrews – Lifeboat volunteer; a baker; son of Margery and Jim.

Detective Inspector Tom Edwards – Lives and works in Falmouth.

Chapter 1

Anna picked up the snow globe and shook it. The tiny orange lifeboat sitting on its plastic waves disappeared in a sparkly cloud, a miniature tornado engulfing the small craft. It made Anna shiver, for it depicted a reality that terrified her. She loved the sea, living near it, being able to hear it and taste it from her own front door. She appreciated its changing moods and powerful beauty but only from the safety of the land, The Lizard, unmoving and solid beneath her feet. Harriet, sitting opposite, had pushed the brown paper bag across to her, suppressing a smile.

"Ha ha very funny!" Anna had said, as she'd tipped her present onto the table. Old, and a little chipped around the edges, but its red Formica was a welcome splash of colour in the vicarage kitchen.

Anna had been asked to go and bless the lifeboat. The crew, what they did, what they represented, mattered on The Lizard. For Anna it was a big deal.

"I thought it would remind you of the moment."

"It's just a blessing." Anna took a sip of tea, also trying not to smile.

"Under the bow of the great *Rose*."

Anna knew that she'd started to grin. She couldn't help herself.

"I know," she said. "Jim will take me beyond the 'crew only' door and out onto the ramp. It does feel like a big step."

"He should have asked you before. You're an important part of life here. So much more so than you realise, or he gives you credit for."

Anna felt herself blush a little, as she tucked a strand of fair hair behind her ear.

"I'll have to say something original, something relevant, though he said I shouldn't go on too long. I don't want to appear out of touch."

Harriet laughed. Anna didn't really want to ask her why. There could be any number of reasons, for Harriet knew her well.

"Just be yourself. You don't need to prove anything to any of them. Especially not Jim."

Anna acknowledged this with a tip of her head, but she knew that being yourself was harder than it looked, particularly when she was being judged by a group of people she was in awe of. People who headed out to sea when the rest of the world was hightailing it back to shore, which didn't make them ordinary people at all.

"Do you think Tom would come, as it's going to be down in the station itself?" Anna asked. "I mean, as it's not at church."

"He might."

"Do you think I should ask him?"

"If you would like him to be there."

Anna was unsure. If she was trying to impress Jim and his crew, knowing that Tom was at the back listening, watching her do her God-thing, might send her stress levels through the roof.

"He probably won't be able to make it; there'll be a nasty murder to solve over in Falmouth."

Harriet shrugged. Anna felt the immediate relief of his absence and then an overwhelming disappointment at his … well, at his absence. Then the absurdity of it all, because she probably wouldn't get around to asking him.

Harriet rubbed at a speck of paint on her wrist.

"I ought to get back and do a bit more skirting before Derek decides he wants a different colour."

"Or you could stay and have another coffee. You haven't told me about the utility room saga. You did promise."

"Anna, I can't decide if you're the kindest woman in the world or if there's something you ought to be getting on with."

Anna was up and filling the kettle before Harriet could change her mind. She definitely wasn't the kindest person in the world. Harriet had, as usual, put her finger on it. Anna was putting off writing her sermon for the following Sunday, and a difficult visit to one of her parishioners. She didn't want to do either, and sitting there, in her kitchen, with Harriet, was preferable, by a country mile.

***

Toby caught the line with the hook and began to haul it in. Genni was waiting on the other side. Once they'd secured both ropes over the cleats, the swell lifted the boat and he tensed. It felt as if the hull would slam down onto the ramp, but his dad had done this a thousand times, the throttle opening just a little to keep *Rose* clear. The winch began to wind them in. With the gentlest of bumps the lifeboat hull grounded. There was a narrow gully for the keel, so hardly any leeway at all. Toby always thought it should be impossible to hit the right spot, but up she went, the cable singing with the weight of her. He stared at it, mesmerised until Genni started to laugh at something Caz had shouted from along the deck. He turned away to watch the sea drop back behind them. It was still light but not for long. His dad had gone around and around again, to practise the rescue. Caz had been the body in the water and even in the dry suit she'd got cold. They should really have used 'Dead Fred', the weighted dummy, but Jim hadn't suggested it, so no one mentioned the fact that it wasn't exactly protocol. Caz was chatting to Genni with a mug of tea in her hand, her short dark hair plastered flat about her face. When the tipping cradle at the top gently brought *Rose* to the horizontal he made his way back to the stern. He knew the lads would be itching to get to the pub, but everyone stayed for the tidy-up. They wouldn't dare miss a job, not with Jim watching them. If his dad thought for half a second something wasn't done properly, then it would have to be done again and no one went home until he was satisfied.

Growing up, Toby had always wondered what it would be like crewing for his dad; it had made him hesitate for quite some time before volunteering. He'd quickly discovered it wasn't any different from being at home, except for calling his dad "Jim". Jim yelled at Toby just like he yelled at the others, just a little more frequently, or so it seemed. Toby had learnt to ignore the sympathetic looks when he received a particular bollocking, or when his dad got a bit personal. Mostly, he was just one of the lads.

Genni was rota'd to finish up, make sure all was ready for the next shout, to be the last to leave but when Jim began the jog to the top, Genni was at the door with her coat on.

"I thought it was your turn?" Toby asked, quietly.

She shrugged, her face creasing into a grin.

"Caz said she was happy to do it. Said there were a couple of things she wanted to go over for her final test."

"You know Dad doesn't like people messing with the rota for no good reason," Toby muttered. His dad liked everyone to share the load and more to the point, to do as they were told.

"I know, but you don't have to tell him, and no one else seems to have noticed. I thought you'd be pleased."

"I am," Toby said, but he wasn't really. Being a *couple* after practice wasn't always easy, particularly if Caz was missing. Genni would want to stand next to him, and the guys couldn't be themselves. He couldn't be himself. It was a little annoying.

"You don't sound as if you are," Genni said. "So, I might as well get an early night, I've still got some prep to do for school tomorrow."

"Alright. Wouldn't want the darlings to get less than one hundred percent of your time and effort."

"You're a sarky sod, and they're not babies. Year three, remember," she replied, smiling again. That was the thing about Genni, she never took offence and was happy to go along with everything. The wedding would be a breeze, and a good excuse for a party. Genni climbed into her lime green Fiat, flashed her lights once and drove away. She'd saved for years to get that car, but Toby thought it was ridiculous and when they were married, there was no way he was ever going to be comfortable driving it.

***

As it turned out, Tom hadn't gone down to the lifeboat station with Anna; he'd made some excuse about needing a walk. Now he was waiting at the top of the stairs for her to return. Truthfully, he was still uncomfortable when she did this sort of thing — a service of blessing for the crew of the lifeboat. He did however feel a bit mean because she'd been so excited that they'd finally asked her back, after she'd opened some fundraiser the summer before. Tom wasn't surprised at the invite — the lifeboat crew were a superstitious bunch; a bit like coppers. Having the local vicar on board, literally and metaphorically, would be important to them.

"Is it like naming a boat? Do you break a bottle of something over the bow?" he'd asked, "Perhaps holy water…"

"Oh, Tom. I'm not exorcising a vampire. I'm simply asking God to bless them, what with all the dangerous things these men do."

"Men *and* women, surely," he'd replied.

Anna had simply stated, tucking her hair behind her ear, "There are a few women volunteers." She'd shivered at this point. "I couldn't do what they do for a million pounds." He'd laughed at her, which had made her face crumple a little, which had made him wrap his arms around her. She was right, he couldn't for one second imagine her donning wellingtons and a life preserver, to roar down the ramp into a restless sea.

Now it was Tom's turn to shiver. Soon it would get chilly, and as per usual, Anna was late. The waves were flat, almost dark green. They looked as if they were heavy with algae. There was a gentle scent of gorse, the yellow flowers speckling the bushes along the path. Bright dots in the dimness as the sun began to dip below the headland behind him. The lifeboat station was a long way down. The steps were steep, more than one hundred and seventy. Tom had counted them, not like

Simeon of course. Simeon counted things to root himself back in the world. Tom counted things to see how many there were. He leaned on the rail and peered down. Even if he could see her at the bottom, it would still be a bit of a wait, as it took ages to climb back up, unless the crew took pity and let her use the funicular. Members of the public weren't usually allowed. It was for equipment, or if they'd had a particularly rough shout. But perhaps being the blesser-of and prayer-for the lifeboat *Rose*, would mean Anna would be granted a special dispensation.

He stamped his feet and shivered again, squashing his fingers down into his pockets. There was a whirr of wires, tension pinging along the cable as the cage below him began to rise. He stepped away. After a while he could see her waving, her smile wide, even through the mesh. Around her stood the gang, Simeon, Archie, Harriet and Derek. He shook his head. Now he would have to face the onslaught of kind words, and sad looks, because he'd chosen to go along the cliffs rather than support Anna, in her strange and wonderful calling.

"Tom, did you have a good walk?" Anna called, as she stepped out. She caught his hand. "You're cold. Don't you have any gloves with you?" It was unusual for her to show such affection in front of the others. It bemused him slightly, but he took heart from it, that she was finally settling into the relationship. She ought to be by now, they'd been *giving it a go* for well over a year. Almost as if she'd guessed what he was thinking, Anna stepped back, drawing away a little.

"Did it go well?" Tom asked.

"It did," Archie said, nodding. Tom realised then that the lifeboat crew had allowed them to use the lift because of Archie. Being seventy, having a new stent, and being an ex-lifeboat man had to count for something. Tom thought Archie looked a lot older, as if suddenly his age had caught up with him. His cropped grey hair seemed sparse rather than neat and his cheeks a little sunken. Mind you, he still stood tall and straight. Slouching wasn't part of his makeup. Tom stood up a little straighter, too.

Anna said brightly, "Genni told me all about tying knots and what they're used for. Jim makes them practise a lot, tests them all the time. She reckons she can tell which member of the crew has tied which one by sight."

Tom nodded but it sounded a little boring. A knot was a knot.

Simeon began to edge away. He'd left Belle, his labrador, at home, and he was never completely happy away from her. Reluctantly, he said, "Hello, Tom. You should have come down. Even if the service made you uncomfortable, the station itself is very interesting."

"It wasn't that," Tom said, even though it was. He was used to Simeon's directness; used to him speaking from underneath his parka hood, oversized and pulled down so all you could see was his chin. Tom was also used to Simeon addressing his feet, or if he knew you particularly well, your knees. "I've been doing paperwork for a week. I needed to stretch my legs." Simeon tilted his head to one side and raised his eyes from Tom's shoes right up to his chest. He didn't look any further, but Tom was gratified he'd got that far. It made him say, "But you're right. I haven't been for a while. Perhaps I'll pop down on one of their open days."

"Let me know," said Archie, "I'll show you around."

Tom nodded, even though he knew he wouldn't do any such thing. They began to make their way along the track to the lane leading up from the cove. Harriet slotted in beside them.

"No juicy murders this week?"

He frowned at her. He was never quite sure if she was getting at him. She often was.

"That's a good thing," Anna said, quickly. She didn't like it when Harriet teased Tom. He knew she would feel caught between them. Still, it was nice that she had intervened. It made him feel comforted, hopeful, drawn into the circle. "I'd really much rather you were bored and chained to your desk, than racing around the county chasing bad guys."

"Of course you would, Anna." Harriet smiled, her face crinkling all the way up to her eyes. It made Anna shrug her shoulders, as if they were finishing off a conversation from earlier. They probably were.

"No chance of being bored," Tom replied. "But it is good to get home early for a change." *Now that I've got something to do with my time,* he would have liked to add, except he didn't want to see Harriet's knowing look or to make Anna glow pink with embarrassment.

At the end of the lane Harriet and Derek turned down to the cove. Their new house was just around the corner. It was still a bit of a building site, but liveable. Archie and Simeon, who'd been deep in conversation, strode up towards the church. At the corner they turned back to wave. Tom was relieved. Sometimes, one or the other of them would invite themselves back to the vicarage for a chat, but now Tom was finally able to reach for Anna's hand. It was warm inside his, her small fingers holding on tightly.

"You'll stay won't you?" she asked, a worried frown wrinkling her forehead, her dark eyes, with pale lashes were open, questioning. There was something about her that drew him in each and every time she looked at him. He smoothed away the lines with a fingertip.

"And miss fish and chip Friday! Not on your life."

Chapter 2

Anna yawned. Tom hadn't left until the early hours, which would have been silly if he'd been heading back to his flat in Falmouth. Nowadays, if he didn't have to go to work the following morning, he slipped up to his mother's. Catherine had bought one of the older cottages in the centre of the village, where she'd quickly settled in. Tom had been worried she wouldn't find enough things to do. Anna still laughed at the thought. Catherine was a natural, already in the coffee morning cabal, on merit rather than because she wore a dog collar, on the church cleaning rota, and was planning to set up a book group. She'd even worked in the shop once or twice, when Jean had had to race off for some emergency baby-sitting, up in Helston. Catherine had quickly become part of them, and Anna knew, with the tiniest pang of jealousy, that she was often invited back to Archie's for a cup of tea and a chat. So much so that Anna couldn't remember the last time she, herself, had been asked.

Anna was running out of coffee. Rummaging through the cupboard she pulled out a new bag. She couldn't be bothered to reach for the scissors so wasn't really surprised when it split, half spilling onto the floor, the other half across the counter.

"Bugger," she said out loud, a little half-heartedly. She was tired and still a bit disappointed that Tom hadn't come down to the lifeboat with them; however, he had stayed until she'd fallen asleep, watching some old movie he'd said was a classic.

Anna had hoped to wake up early. She needed to finish off her sermon, to get it done before Tom came back. 'Finish off' was a little euphemistic. She'd had an idea and hoped it would flow from that and she hadn't woken early, because she hadn't set the alarm. Of course she hadn't.

The kitchen was a mess. She began piling the dirty plates into the dishwasher. Breakfast would be nice, but she really needed to get to grips with her idea. She was pouring coffee when the doorbell rang. Derek had installed a new one that reverberated around the house so there was no excuse for missing it. It could also disturb the rooks along the lane and certainly made her jump. She must ask him if it was possible to tone it down a bit.

Anna dutifully checked her appearance in the hall mirror which Harriet had hung, for that very purpose. She looked a little paler than she would like, and there were lines under her eyes that wouldn't rub away. Too many late nights, trying to cram in a boyfriend alongside the day job. A job that spilled over into the precious moments that she would have liked to call her own. She'd had her fair, straight hair chopped again recently, so that it was neat and tidy but after she'd slept on it one side was flat and the other side stuck out in odd directions. She sighed and tucked it behind her ear.

The young woman on the doorstep was small. She had very short dark hair with a long fringe, naturally wavy so that even after a rough night it would look as if it was meant to be that way.

"Hello, Reverend."

Anna usually hated this bit. Everyone knew who she was, felt able to pop in whenever they wanted to, while she would have to spend an excruciating ten minutes trying to work out where they'd met before. This young woman was easy.

"I was down at the lifeboat yesterday. I'm Caz."

"Of course." Anna had actually spent quite a bit of time talking to the other young woman, Genni, about her upcoming wedding. Caz had been on the boat deck doing things with a rope. Anna had only managed to smile at her, after she'd caught her eye. The exchanged glance was no more than that, as Caz had quickly looked away.

"Come on in. I've just made coffee. Would you like a cup?"

"Yes, please. I have to go down to the station, but I've got half an hour." Anna began to feel a little annoyed. It felt as if

Caz was doing her a favour, as if she'd completely discounted the fact that it was she who'd decided to call. Anna showed her into the large front room. It still looked a little dishevelled from the last retreat. Harriet had offered to have a tidy round, but Anna had wanted the house back. Four ladies from Catherine's old church had come for the week, in a rather nice Volvo. It had been more of a sightseeing tour than time out with God. They were obviously checking that Catherine was alright, that her move away from them hadn't been a terrible mistake. It had meant that apart from the meals, morning and evening prayer, Anna hadn't had a lot to do. Archie had. They'd taken a shine to him, particularly after the first night's meditation. Catherine had been a little uncomfortable that he had been so embarrassed at all the attention. Four single ladies making sure he was taking note and quizzing him on his life. They'd gathered him up and, by the Wednesday, he'd been joining them on their walks around The Lizard.

Anna almost had to pinch herself. She needed to concentrate on the present moment. She left Caz trying to find a comfortable chair while she went to fetch the coffee.

"So, Caz, what can I do for you?" Anna finally asked, settling back onto the sofa. The sun disappeared around the corner of the vicarage leaving the room feeling dull, and chilly. Caz was sitting on the edge of one of the single chairs, upright and clearly not relaxed. Anna thought she seemed nervous, her fingers, lying in her lap, looked tight with tension. Anna hadn't seen a new parishioner for a while. Hadn't seen Caz before the lifeboat blessing. She was young, her face round and smooth, not much of a chin. Red cheeks as if she'd high blood pressure and eyes that were small. She looked past Anna, rather than at her. She shouldn't have been attractive, but there was something about those curls across the forehead that made everything fit. Caz ran a hand through her hair.

"I don't know if you can help," she said.

There was an odd silence. Anna assumed it was because Caz

didn't know how to say what she wanted to say.

"Have you lived here long? I don't think I've seen you in the village."

Anna thought a bit of small talk might help.

"I'm away three days up in Exeter. The rest of the week I work from home, so I don't get much time to do anything else other than crew the lifeboat."

"It's a brave thing to do. A tough thing to do. The lifeboat, I mean." Anna could see that Caz hadn't been sure what she was talking about. "It's right out of my comfort zone." She realised she was now squeezing her hands together and tensing her shoulders. She liked to see the bottom of anything she was floating on. Not knowing how deep the water was, what was lurking underneath, made her feel horribly uncomfortable. And she wasn't thinking sea-monsters, she was thinking wrecks. Tall masts and funnels reaching up, to tear through the hull, no matter what it was made of. This time she couldn't help herself and shivered. Caz shrugged and then leaned forward just a little. It reminded Anna of a dog straining at a leash.

"I haven't been out yet on an actual shout. I'm hoping to in the next few weeks. Jim, Mr Andrews, makes us practise and practise, so I'm quite ready."

"Is Genni full crew yet?" Anna asked, curious.

"Yes, if the call is out of school hours. She's lucky she gets such long holidays. It's meant she's been able to get her time in without missing work."

Anna had of course recognised Genni at the blessing. She taught up at the primary school, which Anna went into a lot. Anna had been adopted by them, which she secretly loved, particularly when all thirty children chorused, "Good morning, Reverend Anna." It was one of the few things that made her feel like a proper grown-up vicar. If she remembered rightly, Genni had just finished her probation and now took one of the younger classes.

"There is something bothering me." Caz laid a slight emphasis on 'me', as if talking about Genni had been a side-track.

"Yes?" Anna was beginning to feel a little anxious. Tom would appear shortly, and she hadn't even glanced at her sermon.

"You said yesterday that you were available for a chat if any of us wanted someone to talk to."

Anna lifted her mug and took a sip. She wondered what was going on that needed the vicar's input.

"Do you believe in the afterlife?"

Anna swallowed a large mouthful of scalding coffee. She could almost feel it taking a layer of skin off the back of her throat. Caz's eyes narrowed. Anna supposed it might have sounded as though she were trying not to laugh.

"Yes, I believe in an afterlife. It's kind of the point for us."

Blast, she thought. There was a sentence, an assumption, that put up a barrier right from the start. You and me, them and us!

"So you do believe in ghosts and stuff?"

"Well, um ..." Anna wasn't sure. She didn't know if she was supposed to believe in them or not. She'd have to look it up. Perhaps ask the others at their next supper.

"So, is that why you're here?" Anna asked.

"Yes." Caz turned away as if she'd seen something out of the window. There had been another change of light; a cloud chasing across the sun. "A few weeks ago I think I saw one."

Anna was strangely unmoved. She wondered if she ought to have gasped or something. Caz did look a little disappointed at her reaction.

"I was finishing off after a practice. The guys had gone to the pub for a drink." *Phil would've been pleased*, Anna thought. "It was Genni's turn for tidying up, but I need the experience. There was quite a lot to do, it took me longer than I was expecting."

"Isn't it a bit spooky down there all on your own?"

"I suppose."

"What time was it?"

"It was quite late. Past nine when the others left. I don't know what time it was when I'd done all that I needed to do."

Anna was momentarily annoyed. Couldn't Caz have glanced at her watch? As soon as she realised what she'd just thought, she felt ashamed. To cover her slip, she nodded her head a little too enthusiastically, smiling, swallowing down questions, but really disturbed at the swift sloughing off of her vicar persona.

"I switched off the lights and was about to leave when I swear I saw someone moving down under the boat. Something caught my eye, just for a second. My immediate thought was that the guys had sneaked back in and were going to jump out at me."

"Oh no. That's horrible." Anna couldn't imagine anything quite so scary and mean.

"So, you switched the light on and went back?"

Caz looked down at her fingers. She was wearing a single ring, fine silver wires twisted together like hair in a scrunchy. She began to twist it round and round.

"No, I came away. I locked up and began to climb the steps. Halfway up I turned back, and it did look as if someone was inside the boat house. They were standing at the door, looking through the glass.

"Please say you didn't go back." Anna's voice squeaked. Caz had been alone which made Anna feel uncomfortable enough and she wondered if any of the others felt afraid, finishing off by themselves, down there among the waves.

"No, there was really no need. We all have the code for getting in and out. Anyway, if it was the others messing around, I didn't want to give them the satisfaction." She looked down at her hands again. For a moment she stopped twisting the ring. "I carried on up. At the platform near the top

I looked back and wasn't surprised to see someone right down at the bottom. The outside light is always on, but I didn't see what they looked like because I had my foot on the next step and nearly overbalanced. I turned around for half a second to steady myself, and when I turned back, they'd gone."

"Did you go down to check?"

"No, because I could see quite clearly there was no one there. The steps and the platform were empty."

"What did you do?"

Caz was twisting and twisting that ring.

She mumbled, "I ran. I've never climbed up those damn steps so quickly. I got into my car and drove home. I put all the lights on and I didn't switch them off again until the next morning. I was really spooked."

"I'm not surprised. It would have scared me too. Have you asked the others? Were they messing about?"

"I haven't. If it was a prank, I don't want them to know how freaked I was and if it wasn't..."

Anna sat upright. She'd been afraid for Caz. Worried that someone might have been trying to jump out at her, but she needed to be sensible. She was sure it had probably been a trick of the light or more likely, as Caz had said, one of the lads messing around. Wasn't it obvious that someone had stood in the door looking out, gone out onto the ramp to come up but had forgotten something.

"Couldn't it simply have been whoever was still in the building, went back in because they'd forgotten something?"

"I wouldn't have thought so, because to do that, you have to put in the code, which beeps loudly. Even on quite a windy day Genni says she can hear it from the car park. It's always a relief if it's a shout, it means you're not the first there." Caz could see that Anna didn't understand. "It means you don't have to open up and get all the details from the coast guard. And if the person I saw had left the catch on, so they could have slipped back inside without the code, there should still have been a loud beep when they pulled the door. Something to do with the security system."

"I've never heard of anyone else seeing a ghost around here," Anna said.

"But there have been heaps of wrecks just offshore. It's not a place that rests easy, is it?"

Anna didn't know what that meant. She'd never felt uncomfortable anywhere around the Point, for any reason other than people being weird or unkind to each other.

"So why did you think I could help?"

"You believe in a God you can't see or prove, so I thought you'd know all about ghosts."

Anna was nonplussed. Caz didn't sound sarcastic or rude, just as if she were stating a fact. But surely she hadn't just lumped God in with the general supernatural? Ghosties and ghoulies and long-legged beasties, and, oh yes, God, the guy who made the universe!

The back door slammed. Both women jumped. Anna hoped it was Tom letting himself in. She was glad she'd an excuse to bring this to an end. She'd no idea what to do with what Caz had told her.

"I'm so sorry, I've got another appointment."

Caz rose to her feet, a single fluid movement.

"I need to be on my way, too. But let me know what you think I should do?"

Anna smiled.

"Of course." She knew she probably wouldn't think of anything useful, not in a month of Sundays.

She saw Caz out at the front door and went through to the kitchen, checking her face in the mirror as she passed. She was pleased to see that there was a little more colour in her cheeks.

"Tom, you've got the kettle on, already!"

"I need some coffee. You know that Mum gets up at the crack of dawn and doesn't mean to make such a clatter, but she's not used to having someone else in the house."

"Do you think she minds you stopping over?"

"No, we had a nice cup of tea and a chat, once I'd finally managed to get my eyes open. She told me I need a haircut."

It was a little long. It had begun to curl over his ears. Anna quite liked it. For weeks after a trim he looked like a convict, all cheekbones and stubble. Should she mention it? No, she didn't want to set up in competition with his mother, not over something as obvious as a haircut.

"But you don't mind, do you? You're always telling me I cut it too short, so I won't go quite yet."

Anna felt ridiculously pleased.

"What did the young lady want?"

Anna knew he wasn't asking for specifics. They did have some boundaries in place.

"A slightly odd matter. Not personal as such. She wanted to know if I believed in ghosts?"

"And do you?" he asked, putting far too much coffee in the cafetiere.

"If I do, is it a deal breaker?"

"For us?" He laughed, and it made her want to wrap her arms around him and lean her face on his broad sensible back.

"In my view it's normally someone messing about."

Anna relaxed. That was just what she'd been thinking.

***

Jim shoved his plate away, patted his stomach, now nicely stretched. Margery did a good, cooked breakfast, and this was the one day of the week he could really enjoy it. He pushed the crumbs to one side with his hand and lifted the pile of paper from the bench onto the table. It never got any smaller. Being Coxswain of the lifeboat was demanding, often in ways people didn't see. It wasn't all just jumping into the car and sliding down the ramp. He still needed to sort out the next couple of rotas for the station crew and arrange a meeting with the fundraising committee. They had the usual list of events planned for the next few months but over the last couple of years, the money hadn't been coming in quite so abundantly. They'd always managed to raise more than their fair share, but the Newlyn station was catching them up. Jim refused to countenance that; everyone needed to work a little harder. He lifted his tea to sip the last few dregs. It was cold, which made him frown. He wondered what Margery was doing. She hadn't cleared up from breakfast and he couldn't hear her about the house. Toby had gone too. He'd an early shift at the bakery. On Saturdays, they took it in turns to fire up the ovens. Jim had heard his son leave; he always did. Toby never managed to go without waking them up with a door slam, or the roar of his car's engine. The boy was a little heavy on the accelerator, as if he were still a teenager. Well, he'd have to learn to have a lighter touch on old *Rose*. She needed a gentle hand to coax her on and off the ramp. He wondered when Toby would start studying for his next promotion.

Jim ran his finger down the list of names. Most of the newbies were shaping up nicely. His finger hesitated over Caz Denbigh. A blow-in from London, a couple of years before. She was just about ready to go out as crew, which was good because she'd moved into the village which meant that some of the older guys could take it a bit easier. She would make it onto the ramp well within the allotted time. She was keen too, but she had that mouth on her. She didn't fit in the way that Genni did. Now there was a lass who did what she was told, and never made a fuss. Jim had worked with her grandfather for a short time, at the garage. She was definitely less bolshy than he'd been. His finger was still resting on the Denbigh girl, who'd also taken a while to get in the number of hours she needed. She apparently worked away for part of the week. She'd had the cheek to bring it up at one of her appraisals, thought she was being overlooked, treated differently because she was from London. He'd tried to explain that time sheets didn't always tell the full story, but she was having none of it.

For a couple of practices after that there'd been a bit of awkwardness, a slight hesitation before doing what she was told, as if she was deciding whether to obey him or not. He couldn't have that. Still, she'd made a good body in the water. Had taken it on the chin, even when she'd been chucked over the side for a third time. Genni had even offered to take her place as Caz had got a bit cold, but it was all part of the package. He had to be sure she could deal with it, just like one of the lads.

The back door swung open and crashed into the wall. There was a circle of cracked plaster from all the times it had happened before.

"Margery! It's going to need replastering if you're not careful."

"It's been like that forever. Anyway, we needed more logs and you said you'd bring them in last night." She looked pink from the wind and the weight of the wood piled up so she could hardly see where she was going.

"I was about to do it. Give me a break. You know I've got to get the paperwork done this morning and be careful how you stack them this time." Margery didn't seem to have heard him. He shouted after her, "Wouldn't mind a hot cup of tea, luv, before you go out again." The last bit was lost amongst the clatter of the logs dropping onto the hearth, and a swear word which she wouldn't have dreamt of uttering a few years ago. Jim turned back to the rotas and began to fill them in.

Chapter 3

Simeon was sitting in the church. Golden dust motes turned in the air and in a line of brightness around the door, ajar to the world. Belle was lying on his feet, which was comforting; her heavy warmth gently moving with each of her breaths. Simeon was praying, his eyes open. He rarely shut them unless he was safely under his blanket. There were far too many people around for him to sit undisturbed. He'd been mulling over Anna's Easter sermon, which had been rambling and woolly but there had been a couple of things that had caught his attention. She'd talked about the people who'd gone before, who'd laid the ground for them. That they themselves would be laying the ground for those that came after. She'd made it sound as if everyone fitted in, but Simeon wasn't sure that was right, for it assumed the legacy was good.

He believed that God did know what was going to happen next and could bring good from the tangled messiness that normally ensued from people always thinking they knew best. He breathed and released his grip on the back of the pew. His fingers were aching, his thoughts jumping about, which was never a good thing. He had realised that he was glad there was still another two months until the next retreat. The last one had been comprised of just Catherine's friends. Four older ladies that she knew well. They'd been like a flock of twittery birds, never quiet, always flitting about. One of them had tried to talk to him after morning prayer but she'd leaned in a little too closely and had shouted as if he were deaf. He had avoided them after that.

Once they'd come through that second retreat, the Bishop had suggested they only ran them four times a year, at least until they stopped worrying that someone else might end up dead. The next one would be their fifth since the murder and Simeon was still nervous. Georgie, who'd been at the fatal retreat, had said that he needed to give himself some time.

They all needed space to process what'd happened. A year, it seemed, wasn't long enough.

Simeon really couldn't concentrate. Archie was never far from his thoughts, not since the heart attack. There was a gentle anxiety about him, bubbling away most of the time. Simeon would text him later to make sure he was alright, even though he thought that it was beginning to annoy him, but Archie must realise it wasn't all about him, not entirely. The light around the door flickered as someone moved into the porch. Simeon stiffened until he saw that it was Harriet. She lifted a hand to acknowledge him and walked down to her favourite spot, right-hand-side at the front. She liked it there because when the sun shone through the windows it would fall all around her. She said it warmed her up, though often the temperature hadn't changed at all.

Simeon stood up to leave.

"Not on my account, I hope," Harriet said, turning to face him.

He looked past her to the altar.

"No, I was going to go anyway. I can't focus." He began to walk along the back of the pews. "How are you?" he asked, stopping in the sunshine spilling through the door. She was right, it did feel warmer.

"I'm fine, thank you, Simeon. It's kind of you to ask."

Simeon breathed a little deeper, gave a nod and started back to the door. He'd made a point of enquiring because Anna said it was a good thing to do, but it always terrified him that people might actually tell him what was going on in their lives. Even now sometimes Anna would say that she was feeling scratchy or grumpy, or extra tired. He needed time to consider what to say after a comment like that, which apparently could come across as rude, particularly if his silence stretched too long. No one had been able to tell him how long was too long.

From the doorway, Simeon looked into the churchyard. The

air outside sparkled with rain. He had decided to take Belle along the road to the lifeboat station, on around to just past Beacon Point. It would be exactly the right length for her. As he crested the hill, he began to hear voices — two women arguing very loudly. They must be in the lifeboat car park. He was too far up to see them, but he could hear them quite clearly. He stopped. He couldn't walk past a row like that, that would be far too difficult. He hurried back onto the lane and down to Church Cove. He would've liked to have gone right at the bottom, but what if the women were still shouting at each other? Instead, he turned left, to walk north along the coast.

The path soon became muddy to the edges, almost deep enough to slide into the top of his boots, and so he reluctantly turned back, pulling Belle behind him. Just before he turned into his lane, he heard a car roar past, heading up into the village. It was going far too fast and made him jump. He imagined being on the lane moments earlier, having to squash into the hedge as it raced by, frightening Belle. He fished his key from his pocket and hurried around the side of the house, but before he put it in the lock, he rang Archie.

Archie didn't pick up. Simeon felt the anxiety becoming a hole inside him. Before he fell into it completely, he took his book into the bedroom, and crept under the weighted blanket and tried to read. He only called Archie three more times after that.

***

Unaware of Simeon's calls, Archie turned his back on his house, a large, square, granite-faced building. It was a good place to come home to. A place he imagined had put down its own roots over the years, so that when the wind sledgehammered across the Point, it sat firmly, deeply embedded and unmoveable. He walked briskly up the lane and across the green. It was his turn in the lifeboat shop. They were desperate for volunteers, and he'd agreed to do one afternoon a fortnight, which didn't seem too big a commitment. For most of the year it was quiet. He was able to sit and read. If there were visitors, the displays were interesting and quickly drew people in, so that sometimes they bypassed the shop altogether. Anyway, walking back up the one hundred and seventy steps was a good workout. At least that's what he told himself.

It had been nearly eighteen months since his heart attack, which he referred to as 'the blip', but he still didn't quite trust himself. He still felt, if he was being entirely honest, that if he pushed too hard, something, somewhere would give. A blood vessel would split, and spill and he wouldn't have time to say goodbye.

Even worse than that, were all the pills and potions he now had to take — when he woke up, after breakfast and then again just before bed. It felt like he'd given in somehow, that he was now especially vulnerable to living. Being seventy had been quite a difficult milestone in itself. He'd been dreading it. A line in the sand he'd not wanted to step over.

His stint at the shop started at three-fifteen, a shift that most of the other volunteers didn't like doing. He'd planned to walk the long way around but had fallen asleep after lunch and now he needed to get a move-on if he was going to be on time.

Just as he passed the vicarage, he realised he'd left his book and phone behind. They were on the hall stand, propped up, so he wouldn't forget them. He hesitated for a moment but there wasn't anywhere near enough time to go back, and he simply couldn't abide being late. Anna was late all the time; for her it was almost a trademark.

Puffing, he marched across the field and dropped down into the car park. There were two cars there, one bright green and the other Jean's familiar red Honda. She must have a tight schedule today. Jean spent most of her time in the village shop, but a couple of afternoons a week one of the local teenagers looked after it so Jean was able to pick up her grandchildren from school or sometimes help out at the lifeboat. Archie didn't know how she managed to juggle everything and still look so bright and cheerful. He was perhaps a little envious. He would also have to apologise for keeping her. It was usually the other way around, as Jean could talk for England, which often cut into his reading time, though of course he'd forgotten his book, so there wouldn't be any of that today. *What a bother*, he thought.

He began the long climb down, holding onto the handrail rather tightly. It could be quite vertiginous and once or twice he'd felt a little dizzy. Coming back up wasn't so bad if you didn't think about the drop behind you. He knew there were one hundred and seventy steps down. He knew that Simeon would count them each time he used them, as if to check the number hadn't changed. Archie's mouth twitched into a smile. If there were fewer steps someone would've had to have hauled the lifeboat ramp just a little closer to the cliff! It was a silly thought. An odd thought. He was having too many of those lately.

He was nearly at the bottom. From there a large metal platform connected the main door and the bottom of the funicular. There were another two sets of steps, either side of the building, that took you down onto the next level, a narrow walkway leading around to the ramp. Everything was fenced off, caged in for safety, in case any of the tourists wandered out of bounds. It was well-maintained, with clear signage, yet Simeon still worried about him coming here by himself. Archie understood that the heart attack had been difficult for his friend, that it had come at the end of a very demanding time, but he was worried that it seemed to have caused Simeon to go backwards. He'd stopped interacting with anyone he didn't know really well and checked up on Archie almost daily, which was making Archie feel a little smothered.

Jean was putting on her coat. She even thanked him for being on time, though he was a good five minutes late.

"Because this is one of my days for looking after the kids. Their mum does this one long day at work, though of course it's never just the one. They're always finding an excuse for calling her in. If I've told her once, I've told her a hundred times, she ought to stand up to them. Honestly, Archie, can you imagine having a job like that? It's such a shame her husband can't earn more." Jean handed over the book of sales. There were no new entries. "So, I'd best be off. Good to see you around and about again."

Jean was in her sixties, yet there she was almost scampering up the steps as if they were nothing. And as for seeing him around and about again, she always said that, even though it had been months since the blip. Archie fetched a chair from the crew common room. It wouldn't make his back twinge quite so quickly as the stool, though Jean always seemed to manage.

He looked at the leaflets, straightening a couple. There was nothing there he hadn't read a hundred times. The displays along the wall, all the rescues by the different boats through the years, were also well known to him. His own face peered out from one blurry picture. He'd been a volunteer until they started the new build to accommodate *Rose*, the unsinkable Tamar class. A beast of a vessel that dominated the space, though she was named after a flower. He'd liked her to have been the Mighty Bertha, or even the unsinkable Molly Brown; names with a bit of weight behind them. He found himself staring down into the well, *Rose's* orange and grey presence forcing him to step back. The cables and chain were lying quietly, though he still felt she was poised, ready to go. He'd watched them launch many times, but nothing could beat his own memories of the lad swinging the sledgehammer to release the pin, the sudden burst of speed and the crunch as they hit the water. Now that had been living.

He checked his watch. He'd only been there ten minutes, five o'clock was still a long way away. He wandered back to the crew common room and made a cup of tea. Jean always brought down a fresh couple of pints of milk for the volunteers and if they were lucky, a packet of biscuits. Since the blip he'd not eaten quite so many of those, but his nurse had said that he could eat some. He thought one day he might discuss with Simeon what 'some' might mean. That made him smile. Simeon was a man of exactness, definitions and boundaries, which weren't always easy to define.

Archie took his tea back out into the main area, a u-shaped platform around the boat, for when the visitors came and crowded along the rail to watch the practice launches. They still had drills twice a week, so it was quite a commitment to be part of the crew but one that Archie had had no trouble honouring, just for the privilege of being paged. He'd never made coxswain but had been the deputy for his last couple of years. It'd meant that on three of the shouts he had been in charge — a yacht and a fishing vessel losing their engines, rolling with the swell, powerless and gently drifting onto rocks. Always drifting onto rocks!

Then, the very last time they'd been called out to look for a man who'd seemingly lost an oar, just off Cadgwith. It was winter, the sea temperature putting them under an exacting time constraint. They'd searched for eight hours and had found the dinghy, one fragile oar resting in the bottom; they hadn't found anything else. It was a little odd because no one had been reported missing. Archie had felt jumpy for days after, worried that if they'd stayed out just a bit longer, they might have found him.

The mechanic at the time, Will Noble, had said that the bloke had probably got ashore and was too embarrassed to say he was alright. After all, there'd been a helicopter and coast guards searching until it got dark.

Archie couldn't believe anyone would be that selfish. Will and he had agreed to disagree. He'd liked Will, and him dying like that had been a bit of a shock.

It had been a difficult funeral, over in Mullion. Will had a big family and they were terribly upset. A heart attack walking back from his local. Archie suddenly felt a bit hot. Probably hadn't quite recovered from his walk over. He went outside for a breath of air.

Out in the breeze, heavily scented with seaweed and brine, and a hint of oil from the funicular, Archie took a deep breath. This was more like it. He swivelled around at the sound of someone coming down the metal stairs, the clang-clang bouncing off the rocks rearing over him. It was a young woman. She was sensibly concentrating on the steps so didn't look up until she got to the top platform, a third of the way down. There she stopped, her hand flying to her mouth as she emitted a small scream. Archie waved. He hadn't meant to alarm her. She came on down.

"Are you alright?" he called.

"You just gave me a bit of a start, staring up at me like that." The young woman looked a little flushed.

"I'm so sorry. I was just having a breath of air." He knew it sounded silly because the boat house was big, purpose-built, wave-shaped, its roof sweeping between the cliffs on either side. There was a wonderful sense of space within. Outside the wind would blow over it, past it, around it, with aerodynamic grace. "I'm Archie. You're one of the young ladies."

She frowned, dropping her chin as if he'd been a little rude. She extended her hand somewhat aggressively.

"Caz. I'll be proper crew on the next shout if I'm available."

"Oh, well done you! Well done indeed!"

She frowned again and he felt as if he'd made it worse somehow.

"Is anyone else here?" she asked.

"I've not seen anyone," Archie replied.

For a moment she hesitated, and then as if making up her mind about something, she walked past him and into the boat house. She let the door swing shut behind her. He had to reenter the code and by the time he'd managed that, she'd disappeared into the common room. He heard the bang of the heavy fire door as she went into the locker room beyond.

Archie had come up through the Navy so good manners and general politeness had been drummed into him. Anna and Harriet didn't seem to mind such things, though even he'd stopped standing up when either of them joined him at a table. He still stood for Catherine, Tom's mum. She was old school, like him, and seemed to appreciate it, or at least to understand it.

He sat down on his chair. Then he got up and began to rearrange the leaflets again. He wondered what the young woman was doing here.

The afternoon passed slowly, and Archie alternated between watching the clock, drinking lots of tea and re-reading the exhibits.

The young woman didn't reappear. When it was nearing five o'clock, he wondered if he ought to let her know that she would soon be on her own. He went into the common room and knocked on the door that led to the rest of the building. He couldn't go through as there was another combination lock, just for the crew. She must be too busy doing whatever it was she was doing, to come up and he couldn't wait. He needed to get home. They were holding a standing committee at his house that evening, and he still had lots to do. Thinking of the walk to his house, the long climb up the steps to the car park, he wished he'd brought the car.

Chapter 4

March gave way to April, but Harriet was oblivious to the changing seasons. She just wanted the hot water in her new kitchen to work.

For a glorious second it ran hot, and she had quickly put the bowl underneath, only for it to turn icy cold. She was about to shout up to Derek that the water heater wasn't working again when she remembered he'd popped up to the shop to get a paper. She reached for the kettle. The immersion would take far too long to kick in and she was really hoping to get the kitchen clean enough to eat in.

They'd been living in the new house for nearly three months, and true to Derek's predictions, it hadn't been much more than a building site. For the first six weeks she'd managed with a microwave and a standpipe just outside the back door. Now, at last, they were all plumbed in. The new bathroom and kitchen were spacious and shiny, the problem being that the hot water system stubbornly refused to work. She'd been having showers up at the vicarage, but they really needed to find out what the problem was. Harriet thought Derek tended to overcomplicate things so hoped that somewhere there was a switch that was off, which could just be switched on.

She looked around. They'd extracted some stuff from storage but not much, as Harriet wanted the house to feel at least 'together' before they retrieved any more of their things. There was still so much to do.

"It's just the twiddly bits," Derek had said, earlier that morning, and then he'd grinned. Harriet frowned at the thought. Hot water was a little more than a twiddly bit! And the others were coming over soon for a roast!

She picked up a clean sponge and the bag of old clothes that Anna had found down in her cellar. It was lovely wiping away the dust and grime, for hopefully the last time, unless one of Derek's twiddly bits involved more drilling. For an architect, he was a little blasé about the logical order of the work.

Harriet had thought, quite a few times, that she ought to have been able to start painting a room, only to find one of the builders was back, putting in an extra socket, or moving a light fitting. And although she felt a large dose of irritation underpinning most of her days, Derek was so obviously having a ball that she often just swallowed it. He crunched over bits of plaster, happily changed his mind over the tiniest little detail, sometimes two or three times a day, while she followed behind with a dustpan and brush.

She checked her watch. She'd twenty minutes before she was due at the vicarage for the monthly meeting about the next retreat. At least it shouldn't be as boring as Anna and Archie's last Standing Committee. Anna had said that that was dire and had gone on far too long. At this meeting, they were going to discuss numbers, again. They had space in the vicarage for six, as long as four people shared, which made it easier to balance the books, but the sharing wasn't always successful. The time before last, by lunch of the second day, they'd had to ask Phil to have one of the ladies stay at the pub. It'd all got a bit complicated and very catty, even though Archie had picked her up and brought her down to breakfast each day. The woman had left a scathing feedback form.

Anna had wanted to give her her money back, but Archie and Harriet had managed to talk her out of that. Breaking-even by a hair's breadth was doable, losing money was not. That would mean stopping altogether, and Harriet liked her new role of Retreat Coordinator. She really enjoyed it and didn't want to give anyone in the congregation a chance to bring it to an end. The last Church Annual General Meeting had been a bit touch and go. Some of the parishioners didn't like the idea that, during the retreats, their vicar was available to five or six strangers and therefore, not quite so available to them. Anna had sat and squirmed, her bottom lip chewed to soreness.

The odd thing was, that in the end, it had been Jean, from the shop, who'd saved the day. She'd rambled on about how important Anna had been to her own daughter, Ellie. How she'd been instrumental in persuading her to move to Helston with her family, which had probably saved her marriage. Anna had gone very pink and even Archie had begun to fidget. No one could quite see where Jean was going with her interruption. At last, she'd ended with the fact that it would be selfish not to enable Anna a wider ministry, to folk who didn't necessarily live in the parish. That it was, in fact, their Christian duty to share her. Harriet had almost laughed out loud at Anna's look of wide-eyed astonishment. But the lady who'd raised the question had seemed mollified, and perhaps had even started to look at Anna with a small amount of proprietary approval.

Harriet closed the last of the kitchen cupboards. She'd tried to keep the room as simple as possible, which despite Derek's love of a good gadget had been easier than she'd anticipated. Derek seemed to treat any opinion she might have with great enthusiasm. It often made her reticent to say how she truly felt. *How much of this wonderful house was really hers and how much was by permission*, she wondered.

She pulled on her coat and hunted for some keys. She thought about leaving a note for Derek but she'd already told him what she'd got planned for that day. Anyway, he could always text her if he got worried. She went out through the back door, along a short path overhung with trees and stepped down into the lane. It wasn't far up to the vicarage but it was still uphill, so it would be some exercise at least.

***

Anna's responsibility was to chair the meeting, Harriet's to take notes and Archie's to create the agenda. Anna had thought the last retreat had gone well, so she wondered what there was to talk about, apart from the question of numbers. Sometimes Harriet seemed to want to fuss over the details just to remind them that she was still doing a lot of the actual work. At least she was paid for the time she put in. Archie was there almost as much, and he did it for free. He even led some of the morning and evening services now if Anna had other things to get on with. Simeon still locked and unlocked the church but kept a low profile.

Luckily, since the retreat when it had all gone pear-shaped, they'd mostly had older ladies and gentlemen. Anna had never imagined they'd get anyone under fifty, so the three youngsters had been an anomaly, a surprise. It did have one good repercussion though, because Georgie had returned to visit them quite a few times since, to recharge her batteries from her job as a youth worker, to get some good lie-ins, and to eat copious amounts of toast. Anna had quickly worked out that Georgie didn't need much more than a warm welcome and the occasional unpacking of her life over the kitchen table.

Everyone had made a real effort with Georgie, except Simeon of course. Although he was nearest to Georgie's age, he was unwilling to let his guard down. He'd always found the retreats difficult, the influx of strangers who did not abide by the rules, his rules, and since Archie's heart attack, Simeon spent increasingly more time worrying about him, which didn't seem to leave room for anything else. He was certainly checking up on Archie with assiduous regularity, which Anna thought was driving Archie nuts.

Harriet rang the doorbell. During the retreats she used her own key, but at other times she said she didn't like to intrude as the vicarage was still Anna's home. Anna didn't mind one way or the other.

The two of them walked through to the kitchen. Anna nearly had the coffee ready.

"So how was the kitchen cleaning?" she asked.

"All done except for a couple of cupboards in the utility room." Harriet shook her head. "There are so many of them, I don't know what I'm going to use them for."

"Oh, it won't take long to fill them up. Food you never use and contraptions you think are going to change your life."

"But are too difficult to put together or wash afterwards!"

"When actually a pair of scissors or a sharp knife would work just as well."

They both laughed. Anna had a drawer full of things just like that.

"And how's Derek? Still making adjustments?" she asked.

"I've told him the kitchen is finished. There's nothing more to do, then this morning, the blessed water heater didn't work again. Now *that* I wish he would sort out."

"I used to hate not knowing what was going to come out of the hot tap here."

It had been a couple of years ago that Archie had made them fit a new boiler in the vicarage, for which Anna was extremely grateful. It was a large eighteenth-century house, with tall sash windows, big rooms and old fireplaces. The radiators still gurgled and clanged, and apart from her own small private space at the back of the house, it took ages to heat up but at least now it did warm through, eventually. Harriet had also persuaded them to open the chimney so they could light a fire in the lounge, which always made things feel cosier. Now and again, even Tom had managed to set one going, but Anna only ever filled the room with smoke.

The doorbell rang.

"That'll be Archie. I'll let him in," Harriet said, disappearing into the hall.

Anna began to pour coffee. She put out biscuits but not too many. Archie was still being really careful.

"Hello, Archie," she called through the kitchen door. He was shrugging out of his coat, scarf and beanie. Anna had bought the latter for him almost as a joke, but he'd taken to wearing it quite a lot, unless it was unseasonably warm. Spring had been bright and chilly with early April showers sweeping in from the West. One minute there were china-sharp white clouds on a bright-blue backdrop, the next the sky was filled with low glowering dampness that hardly cleared the headland at all.

Anna was glad they'd got past Easter, her line in the sand. She enjoyed the warmer mornings of spring, the green shoots poking through the grass but so often before that Sunday, there might still be a snowstorm or simply a storm that was redolent of the dark winter months. She didn't really trust the weather until Easter had passed, and saying, 'At least it's spring' didn't wash when The Lizard was draped in a cloak of grey heaviness, the wind still gusting bitterly.

"So where shall we start?" Anna asked, once they were seated around the table, coffee poured.

Archie pulled out three agendas from his folder. It looked a little long and detailed and Anna settled in for at least a couple of hours. They weren't due to hold the next retreat until the middle of May, and so far, there were just two people booked in.

They worked through the items. Anna made more coffee.

At last Archie said, "Any other business." She and Harriet quickly shook their heads. The doorbell rang again, making them jump. She really must get Derek to tone it down a bit. When Anna opened the door, Tom was standing outside. She wondered why he'd not come round the back.

"Tom! What are you doing here, and at this time of day? Shouldn't you be writing reports or arresting people?" It would annoy him that she'd distilled his job down to a couple of sentences; she hadn't meant to.

"Lovely to see you too," he said. He didn't smile, in fact, looked a little bleak.

"Sorry, come on in. We've just finished," she said, moving aside. He was about to lean forward and kiss her when she turned towards the dining room and said, "unless there is any other any other business, Archie, Harriet?"

Tom looked windswept. Just a smidgeon past the wrong side of rugged, and he still hadn't found time to have his hair cut. He stepped into the hall without touching her. They'd got quite good at this recently, when she was being a vicar, or he was being a police officer. Harriet was putting the cups back on the tray, Archie was carefully tucking his notes away.

"Hello, Tom," Archie said, but there was always that catch in his voice, that query — what are you doing here, now?

As if Tom were answering the unspoken question, he said, "I'm here about a missing person."

"Oh no," Anna said, immediately thinking that perhaps someone had jumped into the sea. Bodies didn't always reappear, which was just a little worse than when they did.

Tom reached out to touch her arm. He looked around at each of them. He realised that they would be thinking the worst.

"Look, it's probably nothing to worry about. A young woman just hasn't turned up at work for a couple of weeks. She's one of the lifeboat volunteers, so I popped over to interview the skipper."

Anna's heart did a backflip. She didn't want to ask, but she knew she couldn't keep the question inside along with a niggling nausea that she was far too used to. She was terrified that this might be another line in the sand — that this was a before-we-knew, and an after-we-knew moment.

"Not Caz?" she asked, trying to sound calm.

"Caroline Denbigh. Mr Andrews did call her Caz."

Abruptly, Anna sat down on the bottom stair. She peered up at Tom. Archie was standing in the dining room door, framed with light. He looked ashen, too.

Harriet, who'd been halfway down the hall with the tray, said, "Archie, do you need to sit down? You don't look good."

He lifted a hand as if to bat away the question, which if he'd been alright, he wouldn't have dreamt of doing. Anna could see that Harriet was a little taken aback.

"I'm fine. It's just that I think I met her during one of my shifts at the lifeboat."

Tom narrowed his eyes, just a little.

"Can you remember when, exactly?"

"Three weeks ago, the day after tomorrow. My shift that week was on a Wednesday."

Typical Archie. Anna knew that to answer that question she'd have had to go and check the diary.

"It was a little odd," Archie continued. "She disappeared into the locker room, which I don't have access to. When it was time for me to leave, I tried to let her know, I even knocked on the door, but she couldn't have heard me. I've no idea what she was doing there at that time of day."

"Well," Tom said, reassuringly, "it was nearly three weeks ago. I'm sure you can't have been the last person to have seen her, but could I pop up after lunch and have a chat? We need to dot the i's and cross the t's on this one. Her dad's an ex-copper from the Met and is kicking up a stink."

Of course he would, Anna thought. Any parent would be frantic. Then she realised that Tom would want lunch. Blast! They'd have to go up to the pub for a pie. She didn't have a single thing in the fridge that wasn't curling up at the edges or way past its sell-by date. She sighed, and wondered what it must be like to be Harriet, with a kitchen that could always rustle up a sandwich or a salad, without any warning at all. She had to almost pinch herself to stop the envy taking root. She stood up to check that Archie had a little more colour and was feeling alright. Really feeling alright!

Chapter 5

Simeon was waiting outside the shop. There was a stranger inside talking to Jean. If it had been Anna, Archie, Harriet or Derek he would have gone in. Even Georgie, though he knew she wasn't back until May. Belle was also watching the door intently. She liked the shop. Jean often gave her a dog biscuit for being such a good girl. Belle wasn't more well-behaved in the shop than anywhere else but that didn't seem to matter to Jean.

Simeon began to wonder how long the person would be; he was getting cold. He pulled his hood lower over his face. The fur trim, a little matted, obscured the view and made him feel more settled. He hadn't bothered with gloves because it hadn't felt that chilly when he'd checked earlier that morning, standing for a few minutes outside his door, among the dripping shrubs. Some of them had begun to get straggly, their branches creeping over the edge of the path. He liked to have the path clear. He didn't like having to worry about where he was walking. He'd also realised that recently, when he let Belle out, he couldn't see her, which made him uneasy. He needed someone to come and cut the shrubs back.

The shop bell tinkled, which made him jump but he was now able to go in. Jean was wearing flat brown shoes and blue trousers. He saw them as he passed the end of the counter.

"Hello, Simeon. And how is my gorgeous girl?" Jean said.

Simeon let the lead run a little and stepped back. Jean could be overwhelming in the narrow space, her voice too high and loud but Belle loved her, or rather the titbit she would get if she wagged her tail. When Jean was safely back behind the counter, he went to find the bread and milk.

"So have you heard?" Simeon knew that Jean wouldn't wait for him to reply, as she rarely needed anyone else to have a conversation with, just their presence. "One of the young women from the lifeboat crew has disappeared."

Simeon knew that a surprisingly large number of people went missing each year. Some turned up again having been somewhere else, but many did not.

"Apparently, she hasn't been seen for nearly three weeks. Her work rang her dad, and he rang the police. They've asked Tom Edwards to take charge. That'll please Anna, at least." Simeon wondered how Jean found out about these things. Apart from people coming into the shop and chatting, he really couldn't work it out. And as for Anna being pleased, he didn't think that would be true. Anna would be more likely worried about why the young woman was missing, and the effect it would be having on her family and friends. "Is that everything?" Jean asked. Simeon nodded.

"I've got an offer on those biscuits Archie used to like."

"He still likes them," Simeon said to the floor.

"Well, he doesn't buy them much now."

Simeon continued staring at his shoes. Was she expecting him to buy some? He carefully placed a five pound note on the counter.

Simeon pulled out the bag he kept in his pocket, to put the bread and milk in. Once he'd sorted that out, he decided to walk down to see Archie. Of course, it would have been better to have bought his shopping on the way back. That annoyed Simeon. He hadn't really been intending to go and see his friend until Jean had made the comment about the biscuits. It had set his heart beating faster, only a tiny bit, but enough.

As he closed the shop door, the bell tinkling, he heard his name. A voice that was used to shouting into the wind, projected rather than yelled. Simeon turned to wait for Archie who was walking up the road from the church.

"Hello, Simeon. How are you?" Simeon thought Archie looked drawn, even though there was a slash of pink across his cheeks. It wasn't the sort of colour that made Simeon think of good health.

"I'm fine. Are you well?"

"I'm perfectly fine too."

A dark Audi drove past and tooted. It was Tom and Anna.

"Has Tom come about the missing woman?" Simeon asked, watching Tom park just outside the pub.

"Now, how did you know about that?" Archie asked, in surprise.

Simeon lifted up the bag.

"Ah, you've been in the shop. Jean certainly is the first to know what goes on."

"There are many reasons why people go missing," Simeon said. "It's not always that they've been murdered, or have died somewhere, alone."

"Oh, Simeon. I wasn't thinking either of those things, but you do have a point. We both live alone, and sometimes I wonder how long it would take us to be found, if anything happened."

Simeon peered up at him.

"Archie, you must never worry about that. I would know if you didn't pick up your phone and I would never assume you were alright."

Archie smiled, one of his tight smiles, where he squashed his lips together.

"Thank you, Simeon. I am reassured."

Simeon didn't think he sounded as if he was, at all.

He said, "Jean says that Tom is investigating the missing woman. That seems doubtful as he normally deals with suspicious deaths."

"I think it's because her dad's an ex-policeman," Archie replied. "Though Tom seemed a bit put out by that. Plus she hasn't been seen for a good couple of weeks."

Simeon glanced at Archie. He looked sad. Simeon wondered if he ought to say something, but Archie continued, "It makes it much harder to investigate, the longer it goes on. The first twenty-four hours are really important."

"I suppose because people remember things better."

"I may have been one of the last people to see her. I keep trying to wrack my brains as to what happened. It would have been much easier if I'd spoken to Tom the day after. As it is, he's coming over this afternoon."

"Would it help if you told me what you remember?"

"I think it probably would, except it wasn't much. She came down the steps and went into the locker room. What she did beyond that I've no idea."

"Where were you when you first saw her?"

"Outside, taking a breath of air."

Simeon looked up sharply, wondering why Archie had felt the need for air.

"Were you feeling alright?" Simeon asked. Belle was leaning against Simeon's knee, she seemed to be looking up anxiously at Archie, too.

"I was fine. I'm fine. Why don't you come over and I'll make us a sandwich?"

Simeon nodded. He was careful not to walk too fast.

***

Tom stood at the bar. As Phil, the landlord, finished taking their orders, he asked, "So are you here about Caz Denbigh?"

"Now, Phil, you know I can't tell you that."

Phil smiled, his all-knowing smile.

"You also know that I will probably know more about it than you by closing time tonight."

Tom nodded. That might be true, but he still wasn't going to say anything. He glanced across the pub to where Anna was sitting, not quite out of sight. She looked uncomfortable. It wasn't her day off so having lunch would be an indulgence, wouldn't feel quite right to her. It did feel like a treat to see her in the week like this, even though everything was a little out of whack.

Tom wouldn't normally do missing persons, but Caz's dad was ex-CID and was in a bit of a state. He lived in London and hadn't heard from his daughter for over three weeks. To begin with he'd thought she was probably busy. He'd left a couple of messages but nothing urgent. He'd said they didn't speak that regularly, but alarm bells had started to ring when her office had called to ask him how she was. They'd assumed she was sick, though it wasn't like her not to let them know. At the beginning of the second week a colleague had rung her mobile and home number. It had gone through to voicemail again so that was when they'd gone to HR to get his number.

Denbigh had managed to get hold of one of the neighbours. They'd said his daughter's car was on the drive but there were no lights, no sign of her at all and they couldn't remember when they'd last seen her. He'd rung missing persons that night, who hadn't done much with it for the first few days, as there were no indicators to say that she was vulnerable in any way. But Denbigh knew the ropes and had started ringing daily, saying repeatedly how unlike her it was to go off without telling anyone.

Tom had finally been called in by the boss. After all, he was between cases. Tom hadn't been pleased as there was a pile of paperwork half-a-mile high, so he wasn't exactly twiddling his thumbs. He was also still trying to find someone to replace his sergeant, Sandra, who had finally moved on. Got the promotion she'd been looking for and deserved. He'd been looking out for a likely substitute for quite a while, but so far no one had come close. He really missed her.

Tom carried the drinks across to Anna. She was wearing her dog collar with a pale green shirt under a navy-blue jumper. The colours suited her and when she smiled her crooked, crinkly smile he leaned down and kissed her. He knew she didn't like such displays without some warning but sometimes he couldn't help himself. She quickly looked around, there were a few people in, though no one who seemed to be a regular.

"So do you think Archie was the last person to see her?" she asked, her face finally beginning to flush with colour. She was looking at him intently. Of course, that would be the worry for her, how this disappearance would affect her parishioners.

"Goodness, I wouldn't have thought so. But as her dad is an ex-copper, I'll have to pull out all the stops."

"Ahhh," Anna said, as if now she understood everything.

"I'll also have to interview the lifeboat crew and her work colleagues."

"You'll need help. That's a lot of people."

"I know. Where's Sandra when I need her?"

Anna smiled, but not one of her open-hearted-couldn't-help-herself smiles. This one hardly reached her eyes at all.

"Have you found anyone else yet?"

"No."

"I bet you're setting your standards too high. Just try and remember what Sandra was like when you first pulled her out of uniform." Anna giggled.

"Now, Reverend, we'll have none of that smut from you."

He was rewarded with one of the smiles that immediately made him feel that all was right with the world, if only for a very brief moment.

The hour he allowed himself, that he'd carved out of his day, rushed by. He tried to extend it a tiny bit but once Anna had glanced at her watch, she began to pull on her gloves. There was no way she would break the rules, even if they were just their own.

"Can I come over Friday for fish and chips?"

"Yes, but if you're going to be late, ring and let me know so I can pop up and get them before the shop closes. We don't go onto summer opening times for another couple of weeks."

As she walked past, she rested her hand on his shoulder, and he caught hold of it and held it to his cheek.

"That's a date," he said. She shivered, because it seemed to him that she still thought it was a big deal, her and him. Anna and Tom. The policeman and the vicar.

As the door slammed shut behind her, he pulled his

notebook from his pocket. He tried not to feel irritated that she was still a little uptight, even after all this time, about them, but as per usual there wasn't much he could do. And this wasn't the moment to think about it. He began to scan his notes – it was time to visit Archie.

***

As Tom drove in, Simeon was just leaving, pulling his hood over his head. Belle wagged her tail, and he bent down to give her a pat.

"Hello, Simeon," Tom said, carefully keeping his eyes on the dog. "I don't suppose you know anything about the lost woman, do you?"

Simeon hesitated, then turned back to stare at Tom's feet.

"No, but I think I know where she lives. She has a small house on Penmenner Road. Archie probably passes it every day. I will pass it now, in a minute. She works from home two or three days a week. In some form of insurance because she once told Jean she was working on a large claim. One of the big companies based in Exeter. I don't know where she stays when she goes up there to work, but I expect her dad does or perhaps one of her neighbours. It's why she's taken so long to become full crew; she can't make all the practices."

Tom laughed.

"Very useful, thank you. Now, you haven't seen her around, over the last three weeks?"

"Not that I remember."

Simeon began to walk away. Archie was standing in the hall with his arms folded. His almost white hair was neatly cut, brushed flat and for a tiny moment Tom could see the young man, in his Navy uniform, his cap tipped to one side. No, the cap would be on straight. Tom wasn't sure that Archie would ever have had that youthful sparkle, cheekiness, even as a lad. He was a man who thought and worried about things a great deal.

"Come on in, Tom, or should I call you DI Edwards, if this is official business?"

"Tom, of course, Archie." But Tom didn't see any unbending or relaxing of Archie's spine. He followed him into the lounge. It was gloriously warm, and Tom sat back while Archie went to get some coffee.

The leather sofa was comfortable and apart from some pink curtain tiebacks and a couple of cushions, the room was bare and functional. Tom liked it. Nothing surplus to what was needed, though the TV in the corner was a little small. He didn't expect Archie watched much of that. Next to one of the chairs was a large pile of books. In anyone else's house Tom would have gone over to look at what was there, but he didn't want to be caught. It felt like a violation of Archie's personal space, which Tom hoped to be invited into one day, freely and without constraint.

Anna relied on Archie, he was her churchwarden, they were close and yet Tom knew that Archie didn't hold him in the same regard. He was suspicious of him and probably would have preferred Tom to have left Anna alone. Tom flexed his fingers. From Archie's point of view this was all about Anna, and Tom really needed to put that to one side. Archie appeared with a tray. Once he'd handed Tom a cup of coffee and sat down, Tom felt able to begin.

"So, Archie, tell me what happened the last time you saw Caroline Denbigh."

Archie frowned in thought.

"I volunteer for the shop, and I'd just started my shift at about three-twenty, but I felt a bit hot. I went outside for some air, which was when I first saw her coming down the steps. She obviously spotted me about half-way down because she looked really startled. To begin with I thought she was just another visitor. I recognised her when she reached the bottom. I'd known there were two young ladies on the crew, but I'd only chatted to the other one, Genni. She wants to get married next year, and we haven't had a good local wedding for ages."

Tom decided to ignore that. Hoped that Archie wasn't making a point, that he was just pleased that someone had decided to do something nice in the church for a change. Anna had said there were too many funerals and not enough of the happy stuff.

Archie continued, "I had seen Miss Denbigh before, of course, at the lifeboat blessing, but she stayed on the boat deck throughout. She didn't even come down to join us when we had a cup of tea afterwards, but when I last saw her, we shook hands and she introduced herself as Caz. Though I still think I might have upset her. She was telling me about going out on the next shout."

Tom looked up.

"Why do you think you upset her?"

"When we went back into the building, she let the door shut behind her. By the time I got it open again she'd disappeared into the common room, then she must have gone on into the locker room beyond."

Tom looked at Archie. Archie may not like him much, but it would be a true enough reflection of what had happened, at least from Archie's point of view.

"What did you say to her?"

"Something like, 'well done for getting through your training'. I thought I was being kind, but sometimes I don't get my tone right. The world is a little different from when I was a boy but Tom, I would've said the same if she'd been a man."

"You can't remember exactly what you said?"

"No, I've racked my brains. Sadly, I do not have Simeon's power of recall." Archie's face was wrinkled with thought, his hands clasped tightly in his lap. He stared at Tom as if he were the interrogator and not the other way round.

"Can you remember anything else?"

"No, my shift ended at five and I had to leave because I had a meeting later that evening. I went and knocked on the locker room door. Volunteers are allowed in the common room to make tea, otherwise it can be a very long afternoon, but of course we aren't allowed beyond that. I knocked quite hard, but there was no reply. Not that I heard anyway, as my hearing isn't what it was. Also, it's a fire door and very thick. Caz could have been anywhere. There are lots of rooms beyond."

"What about locking up?"

"It's a combination. Everyone has it. When there's a shout, the first one to arrive puts the door on the catch so the rest of them can get in as fast as possible. Last one to leave drops it. And once they're out at sea there are plenty of the shore crew to keep an eye on the place."

"Thanks, Archie. Unless there's anything else, that will be all for now."

Archie looked up, but his eyes slid over Tom's face to the window.

"Was that the last time anyone saw her?" he asked.

"We don't know for sure. I've still got a lot of people to interview."

"You'll need some help."

This time Tom felt the veiled criticism. Archie probably knew all about his reluctance to take on a new *Sandra*. Sometimes Anna could be a little too open with her friends. Of course, Archie was right, he did need more feet on the ground. Tom had given the station a call to get a squad car sent over with a few extra uniforms. There was a lifeboat practice the following Tuesday, so he'd decided that would be a good time to get some statements. Everyone in the same place and the chance to see how they were all behaving around one another.

"Under control, Archie," he said. He'd been going for jovial; it came out a little sharply and Archie dropped his head. He'd certainly aged in the last eighteen months. There was a sagginess about his features that Tom hadn't noticed before. He hoped he was doing alright since the heart attack. Tom didn't think Anna would manage very well without him.

Archie saw him out, but when Tom turned to wave, Archie

had already closed the door, the house immediately resuming its uptight, neat and tidy aura. Tom shrugged. He shouldn't take it personally; Archie would never have meant it to be pointed. He just couldn't shake the notion that Archie had been a little keen to get rid of him.

Chapter 6

Toby put some of his clothes into the laundry basket with another two soggy hankies. His dad had warned him it wouldn't all be plain sailing, in that annoying, listen-to-me-son voice of his. Any engagement would have its stresses and strains, but theirs would, apparently, be harder, because their lives were played out in a small close-knit community. Until now, it had been relatively easy. Genni had been great, a good laugh. She hadn't seemed bothered by anything, even when Toby was grumpy after a long week at work.

Then Caz disappeared, and it was like a switch had been flicked. Lifeboat was family, that was true, and Genni only had her mum, but suddenly she was crying all the time, and so clingy. Toby didn't have anyone else either, but he wasn't making a song and dance about it all. He moved over to the window and leaned on the wide sill. Everything was upside down. He'd even tried to distract Genni by talking about the wedding, but she'd still spent the last hour sobbing.

Toby looked around his bedroom. Today you could see some part of the floor which meant his mum had probably been in to get more of his washing. He ought to make more of an effort to put it all in the laundry basket, but he was too tired more often than not. He folded his arms. He couldn't understand why everyone was taking the disappearance so badly. Caz had hardly been Mrs Popular, and yet even his dad was going around like a storm about to break. His mum, as per usual, was simply waiting for it all to blow over. At dinner, she'd said that she thought Caz would probably re-appear and wonder what all the fuss was about.

Toby collapsed onto his bed. It was a well-practised fall, backwards. He'd been doing it since he was twelve. He was still at home because they were saving for a deposit, and living with his parents was cheap but the room was horribly claustrophobic. He wondered when it had stopped being his space and had just become somewhere to sleep. The curtains were covered in garish superheroes, the walls dotted with Blu Tack, where he'd taken down his posters, and though Genni had found him an old plain duvet cover, in a bid to make it feel less like a teenage boy's room, it just felt like four walls and a bed. The guys teased him about it constantly. They all knew the plan, knew he was doing it for Genni, but they never missed an opportunity to have a dig.

He looked at his watch. He wasn't quite tired yet, even though he needed to be in early at the bakery. His turn to get the ovens on and the first batch in. He could hear the murmur of the TV, a noise he'd been falling asleep to for as long as he could remember. It oozed through the floorboards, reminding him that he was here on sufferance, that this wasn't his home anymore. He checked his phone. Nothing from Genni. She was probably still on her way home. Nothing from anyone except a reminder about the next morning. He pulled on a pair of joggers and slipped downstairs.

He stood in the kitchen wondering whether to make a cup of tea or perhaps to have a beer from the fridge. He knew he'd regret that; the morning was bad enough as it was. Through the window he could see the sky, a dark navy above the hedge – a thin strip of green that ran around the back of the house like a comfort blanket.

Toby opened the door and walked out. There was a bit of gravel at the front where they parked the cars and where his mum had put a small table and chairs, more in hope than expectation, as she never had a spare moment to sit down and in the summer the road was nose-to-tail with tourists. He thought, who wants to be gawped at while drinking coffee? The house had been built at the end of the 1950s, a small two-up-two-down that'd been extended many times. Some bits were alright, others poorly thought out and even more poorly built. The kitchen, single storey, always smelt slightly damp and had covered over the small back garden. His dad was always promising to knock it down and build something less shoddy, but they never had the money. The lifeboat meant he didn't get to do much overtime and working just up the road was important to him. When the pager went off, he could down tools and be ready to hit the ramp in less than ten minutes.

His mum worked in Helston at an engineering firm, something in HR. She brought home gossip and the weekly shop. She was a tall woman, grey-haired, recently dyed blonde. His dad always joked that he'd asked her to marry him simply because he didn't get neck ache when he was with her. Not a joke that sat well with Toby. Partly because he'd heard it about a million times and partly because his sister was nearly five-foot-nine in her socks, but he was only five-six in his shoes. Life was so bloody unfair.

He looked towards the pub. Sadly, also not a good idea, plus he didn't have much of the week's wages left. He pulled on his trainers and closed the door quietly behind him. He turned out of the drive, past the rusting table and chairs and began to make his way down to the Point. There wasn't much light, but he'd done this a thousand times. There was a gentle moon behind the thinnest of clouds, so he couldn't see many stars, but there was enough light to see by. He checked his phone. Here, there was no signal. There wouldn't be any until he got right to the bottom. He began to jog, just a few paces. He stopped, looked around him. Suddenly he couldn't be arsed. It was too cold, and he was too tired. He about-faced and retraced his steps. Back in the house he checked his pager didn't need charging, that there were still no messages on his phone and took himself up to bed.

***

Genni knelt in front of Abigail and handed her a tissue. Abigail was seven going on seventeen and was a clever girl. Genni didn't much like her, but it wasn't the child's fault that she knew all the right buttons to press. She probably didn't get tons of one-on-one time at home.

"Being bullied can be very upsetting," Genni said.

Abigail sniffed and dabbed the tissue under her nose.

"Samantha's been horrible to me all week. I was too scared to tell anyone."

The girl in question, was sitting at her desk watching them, bewildered at the storm of tears she'd seemingly created. And she looked scared. Her parents would want to know all the details, would want to talk about it and Samantha didn't seem to have a clue about what was going on. Genni thought it more likely that Samantha was the one being bullied, because she was obviously struggling in class. Genni had wondered about getting some extra help for her, but there wasn't much money available, and she wasn't exactly failing, just not flourishing.

Genni pushed herself up. Well, Samantha wasn't the only one who was struggling to flourish. She turned away suddenly feeling angry and even Abigail stopped sniffling. Genni walked to the front of the class.

"Right, everyone! Find your reading books. We need to get on."

Abigail stood there for another couple of seconds frowning, then reluctantly joined the melee around the drawers.

Genni knew she wasn't handling the situation well; she wasn't being a good teacher. Neither of the girls would feel the issue was resolved and she wondered which of the parents would be first to pop in for a chat, to get to the bottom of why their daughter was so upset.

At three o'clock, when the last of the children had disappeared through the door she sank back onto her chair, exhausted, her uneaten sandwiches sitting on the desk. She switched her pager back on, just in case. Most shouts happened in the late afternoon, or early evening, when people had finally talked themselves into getting help.

She could be at the station from work within five minutes, sometimes less — fifteen from her mum's house at Mullion, where she was still living. Genni didn't always make it in time from her mum's, so she tried to stay on at school for as long as possible, which meant she had plenty of time to prepare for the following day, even the following week.

She was a good teacher, she told herself, at least most of the time. She'd always loved helping others get to grips with things. She held the tissue under each eye. She checked her pager again, which was pointless because it was loud enough to wake the dead.

Her grandad had been part of the lifeboat crew, and both her uncles, and as her dad wasn't around, she'd felt it was up to her to carry on the family tradition. She knew that some people found it funny but at times she couldn't tell if it was her sex or her colour they were laughing at. One of her uncles had even said that she was starting a tradition all of her own.

With school so close to the station, being on crew made sense. The constant training was hard work but mostly good fun, and as she was one of the few women, the only black one, meant she had been a bit of a novelty. Genni had been flirted with, looked after, and been the mascot right up until Caz had walked down those steps, her head held high, confidence oozing from every pore. Looking back, that was the day that everything had changed. Genni put her head in her hands and wept, dripping tears onto a pile of spelling books that she ought to have given out at home time.

***

Anna was on her way home after seeing Harriet for a chat. She was thinking about her lunch with Tom the previous week. It'd been well over a year since she and Tom had decided to be together and they weren't making such a bad job of it, or so she hoped. They'd settled into a gentle routine that was only really disturbed by the big church celebrations or a particularly difficult murder in Falmouth. Sometimes they met in Helston and had a meal out or went to the cinema but although Helston felt a million miles away from The Lizard there was always someone who said, "Hello, Reverend Maybury. You baptised my baby ... married me ... buried my uncle ..." And she'd find herself edging away from Tom, gently loosening the grip of his hand to step closer to her parishioner.

She supposed that having made the decision to go out with him, she now had to go on making that choice every day. She wondered if this was what it was like for everyone else, though when she'd tried asking Harriet, that morning, she hadn't been able to explain herself very well. Harriet had spent the whole time smiling knowingly, which had got a bit annoying. She and Derek were safely ensconced in the new house, with nothing better to do than decide what colour to paint the walls.

The jealousy exploded through Anna as if a bucket of cold water had been thrown over her. It wasn't as bad as it used to be, she just had to wait for it to pass, but she did feel that life wasn't always fair.

She thought about the bench above Church Cove. It was only another three minutes down the lane and though it was nippy for April, a bit of sea and the distant horizon would help her think.

She patted the back door absent-mindedly as though reassuring herself that she would return soon and pocketed the key. She would go down to Church Cove and pray. It was work; she didn't have to justify it to anyone — apart from herself. She crunched back around the house, but as she turned the corner someone was coming down the drive, which made her jump. Jim, the lifeboat coxswain, was a tall man and moved surprisingly quietly on the gravel.

"Jim. How are you?"

He nodded, as if that were answer enough and then looked over his shoulder, as if to check that no one had spotted him turning into the vicarage. That irritated Anna. What was the big deal?

"Can I help you?" she asked.

"You look as if you're heading out." It sounded like an accusation.

"I can easily put off what I was planning to do. Come on in."

She made coffee because it took longer than tea, while he sat in the large front room. She pretended she needed thinking time, but really, she was just reluctant to go and face him. The last time he'd popped in was to organise the blessing of the lifeboat, something he said he'd been meaning to do for a while. He'd been officious and curt, as if he was only doing it because he felt he had no choice. Anna knew that Archie had been dropping hints for months, but she didn't mention that. Archie's rootedness in the community was something she took for granted and for once it had paid off. She was now more than just *chaplain in name* to the lifeboat. Now, she had invites to a couple of their fundraisers and had been asked to say grace at the annual dinner. She must remember to make sure that Tom kept the date free. There was no way she was going on her own. Mind you, she supposed, she could always ask Archie to accompany her. He'd be going anyway, so it wouldn't put him out at all, and Tom might be busy.

Jim was standing by the window. He also jumped when she pushed open the door which surprised Anna. This was the man who took the wheel when *Rose* headed out to sea, mostly when other craft were hightailing it back to safety. A man who faced danger with a pragmatism that left Anna feeling, at best inadequate, at least, overawed. When he'd last been there, he'd filled the place with his presence, now he felt smaller. Last time, it meant she'd finally arrived because he'd sat in her lounge and asked her to pray over his boat. This time she wondered what he needed from her.

"So, Jim, what can I do for you?"

He sat down at the end of the sofa. The man was over six feet four and not a beanpole; he didn't look comfortable. He stood up and went back to the window. He stared out onto the gravel, his hands clasped behind him.

"It's just the disappearance of Caz, Caroline. It's upset everyone and we wondered if you'd come down and pray through the place." He was patently embarrassed at using such language. Anna couldn't remember ever hearing him use the term 'we'. She felt like saying, 'shall I bring holy water and splash it about a bit?' She bit her lip and reminded herself that a young woman had disappeared, and that people often didn't get the prayer thing. Didn't really get God. Hadn't Caz likened him to a ghost?

"Would the crew like me to come, so they have someone to talk to?" she asked and knew she had sounded a little needy.

Jim stiffened and went back to the sofa. He picked up his mug and took a sip. It was strong coffee and he looked mollified. Anna was glad she'd put in two scoops.

"No offence but they're not the sort to need that."

Anna wanted to argue that there were over forty people — boat and shore crew. That they couldn't all be like Jim, feeling like Jim, coping like Jim thought he was. Anna didn't think he looked like he was managing at all. She thought he might be scared, or even bewildered, which didn't sound right at all.

"Of course I'll come down and pray and let them know that I'm around if they need me."

He nodded, but she didn't think he would.

"Caz is probably abroad somewhere, having a break and when she gets back will be sorry for the fuss she's caused." Anna tried to sound reassuring. Even to her own ears it didn't ring true. No one would go away for more than three weeks, nearly four now, without letting their boss know first.

"No, she'd have told her dad. He's all she's got as her mum left them when she was little."

"Oh, poor girl."

Anna wondered if Tom hadn't appeared quite so early that Saturday morning, when Caz had turned up on her doorstep, and if Anna, herself, had been able to see past the ghosts and getting her sermon finished, whether Caz might have told her that herself.

***

Jim fumbled for his key. He didn't normally come home for lunch, but he'd been working all morning down in the pit, on a truck with a long wheelbase so they hadn't been able to shut the doors. He'd felt a draught on his neck for hours so didn't fancy sitting in the cold office eating a cheese sandwich. He wanted hot tea out of a clean mug.

The kitchen was in its usual state from breakfast. Margery normally had a go at sorting it before she tackled dinner. He carefully pushed everything to one side and switched on the kettle. He turned his back to it and through the frosted glass door into the lounge he saw the TV flickering.

"Bloody hell," he muttered. "We're not made of money." He marched in, stopping when he saw Toby draped along the sofa, his shoes lying where he'd slipped them off, still covered in flour. Toby sat up quickly. Jim had obviously given him a bit of a start.

"What are you doing back at this hour?" Jim almost shouted.

"Not feeling well."

"You look fine. You swinging the lead?"

"No, Dad. Of course not. I'm allowed to feel ill once in a while." Toby peered at his father just like he had when he was a boy, staring through those blonde eyelashes. He'd his mother's family colouring — red hair and freckles across his nose.

Jim felt for his son, he did, but if he wanted to get on in the world, he needed to be able to work hard and take it on the chin.

"So why're you home?" Toby said, kicking his shoes under the coffee table.

"Kettle broke and I wanted a hot cup of tea with my lunch."

Toby switched off the television and stood up. He barely

reached his father's shoulder.

"Shoes!" Jim said. "You're not a teenager anymore. And you could help more around the house. Help your Mum out."

With his trainers dangling from his hand, Toby turned to stare at his dad.

"Like you do, you mean?" The door to the stairs slammed, before Jim could think of something suitable to say. He'd have liked to have asked about Genni, whether she was still blubbing about Caz as she'd been worse than useless at practice. He heard the click of the kettle and went back into the kitchen to make his tea. The place was a bit of a mess, more so than usual because Toby had obviously had lunch and had left everything all over the countertop. So much for feeling unwell! The boy was acting as if he didn't owe them a thing. He lived virtually rent-free; he should be at least a little grateful! Jim pulled a large mug from the cupboard. It was one Toby had given him the Christmas before. "Lifeboat men always have a plan B." He'd found it online and Jim had wondered if they could get a box of them to sell at the shop. Margery had muttered something about sexism, but that was nonsense.

Jim used his arm to make a bit more space around the kettle. With a crash one of Margery's mugs fell to the floor, one of the fancy china ones she liked. She said she got them from the charity shops, said she didn't like drinking out of the normal ones. He used the toe of his boot to push the tea dregs and china shards into a pile. Well, at least it wouldn't have cost too much.

Everything was out of sorts. Caz was making them feel out of sorts and edgy. He sat down at the table and took a bite of his sandwich, but even that tasted dry and bland. If Caz were here now, he'd give her a right bollocking, he'd really let her have it though, of course, if she were here now, he wouldn't have to.

Chapter 7

Harriet was sitting on the bench outside the front door. She'd thought it would be warm enough in the sun but had quickly begun to shiver. She wanted to go and see Anna, to have a moan, but she was fairly sure the Rural Dean was coming over for her usual visit. Earlier that morning, Derek had said he was thinking of going to the dog pound to choose another dog with Simeon. Derek missed Dolly, he missed walking with Simeon first thing, which he'd stopped doing when Dolly had got too doddery to go more than a few yards.

The problem was, she'd always thought that they would choose a new dog together. Why did he want to take Simeon, and not her? Stuff the Rural Dean, she thought. She leaned back against the wall and shut her eyes. The garden had filled with shoots and bulbs they'd never seen before, or previously had been buried under piles of timber and rubble. Even the lawn had mostly recovered, though there were still bare patches where they'd mixed the concrete.

It was a lovely April morning, the house was nearly finished, there was no rain forecast for a couple of days, so why was she feeling so restless and crotchety? Derek would be back soon, but she simply didn't want to talk to him about the water heater, the new dog, his scattergun approach to doing up the house, or any of the other things she hadn't been entirely truthful about. She put her cup down and returned to the hall to find her shoes and coat.

When she reached the centre of the village there was no one about, at least no one she knew. She was beginning to feel irritated, which was a change from restless and ungrateful. She waved to Jean in the shop, turned left and headed down to the Point. She hadn't had a cup of coffee at the cafe for ages. She would treat herself. As she passed the last building the view opened up, land meeting sky with room to breathe. Archie's house was away to the right, the lighthouse and cottages to the left. The clouds had lifted a little, but she was still well wrapped up against the wind. Harriet hadn't warmed up from sitting out, so she'd chosen one of her thick, fleecy jackets, with a high collar. It might be mid-April but the wind blowing up from the sea was cold.

At the end of the path, through the car park, the sea spilled out to the horizon. She stopped to stare, where she always paused, at the top of the steps down onto the coastal path. The waves, slate grey, were criss-crossed with foam where they rebounded off the rocks. It must be closer to low tide than high tide because she could see so many, like broken teeth, with skirts of weed and froth. There was a seal, bobbing about with the swell and she almost waved to it. She breathed in deeply and found a smile was beginning to stretch across her face. This had been a good idea.

Inside the cafe, there were a couple of walkers as well as Catherine, who was sitting quietly on the lower level with a book. She looked up at the sound of the door and waved Harriet over. Harriet wasn't sure if she was pleased to see her or not.

"You look as if you're having a good time. I won't disturb you," Harriet said.

"I'm very happy to be disturbed. I've already been here an hour, so if I want to stay longer, I shall need to order another drink."

"Coffee?"

Catherine shook her head sadly.

"More than one and I get indigestion. Oh, yes, and too much caffeine after two o'clock stops me sleeping. It's no fun getting old. I'll have peppermint tea. Perk me up a bit."

Harriet went back to the counter. She'd been going to have some cake, but she wouldn't do so now. She looked back at Tom's mum. Tall, slim, with short thick grey hair, neatly cut and with disconcerting pale blue eyes that were just like Tom's. Catherine was carefully tucking away her book and removing her glasses. She didn't really look like Tom until she peered at you, then there was that penetrating stare that made you feel you were guilty of something.

"So, how are you?" Harriet asked, sliding in opposite. She would have preferred facing the other way, so that she didn't have to continually stare at the part of the cliff where the man had gone over — the man who had caused such problems on *that* terrible retreat. But Catherine wouldn't want to look at it either.

"Good. Everything that I would like done to the house is nearly done. I might treat myself to a new bathroom next year but apart from that it's lovely. What about yours?"

"Getting there, though we've still quite a few niggles. I genuinely thought we'd be sorted by now, but Derek isn't very good at deciding on final details. He keeps changing his mind and so on it goes."

Catherine looked at her through slightly narrowed eyes and then sat back.

"All I'd like to have is hot water we can rely on," Harriet continued, resting her elbows on the table, "and one room that wasn't covered in brick dust."

"You're welcome to come and use my facilities whenever you like."

"Might be a bit crowded if Tom is there too."

"He tends to turn up on the weekends, and I'm lucky if I see him for more than a few minutes."

Harriet looked down at her hands. Was there the tiniest touch of jealousy in that sentence?

"I guess he may be over a bit more than that now, because of the missing woman," Harriet replied.

"It must be absolutely dreadful having someone simply disappear like that."

"But they'll pull out all the stops," Harriet said, "her father is ex-police."

"Oh, I'm sure Tom would do his best anyway."

They stopped for a moment. The tall lanky boy holding their drinks was new and Harriet wondered how long he'd stay.

"I didn't mean to imply that Tom was anything other than professional, but it must be a bit of a comedown dealing with a missing woman, rather than murder."

"Unless they know something we don't." Catherine turned to stare out at the view. From where they were sitting you could see right across the maelstrom that was the end of The Lizard; the bay of teeth that was so good at ripping holes in boats and tossing them away. In sight of land, yet not close enough. The old lifeboat station below them must have been a real beacon of hope. "They don't tell the public everything and if Tom is involved it might mean things are further on than we realise."

"I still can't imagine someone just disappearing like that," Harriet said.

"I did know a family, back in Wiltshire, whose son went missing. It must have been nearly five years ago. The police didn't seem to take it particularly seriously. They thought he'd probably just gone walkabout. He was nineteen and had had a row with his dad the morning he disappeared, but it felt out of character. He was going off to uni the following September, had everything to live for. His parents spent a fortune on private detectives and searches. They never came close to getting over it." This time there was a catch in her throat. "It was, it is awful. I guess when they're not hoping he'll just walk in the door, they're waiting for someone to find a body. Salisbury Plain is a huge area and if he'd fallen over and hurt himself..."

Harriet shivered. That was horrible.

"I don't think that could have happened to Caz Denbigh, unless she fell into the sea."

They both sipped their drinks. Catherine's hand was curled into a tight fist on the table, her light blue eyes staring over Harriet's shoulder. Just now, she looked unnervingly like Tom, and Harriet wondered what she hadn't done that she ought to have done. Tom always had that effect on her.

"So what can you do about your building site?" Catherine asked, quite cheerfully.

A good subject change, thought Harriet.

"I think I need to be a bit more adamant about some of our choices. Derek is like a kid in a candy store and is loving it, but I'm a bit fed up." Harriet hesitated, took a sip of coffee. "The trouble is, though it's our home, it's all his money. His and his dead wife's."

"Ah," said Catherine, nodding. "That might be why he's changing his mind so often. He's trying to get you to show him what you would like, so that it's your home too."

Harriet frowned. It made sense but also made her feel uncomfortable.

"So do you think Tom and Anna will get married?" she asked.

Catherine's eyes widened.

"Absolutely none of my business."

"I suppose, but what you think may have a bearing on it," Harriet said, carefully.

"Why? I really don't have anything to do with it."

Harriet laughed.

"But it's Anna. Of course, what she thinks you think will have a bearing on it."

"I just want them to be happy."

Harriet shook her head. It was what everyone said, but it wasn't quite true. There was always a caveat, and happiness meant such different things to different people. She wondered what people wanted for her and Derek, what she herself wanted. No, that was too much for her just now.

"So, a new bathroom. What sort of thing were you thinking of?" she said, deciding that that was a much safer subject.

***

Archie sat down at the dining room table and pulled the

church accounts towards him. They were coming up to the annual meeting and the treasurer usually got Archie to present them. He liked figures, not people, and got flustered when asked questions. Whereas, if Archie answered a question wrongly, the treasurer was invariably able to explain, quite succinctly, why Archie was in error. Archie took it on the chin because the one time the treasurer had tried to explain the finances first-hand, he'd ended up talking so quickly that nobody had understood a word he'd said. At least, that year, there hadn't been any difficult questions.

The figures were bad but not as bad as usual. If there'd been fourteen months in the year, they might have been alright. Luckily the retreat was in the black, if only by the tiniest of margins.

Archie wondered if he could afford to bolster the general fund a bit, though he had a feeling that Anna knew exactly where any mysterious donations came from. Perhaps everyone realised. He pushed the ledger away and pulled his latest book towards him. It was another hefty tome on the history of the navy, given to him by the Bishop, because they'd served together on a frigate.

A while later, Archie realised he hadn't read a single word, so he put the book down and picked up the rota for the next retreat. It was more or less sorted, and Catherine had said she would come and sit in the lounge during a couple of the afternoons just in case anything was needed. Way back, they'd decided that if there were more than three guests, there should be at least two of them available at all times for a chat, for topping up the milk jug or simply making the place feel less empty. Catherine was proving useful and might also be the reason the general finances were less dodgy.

Archie stood up. He needed to stretch his back. He would go and make a cup of tea. At the fridge he realised he was a little low on milk. He didn't like running out of things so decided a brisk walk up to the shop wouldn't do any harm. There'd been a brief flash of blue sky, the clouds looked less glowering, and if he didn't chat too long, he'd be back home in the light. He was feeling restless, in need of some exercise. He knew why too. Tom always made him feel inadequate, defensive, no matter how often he prayed about it. And he had prayed about it a lot particularly after Tom's last visit, the week before. Archie simply didn't understand Tom's starting point, that there were more bad guys than good, and of course that there probably wasn't a God.

Archie's house was right at the end of the road, nothing between him and the sea. It was about two hundred metres to the next dwellings, a couple of bungalows, and beyond them, just before the road forked, was Caz Denbigh's place, sitting at the end of a short terrace. It was stone built, right on the road. The kitchen was below ground, presumably in the old cellar, so the bottom of the tall rectangular window was at tyre level. Of course, not that many cars went up and down the lane and while at the sink she would have had a glorious view of the hedge and beyond that, the sky. Archie had never peered in, that would have been rude, but he always had the impression that it was a cheerful home, with daffodil-yellow curtains and a row of plants along the sill.

As usual he carefully averted his eyes and upped his pace. He really was getting to be a bit of an old man and he didn't like that at all.

He had a good chat with Jean. The shop had been busy, but her daughter was picking up the grandchildren, so there was no need to race off to Helston.

When Archie noticed a light flickering on at the pub, he took his leave. He was tempted by an early drink but thought he ought to go and have some tea first. A little reluctantly, he headed into the dimness of an overcast sky, pulling up his collar against the stiffening breeze. It didn't feel like April at all, and he wondered if they were going to get any good weather that spring.

Just as he was walking past Miss Denbigh's house, despite turning to look across the fields, something caught his eye. There seemed to have been a movement down in the kitchen. For a moment he was flooded with relief. She must have returned and yet he couldn't help but look back because something didn't feel right. Archie turned around. Keeping close to the edge of the lane he slowly retraced his steps. The first neighbours were home, lights on in three of the rooms even though it wasn't close to sunset yet. The house in the middle was unlit except for the flickering of Mrs Protheroe's television. Caz's house was at the far end, with its front door around the back.

Facing the road were several hung sash windows of varying sizes. He peered down into the kitchen where he could just make out a pile of papers, as if a drawer had been tipped out. He couldn't see anyone, so he slipped around the corner onto the drive. This side was just a wall of bricks and stone and a width of gravel into the back garden. The other two gardens were accessed from the other end.

Miss Denbigh's car, a dark blue Ford, was still parked where she'd left it. Mrs Protheroe's car was squeezed in beside it. There was a gate in a tall hedge leading from the drive into the small back garden and from the gate, a paved path to the front door of the house. It was a back-front door just like Simeon's, which made Archie smile.

The garden looked well cared for, though the lawn needed cutting. The tiny dining room which led into the kitchen was also dim. The house felt shut up and empty but still Archie slipped along to the door. He found himself creeping and that made him feel really uncomfortable, so he straightened his back. Only he'd been right to feel that something was wrong. The door was the tiniest bit ajar, splinters of white wood showing clearly against the red paint.

Breathing a little heavily, Archie made his way back out onto the road and headed a few yards closer to the village. He phoned Tom. He wondered why he'd done that and not 999 but it was a good idea. Tom was down at the vicarage with Anna.

"I'll be there immediately. Stay out of sight, Archie, but get a description if you see anyone leave."

Archie felt a little aggrieved that Tom had felt the need to spell that out, but he could also hear that Tom was running. Archie was glad that he'd taken him seriously.

Chapter 8

Tom found Archie looking out over the fields. There was nothing beyond apart from flat grass dotted with sheep and edged with a seagull filled sky. He was upright as ever, hands clasped behind his back, as if simply admiring the view. Tom wondered if he ever relaxed. He was a good way up from Caz's house, which was sensible. Tom was glad Archie had listened to him. He'd been worried that he might have spooked the burglar, by hanging around too obviously. Tom pulled in beside him.

"Stay here, Archie. Phone 999 if I'm not out again in five minutes."

Archie raised an eyebrow. Tom shrugged. He wasn't afraid of kids or a single thief taking advantage of a bit of local knowledge. Deep down he hoped that Archie would think he was being just a little courageous. Not brave, courageous. That had more depth, more of a ring to it. He walked down the side of the house and slipped into the back garden. He reckoned by the length of the grass that she'd definitely been gone the full four weeks. That if she'd been intending to go away, she'd have got someone to mow it while she was gone. The more he found out about her, the more he believed she'd been that sort of woman.

Tom pushed the front door a little further, but the junk mail had accumulated alarmingly since he'd first been in. At least that meant it would be difficult for the person, or persons unknown to get out in a hurry. He squeezed through the gap and listened. Sure enough, from upstairs he could hear creaking floorboards. He popped his head around the door leading into the dining area and kitchen and glanced into the lounge. He had to be sure there was no one else there, no one else who could creep up behind him. He pulled out his warrant card and shouted.

"This is the police, come down and make yourself known."

The floorboards stopped protesting. The silence of someone listening poured down the stairs. Would they make a break for it? Try and push past? Or would they come quietly? Tom began to make his way to the bottom of the stairs. He didn't think anyone could get out of the upstairs windows; he was pretty sure most of them had locks. He'd been impressed that the young woman in question had been so sensible. Now he knew that her dad was an ex-copper, a lot of things were beginning to make sense.

"It's alright. Caz is my daughter," a voice shouted from the landing. "I'm coming down."

"Keep your hands where I can see them," Tom said.

"I know the drill. I was in the Met for thirty years."

There was a small window halfway down, where the stairs turned back on themselves. It darkened. The man was big. Well over six foot and wide. Not fat, just very well-built. He wore dark jeans and a corduroy shirt under a leather jacket. He stopped on the tiny landing. Tom stepped away to get out of the man's shadow.

"Do you have any identification?"

"I do, and you?"

Tom waved his card at him. The man frowned and came on down. The hall felt very small.

"You're Tom Edwards. What are you doing checking up on a burglary?"

Tom took the proffered driving licence. Gerald Denbigh.

"I was in the area. What are *you* doing here?"

"It's my daughter's house. She's been missing for four weeks. You've done bugger all to find her, so I thought I'd come and see what was going on."

"It may be your daughter's house, but you don't appear to have a key. What were relations like?"

"She was going to let me have one, she just hadn't got round to it. Caz is tight on security. She's my daughter!" As he looked at Tom, he narrowed his eyes. "She understands that there are a lot of low-lifes out there, who don't care who they damage."

"So, you haven't been here for a while?"

"No, but she's been up to me a couple of times. I have a key for the old locks. She had them changed, not that long ago."

"Why did she do that?"

Denbigh dropped back to sit on the stairs. They were too narrow, so he stood up again. His hair was dark, receding. Tom wondered if he dyed it. His face was lined but currently impassive.

"I don't know why. She never said, I never thought to ask. She said she'd got me a set cut and I could collect them when I next came down, or she came up. I haven't found them."

"When were you last here?"

"September. I stayed in the house while she went off somewhere for her job. I saw her for a couple of days prior to her leaving."

"Have you found anything? You've obviously been searching."

"And you obviously haven't."

Tom bridled at that. They'd had the call just over a week before and were trying to work out a timeline. Archie was still the last person to have spoken to her. No one seemed to have seen her beyond that and obviously, she hadn't taken her car.

Denbigh continued, "Something dodgy has happened. Number one, she would have let me know if she was going away. Number two, her car is still here. Her keys for it are in the drawer in the dining room."

"Someone could have picked her up", said Tom. It was a possibility, though he didn't really think so.

"It's a long way out of anyone's way."

"Someone from here? Can you tell me anything about friends, boyfriends? The people at her office were singularly unhelpful." Denbigh shook his head. "What about the lifeboat crew? She spent a lot of time with them." Again, the man shook his head. With his back to the window that was halfway up the stairs, the light in the quickly dimming hallway made it difficult to see his expression. "I'll have to talk to them."

"You better get some help then. There are a lot of them by all accounts. I guess there's nothing else to do around here."

Tom looked hard at the man, for signs of distress, but all he could see was a copper who knew what was what and exactly how he could make Tom's life a total misery.

"You're going to have to leave. I'll need someone else to corroborate that you and your daughter were on good terms. What do you want to do?"

"I'm going to stay around."

"I wouldn't advise it."

"That's exactly what I would've said if I were you, but she's my daughter and she's still missing. So take a deep breath, DI Edwards, because I'm here for the foreseeable. Anywhere you'd recommend?"

"The pub does rooms," Tom found himself saying, but then added, firmly, "Just let me do my job."

"Of course I will, Officer. But I'm a distraught father so you'll have to cut me some slack."

"Right then, family liaison it is. I'll get a representative to contact you shortly."

Denbigh reached into the inside pocket of his jacket. Tom couldn't help tensing. Denbigh put out a hand to reassure him and produced a card with his name and mobile clearly printed in a neat square script. Gerald Denbigh. Tom took the card and stepped outside. The man was leaning down to clear the mail.

"Leave that," Tom said, sharply. He enjoyed watching Denbigh straighten up and force himself through the gap. It really was a bit of a squeeze.

"You'll get someone to come and secure the residence."

Tom didn't bother replying, he was already on the phone to the station.

Archie had come a little closer and Tom was pleased to see

that his mobile was in his hand. As Caz's father passed Archie, he nodded as if he were out for an evening stroll.

"Is everything alright?" Archie asked, hurrying over.

Tom put his mobile away.

"Oh, Archie. That is my worst nightmare." They both turned to watch Denbigh disappear into the village. Archie frowned. Tom blew out his cheeks, expelling a long breath. He knew he was milking it a bit but Gerald Denbigh poking his nose around wasn't great.

"That was Caz's dad, down from London. He broke in because he doesn't have a key and didn't seem to know that the neighbours have one."

"Surely, he ought to have known that," Archie said, his frown deepening. It was the first thing that Tom was going to do, check with the terrace residents to see what they knew of Caz's father.

Tom turned to face the house, as he did so a squall of rain hit the back of his head, like a slap. When he'd been a young constable, one of the sergeants used to do just that. Creep up behind you, slap the back of your head, then justify it by finding some ridiculous fault with what you were doing.

Tom felt just like he had back then, slightly foolish and very aggrieved. What had he done wrong now? What had he missed? What more should he be doing?

"Archie, get yourself home. I'll wait here for the team. I'll have to do another search now, and hopefully daddy won't have messed up any of the evidence."

Archie, nodded.

"Of course. Come down at any time for a cup of something hot."

For a second Tom was pathetically grateful that Archie seemed to understand what a pain Gerald Denbigh could turn out to be, then he spoiled it all by saying, "That poor man. It must be so terrible for him. His daughter's gone missing and there doesn't seem to be any evidence of anything."

Tom shut his eyes.

"Oh, there'll be evidence of something, I just have to find it."

***

Genni parked her car in the layby by the church. She'd been worried about turning around in the vicarage drive, perhaps even having to reverse back out onto the lane. From the top it had seemed a bit overgrown and narrow. Caz had said she'd been there, but she'd walked, and that the vicar was nice enough.

Genni remembered Anna from the blessing day, and she'd got the impression that she was alright, too. They'd chatted for ages and Anna had seemed really interested in everything. She'd even got excited about the wedding, though they still hadn't managed to set a date. There were one or two details that needed sorting and of course the Caz thing made it virtually impossible to concentrate.

Genni had thought they would get married over in Mullion, as it was where most of her family lived but Jim had said it ought to be close to the lifeboat and then if there was a shout it wouldn't be too far to scramble. Well, as long as he wasn't expecting her to assemble in her wedding dress. Genni felt tears prickling again. She pressed her knuckles into her eyes just as a child would, trying to fill the sockets with her fingers instead of the inevitable tears. Toby would be furious that she was here, would be furious that she was crying again.

It began to rain, gently at first and then it was as if the clouds had simply split open. It thrummed on the top of her car like a drum. She got out, pulling her coat over her head and began to run. She had to talk to someone before she simply ground to a halt — someone who wasn't on the boat, someone who hadn't lived at the end of the world all their lives or were worried she might lose her focus at school.

The vicar opened the door almost immediately, like she'd been waiting for her.

"Come on in before you get washed away."

She looked a little dishevelled, as if she'd been asleep. There was the smell of toast and suddenly Genni was hungry. She hadn't had anything since her snatched lunch just before the kids came back from play time. The last couple of hours before the end of school were always hard. You couldn't do anything too gentle as they'd end up falling asleep but anything too energetic was met with whining and tears.

"I'm sorry to come so late and without making an appointment."

"It's no bother. I don't have a meeting tonight and you've saved me from having to tackle my sermon for Sunday."

Genni looked down at her shoes. Was she expecting them to start coming to church if they were getting married there? It was a bit of a tricky subject. She'd thought they might look into having the ceremony at one of the local hotels, but that hadn't gone down well with either of the parents, though Margery had said that they ought to be allowed to do what they wanted to do. Genni had been momentarily grateful until Jim had pointed out that as he and her own mum were contributing substantially, they would have a say in what happened. Genni had shrugged. Toby had taken her hand under the table and squeezed it.

"The front room's a bit chilly, would you mind coming through to the kitchen?"

The kitchen was a long narrow room. On one side there were units ranged under a large window, and on the other a blank wall against which rested a red Formica table. Her grandfather had had one in his kitchen. It felt familiar.

"Sit down, Genni."

Genni pulled out a chair.

"Tea, coffee?"

"Tea, please."

The vicar pottered about. She stuck bags in mugs but did get a plate for some biscuits. Toby would have raised an eyebrow at Genni eating one before tea. He'd said that if she wanted to look nice, she'd have to shed a few pounds. All brides did that, didn't they?

She took a biscuit and almost dipped it into the cup before she remembered that perhaps the vicar might think it a bit rude. Though when the vicar slid into the seat opposite, she took one and without hesitation dipped it into her tea.

"I know I shouldn't, but sometimes it's the thing to do. Now how can I help you?"

Genni grabbed another biscuit and dunked it. They could always let the dress out. She wondered where she should start. The vicar got up, opened a drawer that squeaked and handed her a teaspoon. Genni looked down. Sure enough half her biscuit had sunk to the bottom.

"Sorry. I've been doing that a lot lately."

"Me too. Now is it about the wedding?"

Genni shook her head and then nodded. How could she tell this stranger how she was feeling? And wasn't her boyfriend the policeman, who was now looking for Caz. Genni hadn't thought of that before.

"Call me Anna."

Genni nodded and then wondered why the vicar had brought her into the kitchen. She'd taken Caz into the front room. Was she being treated differently simply because … it had always been the difference between them.

"Do you have a date yet?"

"No, not quite. Are you getting booked up?"

"Not particularly. The problem is normally the reception afterwards."

"Jim doesn't think it will be too much of an issue. He's known the owner of the Housel Bay Hotel since they were young men. They've probably already got something fixed. From there, if there's a shout, the crew will be able to get down the ramp in no time."

"At least your drinks bill will be reasonable if half your

guests are on standby."

"There'll be a rota and the boys of Newlyn will come and help if it looks like it's a long job."

"That's handy."

"It's what we did for them last year when their coxswain celebrated his twenty-fifth wedding anniversary."

Genni took another sip of her tea and sat a little straighter.

"Can I ask you a question?"

"Of course, as long as it's not about ghosts."

Genni froze. Caz had talked to her about the mysterious figure but if Caz had told this stranger that she had seen a ghost, then she must have been truly scared. More scared than she'd let on. Genni thought for a moment she was going to be alright, then her stomach clenched. She made it to the sink and retched onto a pile of dirty crockery.

The vicar grabbed a towel and some kitchen roll.

"People are often nervous about getting married," she said. "There's something important about tying the knot in a church before God. It can make you think hard about it."

Genni nodded miserably.

"And I expect you miss your friend, whatever Jim says."

Genni nodded once more. She didn't dare speak in case she threw up again. Missing Caz was an understatement. She felt frayed at the edges; her stomach had been churning and upset for weeks, and now she was angry. Why couldn't this woman have taken her into the lounge, like Caz? Why was the kitchen good enough for the black woman?

All her life she'd been bullied, had to listen to the quiet laughter at her expense. All through school, on the bus, even at Guides. But her mum wouldn't do anything, told her to suck it up, to be strong. That she'd be a better person for taking it on the chin. So, Genni had tried but now and again she remembered her dad had left her, and her mum wouldn't talk about him, so she didn't feel anywhere close to being a better person.

"Do you want to sit down? Do you feel well enough?" the vicar asked. Genni sat down. "You remind me of my friend Harriet."

Genni didn't know what to say to that, so took a sip of her tea.

"Do you mind if we don't talk about the wedding?"

"Of course. What would you like to talk about?" She really didn't sound as if she minded at all.

"Have you ever been bullied?" Genni asked, cautiously.

"Yes. Quite a few times. And you?"

"What do you think?" Genni said, looking down at her hands, startlingly dark in the dim light of the kitchen.

"Right. Yes. Have you had a difficult time? I'd hoped our little community would have been better than that."

"Some parts of my life have been worse than others."

The tears were gentle, but Genni knew that if she tried to continue speaking, they would come as a torrent, like the rain earlier.

The vicar simply got up and put the kettle back on.

Chapter 9

Simeon was feeling unsettled, even more so than the usual anxiety bubbling inside. This was how he used to feel, like he'd missed his way somehow.

It'd been well over a year since Archie's heart attack so he didn't think it could still be that. He hoped it wasn't, but something was obviously upsetting him.

He looked around. The gloom of sunset was gathering in the corners, it made the house feel too small and the wind singing through the wires and blowing through the branches was annoying rather than soothing.

One of the shrubs had grown up against the window. Now and again it sounded like someone was scratching their nails down the glass. He should have asked Archie to come and sort it out. To bring over a pair of loppers, to chop it all back. But Simeon hadn't asked him. He hadn't wanted him doing anything strenuous. Simeon thought that Archie hadn't been looking at all well of late.

Today he'd rung him twice already. On the second go Archie had picked up and said that he was alright, that he was preparing for the annual church meeting. Simeon knew he ought to leave him alone, but it wasn't just about Archie. He pulled Belle's lead off the hook. She uncurled from her basket and stretched. He knew she didn't really want to go out, that she didn't need to come with him, but it was getting dark, and he didn't want to be on his own.

"Thank you, Belle," he said, tugging gently on her ears. She looked up at him and wagged her tail. She was quite elderly now, but the vet was still delighted with her joints and weight. At her last annual check he hadn't found anything wrong with her, though he had given her some pills, which he suggested Simeon put inside a treat. Simeon had shaken his head, taken one out of the packet. He'd tossed it in the air and Belle had crunched it down as if it were a treat.

"She's definitely a lab," the vet had said, laughing.

There was no point heading down to the coast. The sky was muddled, white high cirrus clouds over to the east, with heavy unbroken grey clouds flowing in from the west. A strange line down the middle of the sky showed where the two weather fronts met. The setting sun was sparkling between the two systems. Simeon had never seen anything quite like it and knew that it would disappear within seconds. The western weather was on its way in, a nasty low sitting over the Lake District with some very tight isobars.

He heard a car screeching down the road. Then another. He'd forgotten it was a practice night for the lifeboat, so there was no point trying to walk down that way, it would be far too dangerous.

He thought he might go and sit in the church and yet he found himself turning into the vicarage.

The drive dipped down past the house, ran across the front and back up to the small patch of grass that was Anna's back garden, no more than a square of lawn surrounded by very tall straggly shrubs.

Once a year Archie organised a team of people to cut them back hard, but they soon sprouted again, a tangle of privet and laurel. Simeon had a quick look up the side of the house and was glad to see Anna's car, parked at a slightly odd angle. Of late, Tom's dark blue Audi was often there too. Simeon went back to the front door and pushed the bell.

For a while there was no response, then the hall light came on and he could hear Anna fumbling with the keys. He stepped back and Belle's tail began to wag. Anna didn't seem to care much for any other dog, but she seemed fond of Belle and had even looked after her a couple of times, when Derek and Harriet had been too busy with their house.

"Simeon, are you alright?"

"Yes," he said. "I just wondered if we could talk."

"Now?" Anna asked, looking over his shoulder as if

someone else might be coming.

"Yes, please. There's something bothering me, and I didn't want to go into the church."

She hesitated a second more.

"Come on in. Let's go through to the kitchen. You know I'm not very good at getting the fire going in the big lounge."

"I like the kitchen," Simeon said. "I can almost see all the walls at once."

"I like the kitchen too. It's where I keep the tea and biscuits."

Simeon made his way to the small kitchen table. At a pinch you could get three people round it, but then no one could get out without the cooperation of the other two. Simeon slid into the chair furthest away while Anna put the kettle on and found Belle a biscuit. She would make tea for Simeon at this time of night. She wouldn't even bother asking him which he preferred. Simeon sat back and realised that some of the scratchiness had already softened. Unusually, there was a strong smell of bleach, and the sink was clean and shiny, but he didn't mind that.

She slid a mug over to him. It said, 'Vicar's favourite parishioner.' Anna always used it if someone came round to talk. It was her little joke because of course, she couldn't have favourites.

"What can I do for you, Simeon?"

"I'm feeling unsettled. I think I'm worried about Archie. He doesn't seem quite himself. He hasn't been for a while."

"It's not been a great spring. Perhaps he just needs a bit of sunshine."

Simeon tipped his head to one side and narrowed his eyes. He felt as if she wasn't taking him seriously.

Anna sighed. "Ok, so you don't think he's just in need of a bit of vitamin D. What do you think is wrong?"

"It may be that he's upset about the missing woman, Caroline Denbigh."

"Granted," Anna said. "He may have been the last person to see her, but we only found out that she was missing last week, and you said you've been worried for a while."

Simeon took a sip of tea. Belle sat up and put her head on his knee.

"What is it, Simeon? Something is clearly bugging you."

"I wonder if the stent is enough. What if another artery is blocked? He does get very tired and when he goes for a check-up, they rarely do more than take his blood pressure and his cholesterol levels."

"Are you worried he's going to have another heart attack?"

"He's bound to die at some point," Simeon said, and he began to pick at his fingers. It was something he'd started doing recently and he was worried it would become a *thing*.

"But not yet," Anna replied. "Have you prayed about it?"

Simeon nodded, miserably.

"I'm really struggling to put him in God's hands and leave him there."

She smiled one of her very annoying smiles.

"Oh, Simeon. Underneath that straightforward exterior, you're just like us."

That irritated Simeon quite a lot. It now felt as though she were poking fun at him.

"What do you suggest?" he said.

"You know what I'm going to say."

He did.

"Go back to God and tell him how I feel. Ask him to show me the way forward, or the way back. And then wait to see what happens."

She nodded.

"I'm afraid it's all I have. I'm sorry I don't have anything else."

"What happens if the young woman isn't found, or doesn't come home?" he asked, suddenly.

Anna sat back, her eyes widening, which made her forehead

crinkle.

"I don't know. I can't imagine how awful it must be for her dad or her friends."

They both jumped when there was a bang on the front door. A real thump. Simeon suddenly didn't want to be there anymore but knew he couldn't leave Anna until she knew who it was.

"I'll just go and see. I wonder why they didn't use the bell."

It was quite dark in the hall and Anna had to put the light on again. Simeon followed her as far as the kitchen doorway; Belle had come with him. He could feel her pressing against his leg. He would know who it was, as long as it wasn't a stranger. His pulse had begun to beat faster, all across the back of his neck.

When Anna finally got the door open, Simeon dropped his eyes to the floor and began to count the tiles. Belle whined. The man seemed to fill the space, towering above her. Anna took a step back and her voice wobbled.

"Just one moment," she said. Simeon shrank into the corner. She walked back to him and whispered, "Simeon, I want you to go home. Use the kitchen door." Then quieter still, "And everything is fine but text Tom on your way. Tell him Caz's dad has just dropped in for a chat."

Simeon managed to walk down the side of the vicarage, but struggled to cross the front, in case the door opened, and the man came out. He knew he had to get home, had to text Tom. Anna had sounded calm but there had been an edge to her voice that Simeon hadn't liked. A tightness that had made him want to put his fingers in his ears. He pulled out his phone and began to type.

***

"You talked to my daughter, Caz." Anna wondered how he knew that, but then it hadn't been a secret and people's movements about the village were often chatted about, in the pub, in the shop, perhaps even at lifeboat practice. Denbigh stood in the hall taking up far too much space. Anna felt a moment of fear but reminded herself that his daughter was missing.

"I did, but it was quite a while before she ... disappeared." She regretted the choice of word, almost immediately. 'Disappeared' made it sound like a magic trick.

"They don't know when she went missing exactly. They don't seem to know anything."

"I'm sure they're doing all they can," she said. Tom was a good police officer.

"They won't be. She's just a missing woman. There's no evidence of foul play, no evidence of anything."

"Come in, sit down. I'll go and make a drink."

"I don't want anything."

She led him into the main lounge. She could just see her car through the side window, which she seemed to have parked at a bit of a strange angle. She hoped Tom didn't come round the corner too quickly, she wouldn't want him to hit it. The room was a bit chilly, but Mr Denbigh didn't look like he ever felt the cold. He was tall, broad and his hands were large. His hair was a little long, thick and wavy and his nose really did look as if it had been broken and set badly.

She sat down at the end of the sofa by the door. He lowered himself onto one of the single chairs, just where his daughter had sat.

"I met Caz just the once to talk to."

"I didn't think she was religious."

"I'm not sure she was either, but I was down at the lifeboat for a blessing. I mean, they asked me to go down and bless the boat. I told them all they could come and chat anytime."

"What did she want to *chat* about?"

Anna sat back. The sarcasm was a little obvious.

"She told me she was going out on her first shout soon."

He snorted impatiently.

"What else did she say?"

"Look, I'm really sorry, but I'm not comfortable talking about what she said. It's confidential, though please let me assure you it wasn't anything… relevant."

"I'm her dad. Do you want to see some ID?" He began to reach into a pocket of his jacket.

"I am really sorry, Mr Denbigh. I would love to tell you everything, but I don't feel I can. Not yet anyway." She bit her lip. She'd as good as said she would speak to him when they were sure his daughter was dead. Simeon had said, sometimes, in these cases, they never found anything, particularly if she'd simply planned to start a new life somewhere. Anna looked across at the man glowering at her. He might have to spend the rest of his life wondering what his daughter had spoken about to the local vicar. Of course, he might be who Caz was escaping from. Anna looked down at her hands, seemingly tangled in her lap. She straightened them.

Denbigh got up to stare out of the front window, just like Jim Andrews. If you knew where to look through the trees, you could see the top of the church tower, but she didn't think he'd want to know that just this minute. He turned back and Anna sank a little further into her chair. She hoped that Tom was on his way, but then thought that might exacerbate the situation. This man was grieving and bewildered but was also used to getting answers.

"Look, I understand all about confidentiality, but you could be obstructing an investigation," he said, his voice quiet. Anna had to work hard to hear him.

"Don't worry. I've told Tom, DI Edwards. He knows all about Caz's visit."

Denbigh's shoulders drooped just a little. He'd been trying it on, Anna was fairly sure of that, and she had told Tom as much as she could remember. At least how Caz had lumped God in with ghosts and the supernatural. Tom had laughed at that, then he'd apologised for thinking it was funny, because he was sure she wouldn't find it so. She hadn't at the time.

She'd been a little shocked, but since then had fervently wished she'd spent more time with Caz, asking about her life.

"Tom's a good police officer."

"You sound as though you know him. Does he live near here?"

"No, over in Falmouth, but we've had a couple of murders in the last few years, so he's been about quite a bit." She could feel her cheeks beginning to prickle.

"Oh, how lovely for you. Tea and cakes all around."

Anna knew that now she would be glowing pink.

"Look, Mr Denbigh, I'm really sorry I can't be more helpful. I can't imagine what you're going through, but we're here for you if you need us. Do you have anywhere to stay?"

"At the pub, for now."

"Good. I'm sure Tom will keep you informed about progress." She was beginning to sound like one of Tom's PCs and was suddenly not sure what her role ought to be. She loved Tom, but first and foremost she had to be a good vicar. Tom didn't need defending, certainly not by her. She also hadn't been completely upfront about their relationship. She supposed it was none of Mr Denbigh's business.

"He won't, you know. But at least if I'm around breathing down his neck, he might pull his bloody finger out."

Anna didn't know what to say to that.

"So did you see much of Caz?" she asked.

The man narrowed his eyes, as if trying to see what she was getting at. She wasn't trying to get at anything.

"Are you sure I can't make you a drink?"

"No, but if you can think of anything, anything at all, tell that bloody DI. Knowing her last movements is critical."

Anna nodded. It was weeks since anyone had last seen Caz. Hopefully, Tom would find out something from the crew. One of them must have known her, at least a little.

Denbigh moved into the hallway. She followed him. He pulled open the door and simply walked out. Anna waved but he didn't bother looking back. He just jumped a little when the security lamp came on as he was turning the corner. Tom kept saying she should get it fixed. In the halo of startling light the shadows stretched away, striping the drive. It did look a bit spooky. Anna sucked in a lungful of salty air. If she started getting jumpy at dim roads, and unlit pathways, tree shadows blowing in the wind or the sound of rooks cawing along the lane, she may as well give up now, and go seek a parish in the inner city somewhere.

As she began to shut the door, headlamps swept over the trees and a car careered down the drive sending gravel into the undergrowth. Tom was in the passenger seat and there were two others with him. He leapt out and relief swept over her.

"Where is he?"

"He just left. I'm surprised you didn't see him."

"Are you alright?"

"I'm fine." She was becoming more so by the minute.

"Simeon said you were scared."

"I was. He's a big man."

"But you still let him in."

"Yes, of course," she said, a little sharply. This wasn't how this was meant to play out.

"And made him a cup of tea?"

"I offered. Look Tom, he's obviously desperately upset, wants answers. I didn't tell him anything."

"Yet still you invited him in!"

Anna began to feel a little exasperated.

"Of course. It's my job."

He looked over his shoulder. Anna stepped back into the house. It was a bit public, and she didn't want to be cross with him, when he'd come racing to her rescue.

"Look, I have to get to Falmouth. We've interviewed some of the crew, but Mr Denbigh came down while we were right in the middle of it. He blagged his way past the constables at the top. Listened outside till one of the Sandras saw him." Anna had to smile at that. So Tom had at least two in mind to replace her. "He needs to back off, let us do our job. Missing persons deal with this sort of thing all the time."

But you don't, she thought and was worried at the small seed of doubt taking root. She wanted to reset the conversation.

"Tom, have you finally replaced Sandra? You've needed to for weeks. Are you training up more than one of them because you can't make up your mind? Or is it simply that Sandra was so good you need two people?"

Anna tried to peer round him. Tom frowned and then shook his head as if he couldn't quite believe it, but she could see he wasn't really cross.

"Look, I'll give you a ring tomorrow. If he comes back, tell me, but you don't have to let him in or talk to him, particularly if you feel scared at all."

"Oh, Tom, you know that I do."

Tom shrugged and began to walk away. Then he swung back

"Do you think it's worth contacting Simeon? He sounded quite worried when he phoned."

She blew him a kiss, very carefully so that those in the car wouldn't be able to see.

"That's a good idea. You are lovely." She whispered the last bit because she knew that the car windows might be open a little but wouldn't necessarily look as if they were.

Chapter 10

Jim heard the door click shut and the beep from the security system. The lights were still blazing throughout the station so his final job would be to switch them all off. For the first time in his life he felt as if he wasn't in control, that he wasn't quite sure what to do. The guys had all stood around Genni protectively but still the policeman had zeroed in on her. She'd looked frail and her eyes were puffy and she'd not been questioned long before disappearing into the loo, once again gulping for breath. By the time she'd returned, Caz's father had appeared. Jim had been about to go and sort him out when the DI had barged past, looking furious. Jim had even felt a twinge of empathy for the man, his daughter being missing and all that, but causing trouble wasn't going to get her found any quicker.

He looked around the meeting room. They never held meetings there, it was too small. He did use it to interview possible volunteers, and afterwards he would take them out to see *Rose*. It was always their final test. If their faces didn't betray a little awe standing under her bow, then they didn't have what it took. Caz had always been borderline in that respect. Her face had been impassive. It was when he'd begun to lead her away that he'd realised she had been seemingly unable to turn her back on the vessel. That had done it. Respect. Always respect your boat.

Jim walked out onto the lower level. *Rose* reared above him. He patted her hull and began to make his way up, the first door clanging shut behind him. The place was full of hard edges, shiny surfaces. The tiniest noise reverberated around the space, often making people jump, and when the alarm went off, the lights turned and flashed, sometimes making him want to squeeze his eyes shut and put his hands over his ears. Of course, the next minute he'd be pulling on his gear and jumping across the ramp. Once her deck was under his feet and the engines were whining up to speed, nothing could hold him back.

He reached the locker room. It was clear of junk. He'd made them sort it out a couple of weeks ago. He didn't like clutter, clutter was dangerous, could slow you down, might mean precious seconds lost. At some point he'd have to get someone to clear out Caz's locker. The police had been through it but eventually her dad might want her things. Jim walked across to the main door. He peered through and up the steps. The place was definitely empty. Toby had taken Genni home and no one had suggested the pub. Bloody Caz would take some getting over, but it was bound to settle down, at some stage. He couldn't run the station with this kind of tension crackling in the air. He needed everyone focused and and working together. As he pulled the door shut behind him, he wondered about putting in another practice. He didn't do it often but perhaps filling their time with something useful would be better than allowing them to brood on what might have happened to their crewmate. Halfway up, and warm with the effort of the climb he stopped. Yes, he would put in another practice. Some training would sort out the wondering.

***

Torchlight was odd, Harriet thought, moving it slowly backwards and forwards. She was sitting cross legged on the newly fitted loft boards while Derek was playing with the controls of the boiler. They were going to get a proper light fitted up there, they just hadn't got round to it. The torch produced a halo of yellow with a darker patch in the middle. She didn't know which bit to concentrate on the panel.

"A bit higher, love."

"Sorry, Derek, I've never been a lamp stand before."

"I'm sorry, too. I thought it was bound to be something simple, but these instructions are a little odd. Look, I can easily prop the torch up so you can go and get on."

Get on with what? She didn't dare do anything really

constructive in case Derek decided that something else needed adjusting.

"Are we nearly done now?"

"I'm just going to try resetting it again."

"Not the boiler, the building work."

"Oh, yes. Just a few bits and bobs to sort. I was thinking it would be nice to put a deck out over the stream. We don't have a massive amount of space at the back, but it would be good to have somewhere to sit when it's really hot. What do you think?"

"It's a lovely idea," she said, "But let's not begin that until we have actually finished one or two more rooms. I'd like to start unpacking."

"Of course. Though it would probably be worth ordering the stone and wood now, otherwise we might have to wait for delivery. I could put in some tall uprights which we could hang a tarpaulin over, to give us a bit of shade."

"Derek, the sun is in the front. Out back it's mostly overhung with trees, we won't need any extra shade."

"Well, that's easily sorted. We can cut those down, open it up a bit."

"No, don't do that, it's lovely."

"But where will you dry the washing? I know you; you won't want to use the tumble drier too much."

"I thought we could put a line down by the garage."

"Ok," he said, slowly, pushing a lock of hair off his forehead.

His hair was fair with flecks of grey, soft floppy curls now she'd persuaded him to let it grow a little. He had a square face, a large forehead, and puppy dog eyes. He pushed the hair back again. It was definitely time for a cut. She could tell he wasn't keen on the idea of a line of washing flapping across the front garden, but she really did like the tiny space out back, the green canopy of overhung branches, the feeling of sitting in a den sparkling with leaves, twisting and turning in the lightest of breezes. The trees were tall and did block out the sky but you could breathe under them, and on a still summer's day, with the sound of the stream, it would be lovely.

"Right, slip down and turn on the hot tap in the bathroom."

She carefully clambered onto her knees and crawled over to the loft hatch. It was a good storage space but there was no head room. At the bottom of the ladder she brushed down her jeans and wandered into the bathroom. It was chrome-shiny, and everything fitted, butted up against everything else. It was a bit of a man's bathroom. She would have preferred something more seasidey, something a little more pastel, but the shower was wonderful when the boiler worked. Compared to her flat at Mullion it was heaven. There, the water had sometimes managed tepid and no more than a dribble, even on a good day. Flush the loo and you didn't have a hope for at least ten minutes.

She turned on the tap. Found she was crossing her fingers. Apologised to God and ran her hand under the flow. There it was. Hot water. Which was great, but they'd been here before, so the proof would be in the pudding if it still worked in the morning.

She climbed back up the ladder and popped her head into the dark space. Derek had switched off the torch and was crawling towards her. The boiler was making reassuring humming noises behind him.

"For now, we have hot water!" she said. She crossed her arms and leant on them. They kissed.

"So hot water is what it takes?" he asked, grinning.

"Hot water and being able to unpack without worrying that you're going to drill another hole through the ceiling."

"Whatever you want," he said, and leaned in to kiss her again.

She waited for him at the bottom of the ladder.

"A drink?" she asked.

"Tea would be nice," he said, going into the bathroom to try the hot tap for himself. She shrugged away the annoyance. She knew it wasn't anything to do with not trusting her, more the glee of fixing something.

"I was thinking of that bottle of wine that Anna and Tom gave us."

"That would be nice, too."

"And Derek, come down for it. Let's sit together in our new lounge and stare out at the view for a minute."

"You know it's dark, dearest girl."

"Then put on an extra jumper and we'll sit outside on the bench and breathe in the sea air. Let our eyes adjust to the night and plan what needs to be done next."

She would have liked to just sit and do nothing, but she knew talking about the project would be the hook that Derek needed.

For a moment they did just sit and breathe. The old bench had been left by the previous owner. It needed a lick of paint but was in just the right position. It was rapidly becoming Harriet's favourite place. She looked up. There were holes in the cloud through which the stars twinkled. There might even have been a moon, but not from where they were sitting. They began to make out the shape of the roofs of the two houses opposite and could just see the end of their garden stretching to a narrow point down by the garage. The lane was quite steep and a good three feet below the hedge, so it didn't obstruct the view. They couldn't see the actual sea, but it was there, just out of sight beyond the lawn, edged with shrubs that would need a jolly good prune to keep them low. Derek wanted to put in a path so they could get to the car without going out onto the road. Harriet hoped there might be a large enough patch at the bottom for some vegetables. It was technically the front garden, but it didn't matter. Front or back, it was invisible from any passers-by and was going to be lovely.

"So, hot water then," Derek said, squeezing her hand.

"What do you think has happened to that young woman from the lifeboat?" Harriet asked, not wanting to talk about the building work quite yet.

"She's probably gone off on holiday."

"It's been four weeks and she didn't tell her dad, the lifeboat crew or her work mates in Exeter. I hope she's alright."

Derek put his arm around her.

"Just because she's missing doesn't mean anything awful has happened to her."

But Harriet thought that was precisely what missing meant. A car began to grind up the lane, its engine struggling, squealing a little as the headlights swept across the house opposite. Probably one of the holiday makers from the cove. Someone who would glance into their community, just for a week or two, perhaps even envy them a little. Not like Caz, who'd bought a house and joined the lifeboat, so that when she'd disappeared it felt as if something had been ripped out by its roots. Harriet leaned against Derek and decided suddenly that thinking about colours for the lounge walls was quite an attractive option.

***

Archie put the last of the cups away, wiped down the draining board and sighed. He never looked forward to the finance committee and tonight it had lived up to his lowest expectation. The meeting had been long and drawn out. A real drag, as Anna would have said. He wished she'd been there. She'd have asked all sorts of questions that would have been interesting, if not, in all probability, naive. As a church they were in the best shape they'd ever been in, but even in the world of God and grace the bottom line always seemed to have a pound sign. Deep down, he felt it shouldn't be about money and yet you couldn't run anything without it. Even with the lifeboat it was mainly to do with how much they could raise through the year. Archie was tired, worn out really. He would go to bed, try and read another chapter of his book before he fell asleep. Not the big heavy one that the Bishop had given him, but one he'd borrowed from Anna. It was brand new, had hardly been opened, and looked interesting — *Surprised by Hope*. Anna didn't seem to read this sort of thing anymore. She read *unsuitable* novels, to escape, she said. *To escape from what*, he wondered. Perhaps someday, he would ask if he could borrow one of those. When Moira had been alive the house had been littered with all sorts of books. She didn't seem to have had a favourite genre. When she'd died it had taken him months to clear them all out, and he'd had to. The sight of them had been too much for his damaged heart to bear. Now, he was beginning to think he might be ready for something new, a clean slate perhaps where he would try something different. He felt it was time, or perhaps that time was running out.

He switched off the light in the kitchen and walked into the hall, glancing up at the front door. He took a step back and found he'd instinctively put a hand on his chest. There was someone standing on the doorstep. He couldn't see who it was, because etched glass ran floor to ceiling, two narrow slithers on either side of the door, designed for light, not for seeing through. He wondered if it was someone simply waiting for him to go to bed before breaking in. He shook his head impatiently and put on the hall light though he still jumped when the doorbell rang.

"Jim! What's the problem? Is everything alright?"

"Archie, I know it's a bit late, but can I come in?" Archie didn't normally have a queue waiting to see him, certainly not at that time of night. He supposed for some people, just after ten, wasn't late at all. Simeon, in particular, often stayed up until the early hours.

He led Jim into the front room. Jim had visited before, not often, and mostly to discuss fundraising, so Archie was a little surprised to see him. He couldn't imagine what on earth it could be about. Jim didn't take the proffered seat but walked over to the window. Archie hadn't bothered pulling the curtains, there was no one to peer in. Living at the end of the road had its advantages. People did pass by if they were heading onto the coast, using the path down the side of his garden, but it ran behind the head-height Cornish hedge. A tall stone wall topped with furze, that nothing but birds sat on top of.

"Can I get you anything?"

Jim shook his head. Archie perched on the edge of his favourite chair but that didn't feel right. He stood up again.

"Jim, what's troubling you?"

"It's Caz, the missing woman," he said, turning away from the window. "You may have been the last person to see her, but she was one of mine. She had a locker, a place on the crew. She was shaping up nicely. It was all good. We were all good, and … now we're not." He turned back to the darkness, leaning on the sill and pressing his forehead against the glass.

"It is awful. I guess it must be the not knowing."

"We're all pretty upset. Genni keeps crying and no one will go down to the station on their own."

"Surely not, Jim." Archie thought of all the times he'd been in to man the shop. Jean's cheerful chattering, and then the blessed silence when she'd gone. Making himself a cup of tea, just sitting close to a boat he'd give his eye teeth to go out on, just one more time.

"Last practice, when I arrived, Martin and Eddy were fiddling with something in the car. We went down together to open up. The week before Trevor was there with Genni, just waiting. They both know the combination and whoever gets there first unlocks, props the locker room door open and puts the kettle on."

"I'm sure it's just a phase. Once we know what's happened, it'll go back to normal."

"But what if we never know what happened to her? What if

she was on the ramp and a wave took her off? She didn't know the sea that well, she grew up in London. And if it was a falling tide, she could easily have been swept out. Bodies do come ashore but not always." He sounded as if he were repeating something he'd thought about a lot, something he felt needed saying. Archie nodded.

"And no one seems to know anything," Archie said, quietly. He hadn't meant it to sound like a question.

"No, they don't. She was a very private person. Got on with everyone and wasn't touchy-feely like Genni. I liked that. She did all that was asked of her. Was desperate to get out on the boat. She'd have made a fine member of the crew." Jim was standing rigid, his shoulders hunched.

A stirring speech Archie thought, it sounded a bit like a eulogy.

"That policeman came down tonight, interviewed us, him and his henchmen. There was no time to practise and anyway, everyone was far too upset by the time he'd finished."

Tom, thought Archie. He had this way of getting under your skin and if he thought something untoward had happened, he'd worry away at it until he got someone to confess. Like last time. The way he'd grilled the retreat guests. It had been relentless, so that on the very last night he'd forced out the truth. Archie put a hand on his chest again. There was a slight tightening, a memory of pain. That awful moment when he felt as if someone had slapped him in a vice, turning the handle so that when he'd tried to breathe there was nowhere for his ribs to go.

"What can I do, Jim?"

"Nothing, Archie. I just needed someone to talk to."

Archie was flattered. Though he wondered why Jim hadn't talked to his wife. Margery was a good sort, always on the go, always smiling and willing to roll up her sleeves to help. She and Jean were good friends. When Jean was up in Helston, babysitting, Margery would stay after work and meet her.

Apparently, they loved the cinema. Archie had been somewhat surprised at what they'd watched over the years, mostly what they referred to as blockbusters, which had never appealed to him. He'd experienced the reality of an explosion; a whining bullet and it wasn't like in the films.

"Actually, Archie, could you have a word with the vicar?"

"Anna?"

"I asked her to come down and chuck some prayers about, but she didn't seem keen. I think it would make everyone feel better. And have you met Caz's dad yet? He's hanging around the place. Came into the boat house tonight, wanting to know who knew her, what she might have said, and was anyone bullying her? He's a big man. Even I had to look up, just a little."

Jim was tall, with a paunch that he was always going to get sorted. Blamed the beer. Patted it often, called it his friend of many years. It always got a laugh. To Archie it wasn't so funny anymore. The blip had changed everything for surely Jim was prime heart attack material.

"We wondered how the policeman would deal with the situation as he's not exactly a large man."

"But he's trained."

"To be fair, he had him outside before you could say Jack Robinson. Up those steps pretty fast, too. Then he gave his constables a real bollocking." Jim grimaced, but Archie could hear a grudging admiration in his voice. "Made us feel better. Like you couldn't mess with him. Doesn't he normally deal with murder? So why is he looking into Caz? What do the police know that they're not telling us?" Jim sounded really worried.

"Jim, I genuinely think it's because Caz's dad is ex-police and the powers-that-be thought that as Tom wasn't up to his eyes it would show Mr Denbigh that everyone was taking her disappearance seriously."

Jim sat down. Simply folded up. He put his face in his

hands.

"Oh God, Archie, she's really messing with us."

Jim was the coxswain. Jim was the boss. Jim led from the front. No one argued with him. He'd been on the lifeboat for years, knew what he was doing. He could be harsh, but he'd never seemingly doubted himself. Losing Caz seemed to have made him do just that.

Archie sat down, too. He wouldn't be going to bed for a while. Not now. He stood back up and went into the dining room, reappearing a moment later with two whiskey glasses, generously filled and glinting in the lamplight.

Chapter 11

Tom walked through the quiet station, nodding to the duty sergeant, who was suppressing a yawn. It was early, usually Tom's favourite part of the day, when everything was ticking over, when there were possibilities and time to think. He made himself a coffee and took it to his desk, very quickly realising that he was still fuming from the night before, the tension, already sitting in his stomach, beginning to wind up even more. If Sandra had been there Denbigh wouldn't have made it down the steps. Tom had been getting a good picture of the missing woman, but after the yelling, the crew had clammed up like ... clams! He'd got nothing of interest beyond that moment. Genni Rowe seemed unduly upset about someone she said she didn't know that well and he'd liked to have pushed her a little harder. The coxswain, Jim Andrews, had been proprietary over them, Tom had thought unreasonably so. He had hovered, listened, even brought tea. At one point Tom had felt the hairs on the back of his neck prickling to find Jim was standing just inside the door, leaning against the wall, his arms folded. Again, if Sandra had been there, it simply wouldn't have happened.

He'd given the speech, the guidelines that Smith and Kellow, the two new possibilities, were expected to follow. Smith was from the Midlands, Kellow a local boy. Smith had less experience, but Tom thought she showed more promise. Kellow was still trying to be one of the lads and Tom couldn't quite see past that. He'd already decided to send them back to The Lizard Village to start conducting a proper house to house. Someone must know something, but another full and frank discussion about what he expected of them wouldn't go amiss and would be payback for his ruined morning. God, he missed Sandra!

Niggling away at the back of his mind was the fact that Anna hadn't been as upset about Gerald Denbigh's visit as she ought to have been. Tom didn't like him. Tom thought he was a bully, but Anna had been won over by the sheer weight of his circumstances. The grieving father, bewildered and lost because his only child had gone missing, but the man was an ex-copper and knew what was what, had probably been able to sum up Anna in half a minute.

Tom glanced at his watch and thought it likely he would catch Randal at missing persons. Five minutes later, Tom put the phone down feeling a little more aggrieved and not one bit reassured. How bloody hard could it be to find someone who'd gone missing, even if they didn't want to be found?

His mum texted, unusual in itself, unless he was late for something. Tom read the short message and sat back; his eyes raised to the ceiling. She'd been out for an early morning walk and had bumped into the missing woman's father. 'Was it alright if she met him later for a coffee? He wasn't a suspect or anything, was he?' Was she asking his permission? He certainly didn't know what to say. Denbigh could be a suspect, though technically he'd been up in London when Caz was last seen. They'd have to check out time frames, but he certainly wasn't front and centre, not yet. He supposed there wasn't a good reason for his mum not to see the guy. She might even find out something useful. As long as they stayed in public, he thought. Though Tom then wondered what not being in public meant. Was it simply that he didn't want this man knowing where his mother lived? He really didn't want this man popping around for a cup of tea. In his head things were getting a little complicated. Luckily, just as he was about to groan loudly and put his head in his hands both his sergeants appeared at the door. Tom beckoned them in, smiling, a sign they would quickly learn was not necessarily a good thing.

***

Anna was up and dressed slightly earlier than usual. Archie read morning prayer on a Wednesday, and he tended to start right on the dot of eight o'clock. If it wasn't that Archie was pathologically punctual, she might suggest he was making a point. She picked up her coffee, screwed on the lid. The cup was a present from Harriet after Anna had tipped coffee down herself twice in a row because she was a tiny bit late. It was hard to run with a normal mug and though she could have made coffee at the church, she would have had to arrive early enough to do that. Anna took a swig and burned her tongue, swore under her breath and headed out the door. It was just on the hour so not as bad as usual.

She stopped inside the church gate, resting her hand on the tomb where they'd found Fiona, Derek's wife — dead from a nasty head wound. Anna looked at the grass, newly mown because Archie sorted that out now, and realised she was still looking for a bloodied weapon lying about. She pulled herself together. She always went back to Fiona when she was upset. They all did, and Caz disappearing had set the old anxiety gnawing. What she refused to acknowledge was that some of the worry was that Tom was being judged. The village would observe with interest how he managed the investigation, based on the simple criteria of whether they found the young woman or not. It was all a little too close to home. She'd had to defend him occasionally in the past, when either Simeon or Harriet had had a gentle dig but now it felt as though the whole community was watching. Find her, please, she muttered and then wondered who she was talking to, God or Tom.

"Hi, Archie, sorry I'm a bit late."

He looked up and smiled.

"Hardly at all," he said.

"Not for you, anyway," Simeon added, but he didn't look at her. He was sitting at the other end of the pew, motionless, facing forward. Anna was just grateful that he hadn't told them exactly how many minutes it was past the hour. Harriet looked away, obviously amused. She was on the other side of the aisle from Archie, also at the front. Anna plonked herself down next to her.

"Hello, you," Harriet said.

"Hello, you too. Can we do coffee or breakfast after this?" Anna whispered. Harriet nodded and Anna suddenly wanted to skip morning prayer and go straight back to the vicarage. Archie cleared his throat and began.

After a moment Anna realised she wasn't concentrating at all. She found herself staring along the pew at the two men. Simeon's hood was pulled right over his head so she couldn't see his face at all. That old parka covered a multitude of things. Perhaps she ought to pop around later to see him, to make an effort to be a bit more pastoral. Archie began to pray for Caz and her father and then seemingly for the whole of the lifeboat crew, by name. He would know them all and was bound to be finding it tough. Add into the mix Simeon's rather cloying protectiveness, and perhaps she should also go and see Archie.

At last, he spoke the final amen and turned towards her. She and Harriet were both having a surreptitious stretch.

"Anna, could I have a word sometime?" he asked. Anna yawned. She hadn't meant to; it just came so naturally after the stretch.

"Sorry, Archie, I didn't sleep last night." Not true, she'd slept like a log.

"No, I didn't either," he replied. "Jim came round late last night, and I'd like to discuss our strategy with respect to pastoral care for the lifeboat crew through this difficult time." Anna nodded. She didn't think there was a strategy for pastoral care. She just did it whenever the need presented itself.

"You could meet now, I can see you anytime," Harriet said, standing up and taking a tiny step back. Anna felt a wave of disappointment roll up and over. She'd really been looking forward to a coffee with Harriet.

"It's not urgent," Archie said quickly.

"There are actually a couple of important things I'd like to discuss with you, Harriet," Anna continued. Harriet's eyebrows shot up just before she quickly looked away, obviously trying to hide another smile. Sometimes she could be very annoying. "Archie, how about this afternoon? I could walk over, save you a trip back across."

"Thank you," he said, doing up his coat, a warm wool overcoat, navy, that Anna realised was looking a little large on him. It made her feel as if she didn't want to let him out of her sight. By the time she got around to looking for Simeon he'd gone, which wasn't like him. Even when he was feeling jittery, he would wait around for Archie, to walk the short way together to the top of Simeon's lane. She underlined him on her imaginary list and then quickly added Catherine, who hadn't appeared at all.

The church stayed open throughout the day, so no one needed to lock up, but Anna still felt she should be the last to leave. Harriet waited impatiently, folding her arms and humphing a little.

"Sorry," Anna said, watching Archie disappear through the gate at the end of the path. She pulled the door partly closed and they began to make their way after him. Anna stopped once more at Fiona's tomb and rested a hand gently on its gritty stone top.

"I do it too," Harriet said. "Often, I can't help myself, particularly if I'm stressed or upset."

"It's the Caz thing for me. What is it for you?"

"Oh, the usual. Derek, the new house. Working out how to do life."

"Has he said anything more about getting a new dog?"

"Yes, yes, he has. He just doesn't realise how hurtful it is asking Simeon to help him choose one, rather than me."

"Harriet, you must say something."

"But aren't I being really infantile? Pick me! Pick me!"

"No, you're not. It's actually rather grown up. Getting a dog is not something to be taken lightly. They live forever, don't they?"

"Dear Dolly. We do miss her terribly, but I'm quite enjoying the freedom. It got a bit hands-on during her last few months, and Derek wasn't always as helpful as he might've been. He tended to deal with the nice end."

"Yuk, I can imagine."

"It had its moments. How about you and Tom?"

"Oh, you know! I'm worrying about him. I had no idea it would feel as if we were both under a spotlight. What if he can't find Caz? What if he messes up? He's such a police officer!"

"Yes, he is." Harriet began to frown. "Actually, I'm not sure what you mean."

"Well, a young woman has gone missing. I can't imagine how awful that must be for those that knew her, loved her even, so I tend to get really emotional about it, for them, on behalf of them I suppose. But Tom has to be ... professional. Stand back, be dispassionate. He seems a little hard sometimes."

"That feels unfair," Harriet said. Anna was surprised. Harriet rarely took Tom's side, unless Anna herself had completely messed up, which wasn't wholly unknown.

"I am being unfair, but I can't juggle more than one emotional crisis at a time. You know me."

"I do," Harriet said, emphatically. She shrugged out of her coat and hung it on the hooks by the door. "Come on, Mrs Vicar. Let's go and make coffee and you can tell me all about it."

Anna trailed after her, feeling just a little lighter with each step closer to the kitchen.

***

Simeon was taking Belle for his usual walk around the Point. It was beginning to get busy, but he was managing. Sometimes he hardly worried about people following him, demanding too much of him, particularly after Archie had said that even if a stranger wanted to speak to him, he didn't have to respond if he didn't feel up to it. He could simply stand off the path and allow them to pass. Just now he was much more worried that Belle might go too close to the edge, her eyesight wasn't what it was. Usually she didn't range far, and he didn't have to do more than whisper her name for her to come straight back, so he ought not to get anxious.

Earlier, in church, Archie had looked better, and though he was obviously troubled by Jim's visit, it did not seem to be affecting his general health. It wasn't Simeon's day to visit him, but he thought he might go over that way, coming back into the village past his house. It might be too far for Belle, but he could turn back or cut across The Lizard in any number of places. He wondered when Archie's next check-up was due.

As he was passing the top of the steps by the lifeboat, the funicular began moving down its ramp. It made him jump because he wasn't expecting it. It was such a steep drop but if you were inside the cage, it didn't feel so bad. He found watching it, particularly if you were below on the metal stairs, much more troubling; it could make you feel quite dizzy looking up at it coming down. He quickly walked across to the five steps on the other side of the building that housed the winding gear, then through the gate, and back onto the coastal path. Calling Belle to his side he turned to watch the carriage fall out of sight. Someone was down there even though there wasn't a car in the car park.

He walked on until the lifeboat was hidden behind the headland, but it didn't help. The missing woman had left him feeling disconcerted. He'd seen her about, knew that she lived just up from Archie, knew that she worked in Exeter for part of the week. He'd never spoken to her because he hadn't been introduced. Of course, he knew that if Caroline, or Caz as she was generally called, had not been in contact for this long, four weeks since Archie had seen her, there was a good chance that she was dead. Disappearing was quite hard to do. Credit cards, phones and bank accounts would have to go completely silent which meant living off cash, and unless you were incredibly wealthy, that soon ran out. Criminals and the very old were the only exceptions he could think of. Simeon was of the opinion that Caz had fallen into the sea and had been swept away. He hadn't said that to anyone yet, he thought it was one of those logical thoughts that no one wanted to hear.

At Beacon Point, Simeon stepped off the path and walked to the edge, pulling a plastic bag from his pocket to sit down on. It was a warm day for April, at least inside his oversized parka. He knew there were some deep lows coming in later in the week but for now The Lizard was at peace.

"So, God," he said, quietly. "Where is she?" Then he hurriedly added, "I don't want to be the one to find her. By now she'll be in a bit of a state. Please let someone else find the body." He shivered, and though the sun was still shining, the clouds light and wispy, it suddenly felt colder. A movement behind him made him turn. A large man was coming across the grass towards him. Simeon shuffled back from the edge, pulled his hood down further and scrambled to his feet. He clutched the loose fur around Belle's neck. She leaned heavily against his leg.

"Do you live around here?" The man sounded authoritative, and it took all of Simeon's energy not to reply. "Oi, are you deaf or something?"

Simeon wondered if he could pretend that he was, but that would be dishonest.

"No."

"Do you live around here?"

"Yes, but I don't have to tell you where."

"There's no need to take that attitude. I was just wondering if you knew my daughter, Caroline, Caz Denbigh."

Simeon shook his head.

"I need to go now." He took a tiny step forward, but the

man was standing in the way, and he didn't move.

"Now, don't be like that. I'm just trying to find out as much as I can about her movements, the day she disappeared."

"How can you know which day she actually disappeared?" Simeon froze. He didn't want to engage with this man. Over to the left was the gate leading onto the lane that ran up through the fields to his house. If the man would move just a little, Simeon could get by.

"Of course, I can't be sure, but I know when the last sighting was. An old bloke who volunteers down at the lifeboat spoke to her. Now I bet you know where he lives."

"I do, but I won't tell you that either."

"And why not? Has he something to hide, I wonder?"

"No, of course not. He's a kind man, honest and sensible but only he can tell you where he lives."

"Where do you live then?"

"I ... I won't tell you." Simeon knew that he was beginning to mumble. It felt as if his mouth was full of cotton wool.

"I don't expect it will be hard to find out. Where does the odd boy in the parka live? And where does the old man, who volunteers at the lifeboat station, rest his head at night? I expect Jean in the shop will tell me, or perhaps Catherine. A nice woman I met early this morning."

Simeon jumped at Catherine's name. But Catherine wasn't stupid, in fact she was sensible like Archie. She wouldn't hand out addresses without the person's permission. Jean on the other hand wouldn't hesitate, would probably think she was helping.

"I really do need to go now. Please step back, so I can get past."

"What's the problem? There's plenty of room."

There wasn't. Simeon tried to move, but his legs felt shaky. He hadn't stood this close to anyone since he'd been grabbed at the end of *the* retreat. The memory of it made him shudder and suddenly he felt unpleasantly hot. The man wore black boots. He looked as if he kept them well polished, but mud had squelched up the sides a little. The bottoms of the man's trousers were also dark from where he'd obviously pushed across long grass, still wet with dew. Simeon was having difficulty breathing and then Belle did something she'd never done before, she growled, just a quiet little rumble at the back of her throat. The man stepped back.

"Alright, keep your hair on, and keep that dog under control."

Simeon was already hurrying past, almost running.

"Good girl, good girl," he found himself saying, over and over again.

Back home he pulled the curtains closed in the front room and then returned to the kitchen. It was at the rear of the house, overlooking his patch of garden. The lounge and spare room looked out over the lane and a small part of the farmyard. He didn't often go into either of those rooms unless someone came to visit because he didn't like the idea that anyone walking past could look in. Apart from this drawback the house suited his needs and at the time, he'd been able to buy it outright. His mother had left him well cared for, but not wealthy.

Once he'd calmed down a little, he phoned Archie and told him what had happened.

"Oh dear, you will have found that quite difficult," Archie said. "But he must be so desperate to find out about his daughter."

Simeon was disappointed that though Archie had understood why he had phoned, and that he was upset, Archie had still made excuses for the man. Simeon didn't think he'd been desperate at all. He hoped that Archie would invite him to come over, but he didn't.

"Stay in, Simeon. There's a nasty low coming in this afternoon. It'll get colder and will surely bring rain."

"Ok."

Archie hung up. Simeon sat down at the kitchen table. Belle clambered into her basket. The man had been right, he could easily find out where he lived, and Simeon hated the idea of that. He hated that more than he could possibly say. He made himself a sandwich, but couldn't face it, so he took himself into his bedroom and pulled the curtains closed in there too.

Chapter 12

Harriet was late getting back to Derek. Over breakfast, he'd announced that after their previous conversation he wanted to talk paint colours. He'd said that though some of the rooms still needed work, he could get the kitchen, the lounge and the small study finished so she could start arranging their things. Harriet had felt the mantle of 'little woman' settle over her. She walked a bit faster. Derek hadn't meant to relegate her to making things look nice. He'd be bewildered that she had taken it that way. She wondered why she had, why she couldn't err on the side of kindness, and generosity.

A young couple were walking up towards her. She recognised them from the lifeboat station. Genni and Toby. Genni had her arm looped through his but there was a gap between them, a thin narrow space of air and sky. They were puffing a bit as if they'd been moving quickly.

"Hello, Genni and Toby, isn't it?"

"Yes," Genni said, looking up, and then away. "We've been trying to fit in a walk between work and the weather coming in, but it's a bit too cold to be nice."

"It's going to get nasty. Derek keeps an eye on such things," Harriet said laughing, as if it were a slightly eccentric hobby that she was a teeny bit embarrassed by. Then a little sheepishly she continued, "I suppose you guys must have to keep an eye out too."

Toby frowned. Harriet tried again.

"Being on the lifeboat. It must mean you have the shipping forecast on speed-dial." She was making heavy weather of this, which made her want to giggle. Stop thinking about the weather, she told herself sternly.

"Yes," Genni said. "You do kind of tense a little when the weather is bad. Going out when the sea is big can be a bit daunting. I sometimes hope the Launch Authority guy will simply say it's too dangerous." She turned back, to look down the lane, to the sea. Harriet realised that Genni was quite beautiful. There was no other way of describing her. Her skin was smooth and dark, her eyes almost black, cheekbones high and lips full and pink. Her hair, pulled tightly off her face, was long and wavy. Harriet was truly envious of the school mistress from year three, the crew mate in oilskins.

"I'd rather have big waves than a flat day to pick some idiot off the cliffs," Toby said sharply. Harriet didn't quite believe him. Toby's red hair was long and thick. His face a little round, his skin pale and under his eyes there were dark patches.

"I guess," Genni replied, but she didn't sound convinced, either.

"You've been quite busy of late," Harriet said. Something she'd heard Phil say at the pub.

"The first couple of months was unusually so, but we've not been called out since Caz …"

"Disappeared," Toby said, a little harshly, Harriet thought. Genni's eyes began to fill with tears. Toby looked away, his lips tight, his eyes losing focus. He really wanted to be somewhere else.

"You know, if you ever need someone to talk to," Harriet said, "we're open for visitors in the new house, though it's still a bit of a building site."

"We know," Toby said, this time definitely pointedly. Harriet was beginning to really dislike him, though she guessed that even their joint wages might not be enough to afford anything around the Point. He continued, clearly sarcastic, "The Reverend Anna is always available for a chat. But unless she can find Caz, what good is talking?"

"I think a problem shared is a problem halved. It's good to be listened to," Harriet said, knowing she sounded as if she were back in school and scoring points.

"We have each other at the station. There are plenty of people to talk to who understand," Toby said. Just for a second, he looked straight at her, and Harriet felt a frisson of something rather unpleasant up and down her spine.

"Thank you," Genni almost whispered, "I'll bear it in mind."

Toby began to move, Genni followed. Harriet turned to watch them around the bend. Not a happy couple. Not happy at all.

She quickly climbed the steps, up into the garden. Harriet hadn't meant to spend so long talking to Anna after morning prayer, in the end most of the morning, and then she'd popped up to the shop, and called in on Catherine about a book. Time had just flown by, but it had been nice squeezed into Anna's tiny back room, sipping coffee and eating biscuits. Harriet had felt hidden away, special. She knew that very few people were invited beyond the kitchen. Most didn't make it past the large front room. Of course they'd discussed Tom, though Anna had real difficulty articulating how she was feeling, how she thought it was actually going. To move on from simply 'giving it a go' seemed to be a gigantic step for her.

On the whole, Harriet thought they were managing the relationship quite well, though she still noticed from time to time a slight stiffening of Anna's spine, or a flash of disappointment on Tom's face, when they were together. Harriet had used the 'm' word that morning, and Anna's eyes had positively bulged out of her head. But she'd have to think about it, because at some point Tom was going to ask her. It was almost inevitable.

"Harriet, is that you?"

Derek came out of the kitchen with two mugs of coffee. Harriet had already had rather a lot of coffee and would have preferred tea, but she didn't say anything. It was also lukewarm. Her fault again for being so late home.

"I saw a couple of the lifeboat crew out in the lane. Genni and Toby."

"Which ones are they?" he asked, leading her into the lounge, where he'd laid out some colour charts.

"You'd know them if you saw them. He's quite short and has

lovely red hair and she is slightly taller, with long dark hair. The black woman. Quite striking. Mind you, Derek, there are two young women on the crew, and one of them is missing!"

"I know exactly who you mean. Her mum is from Mullion, her father was from Jamaica, and sailed out of Cardiff."

Harriet sat down.

"That's the couple and I'm impressed."

"Jean filled me in. She's very excited about the wedding. She's hoping they'll ask her to do the church flowers. And I agree, she's quite lovely."

Harriet assumed he was talking about Genni, rather than Jean.

"But what can have happened to her friend?" Harriet asked. She really would have to warm up the coffee, it was beyond drinking.

Derek stopped pressing one colour against another and looked up.

"You're really upset about this, aren't you?"

"I suppose, it's the not knowing. And though Caz might have just decided to walk away from her life, it doesn't feel likely."

"No, I can't imagine just leaving."

"Which means something awful has happened to her. We just don't know what yet."

Harriet suddenly snatched up the colour charts.

"In here, we ought to have something dark and warm. It's probably not fashionable but something like this deep red."

Derek frowned.

"I know you'd prefer something lighter, Derek, more architectural, but I want to feel cosy. Somewhere to curl up with a book, perhaps one of Anna's unsuitable novels."

"And a glass of wine, with the log fire going," Derek added, but she could tell he wasn't convinced.

It was a room she'd seen in a magazine, a room she'd imagined walking into, where she could close the door on the world. Of course, back then, she'd never dreamt it might one day become a reality.

"Or perhaps this grey?" she said.

"Mmmm! Grey on three of the walls and where the sun hits it later in the afternoon how about this turquoise?"

Harriet had to admit it might look nice.

"Or perhaps the china blue with a dark blue accent? Tell me what you'd like, and we'll do it."

Harriet sat back and smiled.

"Red it is then … and perhaps a hot cup of coffee?" But teasing Derek wasn't really that much fun. As his eyes crinkled into a worried frown she had to quickly add, "Just joking. The grey and turquoise will look fantastic." He nodded, but he still didn't seem that sure.

"I could get some test pots."

She didn't think they really needed to, but they could also do with going to the supermarket, so for once it would be a less indulgent trip.

"Now, how about warming this up, so we can really enjoy it?"

Derek smiled and handed her his mug.

***

Toby had dropped Genni home. He'd watched her disappear down the side-passage. She and her mum never used the front door. Genni would already be sitting at the kitchen table, her mother putting on the kettle, asking her all the questions that he should have asked, about the latest practice, how everyone was at school. Genni would tell her about meeting Harriet, and what she'd said, without the anger of Toby's responses, the unfairness of the housing market and their inability to earn enough to live in more than a shoebox.

He put the car into gear and drove away, his tyres screeching just a little on the first corner. Perhaps he should have gone to the door with her, perhaps he should have stayed, but since Caz he couldn't settle, and Genni had become this weeping choked-up girl. Had she always been like that? Or would she go back to being her easy-going self when it was all over? He really, really hoped so.

He was sitting at the junction on the main road but instead of turning right, he turned left, heading up to Helston. If he drove really fast, he could catch an early film, at least then his day wouldn't be a total wash out.

The film had been crap and he'd felt odd watching it on his own. No one came and sat near him, and he hoped he hadn't been recognised. Saddo Toby from The Lizard, hasn't got any friends, has to go to the cinema by himself. He drove back to the village in record time, and swung into his parking space outside the house, with a good squeal of brakes. The curtains were closed, the lights on in the lounge. His mum was probably watching television. His dad's car was also back but at this time of night he'd be over at the pub. Toby had his hand on the car key, though he realised he found the rumbling under the bonnet a comfort and he couldn't face the silence just yet. Before his mother's face appeared to check who it was, he reversed out and drove past the football field, turning down to Church Cove. He was going a little fast, but he knew the lane well. He was driving as if his pager had gone off. As he swung past the church the boy with the white dog had to jump out of the way. His hood was up so all Toby could see was his chin. He was an odd bod, wouldn't talk to you, kept his head down so Toby had been really surprised to see him down at the lifeboat when the vicar had come down to do the blessing. What a load of twaddle that had been, but his dad had seemed really keen, so the rest of them had gone along with it. You didn't disagree with Jim, and Toby supposed that when you were out in a big sea, you took all the help you could get.

He bumped over the cattle grid and drove across the field to the station car park. It was empty. He didn't know why he was surprised, almost disappointed. No one would just come down, not on their own, not anymore. He couldn't see much through his windscreen, a bit of sky, the top of the building with the winding gear and the dark gorse bushes, speckled with bright yellow flowers, even in the dark.

Toby knew he was being hard on Genni, but he wasn't used to her taking up so much of his time. He was having to be careful around her and it was exhausting. He finally switched off the engine, suddenly craving the silence. It wasn't silent. Not close. There was the ticking of the engine as it cooled and the noise of the wind buffeting the car and the clink of the catch at the top of the flagpole. Sounds that would normally slide past, on into the background, were filling the air around him, were filling him up so that he felt he couldn't fit another thing inside.

Toby was out of his depth, something he'd been struggling with for a while. Genni was lovely but when he really thought about it, he didn't feel as if he knew her at all. At school, she'd been bullied, a lot. Kids didn't like anyone who stood out, and Genni had. She'd been in the year below him, so there wasn't anything he could or would have done about it. Anyway, at that time he'd had his own problems. He was shorter than average, with red hair. School had been a tightrope and then he'd had to put up with his mother's disappointment that he'd not gone away to college, had in fact accepted the first job offered to him, apart from the one working for his dad.

What she hadn't understood, was that after a couple of weeks at the bakery, he'd fitted in. Finally, he was part of something where he didn't have to agonise over every step or reply, didn't have to worry about what to wear or who to sit by. Work had been a blessed relief, time out from the low-level digs and niggles that he faced daily because of his dad and his height, and stupidly, the colour of his hair. Recently, when he'd realised that he was struggling with all this again, he knew that no one would understand how terrible it was for him, that it was almost unbearable. The oh-no-here-we-go-again feeling that could roar over him like a tidal wave at any moment, his constant companion for months.

The real ramp up had started when Caz had arrived, particularly as she'd begun to settle in. It felt as if she were taking his place among the crew, not making a space of her own. She was pushing him out to the edges. He'd never wanted to feel like that again, ever. Her smart replies, standing up to his dad, joking with Genni, understanding what was going on. She found it all so bloody easy.

Toby looked down at his stomach. Something else that was getting out of control. He knew he ought to make time to go for a run, but just recently he simply couldn't be arsed. Perhaps he'd cultivate one like his dad.

He began to feel cold. The westerly was strong and bringing in the first drops of rain, later than was expected. If there was a shout it would be uncomfortable heading through it, and the swell beyond the Point would be huge. He reached into the back and pulled his jacket clear of all the clutter but in the end, it was hunger that drove him home. He'd not had anything since early afternoon, and he wanted his tea. He wondered what his mum had made. It would be cold by now, but easily warmed up, and tonight he'd treat himself to a beer. Not across at the pub, he still couldn't afford that, what with the wedding and saving for the deposit but there was always plenty in the fridge. One day they'd have their own place and then he wouldn't have to make all these boring decisions and that would surely make life a little easier. Perhaps even make it nice, like other people's.

Chapter 13

It was half past six in the morning when Tom's phone rang. He didn't feel as if he'd been asleep that long. These days it took him ages to drop off; the unfamiliarity of the missing woman dancing around at the edge of his thoughts and his sergeants faffing about really didn't help. He might have just about managed three or four hours. Caz had seemingly disappeared completely, and it was proving impossible to make any progress. Even Randal at missing persons had said there wasn't much more he could do. By now, there should have been a credit card withdrawal or a sighting, unless she'd just fallen into the sea, with her handbag! Tom wondered if he ought to organise a search party, but then the assumption was that they were looking for a body and who knew where to start with that? His budget wouldn't stand that sort of expense, particularly based on simple desperation.

He grabbed the shrill demanding phone and heaved himself upright. Sitting was the only way to understand what was being said to him, after so little sleep. It was Smith. She was on the cliff, just past Beacon Point. A man out walking his dog had chucked a ball over the edge by mistake. He'd leant over to see if he could get it back. He hadn't found his ball but could see a trainer that looked as if it might still be attached to a leg. It had to be the young woman.

Tom grabbed a coffee, putting it in the mug that Anna had bought him, and was on the road in just over five minutes. When he got to the village, he drove down past Derek's old bungalow and then out past Simeon's house — a single storey building that butted onto the lane. As he passed, Simeon came down the side with Belle.

"Damn!" Tom muttered to himself. Simeon would recognise his car and easily put two and two together. He might tell Archie, though Archie wouldn't gossip if his life depended on it. So perhaps Tom was safe, except that at eight they would all meet for morning prayer and Simeon might insist on praying for the lost woman's father. And that would be that. It would be around the village in no time.

He parked behind the two cars already there, knowing he would probably get blocked in by forensics but also knew he didn't have much choice.

Smith was on the lookout for him.

"She's probably been tucked down there the whole time, so we're not sure how easy it's going to be to retrieve the body," she said, as Tom climbed out. It was early enough to be chilly, but it looked like it might be a lovely May day. The wind had dropped, and the sky was cloudless.

"Where's Kellow?"

"On his way. I told him to park at the end of the lane and walk down. We're pretty blocked in as it is."

"Good call. Why on earth wasn't she spotted before?"

Smith pursed her lips.

"I've had a good look from both sides. She's on a ledge, and even with field glasses she'd be hard to spot. Grey trousers and black shoes on granite."

Not granite, serpentine, Tom said to himself.

"So how far down is she? Surely someone looked over the edge before now?"

"Seemingly not," she said. "I think we were lucky to find her at all."

"Well, thank goodness the gentleman couldn't throw. Do we know him?"

"No, he's from the hotel around the corner. Staying for a couple of days."

The sergeant had taped off the edge of the promontory. They'd have to do a fingertip search, though after all this time it would be pretty pointless. Tom turned his back to the edge, desperately trying to remember what weather they'd had over the last few weeks. Too much rain, for sure. God, he wished he'd gone with his gut and organised a search.

"I want all access to this part of the path blocked off. No one is to come through. No one!"

She nodded and scurried off. After the bollocking he'd given them, she wouldn't leave anything to chance this time. Tom hid the smile beginning to form and turned away to see what else could be done.

***

Archie was on his way to church, a little early, even for him. It was Anna's turn to take morning prayer but since Jim's visit he hadn't been sleeping well. He'd walked across the village, allowing the sky to expand above his head, allowing the tightness across his forehead to ease. He'd seen a police car turning into Church Cove Lane and wondered if someone had been burgled. When he saw the constable standing guard, seemingly outside Simeon's house, he felt the band around his chest tighten. He breathed deeply trying not to cough and walked quickly along to the cottage.

"Is he alright?" Archie demanded. "What's happened?"

"Is who alright, Sir?"

"Simeon. Simeon Tyler. Why are you standing outside his house?"

The policeman's shoulders dropped; he took a step back.

"There's been an incident down on the path, Sir, that's all. The gentleman who lives in this house, as far as I'm aware, is fine."

Archie felt his chest tightening again. Simeon always walked Belle down on the path at this time of day. He used to go with Derek but since the death of Dolly he'd been going on his own.

"Can you tell me who's involved?" Archie asked, tentatively.

"Not at the moment, Sir."

Archie still went up the side of the bungalow and banged on the door, though he knew there'd be no reply. The garden was overgrown, almost wild. Branches reached out of the borders, the grass was long and straggly, badly encroaching on the gravel path. Simeon liked it light and weed-free. Why hadn't he asked Archie to come and help him clear it? Archie knew why. Since the heart attack, Simeon had been keeping Archie safe. Archie acknowledged the skin of irritation that began to stretch around him whenever he caught sight of Simeon or heard his knock. He sent a text.

'Are you alright? Let's meet to talk after morning prayer. And later this week we'll have a go at your shrubs and the lawn.'

He checked his watch. Just after seven-thirty. Good enough. He'd go and see Anna. He didn't like to burden her with personal stuff but if this anxiety was just a little bit of what Simeon had been feeling for Archie himself, then he needed to work out how to put it right. He was at the vicarage door within a couple of minutes.

He rang the bell and waited for her footsteps to hurry along from the kitchen. At this time of the morning, she'd be worried that someone had died or was dying.

"I know it's early, Anna, but could we have a talk before morning prayer?"

She was dressed, which was a relief. She ran a hand through her hair which made it stick out, before she turned back to the kitchen.

"The kitchen's a mess, Archie, but it's where my coffee is. Do you want one?"

Archie thought for a moment, his heart was still beating too loudly, and he felt a little clammy.

"No, I'm fine." He squeezed into the chair on the far side of the table.

"Now, tell me what's up," she said, filling her own mug, which was chipped.

"Simeon!" he said.

Anna pursed her lips and tipped her head to one side. A gesture so familiar that for a moment he could breathe again.

"I know that lately he's been a bit of a pain," she replied, frowning and smiling at the same time. He couldn't think of anyone else who did that. "But you know it's just because he's worried about you. He's afraid the stent isn't enough."

Archie nodded.

"I know and I've been holding him off because he's so ... I've been brusque when I should have been understanding. I've avoided the subject when I should have brought it up."

"Archie, this feels like a confession. And for you, of all people, it's totally unnecessary."

Now Archie frowned.

"Anna, I'm not as wonderful as you all keep saying I am. Please allow me to be human. There are things that I have done, a person I have been ..."

She sat back.

"I'm so sorry Archie. Tell me whatever you want to tell me."

She looked across at him earnestly and he knew she would be feeling ashamed. She did rely on him, it usually made him feel useful and in control, but he wasn't holding it together, not like he used to. He was beginning to find there were holes in his life, holes that were growing, and getting ragged around the edges. Some memories were getting so big he was having to purposely step around them, deliberately turn to something else so they wouldn't suck him in.

"Did you know there are police all around Beacon Point?" he said, wishing he'd asked for a cup of tea.

She blanched and yet her face began to flush. He knew how she felt.

"Do you think they've finally found her?"

Archie nodded.

"The poor girl," she whispered.

"Her dad will be devastated. Is he back again yet?"

Archie nodded.

"He returned last week."

He knew that his moment had passed. Whatever he was feeling, there was a man wandering about their village, trying to come to terms with the loss of his daughter. Anna's thoughts had, quite rightly, slipped over him, past him and onto Mr Denbigh. She was probably wondering if there was anything she ought to be doing. Archie would have to find another time, or he would have to find his own way through the next bit. He'd always done so before, with hardly a break in his stride, but this brush with mortality seemed to have stirred things up. And it was extremely selfish of him to have allowed it to act as a shield. Feeling a little sorry for himself was unacceptable when Mr Denbigh had lost his child. Archie needed to pull himself together.

***

Simeon didn't go into church straight away. He didn't want to shut himself behind the thick stone walls. He wanted to be able to see Anna and Archie as soon as he could. The extra few seconds he would gain by waiting outside seemed precious. They came through the gate, Anna enveloped in her long, padded raincoat, her fair hair blowing about her face. Archie was speaking and she was listening, and she smiled at something he said, but her shoulders were rounded and slumped forward, her cheeks flushed. Archie walked a little behind, upright as usual, his coat neatly buttoned, a silk scarf carefully tucked into the collar, a nod to the month of May. His face was saggy, as if he was shrinking from the inside. When Archie noticed Simeon, he immediately strode past Anna, coming quickly down the path towards him. Simeon thought for a moment that Archie might be angry with him.

"I was worried. I heard the police were where you walk Belle."

Simeon glanced down at their feet and then up at his friend's face. Archie's eyes burned with intensity and Simeon had to turn away. Archie looked as if he had high blood pressure.

"They've found a body," Anna said. "Tom has just sent a text. He knew we'd be worried."

"The sea does sometimes return them," Archie whispered.

"If it's her, Caz, someone ought to let her father know," Anna continued.

"Not until they're sure. Let him hope for as long as he can," Archie replied.

Catherine appeared, also hurrying.

"I saw the police," she said.

Anna nodded, went on nodding as if she couldn't stop.

Catherine said, "This is the moment Gerald has been dreading."

"If it is her." Simeon spoke, sharply, beginning to get annoyed. That seemed to reach Anna, for she quickly turned away and led them into the church. She picked up the prayer book and put it down again. She stared at the altar as they settled around her.

"We should start," Simeon said.

"Shall I begin," Archie replied. He would understand how disconcerted Anna was. She nodded miserably just as Harriet arrived. She must have run up the hill, there was a sheen across her forehead. She slid in beside Anna and they leaned into one another. For a few days, no one would simply walk anywhere. There would be an urgency that they wouldn't be able to ignore.

"We must pray for her dad," Catherine said. "To lose a child is devastating." And they knew that she was thinking of Tom. That she lived with the fear that one day he would be hurt, or worse still that he might be killed in the line of duty.

Archie began to read the opening sentences.

Afterwards Simeon waited for him at the back. He couldn't lift his eyes off the floor which worried him. It was as if he were slipping into his old ways. Archie's shoes were shiny, polished, well looked after, familiar. Simeon was getting really concerned as to how hard he was finding it standing there, waiting for Archie to speak.

"I'm sorry you've been so worried," Archie said.

"It's just that you've not really recovered. You're not back to how you were. If it were just a stent you should be better by now."

"I thought I was better."

"You look older. You don't fit your clothes as well."

"I'm scared, Simeon. A little frightened. It came as a bit of a shock. I'm not ready to die. I wasn't ready back there on the Point, I clung on with everything I had. For all our talk of faith, when it came down to it, I needed to survive. To live one more hour."

Anna slipped past them and out into the light. Archie and Simeon were by the door until Archie stepped across to lean on the back of a pew.

"Simeon, we talk to God all the time, but when the moment came, I couldn't find him. And I've been thinking a lot that if Caz had slipped, there might have been a few seconds before she hit the water, when she knew she was going to die."

"Let's go to the cafe on the Point," Simeon said. It surprised him, almost as much as it did Archie.

"Is that alright, Simeon? Or we could go to my house."

"No, I want to buy you coffee. It's what Anna would do if Harriet were upset. And my kitchen has just one chair, your kitchen is tiny, and I don't expect Anna would appreciate us sitting in hers."

When Simeon needed to talk about a book, or about an aspect of faith he went and sat in Archie's front room. Archie lit the fire and they talked for hours. But if Simeon couldn't think straight, or he knew that he'd upset someone, he would go and sit in Anna's kitchen. She would make him tea or coffee in a mug with something silly written on it, slide a plate of biscuits towards him and ask him questions that were difficult to answer or didn't really have an answer at all. Simeon used his friends for different problems. Georgie had noticed that, and she'd said it was completely normal because it was helpful if you knew who to go to when you were troubled. It would be good to see her soon, to tell her some of the things that were happening. Because she lived up in Exeter and only came down now and again, she was able to stand back from all their problems. Though *the* retreat had been horribly difficult, a lot of good things had come from it. Being able to speak to Georgie, was one of them. And when she returned to Exeter, Simeon didn't have to think about her at all.

Archie needed him to be a bit like Anna or Georgie, in some respects at least. And him fearing dying didn't seem unreasonable. Like most people, Simeon was too. He was frightened of the process, because, like everyone else, he hated pain or even the idea of it, but finding out what existed beyond death would be amazing.

The thing that had disturbed Simeon, that he really thought they needed to explore, was that when Archie was having his heart attack, he couldn't find God at all. That didn't sound right, not on any level.

***

Genni had a busy morning, until break time, as her Teaching Assistant was helping out in another classroom. As soon as the last child disappeared into the playground, she gratefully went through to the staff room to grab a coffee. The headmistress was there with two of the others. Genni smiled at them, but her eye was fixed on the coffee pot in the corner. The headmistress stood up abruptly, as if she'd just remembered something, but instead she came over to stand by Genni.

She said, "The police are back. There's a rumour that they may have found the missing woman. She was your friend, wasn't she?"

Genni continued to pour the coffee. The woman looked alarmed.

"Come and sit down. I'll bring your drink over. I expect it's a bit of a shock."

Genni wanted to do as she was told because the headmistress was trying to be kind. She must expect her to be a bit upset, to perhaps shed a few tears, after all she and Caz had been part of the lifeboat crew, and crew was family, but a feeling like panic began to roar up through her and Genni wasn't able to contain it. She needed air. She couldn't stay, couldn't think. She found herself in the schoolyard. She had to go and see for herself whether it was true, that they had found Caz, but when she reached the top of the track, the policeman wouldn't let her through. He wouldn't tell her anything, so she carried on down the lane. She didn't know what else to do.

Genni felt as though she were drunk, dizzy. She stopped walking when she stumbled. The lane felt gritty under her shoes where a storm had scraped mud from the banks either side, but at least she wasn't cold. Finally, summer seemed to be on its way, apart from the wild weather of the night before, which was good because she didn't seem to have a coat. She couldn't understand why. She never went anywhere without one.

"Can I help you?" A face was peering down at her from a gate that must lead into the front garden of one of the cottages. There were three steep steps straight up from the road.

Genni knew the face but couldn't remember the name. The woman opened the gate and came down to her. Genni thought she ought to say something but couldn't work out what.

"You look cold," Harriet said. "It's a bit soon to be out without a coat. Are you alright?"

Genni ran a hand up her bare arm. She was wearing a long-sleeved T-shirt and a cardigan, but she'd pushed the sleeves up to her elbows. It was what she did when she was about to start her day, in the classroom.

She ought to get back. The children needed to get on with their spelling and some of them had to change their reading books.

"Come on inside. I'll make us a drink. You look like you could do with one."

Genni followed the woman, slight and small, her hair tucked into a bun that left dark tendrils all around the top of her neck. Genni couldn't stop staring at her hair. The woman took her into a small lounge and disappeared. Genni couldn't sit down, so she stood by the window, hands on the sill. The stone was cold, and she was able to hang onto it. It felt solid and reassuring.

She began to hear whispering.

"It must be shock. She looks like she's on drugs."

"She didn't have a coat or anything and I can't get her to talk to me at all."

"She teaches at the primary. I think we should give them a call."

Genni looked round. The vicar was there in the hall with the woman with the dark hair, Harriet. They'd spoken out on the road when she and Toby had gone for a walk. She knew they were good friends. In a village like this everyone knew everything. The vicar, Anna, came and stood beside her.

"Do you remember me, Genni? I'm Anna. We met at the lifeboat station and then you came to the vicarage. You're getting married."

Genni did remember. Anna was someone you could talk to. The vicar's hand was resting on the sill in front of her. Genni reached out and grasped it, gripping it tightly.

"They found her. They found her."

"Who've they found, Genni?"

"Who else can it be?"

"We don't know for sure that it's Caz."

Genni snatched her hand away at the sound of the name. She looked down at the round face, fair eyebrows and wispy hair.

"I know! I know it's her."

"Genni, is there someone we should call?"

Genni wanted to call Caz, but Caz's phone went to voicemail. She ought to call Toby or the school or her mum, but she didn't know where to begin. She didn't want to be a nuisance, but it's exactly what she was being right now, and she hated that. It made her feel vulnerable.

"I don't want to be a nuisance."

"That's alright. You stay here. Harriet will make you another cup of tea and I'll go and call someone."

Genni began to cry. Big sobs that came out in hard bubbles that scraped her throat.

"I haven't even got my pager on me. What will Jim say if I haven't got my pager?"

Harriet stepped forward and led Genni to a chair. She gently pushed her down and handed her tissues. Genni was blind with tears, the woman knelt beside her.

"You mustn't think about all this stuff. We can always ring Jim and let him know," she said.

"Not Jim. Please don't contact Jim."

"Look, you've had a shock, you're upset, you're allowed to let go a little."

Genni knew she wasn't. She wasn't allowed to give in, ever.

"Caz has been lying there all these weeks. She would have been so cold, so alone. Why didn't anyone find her sooner? I thought someone would have found her. She was so close by."

Harriet sat back on her heels.

"Though she was not far down, she was in a sort of crevice. She was pushed in deep enough for her to be out of sight. It was a stroke of good luck that anyone found her."

"Good luck. No! Not good luck!" Genni's tears dried. She began to laugh, and Harriet leaned away from her, just a little.

Chapter 14

Anna watched them disappear down into the lane. Genni's mum led her daughter as if she were an old woman, almost having to tell her where to put her feet. Genni leaned on her, leaned over her, being nearly a head taller. Her mum was delicate looking with faded blonde hair and a narrow face with a multitude of fine lines around her eyes. Anna had never met her before as she lived over in Mullion, but Harriet had, and they'd exchanged a few words about the weather and her card business.

Anna knew she ought to go back to the vicarage, get organised for whatever was coming next, but instead she went back inside to Harriet. She didn't want to be home when Caz's dad rang the doorbell and asked difficult questions. Worse still, she wouldn't want Mr Denbigh to see a light on but have no one come to the door, because she was too afraid to face him. She'd even texted Tom to say that she wasn't sure where she would be and to ring her when he was on his way. She thought he'd understand, not about hiding at Harriet's, but her fear of what was about to happen.

She walked into the narrow hall and along to Harriet's new kitchen. Shiny, sparkly, tidy because they still hadn't got everything out of storage. Not quite real yet, though there was a row of dog-eared recipe books that Anna knew had belonged to Fiona, Derek's dead wife. Harriet had said she'd decided to stop being afraid of them, had decided that for Derek's sake she would put them with her own books, and perhaps one day she would open one and have a look.

"It'll take a few days to confirm who the body is," Anna said, seating herself at the breakfast bar. The stools didn't look comfortable but were. All she would have to remember, when it came time to leave, was how high up she was. Previously, she'd slipped rather inelegantly at the unexpected drop.

"At least she wasn't in the sea, then she'd have been in a

state," Harriet said, quietly. She was moving about, making things.

In a state! That was an understatement. Anna put her head in her hands. Derek would be back soon, from yet another trip to Helston to get paint and to pick up another light fitting he wanted to try in the hall. She was amazed at how much time he was spending on these things. Harriet had looked a little pained when she'd said where he was. Anna had one of the paper-ball lamp shades leftover from their makeover of the vicarage; it would look quite nice against the newly chosen moss green walls. Perhaps she should offer it.

"Oh, Harriet, I'm going to have to stop being such a coward and go home. I need to be where people expect to find me."

"But what if Gerald Denbigh comes around, all upset and angry?"

"I'll light a fire and make him tea."

Harriet snorted.

"I'm coming with you. Safety in numbers and you can't light a fire for toffee."

Anna blew a big, long breath from between her lips.

"That would be brilliant, but what about Derek?"

"What about Derek? He's not a child. I'll leave him a note and he can finish dinner off."

Anna couldn't imagine simply leaving a note. She thought of Tom trying to make sense of what she wanted him to do, and then swearing under his breath as he went up to the chippy or made himself a sandwich.

What else should she be doing, apart from imagining the impossible? She was worrying about the questions that she might be asked. Where was God now? And what had Caz wanted when she'd come to see Anna, all those weeks ago?

"Perhaps later we should phone Genni's mum. Find out how Genni is?" Harriet said, handing Anna her coat.

"I think I'll call Jim. Make sure he knows that she's not feeling well." Anna grimaced. She was good at euphemisms.

"Don't do that. Genni really didn't want us to."

Anna nodded. She didn't blame her.

As they turned into the vicarage drive and began to crunch down the gravel, Catherine appeared around the corner of the house.

"I'm sorry to have come. I find I'm quite upset about them finding her and I didn't want to disturb Archie."

"We can't be sure that it's Caz," Anna said, searching through the tissues at the bottom of her pockets for the key. No one would believe that. "Come on in, the two of you." She could see Harriet beginning to edge away. "I need to talk this through, we all do. We need to work out what we should be doing, and I would value both of you being around, just in case."

It was still light, though it always felt a little dimmer on the Church Cove side of The Lizard. It hadn't been a bad day, but now clouds were beginning to pile up around them. It wouldn't be long before it began to rain. Anna hoped against hope that Tom would be able to get away soon, that he would pop in on his way back to Falmouth, for a minute, to let them know, let her know, what was happening.

Harriet disappeared into the lounge to get the fire going. Catherine followed Anna into the kitchen. They'd decided to make a pot of tea, and a flask of coffee as if they were hosting one of the retreats. Catherine suddenly leant her knuckles on the kitchen table and dipped her head.

"If it were me, I wouldn't know what to do. Your child, gone!"

Anna laid a hand on her shoulder and said, "Her father is a former police officer, so he'll know all the procedures, the true meaning of the statements. He'll know what's going on better than us."

"Oh, Anna. What must it be like to be Tom?"

"Tom the police officer, or Tom your son?"

Catherine shook her head.

"I have coffee with Gerald sometimes. Yesterday morning, we met down at the Point. He's always asking questions but yesterday he wanted to know all about us. It was like an interrogation. I don't blame him. It's what I would do."

"He must have been fearsome when interviewing a suspect," Anna replied. She felt guilty because though she'd refused to tell Mr Denbigh what she and Caz had talked about, it was not really because it was breaking confidentiality but because she didn't like him. Also, how could she tell him that Caz didn't seem to be that popular, that she'd been worried that her crew mates might have been playing cruel jokes on her, or that she thought she might have seen a ghost. Which was nonsense.

"Come on, Catherine, let's take the tray through."

The fire was lit, the lamps on, even though it was still bright enough outside. Harriet couldn't help herself; she'd made it look welcoming with just a touch here and there. She jumped to her feet as they entered. When Anna bent her head to put down the tray, Harriet whispered.

"Do you want me to go?"

Anna's hand shot out and gripped her wrist. Gripped it tightly.

"No. Please stay."

Harriet nodded and went over to prod the fire. Catherine sorted out the drinks and they sat down. Anna knew they were waiting for whatever was going to happen next. She prayed, but there was no sense of him. It was like God had set a ball rolling and was standing back to see how they managed.

"I can't do it without you," she whispered. "I genuinely don't have a clue."

Catherine's eyes were shut, and Harriet was staring into the fire. Anna knew that God was there, really, but she totally understood why people thought that when the proverbial hit the fan it felt as if he'd left them.

***

Jim climbed the stairs two at a time. It was a narrow staircase, the carpet almost bald where he placed each foot. He felt the years going up and down these stairs were beginning to add up to a lifetime. He supposed the carpet did need replacing but he'd wait for Margery to moan about it before he'd find the money. At the top was a tiny landing with doors to their bedroom, the bathroom, Toby's room and a box room that they used as an excuse not to get rid of anything. Toby's door was closed. A wooden sign, held on by Blu Tack said, 'Toby's Space'. There was a rocket with a background of stars. Toby's Space! The Christmas they'd given it to him he'd tossed it to one side, dismissing it as childish. Jim supposed looking back that he might've had a point, he'd been nearly thirteen, but Margery had loved it. Said a friend from work had made it specially for him. In the end Toby said that Jim could put it up if it meant they had to knock and wait for permission before entering. Jim and Margery had laughed.

"You'll be doing your own washing, then?" his mum had said, as if she understood what was really going on. Jim hadn't. When Toby had stalked off to his room and left them to finish opening their presents alone, he'd wanted to go and drag the ungrateful brat back down. Margery had said to wait until lunch was ready, which she'd got up to do. Toby really could be a sullen sod, had always been one when Jim thought back on it. That had been the first year their daughter had spent Christmas with her in-laws-to-be and the last time she'd spent it with them. A sad year all round, particularly with Jim's mum mumbling in the corner.

The previous Christmas had been the first one without his mother. Her death happening suddenly on a bright June day when they'd been out on an exercise. At the news he'd felt the weight lift from his shoulders and then had yelled at Margery for not texting him before he got back to the ramp. He'd really yelled, until she'd gone for a walk. He'd shouted at her a lot leading up to the funeral. But for the first time in a long time, he'd looked forward to Christmas, without the tedious task of picking his mum up from the home, and then arguing over who should take her back. Jim had thought it would be a relief not having to listen to her strange remarks and sudden outbursts, but Toby had disappeared off to Genni's straight after lunch and he and Margery hadn't quite known what to do with themselves. It had been strangely silent, and he'd spent a lot of time staring at his mother's favourite chair. He didn't really miss her as such, but now and again he wondered at the space she'd seemingly left empty.

He knocked on Toby's door, hesitated for half a second before opening it. Toby was sprawled on his bed. He looked as if he might have been asleep but jerked upright as his father entered.

"Dad, what is it?"

Jim supposed he hadn't been in there for years. There'd been no need. They did all their talking downstairs over dinner, or at the practices. Recently, Toby had supper with Genni more often than not, which was as it should be, he supposed.

"I've just had a phone call from Genni's mum. Genni had to come home from work today. She's in shock or something. She thought I should know because of the practices. I thought you should know because she's your fiancée."

"She's been crying on and off for weeks."

"She doesn't normally miss work though."

Jim thought Toby had to admit that was true. Even he knew that Genni hardly ever had a day off. Last winter the headmistress had had to send her home when the flu was doing the rounds and it was obvious to everyone but Genni that she was really sick. Genni's mum said she'd even fainted a couple of times on the way to the bathroom but had still insisted on driving in.

"I'll ring her, make sure she's ok," Toby said.

"She's certainly not been herself of late."

"Bloody Caz!"

"We don't know it's her," Jim replied.

Though he knew that it was. They all did. Lying on a rocky outcrop, unseen for nearly two months. Jim also knew what the birds would have done to her. He suddenly felt sick, which was ridiculous. He'd pulled enough corpses from the sea to know what was what. He couldn't afford to get squeamish now.

Toby turned away, clamping his phone to his ear. Jim stood a moment longer and then retreated downstairs. He opened the back door and breathed in some lungfuls of fresh air. Margery was out with friends from work, or she'd have gone up to speak to their son. She was out a lot recently which was beginning to get annoying. So, though it was still early, he grabbed his coat and stalked over to the pub.

"Hi, Phil. A pint of the usual."

"Will do, Jim, and a drop of the hard stuff?" Jim nodded. "Tough day?"

Jim climbed onto a stool. None of the crew were in, no one he could go and join, so Phil would have to do.

Phil owned the pub, and had been a fixture for a couple of decades. He'd stayed even after his wife had left him to return to Birmingham. He was obviously comfortable where he was. For a while they'd all wondered if he and Harriet were having a thing but if they were, then it hadn't panned out. Now she was living with the architect.

"So, how are you?" Phil asked, wiping the already shiny bar. "It's been a difficult time."

"You could say that."

"She probably slipped and fell. Went too close to the edge while out for a run."

"Possibly." Jim knew what Phil was really asking. Caz had often been seen out running, but she favoured the lanes. She'd always said she was worried about turning an ankle on the paths, that she wanted to be able to concentrate on her pace, not where to put her feet. Jim wasn't sure why he knew that.

He'd probably overheard her talking at a practice or afterwards at the pub. She'd been keen, he'd give her that. She'd worked hard on her stamina and her technical know-how. She should have been a good fit. "Where's her dad?"

Phil shook his head. "I don't think he's back yet. Probably down at Beacon Point, hassling the police."

"I don't blame him. But surely, they're not still there?"

"It took a while to get her off," Phil said. "They had to use the helicopter in the end, which didn't leave until about three this afternoon."

Jim hadn't heard it, but he'd been under a Land Rover most of the day, welding.

Phil went to serve another customer. When he returned, he topped up Jim's pint. He said, "How's Genni? Jean said she saw her go by in her mum's car."

"She's upset. I think like the rest of us she'd hoped that Caz had just gone off somewhere for a break."

Phil rubbed his eyes. He still had a head of dark hair, a broad face on broad shoulders, probably from heaving the barrels around. He'd have made a reasonable member of the crew apart from not knowing one end of a boat from the other and had assured Jim, many times, that he got terribly seasick.

"It doesn't seem five minutes ago that they were picking that man out of the sea, off the Point," Phil said.

"The drug pusher! I said to Margery that if the vicar wanted to do these holidays it would end in trouble."

Phil frowned. "I don't think they're holidays. They're called retreats. Anyway, Archie wouldn't let things get out of hand."

Jim nodded, a little reluctantly. Archie was a useful man, had been a good crewman, but he wasn't someone Jim would go for a pint with. He felt Archie looked down on him, that because he'd been in the Navy, he was too good for the rest of them.

Jim shivered. He couldn't bear the thought that one day he might be like Archie. That one day, when the pagers buzzed, and the horn sounded, he would have to stand and watch. No, he was never going to retire. Not ever.

"Where's Margery tonight?"

"Some do at work. There's a whole bunch of them from the industrial estate that get together and go bowling, or to the cinema, not sure which, and not my cup of tea."

"Nor mine. Do you want another whiskey to go with that?" Phil asked.

Jim nodded. Phil was a good man; he'd definitely have been a good crew member.

"How's that boy of yours?"

"Saving to be married. I thought nowadays they simply shacked up together, but apparently that's not what Genni wants."

"I'm not sure I blame her. After all, her dad never came back, did he? Perhaps she's simply looking for a guarantee."

"Well, good luck with that!" Jim said. He knew he sounded snappy, but Phil's wife had left him too, so he'd understand that nowadays there was no such thing as a dead cert. Apart from him and Margery, of course. That went without saying. Perhaps Genni simply wanted what they had.

Chapter 15

Harriet was too cold to move. She'd brought a cup of tea out to sit on the bench at the front of the cottage, but the sun had been swallowed by a wash of flat grey clouds edged with pink. She felt it should've been nice, still light and warm, after all it was May, so she'd put on a thin woollen cardigan but like her tea, she'd quickly cooled down, in her case to near immobility. The splash of sunshine had been an illusion, as insubstantial as the stripes of winter sun in the church that did nothing for the temperature. Derek was walking up to the shop for some coffee. Tomorrow, he wanted to go back to Helston for some more paint and a couple of rugs. They'd decided the slate floor in the front room was still too echoey and he hadn't liked the grey and turquoise at all.

Harriet wanted to think about paint colours and rugs because the alternative was wondering again and again about the body. It was bound to be Caz, everyone thought so. The day before, Harriet had listened to the police sirens and later the helicopter, with dread, even sitting with Catherine and Anna at the vicarage she hadn't been able to find any sort of peace. She supposed at least now they'd get some answers. It felt important, too, that she was no longer just missing, though it didn't make Harriet feel any better. It certainly wouldn't be better for her father, or for her friends. Now there was no possibility that Caz was somewhere else, alive. Harriet realised she'd been hoping that she had hit her head and lost her memory, that she was wandering around Exeter not knowing who she was.

The news of the discovery had devastated Genni. Harriet had never seen anyone succumb to shock so completely. She hoped she was better today. She also hoped Anna was alright, sitting in the vicarage, waiting for people to come and talk to her. You'd have thought she was used to it by now. No that wasn't right, for every scenario was different but this was what

Anna's calling meant for those around her. She guided and journeyed with them but was also available to any stranger in need of advice or a listening ear.

Harriet straightened up. She was freezing. She needed to go and find a warmer jumper. Once inside the front door, she found herself listening, waiting. She wanted to know how she felt about this place. This future with Derek. She'd made her choice, and she would stick to it, but was it a good choice? Would she ever think of this brightly painted place as home?

She found one of Derek's Aran sweaters in the pile of washing at the bottom of the stairs, slipped off her inadequate cardigan and pulled the jumper over her head. Immediately she felt better. She'd go and make sure that Anna was managing, so now, at least, she felt she was off to do something of worth.

***

"Anna, it's me."

Anna peered around the door. Her hair was sticking up and Harriet longed to take a brush and smooth it down.

"Come on in."

"Are you sure? You look as if you've been asleep."

"I think I did drop off for a minute or two. Didn't get a lot last night."

"Have you spoken to Tom?"

"He texted to say he hoped to pop in for a cup of tea in the next couple of hours."

Harriet followed her down the hall to the kitchen. There were breadcrumbs on the kitchen table, so before she sat down Harriet reached under the sink for a clean cloth. Anna was standing next to the kettle.

"You don't have to do that, you know."

"I know. You don't mind, do you?"

"No, of course not." Harriet thought she did, just a little and not because Harriet was going to do it, just that it needed doing in the first place.

"Look, Harriet, it's past lunchtime. Why don't we have a glass of something, instead of more tea. I'm really fed up with tea."

Harriet knew it wasn't a good idea. She hoped that Anna was joking.

"I'll make some sandwiches," Anna continued. "Could you light another fire? It feels a bit cold. Not the warmest May we've ever had."

"I mustn't be too long," Harriet said, hoping that Anna would understand. "Derek's on his way back from the shop and then he wants to talk final paint colours for the lounge and the kitchen."

"Ok, just half an hour."

Harriet lit the fire. Anna made sandwiches and brought them through on a tray with a couple of mugs of tea. For a second Harriet was almost disappointed that there hadn't been a bottle of wine. They took a sofa each, putting their feet up. Harriet leaned her head back against the arm rest.

"Anna, it's just an accident, isn't it?"

"Yes, of course. It must be. Except ..."

"Don't say *except*, Anna. Except nothing. The young woman was out running and she slipped."

"It's just that when she came to see me, she was scared."

"You said she thought she'd seen a ghost."

"It's what she dressed it up as, but what if she was simply frightened that someone was trying to hurt her?"

"Then surely she'd have told you exactly that."

"That's the trouble, Harriet, I don't think she would've done. She wasn't like Genni, who I knew everything about almost straight away. With Caz I feel it would have taken a bit of work to have gotten past her defences. She was tough, like her dad."

"And now you're feeling guilty because you weren't able to get her to drop her guard."

"I wasn't interested in what was really going on. She even

asked me to let her know if I had any ideas about her ghost. She was asking to meet again, to speak again."

"She might not have been. This is you and hindsight having a bit of a dance around a handbag."

"But you know that sometimes I miss the point."

"Anna, I don't know anything of the sort," Harriet said. Her mug tipped a little. A few bubbles of tea spilled onto the wool of her jumper, perfect circles waiting to be wiped in or flicked away. Her phone beeped.

"That'll be Derek, worried about where you are."

And it was. She texted back that she was with Anna and would be home shortly.

She couldn't go quite yet; the fire would need a little more TLC before she dared leave Anna alone with it and she thought that Anna had a lot more to say. Derek could wait. Anna had a calling, but part of Harriet's remit was to be there for her which suddenly felt comforting; Harriet found herself blinking away tears, just a few, and got up to prod the logs.

***

Tom parked outside the shop. He hadn't slept for more than three hours the night before, but, as he was waiting for the postmortem, he had a bit of breathing space. Seeing Anna was what he needed. He had also decided to get a local newspaper. It was always good to know what was being said, before the next press conference. Before he got out, he peered around the village. Now that May had arrived there were quite a few visitors dotted about. He saw a tall man hurrying across the green, up past the loos. Tom squashed down in his seat until he realised what he was doing. He adjusted a wing mirror to make sure it wasn't Denbigh. It wasn't but this had to stop. They'd sent a family liaison officer round to see him at the pub, but Denbigh had sent him packing, angry rather than upset. Tom could understand that but still, he'd be happier knowing where Gerald Denbigh was at all times, as long as it wasn't with his mum.

He climbed out of his car and walked in nonchalantly, but couldn't help a quick glance over his shoulder before smiling at Jean. It was the sort of thing that Simeon did. Tom really needed to pull himself together, though at least now they had a body. He felt he was on much safer ground, more familiar territory. Not something he would ever admit to Anna, that finding the young woman dead meant that he was back in his comfort zone.

Missing persons was a world away from what he normally did though he supposed that to everyone else a crime was a crime, which he just needed to solve. Then his mum and Anna could get on with their lives, without worrying about what the village was thinking.

The village, the people, 'everyone else' had become an amorphous mass, one voice, one judgement, which wasn't good for getting to grips with this death. His boss would definitely have something to say about that.

He swept the hair out of his eyes. It was really beginning to annoy him, and he couldn't be having any distractions, no matter how much Anna liked it longer.

"Hello, Jean. Do you have the local rag?"

She picked one up from the counter.

"It's definitely murder then?" she said. Tom looked up. Jean simply shrugged and smiled. "Well, if it was an accident there wouldn't be so many of you still wandering about the place, would there?"

Jean was a master of gossip. He'd wondered about paying her a retainer to keep an ear out for whatever was going on. He was sure she would know before anyone else.

Tom shrugged in reply which made Jean half-smile, as if she now knew everything. He supposed she could be just really good at making guesses, but he also suspected she quizzed the constables when they snuck in to buy sandwiches and coffee. Perhaps he should put the shop out of bounds.

"Your mum has settled in well."

Tom fumbling around for change, looked up, surprised at the switch of topic.

"Yes. I'm pleased. She lived in Wiltshire a long time. I thought she might find it difficult."

"Oh no, she was never going to find it hard. For a start she's a good friend with our Anna, and she's a good listener which always goes down well with folk. Doesn't jump in with her own opinions too quickly.

Tom knew that about his mum. She was a good listener and not someone who pried. She respected others' privacy. Sometimes he wished she was a bit nosier, asked more questions about people, him in particular. That surprised him. There was still a little boy inside wanting his mum's approval. He shook his head, almost as if he was trying to shake the thought free. He wasn't even sure approval was the right word. He'd be happy if she just wanted to know what he was doing.

"Of course, some folk will take advantage of her kindness, but there might also be those who are desperately in need of a listening ear, just now."

As Tom climbed back into his car, he realised that he ought to have asked Jean who she was referring to but there had been that slightly annoying nod she often used when the subject of *our Anna* came up. Anyway, the shop had filled up with a family who'd walked too far. The children were moaning and whinging, and negotiating with their parents as to what they could have before tea. The dad looked impatient; the mum fraught. There would be no privacy for quite a while. Perhaps he'd send Smith in to talk to her, or better still Kellow. Tom had a feeling a nice young man might feel less threatening than an intense young woman trying to impress her boss.

The headlines were just as lurid as the late edition from the day before, but there was nothing new. None of the important details had leaked out yet. They'd a good relationship with the local papers, on the understanding that when possible, they would be favoured over the nationals.

His phone buzzed. There were two messages. One from Smith, and another from Kellow. He wondered if they were competing. Of course they were! Smith had forwarded the ME's initial report, and Kellow was warning him that the Chief Constable had wandered around the office, just to see how everyone was getting on. Tom thought there'd probably been another complaint from Denbigh about the speed of the investigation, or worse still, how seriously they'd taken the first report. Well, that wasn't Tom's problem. He hadn't been brought in until Denbigh had started shouting, which looked as if it had already been too late for Caroline Denbigh. By the time her father had first come to the village, Caz had already been stuffed into the crevice.

Tom would read the reports, but he hoped it wouldn't be necessary to view the body itself. He found those moments really tough. If he thought carefully, he could probably remember the face of every single victim he'd ever had to deal with. You never really forgot them.

He flung the paper onto the back seat and drove down to the vicarage. He hoped Anna wasn't busy, that she didn't have one of her tedious meetings. He really wanted someone to make a fuss of him.

They must have lit the fire. He could see the glow through the window. For a moment he wondered who she was with. A small pang of jealousy wriggled about in his stomach. Oh, for goodness sake, he thought, he was forty-four, not fifteen.

He parked his car at the side of the house and tried the back door. It was bolted from the inside, so he crunched around to the front. A curtain twitched. So someone had heard him, and the annoying security light came on and it wasn't even dark.

The front door opened quickly, as if Anna didn't know her own strength.

"Tom," Anna said. He guessed from the way she was blushing that she was probably with Harriet and had probably been talking about him. He stepped up into the hall and pulled her into a hug. Bugger Harriet. She stiffened and then softened. As she relaxed, she dropped her mug. It landed on the tiles and shattered into a thousand shiny pieces. Harriet appeared in the doorway. She pulled her large jumper around her thin frame and tucked a strand of dark curly hair behind her ear.

"I'll get the dustpan," she said, and headed to the kitchen.

"Oh, Tom, I'm so clumsy."

"So, what have you two been talking about?"

"What do you think? The body is our missing woman, and though we always kind of knew she might turn up, it's still a bit of a shock. It seems we have to deal with more than our fair share of tragedy. I think we're feeling a bit sorry for ourselves, a bit scared."

"Have you eaten yet?" he asked.

"We had some sandwiches at lunch time and then some crisps."

"Can I make us both an omelette?"

"Of course, Tom. I think I've got some eggs."

Harriet reappeared and they passed each other with a nod. As Tom pulled the kitchen door behind him, he heard them talking quietly, as if what they were saying was a secret. He knew it probably wasn't the case, but he still felt a little left out. He was in need of an ear, a bit of TLC. He'd hoped that Anna would notice.

Not long after, she slid into the kitchen with the full dustpan. She tipped it into the bin.

"Harriet's gone home. We spent the afternoon lying on the sofas. It feels self-indulgent. I didn't mean to give in like that. I let my guard down, and once it dropped, I couldn't put it back up again."

"It's all right, you can't be on duty twenty-four seven."

"You will be. At least until you get to the bottom of the poor girl's death." She took a breath and looked down at the floor, chewing her lip, always a sign she was in trouble. At the end of *the* retreat it had been terribly sore. "And Tom, you've had a dreadful few months, I'm so sorry."

He thought she might cry. Anna didn't do that often; she was tougher than she looked. She began to lift her head and he was once again amazed at her gentle resilience, even when it looked like everything was falling apart.

"Come on you, put out some knives and forks. I'm starving."

Anna pulled open the cutlery drawer.

"How long has she been dead?"

"Probably the whole time, from just after Archie saw her, though we can't be exact."

Anna shuddered. He slid the omelette onto the plate and cut it in half. Anna had got out bread and tomato sauce. They sat down. He wondered when she'd remember they hadn't said grace.

He said, "Try not to think of the details. Try to remember her as she was."

"She hasn't been in the sea?"

"No. Obviously I'll have to wait for the full report. The ledge was about twenty foot down, but still miles above the actual waves."

"Could it have been an accident? When she was out walking or running?"

"No, she was wedged in. If she'd simply fallen, she would have either landed a lot further down, or dropped into the water."

Anna bit her lip but didn't argue. Tom was suddenly sad. She was so accepting of the obvious truth. She'd never have agreed so easily in the past. He was shaping her life more than she seemed to be shaping his. He was bringing nasty, grubby reality to bear and it was roughing her up.

"So, someone killed her and stuffed her body out of sight."

"Yep, pretty much."

"Have you spoken to her dad yet? Gerald."

"He's been informed we've found a body. We need to be completely sure it's her before we go and talk to him with specifics."

"But he'll know by now, won't he?"

"Yes, he'll know. If not from Phil or Jean, simply from the kind sympathetic looks he'll be getting. I've got onto Family Liaison, they've been to see him, he sent them packing but at least they know what's going on. They'll keep visiting whether he likes it or not and the local press have only got what was released previously. There'll be another press conference tomorrow, when we'll give them a bit more, after I've interviewed Denbigh."

There was silence while they finished their food. She pushed away her plate and then looked up and said, "Still hungry?"

"A bit."

"Tea and toast?"

He nodded. He really wanted to stay here, in this tiny kitchen, sitting across from this pale, gentle woman. He didn't want to go back out into the dark, nasty world. For a moment he was managing to hold it all at bay and it was nice.

His phone rang. It was Smith. Gerald Denbigh was chucking rocks at Jim Andrews's place. He'd broken some windows, and Margery Andrews, who'd been inside at the time, had been cut by flying glass.

"Got to go, sorry, Anna. I'll probably try and sleep at Mum's tonight."

She nodded and lifted a hand limply, as he disappeared out the back door. Swinging around the front of the vicarage, he realised he hadn't kissed her goodbye and it became a regret; a missed opportunity which saddened him.

Chapter 16

Toby was on his way back from Mullion. He was really fed up. He'd driven over to see Genni but after all his effort he'd had a wasted journey. She'd been supposedly sleeping. Her mum had folded her arms and wouldn't let him go beyond the kitchen. She'd offered to make him a cup of tea, but said that Genni was struggling with a virus, and needed to rest. It's why she'd been so low of late. Apparently, trying to overcome a virus could be all-consuming. He'd been a little shocked when the woman had actually stood at the bottom of the stairs and barred his way. He'd mumbled that he'd simply come to make sure Genni was alright. This tiny, diminutive woman, whom Toby could have knocked aside in a second, said, "Come back tomorrow, after she's had a good night." Toby couldn't help but wonder if Genni was perhaps just sitting upstairs, out of sight, waiting for him to leave.

He didn't stop for a cup of tea. His mother-in-law-to-be scared him a little. Genni and she were close, too close in some respects, though Genni did still manage to moan about her. He guessed that if he wanted his marriage to work, he'd have to get his fiancée away from Mullion. At least find somewhere in The Lizard, or perhaps even further back up the peninsula. For a moment he felt a weight lift from his shoulders, a loosening of long tight muscles. Did they have to live around here at all? Surely Genni could teach anywhere, and one bakery must be much like another, so even he might find something else. If they could just go, away from all their shared history. A fresh start was all they needed.

He accelerated up the road, and as he turned right to head back to the village he sighed and felt the tension around his neck build up again. He didn't want to go home, or to the pub, his dad would be there, so once he reached the outskirts he branched left. He'd park in the lifeboat car park. There was a pack of Twix in the back. He'd eat one of those, listen to the radio, and send Genni a message so she'd know he'd been over.

As he swung into the lane running down to Church Cove, he slammed on his brakes. Coming up the other way was a blue Audi. It was going like the clappers and then it locked its brakes and began to skid towards the front of Toby's car. If some idiot ran into the front of him that would just about do it for Toby. The other vehicle managed to stop about two inches from his right wing. It reversed and began to carefully edge by. As the driver came alongside, he slid down his window. Toby prepared himself for angry words, until he realised it was the policeman.

"You'd better get yourself home, lad. There's been some trouble."

The Audi sped up the road.

'What about nearly hitting my car, you prat?' he wanted to shout after him. It took a few seconds to calm down and the man's words to filter through. What kind of trouble could there've been at home? Had his mum finally cracked and thrown something at his dad? It didn't seem likely, and anyway, surely his dad would have been at the pub for the last couple of hours. Wednesday was always pub night.

Toby reversed onto the lane and turned around. He allowed himself to put his foot down. The engine roared nicely, as he tore past the school and the football field. The copper had been driving like a madman, so why couldn't he?

There was a proper police car outside the house, blocking their drive, its light flashing. Both his mum's and his dad's cars were there. Toby parked close to the hedge. It would be a bit of a squeeze for anything to pass but at this time of night who'd be wanting to go down to the Point. He jumped out. An ambulance arrived behind him and tooted. Of course, it couldn't get past. He hopped back in to move, ignoring the driver, who was shaking his head. Toby wanted to pull him out of his vehicle and yell, "That's my house!". Instead he moved the car a little further down, blocking one of their neighbour's drives. Just as he was getting out, he saw his mum appear from inside, with a young woman.

Running he managed to get to her just as the ambulance crew did. She had blood dripping down her forehead, and she seemed a little confused.

"Mum! Let me through!"

"I'm alright, Toby. Head wounds always look worse than they really are."

Trust his mum to play it down. The young woman beside her seemed familiar but he wasn't sure from where he knew her. He wondered what could have happened until he saw that the large front window was broken. A jagged hole, on which the curtains were catching; more glass breaking with each gust.

"What on earth's been going on?"

"Let them check your mum out, and I'll fill you in. Toby, isn't it?" the young woman said. She was on his eye level, wore a jacket and trousers. Her hair was neatly tied back and there were freckles across her nose. Toby nodded but he still wanted to get to his mum.

"I'm Sergeant Smith. I was down at the lifeboat station when we interviewed everyone."

Toby remembered. She and her colleague had had a bit of a telling off for letting Caz's dad through. Come to think of it, where was the other copper? The one he'd followed up here.

"Where's the boss?"

"Interviewing the suspect."

"What happened?"

"The DI will explain. When he's finished."

Toby didn't have to wait long for either his mum or the DI. It transpired that Caz's dad had come by to talk. His mum had been in the lounge, watching telly and hadn't heard the doorbell. Mr Denbigh had thought they were ignoring him and got angry. Really angry. He'd thrown a stone through the front window which had hit her. What were the chances! It had caught her on the cheek and a bit of flying glass had landed in her hair, causing most of the blood. Gerald Denbigh was in the back of the police car. Toby hoped they'd book him for something serious. His mother must have been scared witless. And who was going to pay for the window? Worse still, now people would think they'd something to do with Caz's death. Toby would have liked to have sat down, he was beginning to feel a little lightheaded, but didn't want the sergeant to think he was a wuss. The DI began to cross over to them from the police car. Toby could see the huddled shape of Denbigh, his head in his hands. He must know he'd messed up big-time.

"What did he want to talk about, Caz's dad?" he asked the DI.

The man shrugged.

"I hoped you could tell us that."

Toby wasn't going to say anything. He knew his own dad had taken against Caz, but he definitely wasn't going to mention that. No one had liked her. They'd even been planning some pranks. At least the lads had mentioned it a while back when she'd first appeared. One of them had got a bit prissy about jumping out at a single woman, in the dark. He'd said it wasn't good or funny. The others had backed off after that. Toby supposed it might have been a bit mean, and he'd never actually jumped out at her. The only night he might have had a chance to, she'd moved too quickly for him to do more than follow her out. She'd turned around, luckily only for a second, but it had given him the chance to dive around the side of the building. He'd hoped she hadn't seen him, and he had worn his cap to cover his hair.

His mum came over as the ambulance left. The cut above her eye was patched with small white strips.

"See, just a little cut. Is Mr Denbigh alright?"

"Mum! He chucked a rock through our window!"

"He's just lost his little girl. I know how I would feel if it had been you or your sister. I might have gone and chucked some rocks about too, particularly if I wasn't getting any answers." She cast a side-long glance at the DI. Toby was shocked. Was his mum making a point, or taking a stand? "Can we go inside? I'd like to start clearing up before Jim gets back," she added.

Now that was more like her. Pretend nothing had happened. Don't rock the boat.

"Should I go and tell your husband? He's across at the pub isn't he?" the sergeant asked.

"No need. He'll be home soon enough," she replied, brightly.

Toby looked at the DI's face. He was watching them intently, his eyes slightly narrowed as his mum turned away. Toby nodded to him and then followed her. To his surprise the sergeant came too.

"I'll give you a hand," she said.

"There's no need," his mum replied.

"You've just had a bang on the head. You should take it easy. I'll help until your husband gets home."

Toby wanted to jump up and down and yell, I'm still here. I can help! He didn't. He followed the two women into the kitchen, then went to get the dustpan from under the stairs. At least he knew where it was kept.

***

There was a gentle southerly blowing across The Lizard so for once Simeon shook his head when Archie offered to put a match to the kindling – always piled up, always ready. Archie had central heating for use through the winter, but it was a big house and expensive to run.

Archie had a cup of coffee cradled in his hands and was staring into the cold grate as if there was a fire. Since their talk, Simeon had thought it would be easier between them, but nothing seemed to have changed.

Archie still felt remote, fragile, and a little disappointed in himself. That at an important moment his faith had been found wanting. It'd left Archie feeling a bit of a fraud and now, they were once more knee-deep in police.

"I was at the shop this morning and Jean told me there had been an incident at Jim and Margery's house. She said Mr Denbigh threw a brick through the window and that Margery was hurt. Jean was really upset."

Simeon looked across at Archie and frowned. He wasn't sure what Archie needed from him.

"I'm sorry Jean is upset. She and Margery are good friends." Simeon knew how he would feel if someone had tried to hurt Archie. "It seems an odd thing to do," Simeon continued.

"Apparently, she didn't hear the doorbell."

"Mr Denbigh thought they might be ignoring him?"

"I don't expect he's being very rational just now."

"I wish Tom would send him back to London. He's just muddling everybody up," Simeon replied.

Archie nodded which made Simeon feel scratchy. There was something about the way that Archie was reacting that was making Simeon uncomfortable.

"It does sound over the top. Margery must have been frightened out of her wits."

"I know Mr Denbigh had just discovered that his daughter was definitely dead, but why did he think that one of the Andrews's could be of any help to him?" Simeon asked.

"He's an ex-police officer. He must be used to being in the thick of things and here, he has to contend with being off on the sidelines."

"I wonder if he was simply giving the tree a bit of a shake, stirring things up, to see what happened," Simeon replied. "Upsetting Jim is a way of putting pressure on those that knew Caz. Also, Denbigh is a bully and obviously has a bad temper, after all, when I saw him out on the cliff, he tried to stop me from getting past. He wanted to know where you lived and when I refused to tell him he threatened me."

"Oh, Simeon. Are you sure he actually threatened you? He's such a large man, I expect sometimes he comes across as threatening just by being himself."

"I felt really frightened and Belle growled at him." Archie looked up sharply.

"I've never heard Belle growl. Why do you think he wanted to know where I lived?"

"Because, apart from the killer, you seem to be the last person to have seen her alive."

Archie shook his head again.

"Could that have been the day she was killed?" he asked and looked up at Simeon. "I should have stayed and banged on that locker room door until she came out."

Simeon was beginning to feel in need of his parka. He wanted to pull the hood over his head, which was difficult, given he'd left it in the hall. He hadn't had to wear it in Archie's lounge for a long time. He took some gulps of air.

"Are you alright, Simeon?"

"I'm sure banging on the door wouldn't have made a difference. You might have been hurt too."

"Are you sure you're ok?" Archie asked. "Shall I light the fire or make some more coffee? Is there anything else you'd like to say to me?"

"One day, not long after," Simeon said quickly, "I did pass by, and the cage was heading down. There were no cars in the car park. Perhaps that was when they moved the body?"

"That wasn't what I meant. And who are 'they'? Simeon, you must try not to dwell on this so much."

"She could easily have been killed down at the lifeboat station. I think it's entirely possible. She worked away but when she was back here, she was either at home or down at the lifeboat. No one in their right mind would have killed her up in Exeter and then brought her body back here. And only a local would know of the ledge."

"It could have been at her house, though Tom said that forensics didn't find anything." Archie looked across at Simeon, caught his eye for a second. "Perhaps he should check out the lifeboat again, if you're so sure, Simeon."

Simeon didn't feel at all sure.

"I think Tom probably already has and anyway, he'd need more than a suggestion from me to do such a thing."

Archie sighed and said, "Forensics costs lots of money and he told Anna that most of his job is justifying expenditure to his boss. Oh, Simeon, when did it all become about money?"

Simeon guessed this was rhetorical and not all about policing. Archie was once more staring into the grate and Simeon was beginning to feel restless. He'd hoped to talk about Archie's faith, about what had happened during the heart attack but even he could see that this was not the moment. The simple questions he'd thought of on the way over began to merge until Simeon knew he wouldn't be able to ask them coherently. He shivered. He would go home. He needed to pray, and this room suddenly felt cold and a little unwelcoming.

Chapter 17

Anna had been sitting at her desk all morning. Well, at least for the last hour or so. She'd made notes, had ideas, and written whole paragraphs. Nothing worked, nothing hung together. She'd also got up any number of times to check that there was no one at the front door, just in case she hadn't heard the bell. She wasn't sure who she was expecting, not today.

Tom had rung the day before, to say that under no circumstances was she to let Gerald Denbigh in, unless there was someone else with her. Denbigh had lost his temper, and Margery Andrews had got hurt. Not badly, but enough to press charges. Apparently, Margery hadn't wanted to do that, though Tom had had an earful from Jim. Something about getting to grips with Gerald, sending him home, where he belonged and not allowing him to run around the Point causing trouble.

Anna had listened while drinking her morning coffee. She had teetered against the wall of words, his orders and all the what-ifs building up inside her. She knew that Tom was good at what he did, but until they could work out what was going on, everyone, including herself, would lock their doors at night, and listen for the sound of forced entry. She'd even wondered about putting Georgie off. She was supposed to be coming down after Sunday service the following weekend. At least they'd cancelled the retreat, only one person had signed up, so they'd asked him to move to a different date.

Anna looked down at the scribbles on her notepad. She couldn't get Tom's phone call out of her head. At least this time there was little doubt. Tom had told her that Caz's hyoid bone was cracked, which meant she'd been strangled, and with some force. Under the body they'd found a rope. They were checking it for fibres and skin. Unfortunately, it was an ordinary rope. The sort you would find on a lot of boats. The sort peeping from lobster pots, coiled up in *Rose's* lockers, neatly hung from hooks around the lower boat deck in the lifeboat station. It was at the cheaper end of the spectrum, flexible and tough. Tom's only hope was to get some decent skin or hair tags off it. He'd told her that he'd yelled at his sergeant, because she'd been worried about what sort of knots were tied at either end. He'd felt angry at himself, she was just checking on details.

He had sounded so fed up and tired. He'd even admitted to feeling a little out of control and Anna knew that she wasn't really helping.

Tom was always worried that she herself would be a target for the local nutters. He kept giving her safety tips. What to do if this or that happened. But there were no local nutters in her eyes; she found the term offensive and difficult. She lived in a small community, and everyone had a back story. Gerald Denbigh was in Tom's mind, someone for her to avoid, but to Anna he was first and foremost a grieving father.

She jumped as the sound of the doorbell reverberated down the hall. So not broken as she'd feared. She almost jogged to the door and then because she didn't know who it was, opened it slowly. She was relieved to see Genni standing there, relieved and pleased that she'd come back. It must be her lunch break.

"Not on playground duty, then?" she said, opening the door wide. "Come on in."

Genni walked past as if the air were thick and her shoulders were not strong enough to hold up the weight of her head, her skin looked dry, uncared for and she most definitely needed to get some sleep.

"You should have had more time off. If you're fighting a virus, you should spend your time resting."

Genni shrugged. Anna wasn't fooled about the virus, and she hoped Genni knew that.

"Have you got your sandwiches with you?"

Genni looked up in surprise and nodded.

"Come through, I'll make myself some lunch, and we'll have a cup of tea. You probably don't feel much like eating, but you'll feel better for making the effort."

"My mum said the same thing this morning."

That felt like Anna had aged herself away from Genni, but then looking at the young woman, Anna did feel older. Not wiser, never wiser. Genni had lines under her eyes that had no right being there. Her fingers twisted like a hand of slow-worms and her back was hunched. Anna led the way down the hall. She checked that Genni was following her.

Once they were seated, and Genni was shredding her sandwiches, Anna prayed, silently, desperately. Genni pushed her food away.

"When Toby's upset, he eats. I don't. I can't seem to swallow it down."

"Let's try and clear the way a bit," Anna said.

"I've got to tell someone about Caz. But you must promise me you won't tell your boyfriend."

Anna felt as if Genni had just thumped her. She'd used the term boyfriend like a swear word. Genni had put Tom between them like a wall, exactly as Anna felt the rest of the village had done.

Her voice wavered as she said, "As long as you are not being abused in any way, I'll not tell Tom what you've said." Though he'd know almost instantly if Anna was keeping anything back from him.

Genni didn't seem to notice how uncomfortable Anna was feeling, her eyes were turned inward, her shoulders still hunched up. Her voice was so quiet when she began to speak that Anna had to lean forward to hear her.

"You see, Caz and I were good friends. The guys didn't get it because they didn't really see it. She was funny, clever, and she wouldn't be bullied. She was everything that I'm not."

Anna wanted to disagree, but she knew from experience

that Genni wouldn't hear her. When Anna had got to know Harriet, she'd spent most of her time feeling horribly inadequate, fat and ugly because Harriet was so slim and lovely. Now Anna knew that Harriet was insecure too, but for different reasons. Genni might be beautiful but something inside was broken into pieces, and each of those pieces was probably burrowing through her skin. Some bits might hopefully break surface and be dealt with, others might lie niggling away at her for the rest of her life. Now that was depressing.

"Tell me about her. I only met her properly that one time."

"Just after she'd seen the ghost?" Genni said, quietly.

"She told you about it."

"I think it was the lads being cruel. I was going to tell Toby to warn them off. That trying to frighten Caz like that was unacceptable, but what if it was some stranger who wanted to hurt her?" Genni spoke pleadingly, which Anna found disconcerting.

She answered carefully, "She certainly didn't recognise them, but then she was quite freaked out. It was late and being down there on your own must be quite spooky."

"No, it wasn't, and we were often there on our own. Caz had so much to learn, and Jim was tough on her. I tried to help her as much as I could, and I have an hour or two after school before Toby gets home. I'm a good teacher and she felt she had something to prove, more so than the rest of us. I didn't blame her. Jim could be a real dictator."

She took a sip of tea and Anna nudged the box of sandwiches a little closer. "It wasn't just her that Jim had it in for. Toby also had a tough time. He has problems with his left and right, so sometimes knots can be a bit challenging, particularly the bowline. It's the middle loop, he always does it back to front. If Jim notices, he goes nuts. He makes him redo it in front of everyone. It's really humiliating. And it's not like it doesn't work, it just doesn't sit as neatly." Genni began to twist the ring on her finger.

"What about Caz?"

"She said she often rubbed people up the wrong way, but I think she just said things that were true, that people didn't want to hear. That Jim didn't want to hear." Genni looked up for a second, and then said fiercely, "Jim was just plain unreasonable and really quite cruel."

Anna thought how hard it must have been for Genni to have watched the two people she cared for most in the world, Caz and Toby, being bullied by Jim. She said quickly, "I know someone just like Caz. You must know Simeon Tyler. To begin with, I didn't like him much, either. Now I really trust and value him."

"I valued her."

"I can see that."

"The thing is, she valued me. She valued me without strings. She didn't care what colour my skin was or that I didn't have a dad. She did care that I tried to fit in with everyone around me, to the point where I lost myself. Even the last message she ever sent was about standing up to the headmistress now and again." For the first time, Genni sat back. "I was supposed to meet Caz at the lifeboat to go through procedures she had to know for her next exam. I never got there because the headmistress caught me in the staff room and wanted to chat about our more gifted students."

Anna nodded but she was also beginning to wonder if Archie had been the last person to see Caz alive. Apart from the killer, of course.

Genni continued, "Caz challenged me. It was hard to take, but she never gave up. She really seemed to like me too. Now everyone is fed up with me crying. As far as everyone is concerned we were convenient friends, not by choice but by circumstances, and so why am I making such a fuss?"

Anna couldn't help but shake her head. That was nonsense.

"I know," Genni continued. "For me it was much bigger

than that. I didn't have any close buddies growing up, so I didn't know what it was like having someone who really understood. I could tell her anything and I did. I was going to ask her to be my bridesmaid, not just because she was one of the crew, but because I wanted her beside me on the day."

"She sounds great."

"She was. But no one else seemed to see it."

"Have you tried talking to her dad?"

"I wanted to, but everyone told me he was a bit nuts and anyway, we all said we didn't know her that well. If I spoke to him now, he might think I'd been lying."

Genni picked up a sandwich and took a bite. Anna smiled encouragingly.

"How is Toby coping with all this?"

Genni took a swig of tea and glanced at her watch. She stood up quickly.

"Oh, flip. My class starts in less than five minutes. The head will be furious if I let them down again. I'm sorry, I've got to go."

"Come back anytime you want to talk about Caz. I'd be happy to listen."

Anna watched Genni almost run up the drive. She returned to the kitchen and made herself another cup of tea. It sounded like Caz and Genni had begun to grow a friendship that ran deep, really deep. She wondered if Toby might have been a little jealous.

***

As the last of the pupils left the classroom, Genni sighed. She'd only just made it back in time earlier and the afternoon had felt rushed and disorganised. She pulled her pager towards her and switched it on. They hadn't had a call out for a couple of weeks, yet Jim had put in an extra practice the following Saturday afternoon. It hadn't gone down well. Toby was getting a lot of grief from the others. Not that he could do anything about it. He wouldn't dare interfere with the running of the lifeboat. That was firmly his dad's thing.

Genni had agreed to meet Toby after work. He'd seemed a little desperate, so she'd said yes. Now it meant she'd time to kill. She looked around the empty classroom. She wandered about a bit and straightened a pile of books. The top one belonged to Samantha, the girl who'd been accused of bullying by her slightly more streetwise classmate. Sam's parents had appeared, as expected, wanting to know what they could do to help nip this troubling behaviour in the bud. Genni had said she thought that Sam was a lovely child and simply needed a little encouragement to be herself, that she was sure it was a one off. The parents reminded her of her own mum. Stay down, don't draw attention to yourself. Life is tough enough without making it worse by standing out. For Genni, right now, it was as bad as it could be so her mum's advice hadn't worked. The hollowness inside welled up. She couldn't stay there, thinking of some child being squashed and broken by her well-meaning and loving parents, so she grabbed her coat from its hook and strode out across the playground.

She turned down the lane to the sea. She took the first right past the farm and Mr Tyler's house, the guy in the parka. In the winter this track was nearly impassable, deep ruts of sticky mud.

Now, in the middle of May, even after a cold and blustery March, it was mostly firm underfoot. She could easily pick her way around the one or two puddles that were left. At the end, it curved along the cliff edge to the old wireless station and another couple of houses. Genni turned through the gate and onto the coastal path. Here she could look down into a shallow bay, with Beacon Point to the north, where the police tape was still fluttering, and the path to The Lizard running south. Staring at the tape, so scrappy and plastic, she wondered if anyone would come and clear it away. It couldn't be good for the environment and was not a great memorial to Caz. Genni took a long breath and began to make her way towards the edge.

Caz was not a large woman, she'd been tiny, light and wiry, had always made Genni feel large and lumpy. She'd been carried and dragged along the path to the Point, unless they discovered she'd been killed at the Point, then simply tipped over as if she didn't matter. The cliff was stepped just there, so dropping her gave the killer two options. One, that she simply bounced off the grassy ledge below and landed in the sea or two, that she fell onto the grassy ledge and somehow stayed there. It wasn't difficult to climb down to it. As a moody teenager, it was a good place to come and get away from everyone. Back against the rock, bum on soft grass and legs dangling. The crevice was just above, a wide smiling mouth in the rocks. Rolling Caz into that jagged maw made the body invisible, unless you knew what you were looking for or climbed down there. She would have been found eventually by one of the many visitors who swarmed over the place.

Genni made her way slowly forward, past the tape and peered down. She stared for a long time, imagining the shoe, perhaps hanging loosely on a bone. She rocked back and retched. When her stomach had stopped heaving, she looked out across the waves, feeling the damp of the grass through her trousers. No one came near, though there must have been one or two walkers along the path. She jumped when she realised that the sea was turning purple, and the sky was almost navy blue, that there were even one or two stars beginning to twinkle. She felt as if she'd been asleep, though she was sure she hadn't shut her eyes. She tried to stand up, but her legs and arms felt heavy, as if they'd slept for her. She pulled her phone from her pocket, the guilt soaring because she'd switched it to silent. There were about twenty calls from Toby. He'd waited outside the school at five, as arranged since her car was still there. He'd texted, then left a voice message, then another one, shouting. He was beyond worried.

She rang him as her legs came back to life, painful pins and needles, a reminder of the time she'd lost. Time that had passed without any realisation. Blessed blankness.

"Where are you?" he almost screamed.

"Out for a walk. I didn't notice the time. I'm sorry."

"How could you not have realised? I've been so worried. I thought you'd disappeared, like Caz."

"No, not like Caz."

"I know, I know. Not like Caz. But I was still so anxious. You've not been yourself lately."

Genni wondered at the word anxious. It didn't sound right.

"I've been fighting a virus, that's all." She hoped he wouldn't hear the sarcasm, but he wasn't listening.

"I didn't think it would upset you so much, Caz…"

"Being murdered? Why not?"

"Can I see you for just a minute? I need to."

"Not tonight, Toby. I'm so tired. I need to go home."

She began to make her way back up the track. It was too early for the moon, so it was difficult avoiding the puddles. She ploughed right through the middle of one and wondered whether she'd just ruined her good pair of work shoes. Such thoughts, kept what she knew would be waiting for her at the school, at bay. She wasn't really surprised to see Toby leaning on her car.

"I just needed to see you." He sounded angry now, not needy anymore.

She could see him peering down at her feet. The mud had splashed right up to her knees. It looked worse than it really was.

"I'm sorry for worrying you. I'm just tired and let time run away a bit."

He wrapped his arms around her. She was technically a couple of inches taller than he was, and it had never bothered her before, but it was like she couldn't remember how to fit properly.

"You could try making an effort," he muttered.

"How's your mum?" she asked, stepping back so she could breathe again.

"Absolutely fine. The cut is tiny, and of course she doesn't want to press charges. Mr Denbigh has offered to pay for the window. He said he'd had a couple of whiskeys at the pub, and the grief got too much for him, so as far as she's concerned it's all done and dusted. Of course, Dad was at the pub and didn't see Denbigh, he doesn't believe he was there at all, so he's properly angry. He reckons Denbigh was just spinning a story to get the police to go easy on him, that he knows how to work the system. He says the man has taken against us for some unknown reason and that it's way beyond reasonable. He doesn't care how much Denbigh is grieving, you don't go and lob a rock through someone's window."

"Did your mum go to work today?"

"Yes. There really wasn't a good reason not to, and she said she could pop round to the glazier on the industrial estate and organise a visit."

"Do you think Mr Denbigh will stay much longer? There doesn't seem to be anything he can do."

"Make trouble?"

"Do you know why he lobbed a rock through the window?"

"Because he thought dad was ignoring him."

But that wasn't what she'd asked. It felt more like Denbigh was sending a message and wouldn't necessarily have known that Jim would have been in the pub, rather than at home. That Jim would have seen through his story of having one too many. Either way, the message was loud and clear.

"I'd best get off. I'll see you tomorrow, Toby."

As she drove back up into the centre of the village, she watched him in her rear-view mirror. He didn't move, just stood on the pavement staring after her. She was glad when she finally turned the corner.

Chapter 18

This time Archie had left early to get to the lifeboat station. He'd agreed to swap with Mrs Toynbee who usually did Saturdays, but she'd got some relatives staying over the weekend. It didn't make any difference to him; his weekends were normally free.

He turned off the lane and was surprised to see that the five-bar gate over the cattle grid was open. That was unusual unless there was a practice. He decided to close it. Just as he'd clicked it into place Mr Denbigh appeared. Oddly, this morning the leather jacket didn't look tough, it looked seedy, a bit cracked and dull in places. Archie could also see that though he'd shaved that morning, he'd obviously not been too fastidious. There were patches of white bristles feathering his skin.

"Mr Denbigh, my sincere condolences."

The man simply stood there, hands dangling at his side. Archie was a bit alarmed. The lifeboat shop would have to wait. This man seemed so lost, and Archie knew all about that.

"What do you need?"

"You were the last to see her alive, apart from the bastard that hurt her."

This time it was simply a statement, not an accusation.

Archie wasn't sure what had happened to Caz. It was of course being talked of around the village but until he heard the specifics from Tom, albeit via Anna, Archie refused to go down that path.

"Try not to think about that."

The man looked up, in disbelief.

"How do I do that?" he said.

"What about going home again?" Archie asked, gently. Denbigh looked surprised. His eyes widening, almost in fear. He had already popped back to London for a week at the end of April. "Not for ever," Archie said, quickly. "Just for a break.

To get some distance, some perspective."

"I can't. I just can't. I did try, when I went home last time, but I need to be here. I thought if I asked the crew, just once more, what they could tell me about her. Or the vicar."

"Anna?" Archie said, carefully.

Denbigh looked bewildered. It didn't matter what her name was.

"Look, I'm on duty down at the lifeboat station, just in the shop for a couple of hours. Come down with me and I'll make you a cup of tea."

Denbigh nodded and followed Archie through the pedestrian gate on the side.

"It's a lovely view from here," Archie said, as they walked over the rise. Denbigh didn't react, kept his eyes on his feet as if he needed to see where he was putting them.

To Archie's horror he could now see that the car park was full. That meant they were having an extra practice. He stopped.

"Mr Denbigh, this is not a good idea. I didn't know, the crew are down there."

Denbigh shook his head, just once, as if an annoying fly was buzzing around his ears.

"Why not? I won't disturb anyone; I won't get in the way. I'd like to see what she would've been doing. She was determined to be part of the crew even though she came from inner London and before she moved west, the closest she'd ever been to the sea was the Thames."

Archie couldn't work out what the expression was on Denbigh's face. At the gate he'd believed in the depth of the man's misery, but now he felt he was being spun a line, manipulated. He didn't know what to do.

Even from half-way down the steps they could hear the noise inside the building below. Jim was shouting and there was a lot of clattering. It could be they were getting *Rose* ready for going out, but there was also plenty to practise on land.

When Archie pushed the door open, a couple of the crew, up on *Rose's* deck, turned to see who was coming in. There were some waves and nods because of Archie, and then intakes of breath, when Denbigh appeared behind him.

Before the door had clicked shut, Jim was clambering down. It took him seconds to make his way across. Archie stepped between the two men, but he felt like a bug about to be squashed flat.

"What do you think you're doing here?"

"I invited him. He just needs a cup of tea and a sit down."

"Not here, Archie. Not here."

"Why? Got a guilty conscience?" Denbigh said, his lips in a tight line, yet Archie felt as though he was grinning. "You're the guy in charge, you know what goes on."

Jim glowered as Archie turned back to look at him. He'd straightened up, was large and broad shouldered again, as though for a second Denbigh's presence had diminished him.

"Mr Denbigh, I think it would be better if you went home," Archie said, as gently as he could.

"You're all trying to get rid of me. What're you trying to hide?"

Jim's crew shuffled about, turning their heads away, just as if they did have something to hide. They looked guilty. Archie shook his head. This was nonsense. He'd known most of this lot since they were in short trousers.

"Caz said you'd got it in for her," Denbigh spoke quietly, into the silence.

"I treated her fairly. I treat everyone fairly." Jim looked around at the crew. Archie thought there was too much of a hesitation before various heads began to nod, and Toby, well he was staring fixedly at the floor. Archie couldn't see Genni anywhere, but she would surely find this dreadfully upsetting.

"She was a city girl, an incomer. None of you would have liked that, but Caz wouldn't have let that stop her. She'd have worked hard and would have called any of you out if she thought you were in the wrong."

"Archie, get this man out of here. I don't care if he has just lost his daughter. I'm not having him spew this nonsense. We don't know what happened to Caz and it wasn't one of us that did it to her."

Did what to her, Archie wondered. What rumours were spinning round the village?

Denbigh lunged forward, as if Archie wasn't even there. Two of the older crew grabbed Jim's arms as he tried to respond. Archie fell back over the stool and sent the leaflets flying. His head hit the floor. It rang out as if he'd really clonked it, but he wasn't dizzy. He closed his eyes. When he opened them, Jim was leaning over him.

"Archie, are you alright?"

"Jim, I'm fine."

"You didn't black out or anything?"

"No, honestly, I just feel a bit stupid."

"Stupid is right, you shouldn't have brought him down here."

That wasn't what Archie had meant. Jim leaned forward and hauled him to his feet. Archie was relieved to see that there was no sign of Mr Denbigh.

"Perhaps you should go home," Jim said.

"There's no need for that," Archie replied, and began to pick up the brochures strewn all over the floor. Toby appeared at his side with a mug of tea.

"Thought you might want a drink," he said, and began to help.

"Thanks, Toby."

"Toby, here, now. We've lost enough time as it is," Jim shouted. Toby froze for a second, before straightening up and returning to *Rose*.

Archie was quite stiff by the end of his shift. Luckily, they'd had a few visitors, so he'd had to move about. Most of the crew had disappeared onto the lower floor, there was still plenty to see. He was quite sure he hadn't done any real damage but thought he might pop into Anna's on the way home just to catch his breath and to tell her what'd happened. It was the best way of letting Tom know that Denbigh was still around and stirring up trouble. And he didn't want her to find out from anyone else. By the time the village gossip got hold of it, Archie would have been knocked to the floor by an enraged father or coxswain rather than falling over a stool.

***

Derek and Harriet's garden nestled into the side of the hill. From its edge the land rose steeply up to the fields above, over which the road to the lifeboat station ran. Harriet and Anna could hear the cars charging across the fields, as the crew turned up for the extra practice. They were sitting on the bench outside the front door, which was still perfect for coffee, even, as it turned out, on a practice afternoon.

"Don't forget that Georgie is down for a couple of days."

"That's nice. It'll give you something else to think about."

"I nearly cancelled her, but she won't arrive until mid-afternoon tomorrow, and she'll be gone Tuesday morning."

"I'm assuming Simeon knows."

Anna shook her head, just a tiny movement. She wouldn't grace that with a reply. Harriet just smiled. She wasn't sure why everyone was ignoring the obvious. Georgie was good for Simeon. They got on well, what was wrong with that? Another car roared along the road. Someone was late.

"Doesn't it bug you?" Anna asked.

"We hardly ever hear it, and often when we do it's because they're on their way to help someone who's in trouble."

"That's a good way of looking at it."

"More coffee?"

"Tempting though that is, I ought to leave you and Derek in peace."

"You don't have to. He's painting more test squares. He's as happy as Larry!"

"And you?"

"Trying to be more honest. Trying not to remember that I brought very little to this venture."

"You came. I think Derek would say that was the point and was more than enough."

"If you thought I was worth it."

"Really!" Anna said. "You want me to respond to that?"

"I know. But if I can't say the unspeakable to you, who can I say it to?"

Anna laughed.

"God?"

"I do eventually tell him, but I try it out on you first."

"I'm flattered."

The gate squeaked and both women turned in surprise to see Genni climbing up from the road.

"Are you guys busy? Am I interrupting anything? I know I'll get bawled out next time I go to practice, but I couldn't get across that cattle grid, not even to please Jim."

"Come and sit down," Harriet said, and she dragged one of the garden chairs over. "Coffee, tea? Anna was going to have more coffee, so it's no trouble."

Genni came and sat next to Anna on the bench. Harriet hurried to make up the tray because she didn't want to miss anything. She needn't have worried, both women were sitting back with their eyes shut, enjoying the afternoon sun, the last of the rays before it slipped around the end of the house.

"This is lovely. What a clever place to put a bench," Anna said, taking the coffee from Harriet. "So how are you, Genni? Apart from your inability to cross cattle grids."

"It feels as if everyone is watching everything I do. All people say to me is, 'are you alright?' I'm not, but I don't know how to say that. Sometimes I get the feeling that if I really said how I was, they'd run a mile."

"Try us," Anna said.

Genni rubbed her eyes.

"I'm scared."

"I think we all are, a little," Anna replied.

Harriet, squinting as she tried to put into words what was going on inside her, said, "Because we don't know what actually happened to Caz, and we're all a bit worried the murderer might come back?"

Anna nodded.

"Do you think that Caz was simply in the wrong place at the wrong time?" Harriet asked. She didn't.

"That's entirely possible," said Anna. Harriet couldn't help but notice that she was chewing her lip. Anna didn't think any such thing either. They both knew that most murders were carried out by those closest to the victim.

"I'm also a bit scared where all this might lead," Genni said, quietly.

"With Toby?" Anna asked. Harriet almost kicked her. Honestly, that was not the route to go down, just this moment.

"I'm finding him a little irritating and when he wants to talk about the wedding, I feel a bit sick."

"I get that," Anna replied. "There could be any number of reasons why you feel like that, but the best thing to do is to try and admit to them."

"What do you mean?" Genni asked. Harriet agreed, particularly as the phrase 'Doctor, heal yourself' popped into her head.

"Well," Anna continued, her head leaning forward as if she'd spotted something on her lap, "perhaps you're getting cold feet about the wedding, about Toby, but it's all muddled in with how much Caz's death has upset you. Perhaps you're even a little startled by how devastated you are. I think, you're used to keeping your head down, that being the centre of attention is making you uncomfortable. Do you see? There are lots of possibilities."

Clever Anna, Harriet thought, and added, "It might be one of those or something completely different." *Keep the options open*, she reasoned.

"What do I do? Does it matter which of those things is freaking me out?"

"Of course," Anna said, this time looking down the garden, anywhere but at Genni. "Some things you can't do anything about, they just have to unfold. Other things you should try to work out."

"But which is which?"

"Talking to someone might help you with that. Anna and I often go down to the church and talk to God. I find that incredibly helpful."

"You can actually talk to him anywhere," Anna said, a little pedantically and Harriet had another urge to kick her. "He's what Simeon would say is a listening God, so if there is something weighing you down…"

Harriet took a sip of tea. Anna was being a bit pointed.

"So, what about you and the DI? Do you think you might get married?" Genni asked. Harriet smiled as she watched Anna flush and bite her lip. Genni was also very good at dodging the issue. Harriet guessed she'd had a lot of practice over the years.

"I don't know. We've never talked about it. Did you talk about it before Toby popped the question?" Genni shook her head.

"It was a bit of a surprise."

Harriet wanted to shake them both but instead said, "And it's terribly sexist, in this day and age. It means that your happiness is all dependent on a man. What if he doesn't ask you because he's worried you might say no? It shouldn't all be on him."

"So are you saying that I should ask Tom?" Anna retorted, her eyes widening in disbelief or perhaps panic.

"Do you want to?" Harriet asked. Anna's face was beginning to glow. Wrong time, wrong place to discuss this. Harriet took pity on her and said gently, "Perhaps just bring it up, so you both have a chance to get it out there."

If Genni had not been with them, drinking coffee and listening in bewilderment, Harriet thought that perhaps Anna might have kicked her, too.

Chapter 19

Simeon didn't spend a lot of time in the church over the summer months. There were too many visitors popping in and out. Some ignored him, tucked in his pew at the back, others simply spoke a greeting, but some spotted Belle and wanted to pet her or to chat. Sometimes, if he was feeling really stressed, he'd go and hide in the tower room, but people had been known to try and poke around in there, too. He'd made quite a few of them jump, on finding him sitting alone in the dimness.

Today, regardless, Simeon needed to go in, needed the familiar feel of the ancient building around him. At morning prayer, Archie had mentioned what had happened down at the boat house on the previous Saturday. That he'd bumped his head when he fell over, standing between Caz's dad and Jim. Simeon had frozen, all his thoughts and feelings focused on one thing. Why hadn't Archie told him before? There had been plenty of opportunities. The only thing out of the ordinary was that Georgie had been with them and that shouldn't have made a difference.

Simeon felt as if Archie had deliberately kept the incident from him, picked his moment to tell him, protected him. That he had waited until Georgie had gone home so he wouldn't spoil her visit and yet, Simeon felt betrayed.

During her stay, Archie had seemed his usual self. When she'd arrived at morning prayer on the Monday, Archie had made a fuss of her, they all had, as she didn't normally manage to wake up in time. But she and Simeon had planned to take Belle out to the cafe at the Point and he didn't want Belle to have to wait too long for her walk. Georgie was an easy companion, only talking when she had something to ask or to say. There didn't seem to be any incidental prattle, which Simeon liked. When they had reached the cafe, Georgie had gone in to get the drinks. She understood that it was far too busy for Simeon. All he had to do was go and sit with Belle in a quiet spot and wait for her. Anna must have filled her in on the murder of Caz because she had had lots of questions. She was upset, as it had brought up a lot of bad memories of *the* retreat, but she didn't cry. She said she'd done all that with Anna, the day before.

Georgie's hair was still short and spiky but was now its proper colour, a light brown, which sometimes caught the light. When he'd first met her, it had been orange. He hadn't liked that; it had made her too startling to look at.

She said her work was going well, that the youth group was growing. Simeon had told her how anxious he was about Archie, and that he knew he was ringing him too often. Georgie had thought about that for a while and then had told him to ask himself, if he were Archie, what would he want Simeon to do? Which had seemed a good way of looking at it, until Archie had said about falling over the stool and bumping his head. Simeon wished then that Georgie was still with them because he would have liked to have asked her advice as to what to do now.

Simeon was really frightened that Archie had been hurt, though he'd hurriedly assured everyone that he was just a bit bruised, that it was mostly his pride that had taken a knock.

Jim had, of course, roundly and soundly blamed Archie for what had happened, which was a little unfair as he'd been responding to Caz's dad's seeming grief. Then after morning prayer was done, Simeon had tried to walk with Archie up to the shop, but he was still stuck inside his head, so he'd returned to church.

The sunlight sparkled through the windows, splashing the flags at the front with splotches of colour. He supposed it might be considered pretty but it was simply the old leaded glass bending the light this way and that. The door creaked. Belle stood up and stretched.

"We should go," Simeon whispered. Someone was moving

about. He could hear the tip-tap of heels, so probably not a tourist; they normally wore trainers or walking boots. There was now silence and Simeon began to get worried because he didn't know where the person was. He risked a glance. The young woman, Genni Rowe, from the school, was sitting on the front pew. She was staring straight ahead as if concentrating. Simeon stood up as quietly as he could, but Belle stretched again and whined a little. The woman turned around.

"Sorry, the vicar said I should come in." She spoke as if she'd been caught trespassing.

"You're allowed, it's a public space."

"You were down at the lifeboat when Anna, the vicar, came and blessed it." Simeon wasn't sure if it was a statement or a question. "I feel a bit foolish. I've never tried praying before, apart from when I really didn't want to go to school. When I was a kid, not now, of course. And then it was that I would break my leg."

Simeon hesitated. He'd prayed that he would get a cold, but he had, once, desperately hoped for something like a broken leg, as long as it didn't hurt too much. "I used to tell my mother I felt ill, but she always asked, who was bullying me this time."

"You know what it's like?"

"Yes."

"For me it was because I look different, and Dad didn't bother marrying my mum. He simply went away one day and never came back."

Simeon was suddenly irritated, which was slightly better than feeling anxious. He knew Genni's story, everyone around the Point did, but why didn't people think things through?

He said, "People disappear all the time and are never found. Any number of things might have happened to him. Twenty years ago there weren't so many mobile phones, some people even refused to have one. Your dad might have been mugged and all his documents stolen. He might have been run over and they couldn't find any relatives. He might have drowned and been carried out to sea. He might have decided never to come back because he didn't want to, but there are lots of other possibilities."

There was silence. Simeon wanted to leave but he didn't know if she might have moved or not. After a long time, she cleared her throat and spoke so now he knew she was still sitting in the front pew, facing forward.

"I've spent a long, long time thinking it was my fault. It made me keep my head down, it made me try to stay unnoticed. Now, you're saying he might have had an accident."

"It's possible. What did he do for a living?" Simeon took a couple of deep breaths.

"He was a sailor out of Cardiff. He originally came from Montego Bay. Mum met him when she was at art school. They came back here to be near her family because he said he could easily get a job in Falmouth."

Simeon shivered. Why couldn't people just answer the question? He didn't need to know the rest of it.

"What should I do?"

Simeon found himself answering. He didn't want to. If he gave advice, people felt they owned him.

"Where did he say he was going the day he disappeared? Start there. Then use the internet. Look for incidents that happened around the same time. There are also the libraries, archives, and old newspapers." It made perfect sense to him.

"So how do I pray?" she asked, suddenly. This time he could feel her eyes on him, even though that was impossible. It made him feel hot.

"You can talk to God, which feels odd to begin with, but the more you do it, the easier it gets. Or you can just sit with him."

"Does he talk back?" She sounded a little scared.

"In different ways. Archie finds him in books, in the Bible. I often hear him in what people say. Anna sort of finds him everywhere when she remembers to look. Harriet finds him in sunsets and trees. Tom hasn't found him at all, yet, unless it's in Anna."

"Tom is the detective looking into Caz's death." Her voice trembled and faded.

"Yes. He is Anna's boyfriend. Though he seems to make her more worried than happy."

"Boyfriends can do that to you."

Simeon suddenly had a horrible feeling that she was about to tell him all about the guy from the lifeboat, who she was engaged to. It was too much. His hands began to sweat.

"Thank you," she said. "I may not have managed to meet God, but I have met you and I feel a bit better. I'll give it a go, what you said, about my dad. Thanks for being so …" Simeon knew that she'd stood up and had begun to make her way to the back of the church. She didn't come down his aisle for which he was grateful. He lifted his eyes when he was sure she was nearly through the door, and he saw Anna sitting on the bench in the porch. She stood up as the young woman passed her. Anna said something and the woman nodded but kept on walking up the path.

Simeon slipped out of his pew as Anna came in.

"I don't want to talk about it."

"Neither do I," she said. "But I am glad she kept going, even when you were a little short with her. She's not very good at standing up for herself."

Simeon had to ask Anna to explain which part she had thought was a bit short.

***

Jim walked into the kitchen. It was just after six, the sun still slanting into the window. Another five minutes and it would be gone from that side of the house, leaving the room dull. Margery wasn't home. She hadn't said anything about being late, again. It was beginning to really annoy him.

He stuck some bread in the toaster and opened a can of beans. Even if she returned in the next half hour, dinner wouldn't be ready for ages. He made a cup of tea. The sun disappeared and Jim suddenly shivered. He wondered if the madman had gone home yet. After Saturday at the practice, he'd thought about ringing the police and making a complaint, but he didn't want them coming down and asking more questions. He didn't want anyone else looking around his lifeboat station. It had been sullied by far too many strangers prodding and poking around and he was sure that Archie would play the incident down. God, the man was so up himself. Just because he'd been in the navy, he thought he was untouchable.

Jim had been glad to see him fall backwards. He'd momentarily worried that he might have broken his hip or some other bone, as the paperwork for that claim would be a bit all-consuming but once Archie was on his feet, Jim could tell it was just his ego that was bruised. What did he think would happen, bringing Caz's dad into the boat house during a practice?

The door crashed back against the wall and Toby burst in. He looked around the kitchen.

"No Mum?"

"Bit of a stupid question as you can plainly see I've just eaten beans on toast."

"Did she leave us anything in the fridge?"

Toby pulled out a lasagne. It just needed warming through. Jim could see he was trying not to laugh. Jim should have checked the fridge, but couldn't she have left a note or something? Mind you, after the day he'd had he'd still eat his share. Beans on toast was no more than a snack, and was it any wonder he'd assumed Margery had left them to fend for themselves? She'd been off lately, not her usual self at all.

"So, have you had a word with Genni yet?"

"What about?" Toby said, cutting some bread.

"Not turning up to practise on Saturday."

"You know she's not been well."

"She should've let someone know." He meant, she should've let him, Jim, know she wasn't coming. Toby shrugged. Jim could see he didn't want it to be his problem, but surely, that wasn't right. They were getting married, weren't they? It was costing a fortune and Jim was fed up with sorting everything out for his son, making all the decisions. Making sure he got what was due to him, that he wasn't overlooked, and did he ever say thank you? No, not once, not ever. Jim could feel his temper beginning to rise.

"She's your bloody fiancée. You know the rules. She should've let me know."

"Her friend has just been murdered. We all need a bit of slack at the moment. Some more than others." Jim disagreed. That was when you needed to tighten things up. That was the time when things began to slip, and he was just about to say so when Toby turned around, butter knife in hand and said, "God, Dad, you can be such an arse sometimes."

Jim hit him. He hadn't meant to. In fact, he'd mostly made a point of not hitting him, as Jim felt his son already had it tough. Toby fell hard against the counter, his head snapping back. He stood, as if he were seeing stars and then put his hand up to his nose. It wasn't bleeding but it was already beginning to swell.

Just for a second, Toby looked at Jim in a way that chilled him to the bone. There was no fear, no anger, just a cold stare that Jim felt went straight through him.

"Like I said, an arse." Toby picked up his coat and walked out.

Jim looked down at his fist. He hadn't lost his rag for a long time and now he couldn't seem to keep it. Bloody Margery and her after-work socials, and her film nights and her book club. She should be at home where she belonged.

He switched on the kitchen light and sat down at the table. Then he got back up and switched on the kettle, wandered through to the lounge and put on the television for the local news. Toby would come home once he'd calmed down, once he was hungry.

The wind was getting up. Jim hoped there wouldn't be a shout. Deep inside, he really hoped there would be. It was what everyone needed, to concentrate on something other than themselves and to thank Jim that he'd organised the extra practice. For them to acknowledge that it'd been a good idea after all.

At eight, Toby wasn't back, and neither was Margery. Jim had left her a couple of messages to say he thought she ought to come home but she'd not bothered to pick up or send him a text. Honestly, she was getting more and more selfish. When his pager began to vibrate and then to ring, he was up and out the door before he'd even checked the message, hoping it was *launch* and not just *crew assemble*. He wondered if Toby and Genni were still around The Lizard, whether they'd make it down onto the ramp before *Rose* was launched.

He was the third car to arrive, and luckily for the early arrivals they were already clattering down the stairs ahead of him. As he began the descent, he heard at least another two cars coming in. This was the bit he tried not to think about. This was the bit when his heart started to pump. It was not knowing how far they'd have to go, and what they'd find when they got there. In the locker room, he finally found out that the coast guard had a mayday from a trawler off the Point. A mayday meant urgency, meant they'd need to work slick and fast.

Ten minutes later, he had the full complement and pushed the button. *Rose* tipped and slid and everyone braced for the moment she hit the water. There was quite a swell but a clear sky. That shouldn't change until the early hours. The trawler was about half an hour out, taking in water, so it was a race against time. He ordered the pump primed, so they'd be ready. Once clear of the ramp he opened up the throttle and they began the relentless thump, thump across the waves. It would be a lot easier coming back, as they'd have the wind behind them and they could slow down a bit, as long as no one needed medical attention. Genni and Toby were down in the cabin, strapped in. You only floated free if you had a job to do, and right now their job was to be ready.

Jim had calmed a little by the time the trawler appeared, listing badly. The first job was to get one of his crew over there to assess what was going on. It should really have been Toby, but when Jim began to move towards him, Toby deliberately looked away. Jim wanted to yell but for once decided that one of the others could go over instead. There was a problem with one of the trawler's bilge pumps which the skipper hadn't been able to fix. It might have been a lovely May day back on the Point, but out here in the grey swell, the sun dropping swiftly below the horizon, it felt cold and lonely. Jim put a couple more men across with their own pump.

Once they'd managed to get most of the water out, both boats began to make their way back to Cadgwith, *Rose* staying astern, a bright orange escort. It would take a while to get home as the trawler was setting the pace. *Rose* rolled and turned so a few of the crew got a bit green, but it was all part of the job. Now the adrenalin was done with, you just had to hold on.

It was the early hours when they hauled *Rose* back up the ramp. The shore crew were ready, and it didn't take long to get everything stowed. Toby still hadn't spoken to him but had followed orders which was all Jim expected. He and Genni were the first out the door. They ought to have checked that there wasn't anything else to do but Jim was too tired to call them back.

When Jim arrived home Toby's car was parked as usual but there was no sign of him downstairs. Margery was still up, waiting for him at the kitchen table. Well, if she wanted a chat, he'd got a few things he'd like to say, too.

***

Tom was going to drive straight past the vicarage. It was the middle of the week, and he ought not to pop in but suddenly he longed to see Anna. She'd probably be out, holding a meeting or writing a sermon but he swung in, anyway. Her car was there but no one answered the door. Tom shrugged-off his disappointment. The desire to put his arms around her had become a need. As he'd driven across the green, he'd seen his mum heading down to the Point with Gerald Denbigh. He'd thought the man had gone home, had hoped the man had gone home. Phil must be doing a good rate if he could afford to stay at the pub so long.

Tom had come back to visit the lifeboat. There were a few things bugging him. Caz had been strangled. There wasn't much solid flesh left but her hyoid was cracked. The ME said it had to be someone strong to have exerted that much force, that they had probably slipped the rope over her head, crossed the two ends and pulled tight. It didn't look as if she'd been sexually assaulted but after eight weeks exposed to the weather there wasn't much to go on. Tom swallowed. He tried hard to think about the young woman pictured in the photographs her dad had provided. To think about her living, not about the mess on the table in pathology. Of course, what was really bothering him, the real blow, was that the rope was clean. The ME hadn't been able to find a trace of anyone apart from Caz.

Tom began to reverse around the side of the house. Then stopped. It was worth a try. She was probably out visiting, but she might be down at the church.

They were well into May, so there were a couple of extra cars parked in the layby. Anna moaned about that, as some of her parishioners needed to drive down to the services and there wasn't always space for them. She'd tried bollards and signs, but it didn't seem to make any difference. Tom wondered if he could do anything to help, though he had a feeling Anna wouldn't want him to.

Just through the gate he rested his hand on the tomb where Derek's wife had died. That had been a difficult year but had been the first time he'd met Anna. She'd annoyed him, challenged him, and then totally disregarded his advice. She'd crept under his skin until nothing felt quite right when he wasn't able to see her. It'd taken him a while to work it out, but with her he felt ordinary, not a police officer or a son or a boss. Just Tom Edwards.

She was lovely but more to the point, she really didn't think that she was. She *was* a little chubby, her hair was always a bit of a mess, but when she smiled, her eyes sparkled and when she looked at him intently, even when she was cross with him, he sometimes forgot what he was going to say next.

He walked to the door of the church, slightly ajar, the sunlight a sharp rectangle across the flags. He pushed it open a little further, but not too far because then it would squeal and if someone was inside trying to pray, it would make them jump.

She was sitting at the front, off to the left, looking forward, a cardigan draped around her shoulders. She held a mug to her lips, and she looked as if she were talking. He went to the table at the back and switched on the kettle. He watched her turn at the hiss and click.

"Tom, what a lovely surprise."

"I'm not disturbing you, am I?" Though clearly he was.

"No. I can do this anytime."

She'd looked as if she might join him, then she turned back to face the altar.

"It's nice when it's so warm outside. I love this time of year," she said.

He plonked down beside her, stretched his feet out in front of him and reached for her hand. She checked over her shoulder and then squeezed his fingers.

"How's your day?" she asked.

"Bloody awful. I'm getting nowhere."

"I'm sorry Tom. I wish I could help."

"You can."

She looked at him, eyes wide. He reckoned he could ask her anything and she'd try and answer him, unless it went against her God or upset one of her precious parishioners.

"Just don't change."

She laughed.

"Very romantic, but everyone changes. Hopefully, for the better in the long run."

"You have such a positive outlook on people."

"Oh, Tom, you know that's not true."

He enclosed her small fingers in both his hands. Hoped no one would come in, not because he was afraid they'd be caught but because he didn't want this moment to end.

"So why is your day so bad?" she asked.

"Are you sure you want me to talk about it?"

"Isn't it why you're here?"

Definitely, he thought. That's exactly why I'm here.

"She was strangled with the rope we found with the body; the ME is sure of that. We're not sure where it happened and whoever did it must have been reasonably strong to have got her out to Beacon Point, particularly as they then shoved her into the gap between the rocks."

"The village has already been speculating. I've discussed this in the shop, at the start of at least two of our church meetings, and even Mrs Protheroe stopped me after the service on Sunday." Anna sounded weary and sad. "The Point is not far from the top of the lifeboat station or where the track runs alongside the coastal path. At this time of year you could get a car down it, easily enough," she continued, thoughtfully.

"Yes but wouldn't they have been spotted by the farm or even perhaps by Simeon?" he replied.

"I guess. You said they? It would make a lot more sense if there were two people. You'd have to be quite fit, either way."

"Most of my suspects are lifeboat crew, purely because they would be physically capable of doing it."

"And they'd know that there was a crevice just there. I bet you can easily see it from the water, say from when they were out on a practice."

Tom nodded and sipped his tea. That made sense.

"Who've you got in mind? Because I know you won't believe it's a random stranger," she said. She sounded so very troubled.

"Anna, you've changed. Even last year you would have argued the opposite. Told me that not one of those people could have done it. Have I ruined you?"

"Not you, Tom. Just the realisation that people are sometimes so damaged. Broken. Often, so very broken."

"Ah, there she is."

"There's who?" Anna said, twisting round to check the door.

"My Anna."

Even though he knew she'd be horribly uncomfortable he pulled her into his arms.

He whispered, "Don't push me away for a minute. This is for me. I need this."

After that, she made him another cup of tea and they watched the sun dappling the floor with spots of light.

"So you never said. Who's on the list?" Anna asked.

Tom did have a list in his head.

"Her dad, purely because he'd know exactly what to do to cover it up. Jim because he didn't like her. That much is obvious. Anyone from the crew who she'd rubbed up the wrong way."

"Genni because she was so very close to her, and that can so often flip in a moment, or Toby because he was jealous."

"What do you know, Anna?"

"Nothing really. Genni is just so devastated."

"Are we talking love affair here?"

"Not sure, and to keep it a secret nowadays seems a bit off. I suppose if Toby found out, then anger could be a factor, but I don't quite believe that."

"People get murdered for far less."

"I know, but I don't want it to be Toby or Genni, because I want them to work out their problems, to get married and be happy."

He didn't know what he wanted for them. The truth, he supposed, and he knew that people were often killed for simply being in the wrong place at the wrong time, for saying the wrong thing at a bad moment or because they'd been a little irritating for a long while.

He drained the last of his tea, kissed the top of her head and left her to pray. Left her to ask God to take care of everyone she was responsible for, which seemed to be most of the people within a five-mile radius. Well, just so long as she included a certain DI from as far away as Falmouth, he didn't mind.

Chapter 20

Genni rubbed a bit more arnica into Toby's bruised nose.

"Ow! Can't you be a bit gentler?"

"I can't believe your dad did this. It's nasty."

"It's happened a couple of times before." He didn't know what he was trying to say, what he was telling her.

"Has he ever hit your mum?"

"Once, I think when I was quite young. She said it didn't hurt at all and not to worry. I was five or six, so I didn't. She's so easy going. I think sometimes Dad gets mad because she goes along with whatever he wants, she never stands up to him, or tries to get her own way."

"Are you defending him?"

"No, of course not. I can just see how annoying it could be to have someone agree with you all the time."

"I'm a bit afraid of him."

"He won't touch you."

He climbed out of her car, while she packed away her first aid kit. It was Thursday, but they were both having a crap week so had decided a drink at the pub was what they needed. Stuff the savings! They would tuck themselves out of sight, around the corner, away from the bar. Neither felt up to the smiles and knowing looks of the other regulars, or worse still the sympathy. Nobody would believe he'd bumped into something at work.

Genni brought the drinks to their table.

"I've been doing some research," she said, sitting down.

"On what? I thought the wedding arrangements were going quite well."

"On my dad."

Toby felt an odd sensation, down in his gut. He squashed it with some beer.

"He left you. End of. What's to find out?"

"I was chatting to Simeon Tyler."

"The weird guy with the dog?"

"That's the one. He's actually quite nice." There was that feeling again. Toby took another swig. "He won't look at you and gets anxious, but he talks sense. More sense than most." She was dragging her finger down the side of the glass, wiping away the condensation. "And Mum won't tell me anything, so there's this gap in me."

"Aren't I enough for you, Genni?"

He'd said it so quietly she couldn't have heard him. He was ashamed of his own neediness. Any other bloke would have simply assumed that he was plenty enough.

"So, after yelling a bit, quite a lot actually, I finally got the date of when he left. Mum almost remembered the exact time, which doesn't surprise me. Before that moment she was happy, after that, not so much. He was heading into Falmouth to sign onto a ship. She didn't know which one. He said he'd be back with the details. I didn't know any of that."

"Why didn't you ask before?"

"Because there was no point. Mum always evaded the question, and I didn't want to upset her."

Toby didn't really understand, but then why didn't he stand up to his dad more often? Perhaps his mum, and Genni's mum for that matter, had a point.

"Anyway, I went on the internet and looked for accidents that happened in Falmouth around that time, where the person was a John Doe. You know, someone without a name."

"I know what a John Doe is. I'm not entirely stupid."

"I know that," and she smiled at him, put her hand on top of his. He grabbed the moment and held onto it. She hadn't looked at him like that for a while.

"Anyway, there are more accidents than you'd think. I'll need to go into Falmouth, a lot of the records aren't digitised yet, but he's quite distinctive."

"Wouldn't he have had some ID on him?"

"Like what? He apparently didn't have a phone, and no

bank card that Mum knew about. We carry that stuff all the time now, but back then, I suppose, you could get away with just cash!"

Toby took another swig and they both stiffened as they heard the door bang shut and his dad shout a greeting to the pub, a general hello. Toby hoped no one would mention they were there but it still meant they couldn't have another drink, which was a bore.

Genni was looking at him strangely, her eyes had narrowed and there was a line running down to her nose, he'd not noticed before. She was beginning to look a little thin, which made her look taller, though she'd promised to wear flatties for the wedding itself.

"What is it now?" he said, feeling as if he'd missed something.

"We're not going to turn into your mum and dad, are we?"

"Better than turning into your mum and dad!"

He'd meant it as a joke, he'd certainly not meant to upset her, but her mouth formed a perfect 'o' shape and her eyes stopped focussing on him altogether.

Shit, he thought. How long before she'd forgive him that little slip?

They left through the back door, so they didn't have to go through the main lounge. Toby took her to her car, and she kissed him, long and hard.

"Let's not be like either of our parents," she said. "Let's just be like you and me."

Then she was gone. Toby watched the empty road for a while and then ambled across the green.

She was right. They got to choose how they were, who they would be. Perhaps they ought to start looking for somewhere to live, get away from the parents. Even if they couldn't afford much, at least they'd be together.

***

Archie stood in his garden. There'd been some beautiful days through May, when the tourists had appeared. A stream of cars coming down the main road, splitting so that half turned down the lane to Kynance, the others meandering through the village and on down to the Point. Today was one of those days, light and balmy. Balmy was exactly the right word to use, he thought. The sea would be a deep blue with the odd white horse. The air would smell of sea pinks and grass and salt.

Archie fancied a walk over to Kynance but wanted to get some weeding done first. He'd worked hard in early spring but had let things go a little since. He knelt and began to fill the wheelbarrow. Annoyingly, it wasn't long before his back began to twinge so he was quite glad when he heard the doorbell ring. He straightened up slowly and hurried around the side of the house. He was worried in case it was Simeon in a tizz, or Anna had a problem with church. It was Anna.

"Hello, Archie. You look busy."

"Not at all. Just doing a bit of weeding."

Anna bit her lip. Archie knew why. She didn't do weeding. She did mowing but not a lot else. Archie had once given her a pot of summer bedding plants, to put outside the front door but she'd forgotten to water them. For a few days they had looked really pretty, a bit of colour and then for months after, brown desiccated sticks that made both of them feel bad.

"I just wanted to make sure you were alright and thought perhaps we could have a chat about Caz and her dad."

"I'll make us some tea and we can have it in the garden. Just round the back is a bit of a sun trap."

"Thanks, Archie. That would be nice. Perhaps I ought to do something with the vicarage garden."

The first thing Archie would do would be to cut down all the shrubs around the back lawn. They were so big and straggly there was hardly any grass left, and definitely no sky. It would mean a lot more light in the kitchen, brighten the place up a great deal.

When he returned, she was sitting with her eyes closed, and

for a moment he hesitated. She looked quite peaceful, her hair tucked behind her ears, her normally pale cheeks a little flushed from the walk over. She was wearing her dog collar, with a rose-pink shirt and a navy cardigan. He'd seen her in mufti, but not often. He placed the tray on the small wrought iron table, which could do with a bit of a lick and a rub. He might even have some paint left from last time he'd given it a coat.

"This is lovely, Archie."

"It's a good spot."

"And you keep everything so beautiful."

"The navy. Maintenance, maintenance, maintenance."

She laughed and then she turned to him with a worried frown.

"Archie, what would I do without you?"

"I'm not going anywhere," he said, feeling at a loss at the abrupt subject change, then a bit cross. Why did everyone think he was going to die all of a sudden? Simeon yes, but not Anna too.

"I'm sorry, Archie, I didn't mean anything by it. I was just enjoying being here, remembering all that you do for me, for us."

"Now *I'm* sorry. I'm such a grump at the moment."

"We're all struggling. And you've had to put up with Simeon worrying about you."

"I don't think I've handled that very well."

"He seems better after your chat," she said. It could have been a question, but Archie thought she was just being hopeful. Anna needed him firing on all cylinders. "I'm a little worried about Catherine. She's been out with Gerald Denbigh quite a lot. That must be difficult for her."

Archie felt a small pang of jealousy. He'd wondered why Catherine hadn't popped round for a cup of tea recently. He enjoyed their chats immensely. They didn't feel quite so weighty as when he spoke to the others, things felt shared rather than carried.

"She's a wise and sensible woman."

"But Archie, we don't know who hurt Caz. What if it were her dad?"

Archie shook his head. He didn't believe that. That any father could kill their child.

"Do you think I ought to have a word with Catherine?" Anna asked.

"I'd have thought Tom might."

"Tom tries not to interfere, but I'm sure he's worried."

"Why don't you let me give her a call? I haven't had a cup of tea with her for ages. It will give me a good excuse. I'll make sure she's being sensible, and that she knows we're around if she needs us," he added.

Archie didn't doubt for a minute that Catherine was being sensible, but she was also a very kind woman, and spending time with a man whom Tom had had a couple of run-ins with would make her feel uncomfortable or disconcerted at best. Archie was in no doubt that she was trying to help Mr Denbigh. He tried to feel kinder towards the man, but after the incident at the lifeboat he'd felt quite used by him.

He also didn't like the fact that Jim had been less than understanding. He wished Tom would get on with the investigation, so they could get on with ... get on with what? Living as long as possible? Helping Anna when she needed him, chatting to Phil about church, looking out for Simeon? Archie felt himself slumping.

He'd had a heart attack; he hadn't wanted to die. He wasn't ready but he also wasn't quite sure how to live. He couldn't find God in anything. He'd looked and looked. Waited and waited and now he was beginning to know why too.

"Anna, I know you've got a lot going on, but could I talk to you?"

For a moment her grey eyes widened, then she smiled. Poured more tea and said, "What is it?" That was all she said, and Archie felt tears welling up behind his eyes. He stood and turned his back. Anna didn't say a word. He took some deep breaths, got a grip.

"I'm struggling to find God. I'm sure it's just a temporary thing, but since the heart attack I've not been quite so sure as I was before. Quite unsure, in fact."

"I thought it might be something like that. You've had your cage rattled. Substantially rattled. You've looked at death, square in the face. You didn't get any warning. It must have been such a shock!" Archie nodded. It had been like a bolt of lightning. "Did you feel a little aggrieved, particularly afterwards?" He nodded again. "Afraid?"

"Yes."

"I bet you've hardly ever questioned God before this."

"Of course not. He's ... well, he's God!"

"I question him all the time. 'What did you do that for? Why did that happen?' Caz had most of her life ahead of her. She was an only child, for goodness sake. God is still God, and I don't doubt that he sees the bigger picture, but I still think it's important we get our questions out in the open, particularly if they're upsetting us."

It made sense. It was probably why he was so irritated with Simeon. Simeon had said he wasn't his usual self, that he didn't seem to have recovered properly. Well, he hadn't, had he! Because though his health was probably back to normal, his faith wasn't, and he needed to come clean.

Anna stood up.

"Won't you have another cup of tea? You've hardly been here five minutes."

"I'm going to leave you to have a full and frank discussion with God. Get some stuff out in the open. You'll find him again, but you may have to look at him differently."

He didn't know what to say to that. At the corner, Anna turned back.

"Thanks, Archie, for letting me be the vicar. It may not have helped you, but it's done me a power of good." As she turned away, he could see she was smiling.

***

Anna walked across the village, with a little bounce in her step. She didn't know why she was feeling so happy. Archie was struggling and yet she wanted to cartwheel across the grass. She popped into the shop. There were quite a few people squashed in there already, but Anna needed milk. Jean looked a little harassed, and not for the first time, Anna wondered what they'd do if she ever decided to retire.

Carrying her milk, she continued down past the sports field and the school, past Derek's old bungalow, now owned by a couple with a large number of cats and a 4x4, and into Church Cove Lane. She was going to go home and for once get to grips with her sermon, early. She still had no idea what she would say, but right now she could conquer the world. In the end she didn't turn in at the vicarage drive but continued down to the lifeboat gate and headed across the field to the car park.

Everyone was struggling and Anna wanted to go and wander around *Rose*. The lifeboat was at the centre of all this, so she'd go down and chuck a few prayers about, as Jim had so eloquently put it. There shouldn't be anyone there apart from whoever was manning the shop. She wanted to take God, show him all the people on the board, talk about the real tragedy of losing Caz and what it was doing to everyone. It's what a good vicar would do. And she was a good vicar. At least she was today.

As she walked into the car park, she noticed a couple leaning on the railings above the steps. She soon realised it was Gerald Denbigh and Catherine.

"Hello," she said, trying not to sound too cheerful.

"Hello, Anna," Catherine replied, looking away as if she were embarrassed. Anna wondered if they'd been talking about her. Not her, of course, but Tom, which meant that Catherine would be in an intolerable position.

"How are you doing, Mr Denbigh?" she asked. She gave Catherine a quick smile. "Are you still at the pub?"

"Yes. Though the police said I can move into Caz's place at the end of the month."

"That must be good and bad."

"Yes. Has that boyfriend of yours made any more progress?" Anna saw Catherine wince, out of the corner of her eye.

"You know I couldn't tell you, even if I did know anything."

"Your confidentiality seems patchy at best."

Anna's morning trembled and crumbled. She knew full well she wasn't always as straightforward as she ought to be. That when people told her things, sometimes she didn't manage to keep them as private as she should, that occasionally lines got blurred. Would he make a complaint?

"Well, if you do need to talk, you know where I live." She turned left onto the coastal path, as if that had been what she'd meant to do all along. She walked through the gorse until she was standing above Church Cove, looking down on the holiday cottages. There were people everywhere. The tide was out and the sound of voices from the steep cove filled the air, children squealing, demanding attention, towels draped over rocks, the sea blue, the waves tiny. At least three people were swimming out in the deeper water. It looked wonderful. Anna would have to go back to her dim, cool vicarage and hope that Mr Denbigh didn't come and bang on her door. She did find him frightening and of course, she felt guilty at abandoning Catherine.

She made herself a cup of tea and sat on the step outside the back door. Her tiny patch of grass needed cutting again, and some of the shrubs could do with a tidy up. She remembered Archie's back garden, full of colour, the lawn short and open. Even the wall that ran down the side sprouted ferns and daisies as if planted deliberately. The vicarage was too much for her. It was all too much for her.

The front doorbell rang. It made her jump. It always made

her jump. Reluctantly she put her cup down and went to see who it was.

Catherine was standing in the drive, and Anna was deeply, profoundly grateful she was alone.

"Come on in. You look ... exhausted."

"I'm tired. Quite tired."

Anna led her into the front room. For once a good temperature. No need to battle with the fire.

"Tea?"

"Something cold?"

Anna came back with a couple of glasses of orange juice. A good moment to try and drink less caffeine, though she'd just read an article that said too much fruit juice was as bad as eating a bag of sweets. How could orange juice have turned into a guilty pleasure? She'd run out of biscuits, but they didn't really go with juice, and she knew Catherine wouldn't mind.

"I know you won't tell anyone, but please can we keep this between ourselves?"

What she meant was, please don't tell Tom — my son, the police officer.

"Of course."

"It's just that I've been spending quite a bit of time with Gerald. I know he doesn't always seem it, but he's really devastated by the death of his daughter, and we must remember that he's been a police officer all his working life. He's used to throwing his weight around to get what he wants. He's a bit of a cliché really. Plus Caz was all he felt he had, after his wife left him."

"I haven't particularly warmed to him, but I've never forgotten his loss. The last couple of months must have been hell for him."

"I'm amazed he hasn't hurt someone, more than Mrs Andrews, that is. He says he's truly trying to hold it together, but the longer it goes on the less chance there is of finding out who killed her." Catherine looked down at her hands, clasped tightly in her lap. "He keeps asking me what Tom has told me, what the gossip is, but Tom has hardly said a word to me, apart from telling me to be really careful."

"Tom's just worried about you spending so much time with a man who looks as if he might thump someone."

"He must be a bit worried how it might look, if work found out that one of the suspects was having coffee with his mother!" Anna almost sighed with relief. For once it wasn't her who was putting Tom in a difficult position.

"Do you think Gerald is a suspect?" Catherine asked.

"Of course. He might be ruled out if they could narrow down where she was strangled or exactly when."

"I thought it was the boat house."

"Not for sure. Forensics have been over the place with a fine toothcomb, but of course *Rose* gets hosed down after each practice or call out. So, if there was any trace it would have been washed away."

"And someone would've had to carry her body up the steps and onto the path, probably in the dark."

Anna shook her head.

"There's always the funicular and Jim uses the steps for training. He's had all the crew carrying sandbags up and down, against the clock." Anna supposed if they could do that, they could probably have carried Caz from the top of the lift to Beacon Point, then heaved her over. Even at night it would've been fairly easy to clamber down and stuff her out of sight, in the crevice. That would therefore mean it was a local. Someone who'd walked the paths all their lives. Which did rule out Gerald Denbigh.

Catherine's eyes began to blink as if she were trying to stay awake. She did look as if she could do with a good sleep.

She said, "I just wanted to tell you what was going on. That I was trying to listen to Gerald, that I was trying hard to help him carry his burden. It's taken me a while to realise I can't.

I'm not up to it."

"Catherine, there is no possible way for you to make this better. He's carrying a pain that no one else can come to terms with. I expect it'll take years, but you tried, you went with him when the rest of us were keeping him at arm's length."

Anna ignored the obvious fact that though Catherine was talking to her, she was really speaking to Tom. It was him that she wanted to tell.

"How do you do it, Anna? There's a murderer on the loose and you sound so calm, so wise."

"You know that's not true. This morning, because dear Archie confessed to struggling, I felt on an absolute high. He doesn't always confide in me. Then I bumped into you and Gerald, and everything faltered."

Catherine nodded. She'd realised, noticed, understood. Of course she had.

"I haven't seen Archie for a while. Perhaps I should pop over."

"I'm sure he'd like that." Anna thought he'd be delighted. She hoped that Catherine wouldn't misinterpret her smile as a knowing smile. The sort she got whenever anyone caught sight of her in the village, holding hands with Tom.

Chapter 21

Harriet walked into her lounge. It would be lovely once they'd decided what colour to paint the walls. She'd just popped through to tidy up a bit. Derek's wine glass from the night before was on a side table, the fireplace was dotted with ash. It looked homely, used. She hugged her arms around herself. This was all hers, all theirs. She smiled at the many squares of paint splashed across the walls. She quite liked the patchwork of colours, it reminded her of the sun speckling the flags in the church, through the old glass.

For a second, she almost did a little jig on the spot, then she remembered that she'd told Anna she was going to try and be more honest. Perhaps she was ready. She should at least try to express her opinions without feeling guilty or unworthy. She looked carefully at each of the squares, trying to imagine the room finished, a small, neat set of curtains hanging either side of the window, framing the sky and the not-quite view of the sea.

It was no good, she simply couldn't picture any of them. As she turned away once more, a small patch caught her eye, down behind the chair in the corner. She went over and sure enough it was her red. The colour she'd laughingly suggested. Immediately, she couldn't imagine anything else. It would be gorgeous. Dark and cosy and old fashioned. Derek had given it a try after all. She heard a drill up in the front bedroom. Derek was putting up a curtain pole.

He was at the top of a set of steps, so she thought she'd better wait, though it was obvious she was hovering. He clambered down.

"What do you think?" he asked. It's a curtain pole, she thought.

"It looks straight." That seemed to be the right answer. He began to coil the flex around the drill. "I've been looking at all your test squares down in the lounge," she said.

"It's difficult, isn't it? None of them seem quite right."

"I did notice that red square down behind the chair. I quite like it."

He looked up and smiled.

"I do too. It might make the room feel smaller, but does that really matter?"

"No, I don't think it does. I love that colour. I'll do you a deal. Let's give it a go, and if we really can't bear it, then I promise we can paint everything white!"

Derek carefully put down the drill.

"You'd hate white. The thing is, Harriet, I've never done this before. Fiona used to choose everything, and I never saw a client's project until they'd put their own stamp on it. So, I'm loving all this decision-making, but I'm aware that it's not just about me. It's about us, but I can't always tell what you're thinking, whether you like something or not."

"I'm not used to someone really wanting my opinion."

"Anna does, all the time!" Which Harriet had to admit was a fair point.

"Ok, Derek, you lovely man. I will tell you what I really think, I really will." He reached forward to grasp her hand. "There was one other thing," she said. He grinned.

"Anything. Anything at all."

"When you go to the dog pound to choose another Dolly, please may I come? Choosing a dog is something we should do together, so that she's our dog."

Derek frowned.

"You want to come?"

She nodded.

"With Simeon and me?"

So Rome wasn't built in a day.

"Of course Simeon can come too, but it's our dog."

She went down to make coffee. Anna would be proud of her. On a whim she put the coffee in a flask and when Derek came into the kitchen she said, "Let's go and have this up on Beacon

Point. It won't take ten minutes to get there and on a day like today it'll be lovely. We don't have to be hours, because I know you've got things you want to get on with, and I have a meeting with Catherine and Archie about the retreat, but let's …"

He reappeared holding their boots. Harriet laughed.

"You're ready! Now all we need is a dog!"

It didn't take them long to walk down the lane and onto the path. Four or five minutes to the steps down to the lifeboat station and another two minutes around the corner onto Beacon Point. Harriet didn't want to sit right at the end, it was too close to where the body had been found, but halfway along they would be facing south, looking down at the sea and along the cliffs to The Lizard. It was a warm sparkly day and though the cove had been full of people the path was empty. She guessed everyone was on a beach somewhere. Up here, with the gulls, was the tiniest breath of wind that prevented it from being oppressively hot. They didn't really need the rug; the grass was quite dry, but it stopped it being prickly. Harriet had brought some biscuits and a couple of mugs. This was one of the things they'd said they'd like to do but had never quite got around to.

"This is bliss," Harriet said, with her eyes shut. Even through closed lids she could see and feel the sun sparkling on the waves.

"Isn't that Simeon?" Derek said, a few moments later. He was standing up and waving before Harriet could sigh. He hauled her to her feet so that she could wave too. For a moment she thought Simeon was going to ignore them, walk back up his lane. He did hesitate and she could imagine the conversation going on inside his head. Then with a half wave he came on up the path, making his way over to them.

"Hello, Simeon," Derek said. "Harriet wants to come and choose a dog with us. I think it's time we set a date."

Simeon nodded.

"Would you like some coffee? I could wipe out one of our mugs." Harriet knew that wouldn't be good enough and so wasn't surprised when Simeon shook his head.

"We're just sitting for a minute, enjoying the view. Why don't you join us?"

Simeon looked around him, turning his head this way and that.

"I know, Simeon, it's really hard not to think of Caz," Harriet said.

"I will definitely be uncomfortable here for a long time. I might have to ask Anna to move the Easter morning celebration."

"Oh, now, that's a long way off," Derek said. But Harriet nodded, she agreed. How could they speak of resurrection when a young woman had been hidden away, abandoned, just below their feet.

"The question is whether someone put her there temporarily, or whether they put her there in the hope that someone would find her?" Simeon said.

"That is an interesting question." Like everyone else, Derek had been thinking about it. "Or the person who killed her may have thought it was only a temporary solution and then when they came back to move her, couldn't bring themselves to do it."

"Why didn't they just drop her into the sea?" Harriet said.

"Because sometimes bodies come back. Once the sea has finished with them," Simeon replied.

Harriet shivered. Even sitting back from the edge, it felt too close. She could almost smell a sweet cloying tang in the air. She knew she was being silly, that it was just the seaweed and gulls, but for the moment it was enough.

"Come on, Derek, it's time to go. We've had our break, and I need to get back for my meeting."

**

Tom had said he would be late. Anna was going to sit in her

210

back room and read her book but instead had decided to come down and sit in the church. It was so bright outside that the soft dimness inside was just what she needed.

She tried to look forward to the gently forming darkness, filled with the smell of flowers and the sea, warm splinters of a perfect day. It was still only late May, but it felt just like June ought to feel. Anna normally loved this time of year, but she was worried, and the worry was spoiling a moment of peace.

She stood and began to pace in front of the altar, then she made her way to the back and wondered about making a cup of tea, but she'd already had so much tea — a sure sign that she was bored or that something was niggling her. Perhaps she should simply lock up and go home — get out some glasses.

Anna moved to the door, pulled it open so that the warmth spilled inside. As she stepped into the porch, with the key already in her hand, she felt she sensed the word, 'wait!'. Anna hadn't particularly wanted to leave anyway. She didn't need much of an excuse to stay a little longer in the blissful quiet. She left the lights off even though it was now quite dark inside. Outside, it continued to look bright, so she sat in the back pew where she could see the path.

She knew that Tom would ring when he got to the vicarage, and she could be home in a couple of minutes. That didn't worry her as she sat for another quarter of an hour, waiting. Every minute long and spiky, the tranquil peace of earlier having fled with every noise, every rustle of leaves. Could this be someone? No, but what about that?

"Well, you've had your chance," she said, and then laughed out loud. "Sorry, you don't need a chance to do right. It's me that misses the moment. Mostly on purpose. I know that, and you know that. Do you mind?" She realised she was getting a little stuck in a maze of ideas. She stood up, jumping out of her skin at the figure in the doorway, and then quickly breathing a sigh of relief when she realised it was Genni.

"Oh, I do hope I didn't make you jump?" Genni said.

Anna shrugged.

"A little. Not your fault though, I should have put the lights on."

Anna's heart ran a little cold when she realised that Genni might have heard her chatting to God. She wished she'd been more articulate.

"I'm really sorry to disturb you. You were obviously busy."

"Not obvious at all. If you heard me rambling on at God, you'll know that praying doesn't take much intellect."

Genni moved into the church, and for a second the light dimmed completely. Anna stepped back. She didn't know why she'd done that. Perhaps because Genni was tall and strong and was obviously in a bit of a muddle about life.

"It made me sad, listening to you. You sounded as if you were talking to your best friend. I don't have one of those anymore." She turned away and looked down the path to the gate. "It took me ages to realise I'd got one at all and now she's gone." Turning back to Anna, she said, "wasn't that rather cruel of your God?"

"Oh, no, Genni. It was cruel of whoever killed her." Anna had used that line more times than she was comfortable with, though it was true. Someone had overpowered Caz, even though she was obviously fit, but she was still quite short and slim. Anna felt a wave of envy. She swallowed it down as it was not an appropriate moment for diet regret.

"Come on in. It's very peaceful at this time of night."

"Don't you want to lock up and go home?"

"I can slip back later. Or I can stay awhile if you'd rather."

Genni took another step, Anna, again, took a step back. She was getting really annoyed with herself and hoped Genni hadn't noticed or would read too much into it.

"I'm a bit of a slow burner," Genni said, as she followed Anna to the front.

"Are you? What do you mean?"

"It takes me a while to realise things." They sat down.

"People can be rude or mean and I don't see it, not until much later when there is nothing I can do, nothing I can say. It means that people think I don't care. But I do."

"Does that mean the converse is true? That when someone says or does something nice you don't always see that, either?"

Genni nodded her head.

"When Toby asked me to marry him, I didn't realise that was what he was doing. How important it was. It really hurt him, made him angry."

"Did he have a ring?"

"No, he said he didn't want to get one until he knew my answer."

Sensible perhaps, but not very romantic.

"I was so busy apologising that I realise now I said yes, without actually saying yes."

"Do you love him?"

"I thought so. He's funny and kind as long as he doesn't lose it and he looks at me, not just at my breasts."

Anna was suddenly glad she was herself. Glad she could be with someone without wondering if they were looking for something else.

"Does he often lose it?"

"No, hardly ever. Not with me anyway."

"Because …?"

"Because I've got really good at reading the signs. I'm brilliant at it." Tears began to roll down Genni's cheeks.

"Then what happens, if what he wants doesn't coincide with what you want?"

"I always do what he wants."

"Then you met Caz."

Genni's tears fell dripping onto her lap, Anna pressed tissues into her hand. It was getting quite dark, Anna thought she really ought to put on the lights, but she didn't dare move. Finally, Genni sighed and began to speak again.

"She always joked that she stared at my breasts because she didn't have a choice. She was so much shorter than me."

"You are lovely and tall."

"A giraffe, a lamppost, a beanpole."

"Willowy, lithe, slim. All the things I'm not."

"The DI doesn't seem to mind."

Anna was a little miffed that Genni had tacitly agreed that she was not willowy or slim, but again, not the moment for diet regret.

"No, he doesn't."

"Do you love him?"

"Sometimes I'm sure I do. Sometimes I don't know. I get worried when he's going to arrest someone. I hate it that he has to deal with the nasty side of life, all the time. He makes me laugh, and he worries about me, even when I've just invited someone in for a cup of tea."

"That's your job, isn't it?"

"Yes, kind of. There is a little bit more to it than that."

"You spoke to Caz when she wanted to talk to someone. She said you were easy to talk to."

Anna thought perhaps that God may have taken her very mediocre listening skills and turned them into good enough.

"She was frightened," Anna said. "She put on a brave face, but I don't think for one second, she thought she'd seen a ghost. Why did she spend so much time down at the lifeboat station?"

Genni sat up.

"She practised things, and it helped her if she could see *Rose* when she was working on a procedure. You know, what to do when a boat needs a tow, or when there are people in the water. Which knot to use for which exercise. She'd worked hard, she would have walked her final assessment."

"What reason could anyone have to kill her? Did she find out something to do with one of the crew? Or did she simply make someone angry enough to lose their temper?"

Genni slumped back.

"I could see the scar from the boat when we were out on a practice. We all could." She shuddered. The long shadows that had stretched across the church had merged into darkness and Anna could not read her expression.

"You knew her best, Genni, by the sound of it. What do you think happened to her?"

Anna's phone had been vibrating in her pocket for quite a few minutes. She knew it would be Tom but didn't want to break the moment.

"Sometimes, the truth is hard and cruel and needs to stay hidden."

"What truth is hard and cruel, Genni? What did Caz tell you that you didn't like?"

Genni turned just a little, seeming to look past Anna. It made her want to look over her shoulder. She couldn't read the young woman, who seemed frozen somewhere else. Then Anna heard someone running down the path, calling her name.

Bugger! Tom was coming to the rescue. Genni unfolded and stepped out of the pew.

"I'll leave you to your evening. You're right about this place, though. I wish I'd discovered it earlier."

She spoke with such regret that Anna ached for her.

Tom was coming into the porch as Genni walked out.

"Good evening," she said. "Anna's inside. She's quite safe."

Tom came on in, panting a little.

"Are you ok? You didn't answer your phone." He said it quietly. He didn't seem to be particularly upset. "You know I worry."

Anna made her way up to the door and wrapped her arms around him. After a while he whispered into her hair, "Are you alright, love?"

Anna shook her head, then nodded.

"I need to lock up and I expect you're hungry." Anna was

ravenous, she wanted something warm in her stomach, something warm deep down inside.

On the way back up the lane he said, "Do you think she could have done it?"

Anna thought it was a little unfair of him. He knew that she'd react, that most of the time he could read her like a book. She dropped his hand.

"I thought tonight you were Tom, not DI Edwards."

"I'm always Tom for you, but people tell you things and I need a pointer or someone I can lean on. You know how it is."

She did. They walked around the back.

"I'll make some eggs, he said".

Anna was grateful. She poured wine, though it was a little late. Normally they would've gone into her small back room but tonight, they stayed in the kitchen.

Anna felt the gap between them, between their roles, their callings and wondered if it were possible to reconcile their lives, one with the other. She sat down at the table and hoped that they could.

Chapter 22

Genni was reviewing the reading cards of the children who were struggling. It seemed a good thing to do, to kill some time before she was due to meet Toby. She'd just managed to arrange an appointment at the records office at Falmouth. The lady had sounded intrigued and eager to help her. For the thousandth time that day, Genni wondered what difference it would make if she did discover that her father had died, rather than simply leaving them. Abandoning her and her mum. Her mother had stated that it wouldn't matter one way or the other. Genni wasn't so sure. After all, she'd never married, had never, to Genni's knowledge, ever gone out with anyone again. So perhaps like Genni she was still waiting for him to come back. To explain away the twenty odd years of absence with a wonderful story of mishap and lost letters. She stood up from where she'd been kneeling, the reading cards in a mess in front of her. She piled them up neatly, as if she had already finished her task and went to grab her bag and coat from the staff room. The headmistress was there, staring into space, nursing a cup of tea.

"I thought you'd still be here," she said, smiling.

"To get my bag. I'm going to meet Toby."

"I'm looking forward to the summer holidays. Are you off anywhere nice this year?"

"No, still saving like mad for the wedding and a deposit for a house. If we didn't live at home, we wouldn't stand a chance."

"You're doing alright, Genni. You're a good teacher. And though we absolutely love you, we're a very small school. You could go somewhere bigger, get some different experience. It wouldn't do you any harm. There are other places where you wouldn't have to live with ..." Genni wondered what the woman was trying to say. "Anyway, have a good evening."

Genni nodded. She liked the school. It was small, but she'd

grown fond of the kids and the other teachers. She wondered if the headmistress was trying to say that she didn't fit in. She was used to feeling like that.

She dropped her bag in the boot and was about to ring Toby when her name was called, from a long way away. For a moment she wondered if she could ignore it, pretend she hadn't heard, only to her surprise, she saw Margery striding towards her.

"Genni, I'm so glad I caught you. I took the afternoon off especially and then went for a coffee with a friend and time ran away with me."

Genni wasn't sure what to say. That sentence left a lot of questions hanging in the air, the main one being that surely if Margery had wanted to talk to her, she could have done it at any time.

"Have you a moment? Or are you going home?" Margery asked.

"I'm meeting Toby, but not for another half hour."

"Good. Let's head down to the cove."

Genni nodded. She'd not really spoken to Margery on her own. Margery came as a set with Jim and Toby. She'd been sweet about the wedding, trying to get Jim to back off a bit, but, as Toby often pointed out, she never made waves, or stood up for herself, so why would she bother standing up for them?

They began to walk down the lane.

"I don't normally have time to do anything like this. It's mad really, living here, but there's always something to be getting on with. I shall regret not getting out more on the coastal path."

Genni nodded.

"I've walked a lot since Caz disappeared. Sometimes I simply can't keep still."

Genni felt Margery's eyes on her, a tiny flicker of movement that made Genni want to look away, as if Margery were seeing her for the first time.

"I did wonder how you were getting on. Really getting on. And let me say, I didn't for one minute believe in the virus."

"Mum hates anything emotional. We must soldier on, whatever happens. Sometimes, it's hard."

"Caz was really special to you, wasn't she?"

"Yes."

"And Toby and Jim don't seem to care."

"I guess not." Genni felt the ache of her emptiness. "I didn't notice at first. We began to chat at the pub, after practice. Sometimes she stayed when it was my turn to close up, or vice versa. Then I began to help her learn some of the stuff she needed to know, mostly after school. She was a real city girl. She'd no idea there were so many different knots and different wind speeds, knots, again, not miles per hour. It was all new to her."

"You've lived here all your life. Like me. I guess we've absorbed the place, which isn't necessarily the best thing for us, long term."

They turned up onto the coastal path. It was narrow just there and they had to walk one behind the other. Genni went first and found herself checking out of the corner of her eye that Margery was still following.

Past the top of the steps leading down to the lifeboat station she found that she was breathing again, that until she'd come past the familiar drop, she'd held her breath.

"God, I hate that place," Margery said, fiercely.

Genni looked back at her in surprise.

"Why?"

"Because I couldn't compete, and I stopped trying a long time ago." Margery was staring down at the station. "Now I've lost them both. Compromise is good to a point when the two of you share it. If it's just you doing it all the time, it sucks the life out of everything."

They started walking again. Genni knew what she meant. Knew that it was what her mother had done. Knew it was what she would probably end up doing. She stopped. They were just at Beacon Point, and she couldn't help but stare out to the end.

"Was this where they found her?" Margery asked.

Genni nodded.

"The poor girl. It must have been dreadful." Fiercely again, Margery continued, "Look, don't be me. Don't be your mum. You don't have to, you know. I've put up with a lot and sometimes I get scared. Jim can be mean, and I don't have the energy to fight him, not anymore. He's hurting Toby and Toby needs to make his own way, even if it means facing some difficult issues."

Genni was still blinking tears.

"Toby said Jim's not hit him for ages."

"That's not what I meant." Then Margery sighed. She seemed defeated. "I can be so stupid sometimes. I believed Toby when he said he'd had a bump at work. I always believe whatever he tells me." She put her hands up to her own cheeks and dragged them down as if she were trying to squash her face between her fingers. "Jim needs to be reined in. Hitting our boy is unacceptable. It always was." Margery turned away. She was trembling.

It was odd, but Genni was unmoved by the woman's pain. For some reason all Genni could see was an image of Caz yelling at her in the car park. Genni had yelled back, because she was so scared she was going to lose her, that Caz would despise her for her cowardice and walk away. Screaming had put Genni way beyond feeling in control, and for a moment she felt a tiny shard of empathy for Jim, which made her feel a little sick.

Yelling at Caz had made Genni realise how frustrated she was at being unable to step beyond herself. Caz seemed to understand that and yet didn't understand at all. Then Genni had lost her anyway, which was hemming her in and was making her selfish and deaf. She simply didn't know how to listen to what Margery was trying to say to her, out here on the cliff.

"I love Toby. He's my son, though I know I've not been the best mum there ever was. But are you sure you love him?"

Genni frowned. Was a mother allowed to ask her son's fiancée such a question? It seemed as if Margery had just crossed a line. She hadn't had an opinion on anything before this, so why now?

"I love him. He's kind, and he doesn't mind my history."

"Oh, Genni, there's nothing wrong with your history. You had a black dad. It means you have a black heritage. Do you even know what that might mean for you?"

"It doesn't matter. I am who I am."

"But you're not, are you? What would Caz have had to say about that?"

Caz had had a lot to say about that.

"Get away from here," Margery said, fiercely. "I'm not saying you can't ever come back, but there's a whole world out there, filled with beautiful Gennis who know who they are and what they really want. Find out how to do this life, so you won't be filled with regrets like me."

Genni felt the anger rise from within. How dare this woman tell her how she felt! Why did everyone think they knew what was in her heart, that they could see clearly what was hidden from her?

She turned away, abruptly, to stare over the sea. For a moment she wondered if she could simply run, flinging herself over the edge.

"I'm sorry. It's not my place. It'll never be my place to tell you what to do. And I'm sorry because I'm more of a coward than I realised. Forgive me, Genni. But I do hope that one day, you might remember that I tried."

Margery walked back the way they'd come, leaving Genni bristling with hurt. Even Margery wanted Genni to leave Toby alone. That she didn't think Genni was good enough. Finding out what happened to her dad was rapidly becoming the only thing that might save her.

***

Summer wasn't Simeon's favourite season. It wasn't that he didn't like the warmth, which sometimes meant that wearing his parka could get a little uncomfortable, it was just that the place filled up with tourists. For June, July and August, he took Belle for her walk early, often before six o'clock. He still went on his normal days to see Archie but cut across the village. The coastal path was too narrow to be constantly meeting people, constantly stepping aside and turning away. Cutting through the village meant that there was space to walk alone.

Simeon was staring at the ceiling waiting for his alarm to go off. He knew it wasn't logical, that because he was already awake he should just get up but there was a strange reluctance to move.

He knew he was still anxious about Archie's health, and it didn't help that since they'd talked, Archie seemed to think that all was well between them, that Simeon was reassured. Simeon now didn't feel able to ring him quite so often. It was beginning to become a bit of a thing.

He wanted to ring Archie right now. Simeon knew that he'd got stuck, and that usually he would go to Archie to talk it through. He was stuck, stuck, stuck and somehow Archie wasn't available. He drummed his fists against the mattress, feeling the muscles in his arms tense until they ached.

He stopped when he heard Belle whine, and then stretch and then the comforting sound of her claws clattering over the tiles. She pushed open his bedroom door and came to find him under the covers. He deliberately relaxed his fingers so that he could stroke her ears.

"I'll take you for a walk, then I'll go to morning prayer, and then I'll make an appointment to speak to Anna about my anxiety. I'm getting into a loop, Belle."

He knew she didn't really understand what he was saying,

but she always seemed to guess his mood, for when he got anxious or scared, she always leaned in harder, snuffled her nose against his hand more frequently. Getting her had been a really good idea. She'd changed everything.

Anna read morning prayer a little wearily. She yawned a lot, which meant that she probably hadn't slept or that Tom had stayed late, though being mid-week Simeon thought it unlikely that Tom had been the cause. For the last couple of weeks he hadn't been around as much, but either way, the tiredness would mean that when he asked to speak to her, she'd probably insist on sitting in the kitchen and making lots of coffee. Simeon didn't mind. The kitchen was a small room and he liked to be able to see the walls around him, and if some were within touching distance, then all the better.

Archie had sat next to him in church. He'd seemed relaxed, his face tanned by the sun. Simeon supposed he'd been out in his garden a lot, weeding, planting and feeding. He'd waved jauntily to Simeon as he'd left, walking briskly up the path. Anna had chatted to everyone. Simeon had to wait quite a while for her to finish. When she turned around and saw him standing in the shadow of the door, she jumped.

"Simeon, waiting for me or waiting for me to go, so you can have the church to yourself?"

"Waiting for you."

"What can I do for you?"

"I would like to talk. I would like you to help me with my anxiety."

"Come on, then. I had a terrible night, so I will need coffee."

She led them round the back of the vicarage and straight into the kitchen. She'd obviously not locked the back door. Tom would be cross with her for that.

"I thought you and Archie had had a long chat about this, that things were better now."

She began to fill the kettle. Simeon waited until she'd turned off the tap so that he wouldn't have to raise his voice.

"We did have a talk about it. He apologised for not realising how difficult I'd found his heart attack, but Anna, the basic situation hasn't changed. Archie still isn't quite himself, no matter what he thinks, and I can't help thinking that there is something underlying that. That the stent is not doing its job, or something is leaking or …"

"Stop right there, Simeon. You're not an X-ray machine, and unless you've one in your pocket you're not going to be able to check out any of those things."

Simeon didn't tell Anna that to check up on your heart you didn't use X-rays.

"I know that, but I can't switch off the worry. And I have prayed about it a lot."

Anna made the coffee and fetched a pint of milk from the fridge.

"I wonder if something else is bothering you."

She brought the mugs over. Simeon was disappointed that his was an ordinary mug, with a picture of her nephew and niece. Normally he'd get something which said, "Vicar's Favourite." He knew it was silly, but somehow it mattered.

"Tell me all the things that are bugging you, even if, like Archie, you feel they've been sorted."

Archie wasn't close to being sorted but Simeon supposed he knew what she meant. He sipped his coffee. Anna didn't make it as strong as the others, but it was still nice.

"I suppose the obvious one is that Archie is going to die before I'm ready."

"You'll never be ready. Death cannot be prepared for."

"Actually, I'm not sure this is about me at all. Archie was scared when he had his heart attack. He thought God would draw close, but he says, in the moment, he couldn't find him."

Anna bit her lip. She sipped her coffee, then stood up to reach a little more milk, which she'd left on the side.

"I think if I were concentrating on breathing, and the pain was so strong I couldn't see beyond the end of it, I wouldn't worry about finding God, I would simply hope that he was there holding me through it. Archie's job at that moment was to take another breath. He did his bit and God most definitely played his part because Archie is still here."

Simeon smiled.

"Good answer. May I say that to him when I see him tomorrow?"

"Of course. You know him best. You know what he needs."

Simeon nodded.

"Now how about you, yourself? You've been so anxious of late. Is it simply about Archie or might there be something else?"

Simeon sat back, then sat forward again so he could reach down and smooth the top of Belle's ears.

"I am scared about Archie dying. I am also scared that Caz's father will come and shout at me, or even worse. I don't like the fact that he's still here and that he keeps seeking out Catherine. Even though she's sensible, she is also very kind-hearted."

"I agree about Catherine. Tom's very worried about her, too, but unless it conflicts with the investigation, or puts his mum in danger, he simply won't interfere. Something about professionalism."

"He must have to make that kind of decision about everything, all the time."

"What do you mean?" she asked.

"Well, how much should he tell you? He knows your role within the village, but he also knows that sometimes that might make it awkward for you. Do you tell him everything you hear?"

"No, of course not. But it's a fine line, and sometimes I have to make a judgement, too."

Simeon knew she wasn't always as good at that as she ought to be.

"If you think about it first or you're not angry, or upset," he said.

"Yes, that's true." She dropped her gaze to the table. He could tell because when he glanced up, he could only see the top of her head.

"People say all sorts of things they don't mean when they're angry."

"Oh," Simeon said, suddenly remembering the two women in the lifeboat car park. The yelling, the intensity of their voices.

"Anna, I need to tell you something I've just remembered, because I don't know if I need to let Tom know about it or not. It's not much, but it might add more to the picture."

She nodded.

"Of course, but first, more coffee?"

Simeon did have another cup.

"I was out with Belle, walking towards the car park, at the top of the steps, leading down to the lifeboat. Well before I got there, I could hear two women arguing. They were really angry with each other. One of them said, "You don't understand." And the other one replied, "Oh, I do. You're a coward and it would serve you right if I just went and told him who you really are." I didn't recognise the voices, but I knew I couldn't go near them. I turned around and went back. I don't remember anything else they said.

"When was this, Simeon?"

"Before Archie saw Caz for the last time."

"And you think it might have been Caz and Genni?"

Simeon supposed he did, though he'd no real proof of that. The voices had been hard to recognise because they were screaming so loudly.

"Genni did say that Caz challenged her, didn't like some of the things she did, but screaming at each other sounds a little more than that. You'd better tell Tom. He might send one of the Sandras to get a statement from you."

"A Sandra?" Simeon asked.

Anna explained that Tom still hadn't replaced Sandra and was trying out a couple of sergeants, but that it wasn't going well.

"I'd rather tell him than a new sergeant." He didn't want some stranger coming to his house, even to take a short statement. Simeon knew Tom well enough to trust him.

"Is there anything else you want to talk about?" Anna asked.

Simeon thought not.

"I feel better. Less fuzzy. So no, not for the moment. And despite having two cups of coffee, I feel calmer. Thank you."

Anna smiled, a big wide grin that smoothed out the wrinkles, and lightened the dull patches under her eyes. He nodded and stood up. He would take Belle to the shop to get some bread and milk. Hopefully, there wouldn't be too many visitors around at this time of day.

Chapter 23

Tom was stuck behind a queue of cars heading down the peninsula. He thought perhaps that the schools had broken up, but it was still only the end of June, so it was far too soon for that. It was probably just the weather. They'd had some lovely weeks, warm and balmy, so where better to head than down to the Point, to Kynance or Mullion. Still, he was going to be late, and they'd struggle to find somewhere to park.

He'd booked a table at the pub in Cadgwith, wanted to get Anna away from The Lizard. The investigation had pretty much ground to a halt, and though Caz's dad had been on the phone again, yelling at the desk sergeant, the man had refused to put him through unless he'd calmed down. Tom knew he'd have to phone Denbigh to tell him there was no further progress since the last time he'd asked. The body had given them a window for the time of death, but it wasn't that specific; definitely not long after Archie had spoken to Caz, but she'd been out in the elements for a whole eight weeks. He tried not to think about the putrefaction and bird mutilation. She had been identified with dental records, that was all anyone needed to know.

Thankfully Anna was ready, waiting for him and he realised it'd been a good call. She too didn't mind going up the coast a bit. She wasn't wearing her dog collar either, so she was treating it like a proper date. She was still carrying her rain mac because no one who lived on The Lizard went anywhere without access to some form of weatherproof coat.

"What a treat," she said, getting into the car. "I even brushed my hair."

He leaned over and kissed her. If she was taking a moment off, then he wasn't going to miss the opportunity. What a contrast with the last time they'd had lunch, when she'd been ill at ease and had clock-watched through the hour. He decided it was all to do with notice, warning.

"So, a busy morning?" he asked.

"Yes and no. I had a meeting with Archie and Harriet. We're going to plough on with the retreat in September, even though there are only two guests, as we had to cancel the one in May."

"Two people should be easier than six, and I know Mum will help out."

The car park above Cadgwith was quite full but Tom found a space in the corner. They'd be ten minutes late; it could have been worse. They began the walk into the tiny village, the road dipping steeply, then almost immediately back up again. The beach was empty of boats, but there were plenty of people around. It was another fair day, and no one was missing an opportunity for a bit of fresh air and sunshine.

The landlord came out of the bar to greet Anna. She'd taken his mother's funeral, and nothing was too much trouble. The other punters kept looking over at her as if she was some minor celebrity that they couldn't quite place. Anna of course blushed pink, and her dark grey eyes kept darting around, as if looking for a way to escape. The man led them to the back of the room, furthest from the bar, where there was a small table in the corner. Tom left Anna with the menus while he fetched their drinks. Anna took a big gulp of her white wine.

"You should be used to being a bit of a VIP, you know."

"I'm just the local vicar."

"You are Anna Maybury. People know the real deal when they see it."

She began to blush again.

"This *is* a bit of a treat," he said, trying to distract her.

"You don't normally take time off in the week, particularly in the middle of a murder investigation," she replied. The last few words were whispered.

"I've got the sergeants reviewing any evidence we have. I even bought another paper from the village shop in the hope that Jean might let something useful slip."

Anna laughed.

"You are desperate. I do have something extra, though it may not have anything to do with the case."

She told him what Simeon had told her about the arguing women, that she and Simeon thought it might have been Caz and Genni. Tom winced at the vagueness but said that he himself would go around to speak to him.

"Thanks. If you send one of the Sandras, it might freak him out. He's been under a bit of strain these past months worrying about Archie."

"Are you worried about Archie?"

"Not so much now. Though I think he might be a little jealous of Mr Denbigh."

"Are you talking about my mother?" Suddenly he wanted to laugh out loud. Mothers didn't have lives beyond the love for their sons. Didn't Anna know that?

Anna looked really embarrassed. He was trying to lighten the mood but at the very mention of Denbigh's name, Tom felt his hands curl into fists. There was something about that man that left him feeling pared down to the bone.

Anna reached across and laid her hand over his. He quickly grasped it and squeezed.

"He's a bit of a pain, isn't he?" she said.

"He's doing what any of us would do if our daughter had been murdered. And he knows how it all works, so nothing I can say will help him. I'm sorry, Anna, let's talk about something else."

"What would you like to talk about?"

"How about us taking a break? Let's go somewhere else. You must be allowed to take a holiday, and I've got plenty owing to me?"

She froze, just for a second, then narrowed her eyes as if she hadn't quite heard him properly. Their food arrived. He fetched another glass of wine. He sat down and at last she smiled.

"I'd like that. Somewhere inland. Somewhere green and

hilly."

"Somewhere with a log fire and you can bring lots of unsuitable novels."

"And we can switch off our phones."

He knew she wouldn't do that, just in case one of them needed her. And of course, they'd have to wait for him to catch the murderer.

On the way back to the vicarage, they passed the school.

"Anna, isn't that Genni's green Fiat? It's well past three. When do they break up?"

"A few more weeks yet. And Genni stays late just in case there's a shout. The headmistress gets quite worried about her."

"Archie mentioned a green car, parked in the lifeboat car park the day he saw Caz," Tom said, thoughtfully.

"What time did he go down for his shift?" she asked.

"About three-fifteen."

"Genni might have already been down in the boat house if she left school on the dot of three. I bet Caz was on her way to meet her to do some more revision. Except hadn't they supposedly had a row earlier that day when Genni should have still been in school?"

"I need to talk to her again. Perhaps Archie was not the last person to see her alive."

They swung into the vicarage drive. He automatically checked that there was no one lurking.

"Anna, that was great. I really needed it."

"Me too," she said. He left her standing on the front doorstep waving. As he drove back up the lane, the case consumed him again except now, locked away in a deep place was a spark of excitement that they might go away together, perhaps for a few days. That's when he would ask her.

***

Jim was sitting in the dark. They both jumped when Toby flicked on the kitchen light. It was past eleven. Late for the working week but Genni's summer term was never as hard as the others, so she didn't care so much about early nights. She could be a bit selfish like that, Jim thought.

"Honestly, Dad, what are you doing in the dark? You gave me the shock of my life."

"Waiting for your mother," Jim growled.

"She's not out again! What is it tonight? Film club, knitting or art?"

Jim shook his head. He kept his lips tightly closed, his fists balled in his lap, under the table.

Toby was running the tap. He always took a glass of water up to bed.

"Is something wrong?" Toby leant back against the sink, the window behind him was black and shiny.

Jim swallowed, thought about shaking his head but any movement would cause everything to spill over, would make it solidify into something he couldn't control. Instead, he lifted the note in his hand and read aloud:

"I'm sorry, I'm not coming back. I love someone else. He's got a job, away from here, and I'm going with him."

Jim slid the note across the table. Toby frowned and picked it up. He didn't seem able to tear his eyes away from the words on the square of paper, when he did look up, he said, "Did you know?"

What a bloody stupid question and he couldn't tell the boy because Toby loved his mum.

"Did you hurt her? Hit her like you did me?"

Jim couldn't believe the unfairness of that. All the times he'd thumped the wall in the shed, all the times he'd walked out rather than raise a hand and it hadn't made a ha'p'orth of difference.

"She'll be back. She can't have gone, not just like that," Toby said. Jim thought he sounded like he was ten years old.

Jim shook his head. He wished that Toby would go up to bed, turn out the light, leave him sitting in the kitchen. He didn't want to have to deal with him as well. Margery was messing with him, wasn't that enough?

"Are you alright?" Toby asked.

Jim looked at the back door and then down at the table. Finally, he managed to glance at Toby and nodded.

"Get up to bed. You've got work in the morning." He knew he sounded angry, as if it were Toby's fault, but the boy would have to suck it up, man up. Right now, Jim couldn't be responsible for him as well.

Toby picked up his glass and disappeared into the hall. Jim listened to the familiar creaking as he climbed the stairs, the click of the latch when he closed his door.

This time he hadn't had to work it out for himself or go around to explain to the man that Margery wasn't available. This time he hadn't needed to thump anyone. She just wasn't here anymore.

Minutes had become hours, and were hard, like concrete. He was pinned up against its unyielding roughness. How dare she do this to him? How dare she! And for a terrifying moment he couldn't remember what she looked like. He certainly couldn't remember what she'd been wearing when she'd left for work that morning.

Jim got up and leaned over the sink. He was trembling, his hands shaking like an old man. He wanted to switch off the light, which meant crossing the room to the back door. In a rush of adrenaline, he grabbed his coat and flung himself out. He was in his pickup and driving fast, down through the village before he realised what he was doing. It was cloudy, there was no moon and nearly midnight so there was no one around. He kept checking his phone as if he were waiting for a call. He'd left messages for her, though her phone was switched off.

In the car park he waited and listened. He couldn't see anyone, couldn't hear anyone. He took the steps carefully until he reached the platform, lit by the light above the door. He entered the code and walked into the boat house. *Rose* filled the space and he wanted to lean out and touch her hull. Instead, he took himself downstairs and out onto the ramp. The tide was high, the sea flat. All he could hear was the slapping of the waves under the pilings. He didn't cry, he simply stared out into the dark vastness. She'd left him. He'd have to practise saying it, until it became a reality. Still he didn't want the village gossiping, having an opinion. He'd have to tell Toby not to say a word. This was his business, no one else's.

He'd be better off without her. They both would. After all, he was better off without Caz or at least he would be once the rawness had worn off, once everyone had stopped wallowing. Caz had been trouble from the start. Caz wouldn't play the game. Caz was a stirrer, which was why Margery was such a blow. They'd had their problems but since Toby, Margery had never made waves, argued back, put her foot down. She'd become a good wife, never went against him, always provided a meal even when she was out at one of her stupid clubs.

Jim was cold now. It was June but there was still a chill to the nights. He had to get moving, keep moving. Later he'd come back to his beloved *Rose*. She would never let him down.

Chapter 24

Harriet walked up to the shop, briskly because it was still a bit chilly and because she needed to stretch her legs. Anna was coming over for coffee later and they'd run out of milk. For a minute she'd been irritated but then had thought it would be a good opportunity to get some exercise. They'd been painting the front room over the weekend, and she'd got a lot of tight, achy muscles, and some strange bruises around her knees where she must have leaned on the step ladder awkwardly. Still, it was beginning to come together. The red was quite dark, but it did remind her of that room she'd seen all those years ago in that magazine. Derek was reserving judgement until they got the furniture uncovered but she was quite sure it would look fabulous. She really wanted Derek to see that, that she'd been right. They were really beginning to tick things off now, walls, ceilings, curtains. It was beginning to feel like home.

Jean was serving when Harriet walked in, but the shop soon emptied, the group browsing the shelves, eager to get out and begin their day. There was supposed to be some rain coming in later, though Harriet hoped it would hold off until lunch time.

"Hello, Jean. We ran out of milk and Anna's coming over. For a meeting," she added quickly.

It wasn't really a meeting, and she knew that Jean probably knew that, too, and wondered why she bothered making excuses to Jean.

"How is she? She's having to be there for everyone again, particularly the lifeboat crew. What a terrible thing," Jean said, beginning to count the newspapers in a pile in front of her.

Harriet thought they were all shouldering a bit of the load, that Anna wasn't having to manage entirely by herself. Catherine was helping Mr Denbigh. She, herself, was helping with Genni, and Archie was talking to Jim. They were all finding it difficult.

"How's the great romance coming along?"

Harriet bristled until she realised that Jean was asking about Tom and Anna, that she wasn't asking about herself and Derek. She supposed they were a done deal, whereas Anna and Tom were still the subject of some speculation.

"They continue to go out," she said, which she hoped was communicative enough. Jean started to count the newspapers again. She seemed a little distracted.

"Jean, is something bothering you?" Harriet asked. Jean looked up and for a moment Harriet wondered if she was going to cry.

"Margery Andrews has disappeared."

Harriet frowned.

"What do you mean, she's disappeared? Are the police involved?"

"I don't think so. Jim isn't saying anything, but Toby told Genni she's run off with another man. That she'd left a note, but she didn't say a word to me, and we were supposed to be going to the cinema this week."

Harriet wasn't surprised that Margery hadn't confided in Jean. Tell Jean, you told the whole village and if something like that got back to Jim, Harriet wouldn't like to speculate as to what might happen.

"What if she hasn't run off?" Jean said, a little quietly. "What if something has happened to her, like Caz?"

"If there wasn't a satisfactory explanation, then Jim would be yelling from the rooftops."

Jean nodded, but she didn't seem convinced, she looked worried. She and Margery were good friends.

"Jean, if you're that worried, why not have a chat with Tom? Particularly if he might be able to put your mind at rest. Toby might have heard from her, or Jim, and they're just not saying."

Jean nodded, but she was still trying to count the newspapers. There weren't that many. Harriet thought her face looked puffy; fine lines seemed to have appeared across her forehead and under her eyes.

They all wondered what they would do if Jean decided to give up the shop. She was well past sixty, and her daughter and family now lived in Helston. She might want to spend a bit more time with them. Harriet wasn't even sure who owned the building. She must ask Derek, or perhaps Phil, at the pub, might know better.

"Talk to Tom or Anna. I would if I were you."

***

Anna and Harriet decided to sit in the kitchen while Derek continued painting the woodwork in the lounge. Anna had been impressed with the colour, Harriet could tell, and it made her feel inordinately pleased with herself. Once ensconced in the shiny new kitchen she told Anna what Jean had told her that morning.

"Do you think you should tell Tom? What if something has happened to Margery and Jim is simply covering his tracks? It would be easy to forge a note if you'd been married that long."

Anna nodded slowly, but a crinkled line was forming between her eyes.

"Jean did ring me. She said there was a man that Margery met at work, years ago, that Jim had warned him off even though there was really nothing in it. Simply two people who got on well. Margery was really embarrassed and not long after changed her job. I suppose, if they met again recently, it might have blossomed into something else."

"It's possible. And if Jim found out? Do you think he would have just let her go?"

Anna pressed her lips together as if she wasn't sure what to say.

Finally, she said, "No, I don't suppose he would. Jim reminds me of Gerald Denbigh. There's a wound up spring behind their eyes that's a bit scary. They're both so big and powerful."

"And if Gerald did lose his temper with Caz, would he have known where to take her body to hide her?" How easily they had slipped back into talking of Caz, Harriet thought.

"He's been down to visit before, perhaps Caz took her dad to Beacon Point for a picnic or something. He might have found the gash then. You can get down onto the lower level, if you're careful and from there the ledge, crack, crevice, whatever, would be visible, particularly if you're tall. Genni said that, from the sea, it looked like a scar in the cliff."

"You spoke to Genni about it?" Harriet asked, a little surprised.

"I bumped into her in church. She's not very happy."

Anna picked up her tea. Harriet knew by the way her eyes slid around the room without seeing anything, that there was something else niggling away at her. Any second now it would spill out.

"Harriet, do you think that Caz and Genni were more than friends?"

"Yes, it's possible. Genni may not have realised it of course."

"She constantly talks about friendship, but do you think that she doth protest too much?" She took a gulp of tea and almost choked. "After all, Harriet, we're good friends and I would be devastated if anything happened to you." For a second Harriet thought Anna was going to cry.

"Who else would you find to gossip with, or to tell all about your dates with Tom?"

Anna smiled with relief.

"So would you like to hear about last week?"

"I would."

"I was quite nervous, but you were right. I treated it like a proper date and so did Tom, though we still talked about the case quite a lot."

"You're bound to, to some extent. I'm still amazed that he took time out in the middle of an investigation."

"I think it's because he's a bit stuck. He really doesn't know what to do next and if there's another murder somewhere else, he'll have to put this one on the back burner. It's always a worry for him."

"He won't want you to be living so close to a possible killer, either."

"Any of us." Anna looked through the window to the canopy of trees behind. Sitting there was just like being in a tree house, and Derek was getting quite excited about putting in the raised platform over the stream. It would be gorgeous the following summer. "Tom is actually quite fond of you all," Anna continued.

"Possibly, but he loves you. He's simply learning to like us because of you."

"He wants us to go away on holiday, for a short break," Anna whispered, and stared down at her hands. If she'd been in the pub, she would have been shredding a beer mat.

"It is kind of the next step. Are you excited or scared?" Harriet asked.

"A bit of both. Will it mean going to the next level?"

Harriet laughed. She grabbed Anna's hand.

"Oh, you silly old bear! Do you mean will you sleep together?"

"Yes. And I wish you wouldn't refer to me as a fat bear with a very small brain."

Harriet wasn't going to be distracted.

"Sleeping with Tom will happen when you decide. And you really will have to be ready because otherwise you'll get yourself into the most awful muddle. You know you will."

Anna nodded miserably.

"Try not to get into a state. Going away together could be lovely. And you do need to know how you get on beyond a couple of snatched hours when you're both tired. Working out that you can spend all day together without either dying of boredom or wanting to kill each other would be a good thing."

"It's been a while."

"Anna, don't blow this up into something it's not. Tom loves you and will go at your pace. The big question is where, and will it be a romantic cottage or a hotel? And then twin beds or …"

Harriet had to laugh at the panic flitting across Anna's face, like clouds around the Point on a blustery day.

"You really do have to talk to him about it," Harriet added.

She made them more tea and took a cup through to the lounge. Derek had paint in his hair, but the skirting was nearly finished. She bent down and kissed him. A proper kiss that made him rock back onto his heels.

"This is looking really good," he said.

"It is, isn't it," she replied. "So, the next thing is for us to go and choose a dog together, ok?"

Derek frowned, confused by the rapid change in subject, but Harriet wasn't worried. He'd get used to it. She was going to start asking more of him. It made things feel real and solid, and she wouldn't give up that feeling for the world.

***

Two days later Anna still hadn't heard from Tom, but their lunch seemed to have filled the gap, for the time being. She hoped he was making some progress, and at the first opportunity she would tell him about Margery leaving. Even if it had nothing to do with the murder, he still ought to know.

The end of June was beginning to be a little disappointing, and she felt sorry for all the young families who were battling with the cold winds driving in rain from the west. She turned into the church. The vicarage would be a bit nippy and after Harriet's wonderful new house she couldn't quite face it.

She made herself another cup of tea and took it down to the front pew. To her place. Her seat facing the simple altar and cross. It was odd, they all had somewhere they came to, and no one encroached on anyone else's territory. None of them would dare sit in Simeon's pew at the back. Archie tended to make himself comfortable in the second row on the left, which probably said more about him as a person than anything else. At morning prayer he and Simeon sat in the front middle pew. Harriet sat at the front on the right, where the sun sparkled across the floor, when it deigned to make an appearance.

Anna breathed out, and then zipped her coat up, sipped her tea and breathed deeply again. She tried to suppress the thoughts of Tom and going away together so she could concentrate on the others, on the murder, on Gerald Denbigh. On Simeon, who was better but still not quite right. She was also a little concerned about Archie. Something in him was beginning to move. Something deep down inside was beginning to demand attention. Anna thought the heart attack had woken it up and now he'd have to deal with it. But she soon found herself praying for Tom again. When the door creaked, she was relieved to be able to turn around.

"Toby!"

"I'm looking for Genni. She said she'd be here."

"She's not appeared yet. Come in and wait here, if you like. Can I make you a cup of tea?"

"No, thank you," he said. Anna thought it had been an automatic response rather than a decision and that he'd rather be out in the churchyard. Rain began to spot the stones outside.

"I'm not disturbing you?" he said, coming a little further in.

"No, certainly not." He did look a little washed out, but then he always looked either pale or red-cheeked. Surely Genni could do better? Anna immediately felt bad, she'd just judged him on his outward appearance. That was unforgivable. "I was so very sorry to hear about your mum."

Toby sat down suddenly and shook his head.

"Dad wanted to keep it to ourselves, but I don't know how he thought we were going to do that."

"I love The Lizard, but sometimes it's like living in a fishbowl," she replied.

Toby nodded.

"All my life! I couldn't even misbehave when I was a kid, because someone always recognised me, they would tell my dad, and he would ..." Toby stopped, he straightened up, his eyes roving about, though he still managed to avoid looking at her. He'd sat where Harriet normally sat, so Anna was quite comfortable swivelling around to talk to him.

"You have a sister, don't you?" she asked.

"Sensibly married, living up near Bodmin. Some tiny village, where they keep chickens and ponies."

"Have you got some nephews and nieces?"

"Nieces. Three. She was always glad she didn't have a boy, was glad that Dad was a bit disappointed. And he doesn't like her husband, who's from London and has never been to sea."

"Like Caz, then?"

Toby stood up and shoved his hands in his pocket, and then, to Anna's surprise, he sat down again.

"She was a bitch. I couldn't make Genni see that. None of the others liked her. She was always causing trouble, getting Dad riled and of course, he'd take it out on the rest of us. She just wouldn't let stuff lie. Kept telling Dad that he was breaking this regulation, or that regulation. Before she came, it was better. Not great, but definitely better."

"What sort of stuff did she accuse your dad of doing?"

"Oh, you know, gender discrimination, favouring locals, making her work twice as hard as everyone else."

"And did he do those things?"

Toby looked across at her.

"Are you just going to tell that policeman all this?"

"No, Toby. I will not," she said, fiercely.

"I suppose he did do some of it. I think we'd kind of got used to how he was. And I'm talking as a crew member now, not as his son. As his son I never stood a chance. He may have had it in for Caz, but he never let up on me either, not for a second."

"Have you ever thought about getting away?"

"You mean like Mum?"

"Yes, I suppose, just like your mum."

He shook his head, as if dismissing the thought.

"I saw the note, she's not been murdered despite what the village is saying."

"It was definitely her handwriting?" Anna asked, suddenly feeling terribly sorry for this young man and a little shocked at the turn of the conversation. However she felt, with respect to Tom and the investigation, this boy had lived under the spotlight all his life and it must have made everything really hard.

"It was her handwriting," Toby replied angrily. "Not you as well. Even a couple of the lads asked me if it was really true. Asked me if I was sure that mum had actually gone. Had I heard from her, etc, etc. They had to get well-oiled up before they dared, of course."

"And have you heard from her?"

"No, I bloody haven't. What kind of mother leaves and doesn't let her son know where she is?"

He stood up again, as if he were about to storm out of the church.

"Have you checked with your sister?" Anna asked, a little desperately.

"Yes. She didn't know anything, or at least that's what she told me, and she doesn't usually lie to me."

Anna wondered how he might know that.

"Toby, I'm really sorry about your mum. It must have come as a terrible shock."

"And yet, not such a shock really. Looking back, she can't have been happy. Why didn't she ever fight back? She never stood up for herself."

"And do you?"

He sat down again, this time his head drooped, his eyes staring at the floor.

"No, I suppose I don't either. And I guess it means Genni and I now have to stay."

"Oh no, Toby. You're not responsible for him. If your mum can leave, so can you."

He shook his head. The door creaked, they both looked around. Genni saw Toby and came on in. She was wearing tight black jeans and a dark blue T-shirt, her hair was scraped back from her face as usual, but a single tendril of dark hair curled over her cheek. Anna thought again how exquisite she was. Then she chastised herself for once again judging someone by what they looked like. Anyway, it wasn't like that with Genni. She seemed completely unaware of her outward beauty. Toby didn't seem to realise it either.

"Any news?" Genni asked.

Toby shook his head and nodded towards Anna.

Genni jumped.

"I'm sorry, I didn't realise you were here, too."

"No, problem. We've just been chatting. It was good," she said to Toby. She wanted him to know that he could come and see her again, if he liked, but she didn't want to say so in front of Genni. "I'll leave you to it. Time together is precious."

Anna could hear their voices as she walked down the path. They were talking about Margery. She couldn't help but hear Genni say, "But your mum came and found me the day she left. She asked me to forgive her."

Anna hoped that God had his fingers in his ears, because Toby's reply was loud and the swear words he yelled poured into the churchyard with such anger and hurt, that she hesitated. She wondered if she ought to go back in, but then she could hear Genni's voice soothing and gentle, her words unintelligible from where Anna stood frozen. Perhaps those two were meant to be together, both of them having to stand alone, their parents seemingly with enough troubles of their own.

Anna did text Tom, to let him know that Margery had gone,

and had seemingly left no forwarding address. She didn't add anything else. Tom could do his own detective work on this one.

Chapter 25

Archie walked past the house for the third time. It was just after six in the evening. Phil had told him the rumours and Archie felt he should go and visit Jim, but each time he got level with the path that ran up past Jim's car, he swerved away and continued around the triangle of roads.

"What on earth is wrong with you?" he hissed to himself. A man was sitting inside that house, his wife had left him, he must be feeling absolutely terrible, and Archie couldn't get beyond the front drive. It was a matter of walking twenty feet.

"God, I need you to help me do the right thing."

He began his fourth run and as he did so, Toby drove in.

"Hi, Archie. Are you here to see Dad?"

Archie nodded.

"You're a brave man," Toby said, and led the way around the side. "Archie's here to see you," he yelled, as he opened the door. There was a tiny porch filled with shoes and a half glass door into the kitchen beyond. Jim was sitting facing them, a tin of beer on the table beside him. He looked up at the sound of Toby, but his focus didn't seem to clear. Archie hoped he hadn't been drinking long.

"Archie. What do you want?" Jim's voice sounded gravelly.

"I came to see how you are. Whether there was anything I could do."

Toby leant back against the sink. His eyes roved over the space that his father filled but Archie could see that Toby wasn't really looking. It was how Anna used to be, when her eyes skated across someone for fear of what she might find.

Toby turned to Archie and said, "I bumped into Anna today."

"You did?" Archie knew he sounded surprised, as if Toby had come across her popping out of the ground, somewhere.

"She was at church. I was meeting Genni," Toby said hurriedly, glancing at his dad. Archie felt a wave of annoyance, because people always had to excuse themselves for visiting a church, for anything other than historical interest.

"You were lucky," Archie said, "She's not in there as much as you would think."

That sounded terrible. Archie told himself to get a grip. He'd faced far worse things in his life. He'd pulled young men from the burning water. He'd held their hands while they wept or screamed in agony. He should be able to face Jim Andrews, even after his wife had left him. Archie sat down at the table, opposite him.

"May I?" he asked, a little belatedly.

"You may," Jim said, but his mouth was twisted, almost like a snarl. Archie was struggling to recognise the man at all.

"I want to tell you, that when you're ready, I'm here."

"That's good of you, Archie," Toby said, nodding. Archie couldn't quite get over the idea that he was enjoying this. "Anyway, I'm off to Genni's for tea."

"Are you managing to cook?" Archie asked Jim, relieved that Toby had gone. Hoping that the brief visit had been to check that his dad was alright.

"I'm not ill, Archie. Margery is just playing silly buggers."

Archie wanted it to be true. Wanted her to come back, so that Jim would stop being this terrifying man.

"Have you heard from her?"

"It's none of your business."

"Of course not, Jim. We're just worried, that's all."

He shouldn't have used the term 'we', it implied he'd talked about this with someone else. Apart from Phil telling him the news, Archie wouldn't dream of doing that.

"Worried about what, Archie? Worried about what?" Jim said, the anger rising. His hands were beginning to form fists on the table in front of him.

"That you're alright."

Jim laughed and took a long swig of beer.

"Well, if that will be all, perhaps you'll leave me to sort out my tea."

Archie stood up. There were dirty plates and cups piled high on the draining board, crumbs scattered across the work surface. The bin wouldn't shut properly, cartons and scraps spilling out. Archie shuddered. He couldn't live like this. After Moira had died, he'd gone quite the other way. Everything had become very clean and shiny. After every meal or cup of tea, he'd filled the sink and washed up his crockery and any cutlery, carefully drying them, before putting them away.

"You know where I am, Jim. Whatever you need."

Archie hurried out and gulped in a couple of good breaths of fresh air. He put his hand on his chest and willed away the tightness gathering there. Jim was a proud man, Archie knew that, a man who shouted and reacted. If truth be told, Archie didn't much like him, but that was unkind and was more about Archie than Jim.

Archie found himself standing outside his own house, having no recollection of the walk back. He let himself in. The house sighed and settled as he closed the door and pulled the curtain across. If someone came to call, he didn't want to see them before they rang the bell.

He wondered if Jim had realised that Margery was going to go. Had he known in advance? Surely she wouldn't have just left him, with no warning at all. That would have been cruel, though perhaps understandable. Archie had seen Jim angry, and it hadn't been rational. Archie liked rational, liked to understand why things were how they were.

He undid his coat. The weather was getting colder. Not pleasant at all. He was checking the pockets to make sure he didn't leave anything important in them when he was suddenly gripped by an awful dread. His heart hammered in his chest, and he could hardly turn around for fear that he would see her at the top of the stairs, or standing in the doorway of the kitchen, her arms crossed, waiting.

He pulled himself together, but he did need to talk to Anna

about Moira. About her death. God had been bringing him to this moment since he'd first met their gloriously flawed vicar and for quite a few months lately the shadow wouldn't entirely disappear. He knew it was time.

He rang Anna straightaway and asked to meet her the following day. He'd hoped that would mean that he could relegate the memories to the back of his mind, but they simply wouldn't be quiet. When the doorbell rang, he was still sitting in the front room in his coat staring at the empty fire and then he did something he'd never done before, ever. He peeped out of the window to see who it was. When he recognised Catherine, the relief was immediate.

"Come on in."

"You've just got back yourself. I can come another time."

"No, I've been home for ages. But it's cold. Aren't you finding it a bit chilly for this time of year?"

"Yes, I am."

"Let me light a fire. I always have one laid up because Simeon likes to be warm."

"If you're sure I'm not bothering you. This is teatime for a lot of people."

"Not for me. I'll have something later. Would you like a drink while we're waiting for the room to warm up."

"Archie, do you just mean tea or coffee?"

"What about a whiskey?"

"Perfect. Just a little one."

The fire caught almost immediately, the kindling bursting into a lively flame. He'd need more logs for next winter, but these were dry and seasoned, burning well. It made him feel better.

"You look thoughtful," she said, when he returned with the glasses and a jug of water.

"I suppose I am. A ghost has come back to haunt me."

"Can I help? I'm a good listener."

"You are but you're also carrying a lot of other people's

problems at the moment."

"Don't you worry about that. I know the more people you share with the better it gets. When Tom's dad left me, and then had the audacity to die, once the funeral was over, I went to each of my girlfriends and told them, one by one, everything. And I mean everything. It did me the world of good."

"I suppose Tom was too young."

"Yes, and sadly, I think perhaps that moment may have passed. I should have tried to tell him all about it, for his sake." She smiled, except her lips were pressed tightly together.

"Perhaps you'll get another opportunity. God isn't mean and he knows we're incredibly slow off the mark sometimes. How are you managing with Gerald?"

She sat back a little, took another sip of whiskey.

"I thought I was being so helpful, but I simply felt, feel used, which is incredibly mean, because of what he's going through."

"Me too when he came with me down to the lifeboat station. He looked so lost and then he changed, once he'd got his way, I suppose."

"Oh, Archie, I don't think it's that straightforward. I think he's all those things, lost, grieving, bewildered, angry, manipulative. We all are on some level to a greater or lesser extent."

She took another sip and Archie took his coat off. She was right and she would understand about Moira.

"So tell me about this ghost?"

Archie took a deep breath. The lump in his chest felt real and hard but it wasn't a heart attack waiting to grab him, this was an old sadness waiting to be brought out into the air, at last.

"Moira," he started, staring at the fire. Archie paused. He wanted to say this right. After a few seconds he tried again.

"I loved Moira, but we were hardly married five minutes

before I was away at sea. I so looked forward to coming home but somehow it was never quite as wonderful as I thought it should be. I didn't know how to be a good husband. We didn't seem able to talk about things without hurting each other." Archie was surprised at the flow of words, as if they had been waiting a long time to break surface. "She always tried so hard to be a good wife. The house was always spotless, my clothes ironed and neatly piled or hung up. I never saw her cleaning, but everything was just so. Gradually everything became more and more formal between us. Of course, I knew she liked to read, there were books everywhere but I'm now beginning to wonder if that was all she had. And when she died, I was so very…" Archie petered off.

"Cross, angry, bewildered, confused?"

Archie closed his eyes. For a moment he was back there, clearing out those books. She'd loved a good romance, he'd said to some distant relative, a little ashamed of her, now ashamed of his lack of understanding that they might have been all she had to fill the void of their own rather stilted marriage. He'd never been very good at sharing his feelings and it had been Moira who had suffered. No wonder she'd turned to food, no wonder she'd eaten herself to an early grave — a heart attack, which had been his fault. So when he'd faced his own mortality Moira had appeared like a real ghost, laughing. A heart attack, she had seemed to say, oh dear Archie, the irony of it.

Forgiveness and peace were what he needed, but as it turned out, he really didn't know where to begin.

***

Jim woke late, his head thumping. He'd not heard Toby leave, but then neither had he heard him come home the night before. He supposed he might have stayed over at Genni's. Jim rolled over. Her side of the bed was still neat, unruffled, her pillow smooth and cold. For a second, he wanted to bury his face in it, to breathe in her shampoo, her face cream, but the very thought of doing so horrified him. She wasn't dead, she'd left him. He had to keep reminding himself of that. He got up and went into the bathroom. He looked along the shelf. It didn't look like she'd taken much. He should clear more of her things out just in case someone got nosy. Her side of the wardrobe was still too full, as well. A couple of bin bags would do it.

Just now, he didn't want to have to argue with anyone and he knew there were rumours flying about. It was getting a bit complicated. Jim sighed. If the police came and accused him of murdering her, he might just go quietly.

There was no bread, and he couldn't face the shop. That woman had a way of asking a question that left you feeling scraped bare. Well, not today. He climbed into his car but instead of driving along the main road to the garage he found himself turning into Church Cove Lane. As he passed the entrance to the church, he saw the vicar standing under the gate arch. She looked undecided about where to go. He accelerated and lower down he sent the woman from the pub and her architect friend scurrying into a drive. She looked scared as she jumped out of his way. He was glad he'd managed to affect someone this morning.

Turning across the cattle grid, the familiar rumble slowed him down. There was no one in the car park for which he was grateful. The shop wouldn't open until later so he would have *Rose* to himself. It was what he needed. And while he was at it, he would clear out Caz's locker. The police had been through it, but they might not have known what they were looking for.

At the top of the steps, he checked both ways along the path. You couldn't see far, but he was still glad that no one was about. He had just reached the bottom when he heard the clang of someone coming down behind him. He groaned. So much for a quiet five minutes. He turned to check who it was and swore. It was Caz's dad. So he hadn't gone home, which was a pity.

Jim didn't go inside, which he could have done, locking the door behind him. Instead, he waited, arms folded, a glare on his face that would have brought the crew to silent stillness within moments.

Denbigh stopped about twenty feet up and put a hand out.

"I'm not here to cause trouble."

"What do you want?"

"Could I have her stuff, from her locker? The police are done with it. They'll have taken what they need."

"No, you can't. Not yet. There are procedures we have to follow."

Jim expected somewhere there'd be a regulation covering the removal of a dead colleague's property. Anyway, at some point they'd need the space for the next recruit. Hopefully a bloke. Jim wasn't prejudiced, ask any of them, but he needed someone familiar to whip into shape. Someone local, who wouldn't talk back, question the way he did things, argue the toss every bloody time. She'd been so irritating.

"I'm going home to sort things out for a couple of weeks. Have a bit of space from this place. I'd like to take them with me."

"When are you leaving?"

"Saturday morning."

"Are you still at the pub?" The man nodded. "I'll drop them off there in the next couple of days. I won't break regulations." Not for you, he thought. "I'll need to do the paperwork," Jim added.

Caz's dad laughed.

"It's funny, you don't strike me as the sort of bloke who needs to play by the rules."

"You don't know me. You don't know anything about me." Jim willed him to come a little further down. He wouldn't need much of an excuse for thumping him. And it would feel so good.

"I know your wife has supposedly left you. If it was me, I'd be checking out where she was, just in case she was stuffed somewhere the birds could strip her back to the bone."

"You don't know what you're talking about." But that finished it for Jim. He would definitely slip back and clear out a bit more of Margery's stuff. Make it look more obvious. How could she still be causing so much trouble? She and Caz refused to go away, even though they'd both gone away,

Denbigh stepped down one more step, quite deliberately. They both jumped at the clatter of feet from above. It was like Piccadilly Circus. Jim was surprised to see the vicar hurrying towards them. Very out of breath she slipped past Denbigh and stood between the men. Jim almost laughed out loud. What did she think she was going to do?

"Now, Reverend, there's no need to worry. We were just having a chat," Denbigh said, though he couldn't entirely keep the sarcasm out of his voice. Jim wasn't having any of it.

"Anna, I've asked him to leave. He just wants to make trouble again." Jim folded his arms.

She was looking very pink, and her hair kept blowing across her face. She repeatedly pulled it behind her ears, to no avail. She turned around to look up at Denbigh.

"I'm so sorry, but perhaps it would be better if you left."

"I came to get her stuff. He won't give it to me. Ask yourself why not? It's just the things from her locker."

"I said I'd take them to the pub, but I'm not having him in my boat house." Jim stepped forward, just to make himself clear.

"You'd love to, wouldn't you? I may be retired, but I'm a copper and I know how to deal with slobs like you."

"Stop it, both of you. Mr Denbigh, go home. Now! And Jim, just go inside and do whatever it was you came down to do."

"You could always phone the boyfriend," Denbigh said, quietly.

Jim didn't want that. He glowered but backed off. He turned and quickly entered the code, carefully watching the man's reflection in the door. Denbigh was smiling, perhaps triumphantly, but when the vicar turned back to look up at him, his face changed to one of sadness. He was an actor, that was for sure.

Jim dropped the catch so that no one could follow him in. He found he was breathing a little heavily but that would soon settle down. He watched Anna and Denbigh exchange a few words and then they both headed back up to the path above. He watched them until they were out of sight.

He very carefully took the pile of books from Caz's locker. He went through each of them, shook them out, just in case. At the back of the book of regulations, on a blank page, was a list of dates. Jim didn't need a calendar to check what they were. He carefully tore the page out and put it in his pocket. He couldn't find anything else. There were packs of tissues, a couple of notebooks that were full of stuff about *Rose*, and a magazine, all about weddings. Jim couldn't quite believe there were a whole fifty pages dedicated to the special day. Things had certainly changed a lot since he and Margery had got married. Caz was probably going to give it to Genni. Well, Denbigh wouldn't want it, so Jim put it on the pile that he wasn't taking to the pub.

Driving back up the lane he almost got past the vicarage, except he felt he ought to check that the stupid woman was alright. Denbigh was a troublemaker, and it wouldn't do any harm to find out what lies he'd fed her. Jim felt he needed to keep her on side as much as possible. She was, after all, good friends with the policeman.

"Jim, come on in."

"Is it safe?"

"Do you mean, is Mr Denbigh here? No, he left a while ago."

"I know he's lost his daughter and all that, but he's really making life difficult for everyone."

"Sit there a minute, and I'll get some coffee."

She disappeared down the corridor. The room was still big

and cold, devoid of anything personal. The fireplace swept clean, on the mantelpiece a wooden cross, on the coffee table a pile of Bibles. Jim sat down on the lumpy sofa. He closed his eyes. Surprisingly, he felt he could've dropped off. He'd been up quite late the night before, had drunk more than usual for a weekday and he hadn't slept well. He ought to have phoned the garage to let them know he'd be in later, but he expected they'd have worked something out by now.

"You look tired," she said.

"I'm fine."

"Your wife has gone. You can't be fine."

For a moment he felt his anger swell and then it sort of popped. She was right.

"It has been a bit difficult."

She handed him a cup, offered sugar. He took it and gave himself an extra spoonful.

"You've been through the mill. I expect you're exhausted. Have you heard from her?"

"You know it's none of your business," he replied, but he couldn't seem to find the energy to fuel his temper.

"Of course it isn't. But talking really does help and I'm honour bound to keep it confidential."

For a second Jim was tempted. He wondered what it would feel like to tell her what had happened over the last few months. Give her his side of the story.

"There's nothing I've got to say that would need to be kept confidential. Now, why would you think there was?"

There it was again, that fleeting look of fear. To be fair, she seemed to get a grip quite quickly, taking a gulp of coffee.

"Well, if not me, then Archie. He's a good man in a crisis."

"But I'm not in a crisis."

"Ok, Jim. It is none of our business and you're managing to hold it together really well."

"Are you being sarcastic?"

"No, well, perhaps a little." She smiled as if everything was now okay. Jim wanted that to be true, but it wasn't and the feeling of wanting to hit someone was beginning to grow again. He carefully put his cup down.

"Did you get all of Caz's things for Mr Denbigh?"

"There wasn't much. A change of clothes and some books she was using to work towards her next test."

"Genni said she was really eager to go out on a shout. That she was working hard."

"She would've been alright, in the end, though she was like her dad, a real troublemaker."

"Was she? What sort of trouble?"

Jim shook his head.

"Lifeboat business."

"And so not mine," Anna said, and looked out of one of the large windows. It rattled a little as the wind blustered past.

Jim stood up. He needed to go.

"Don't forget I'm still around if anyone else needs to talk," she said, moving past him to open the front door. He stepped down onto the drive, then turned back, feeling the gravel swivel under his feet.

"No one needs to talk. We need to get on. Forget what's happened." She tipped her head to one side as if she expected him to say something else. He stepped towards her, and still she didn't flinch or move back. For a second, she reminded him of Caz and that insolent look of hers.

"Stay out of it, Reverend. The guys don't need a soft-soppy-shoulder, they need to man up and get on with it."

"Even Genni?"

"Just stop poking your nose in places where it isn't wanted or needed. Back off." He knew he'd begun to shout; he knew he was trying to intimidate her. She flushed and then blanched, the colour draining from her cheeks, but she didn't back down. She should have backed down. He leant forward just to push her a little. As he did so, she began to slam the door. He stumbled forward. Off balance he couldn't get out of the way, and she must have been stronger than she looked because the bottom of the door smashed against his foot. He yelled in pain and rage.

"What've you done?" he cried out, hopping backwards.

She re-opened the door, immediately, her phone to her ear.

"Who are you calling?" he shouted. He wanted her to do what he wanted , by sheer force of will. She wouldn't. If he could just get hold of her for half a second, he'd put the fear of God into her. Then he began to laugh. Put the fear of God into her! She was a vicar, and he was trying to frighten her with God. What the hell did he think he was doing? He leant against the wall.

"Jim, sit down on the step. I've phoned for some help."

He managed to hop closer but still couldn't help groaning as he lowered himself down.

The architect, Derek, and his partner, Harriet, appeared. They'd obviously run up from their new house. Anna went out to them, carefully stepping around him.

"I got frightened, and I tried to shut the door, which caught Jim's foot and I think I've really hurt him."

Jim put his head in his hands and wondered if life could get any worse. His pager began to vibrate in his pocket. He reared up, ready to run but couldn't put any weight on the rapidly swelling foot. There was a yacht with a cracked mast past the twelve-mile limit and he began to cry. Tears ran down his face and there seemed nothing he could do to stop them. He frowned. What was happening? What had the stupid woman done to him? Faintly, in the distance, rapidly getting closer, he began to hear the roar of cars heading down the lane.

Chapter 26

Tom deliberately slowed right down as he turned off the main road. He was so agitated he thought he probably shouldn't be behind the wheel, which was ridiculous as he'd driven to emergencies a thousand times, and not once had he panicked like this. Smith had phoned him to say that Anna seemed to have broken Jim Andrews's foot, that the man would have to go to hospital, that it had been her friend who'd phoned it in.

Tom had been on his way back from a meeting with his boss and when he'd switched his phone off silent there were so many missed calls and texts he'd run straight out to his car. It was bound to have been an accident, but it might complicate matters. Jim was a man who loomed large in the community, even if his wife had disappeared without a trace. The so-called lover didn't seem to have existed so if she had run off with someone then she'd managed to keep it incredibly quiet. Tom couldn't quite believe that, not around here. He'd got both Smith and Kellow trying to find her. He'd given them two days. Any longer and the Boss would really want to check out the time sheets.

He swung onto the drive scattering gravel into the hedge — so not going as slowly as he'd thought. Before he could climb out Anna was already standing beside the car.

"You didn't need to come," she said, a little breathlessly.

"Well, I'm here now. Are you alright? What happened?"

She sighed.

"I know what you're going to think. And I know you're going to be cross."

"Anna, what happened?"

She turned around and led him into the vicarage, the back door still open from where she'd run out to meet him.

Harriet was in the kitchen. She was piling sandwiches onto a plate. Derek was nowhere to be seen. Harriet nodded to Tom, before kissing Anna on the cheek. She said, as she moved towards the door, "Tom will need to hear all of it." She even patted him on the arm as she passed. He was grateful that she wasn't going to hang around, so he didn't even wait for her to shut the door before turning to Anna.

"Pour me coffee and tell me everything."

Anna bit her lip repeatedly and it looked quite sore by the time she got to the part where she'd slammed the front door. The foot was obviously broken, and he was off to hospital to have it X-rayed. Anna had offered to take him, but Harriet and Derek had persuaded her that an ambulance would be better. The pager going off had proved one step too far for Jim and neither Harriet nor Derek thought he was behaving rationally.

"Oh, Tom, he cried because he couldn't go out on the lifeboat. He was so upset." Her eyes filled with tears.

"What did he say?"

"He just kept repeating over and over, what have I done?"

"He was admitting it was his fault?"

"I think he lost his balance and slipped. Though I was quite scared," she said, looking down at the table. "I was trying to slam the door, but looking back on it, he was just angry about his wife and Caz. It's been horribly difficult for him. Tom, I heard the bones crunch. It was awful."

"What did he want? Why was he here?"

She began to bite her lip once more, began to twist her fingers around and around. She was staring down at the table. He gently leaned forward and put his hand on top of hers. She stopped and looked up, barely able to hold his gaze.

"Um, earlier he had a bit of a do with Gerald Denbigh. At the bottom of the steps at the lifeboat station. I went down to make sure they didn't end up hitting each other."

Tom put his face in his hands.

"What were you expecting to do?" he said, his voice muffled.

"I just thought, if I was there, they'd be less likely to do anything silly."

He straightened up. "You stepped between Jim and Gerald. Two men, well over six feet tall, both with anger management issues. And you did this to stop them hurting each other?"

"It worked."

"Then Jim turned up to what... finish the job?"

"What job? Finish what?"

"Anna, you drive me mad. It's when you do things like this that I don't know what to do. I feel quite powerless, and I'm a DI. What if something had happened to you? What if one of them had hit you, or pushed you? I'm scared, really scared. I'm a police officer, with years of experience, but you terrify me."

"It's just as bad for me," she said, angrily. "What you see, what you have to deal with day by day. When you walk into an incident, when you give chase or have to knock someone to the ground to handcuff them, isn't it the same?"

He laughed, though he felt like crying.

"No, it's not the same. This is what I do. You're not trained, you're not large, most of the time you don't even realise the danger you're in. You always think the best of everyone when you should be terrified. You should be running away, not stepping forward."

"But I did try and run away today and look what happened. I broke Jim's foot. And he wept in front of me." Once again, her face fell, and he reached forward and grasped both her hands.

"It will have dented his pride, that's all."

"I don't think he'll ever want to have anything more to do with me."

"That makes you sad, but it makes me feel really happy. Anna, I can't be here all the time."

"Of course not. I wouldn't expect you to be."

"But who's going to protect you?"

"I don't need protecting. This is what I do, and I do try to see the best in people because mostly no one else does. That's important and I know I won't be able to change anything much by doing that, but God can. I have to believe that, that my life, my calling, is making a difference." She scraped a tissue across her eyes and looked defiantly at him.

Tom drank some coffee, which he assumed Harriet had left for him and even thought about taking a bite of a sandwich, because he needed time to think.

"You do make a difference. You do to me. If we were married, at least I'd be around."

"I don't want to marry you because you think it will keep me safe," she said.

"What's wrong with that?"

Tom kicked himself, this wasn't how he'd planned it. He'd wanted them to be away from here, wanted to make it special, get a ring, buy champagne.

Anna looked a little flushed and her eyes were getting bigger by the minute.

"I want to marry you," he said, "because I want to be with you at the beginning and the end of every day. But I wanted to ask you when all this was over. And now something really special is all muddled up with a murder investigation. It's not how I wanted it to be. It's not how it should be."

She laughed and shook her head.

"It was always going to be like this. And I'm still really upset with you." She narrowed her eyes, but couldn't keep it up, instead she leaned forward and grasped his hands. "I thought I'd be totally scared and wouldn't know what to say, but you're right, I want to start and end the day with you, too. Make this barn of a house into a home."

Tom swallowed a large lump of bread he'd torn from the sandwich. He nearly choked.

"Did you just say yes?"

"Wasn't I supposed to? Were you expecting me to say no or at least to ask for some thinking time?"

"Yes, no! Oh, for goodness sake. Anna, we've just got engaged. I should have got a ring or something. I should have …"

She smiled. Her eyes crinkling and her cheeks glowing pink. She tucked a piece of hair behind her ear and picked up a sandwich. She looked at it as if she'd never seen one before and then she put it down again.

"I don't know what to do now," she said.

"Neither do I." Then his phone rang. It was Kellow.

"I have to go. I'll pop back and see Jim another day. Promise me you won't get involved in any more fights."

"No, I won't promise that."

"Of course you won't. You're changing me, but why can't I change you?"

"Because I am already just how you like me."

Tom looked across at her a little taken aback. Even Anna looked slightly surprised at what she'd said, but in a way she was right. She would still probably have a panic once he'd gone, have to run down to Harriet to talk it through. She would still, no doubt, get cold feet, any number of times and no doubt interfere in the case when she had a moment. Climbing into his car he shook his head and then he smiled, a big wide grin, which he couldn't help. She'd said yes, at least for now.

***

The lifeboat had gone out twice since Jim had hurt his foot. On the second shout he'd insisted that Toby pick him up and take him down, which meant that Toby had been too late to make up the crew and he'd missed an afternoon of work for nothing. Genni had made it worse by waving forlornly from the foredeck. They wouldn't be out for long, as it was just a man on the cliff a couple of miles down the coast. He'd gone after his dog and got stuck but he wasn't in any danger, he just couldn't manage the climb back up. The coastguard had decided that *Rose* had the best chance of pulling him off with minimum fuss. It was the sort of job Toby hated but he would still rather have been out on the boat than sitting with his dad and the shore crew. He went and made a cup of tea. Jim had managed to get down to the lower deck where the others had found him a seat.

Well, if his dad was down there Toby would go and find a space up top. Archie was looking after the shop so there was no possibility of being talked to unless Toby wanted a conversation.

Archie nodded but true to form, when Toby walked down to the far end and leaned over the railing with his cup. Archie remained reading behind the counter. Toby couldn't see the others, the waiting guys, the shore crew, as they were tucked out of the wind. He could hear his dad waxing lyrical about the sea conditions, and how close they'd be able to take *Rose* safely, and from which side to launch the Y Boat. Honestly, Toby had never realised how grating his father's voice was. He straightened up. Without *Rose* sitting on her rollers, and with the main door open to the waves, the space felt huge. Too big, the roof too far away.

Toby shivered. He didn't want to be here, didn't want to be part of this anymore. He needed to leave, like his mum, and he wasn't sure that Genni needed to come with him. Since Caz, everything had changed. Perhaps this was the wake-up call, the kick up the bum that would prevent everything else from spiralling even further downwards. He tried to imagine the ceremony, Genni standing beside him, but he couldn't. There was a blank space in the aisle, and he didn't want to get married without his mum sitting there, mellowing his dad, helping it be about Toby rather than all about Jim.

Toby was still monstrously hurt that she'd obviously tried to tell Genni and not him that she was going, but he supposed Genni had been easier because she was one step removed. His mum wouldn't have been able to face him because she loved him, and it would have been too difficult. Genni was easy to talk to, was usually easy to be with. Perhaps she *should* stay. She was meant to be part of the crew; she was meant to teach in the tiny school. She'd probably end up being the headmistress one day. She might even begin standing up for herself. And one evening a tourist would see her in the pub and ask for her number, because she was so beautiful. If he wasn't here, he could maybe forget bloody, bloody Caz, standing there, laughing at him. Telling him how he'd got it all wrong about Genni. How bent out of shape his father was, and asking why Toby hadn't the balls to fight back now and again? Toby shivered and walked back to Archie.

"Hello, Toby. Sorry you didn't make it in time to go out."

"It's no biggie. It's quite nice actually. I'm not a natural like Dad and Genni."

"I didn't always find it easy."

"I thought you were acting coxswain."

"Three times."

"Was it tough?"

"The worst one was when we were looking for a man in the water. I kept the boat out far longer than I should have, just in case. The crew really grumbled."

"We do that. Grumbling is par for the course. Did you find him?"

"No. There was never any news one way or the other."

"And you were waiting for a body to come ashore," Toby said.

Archie nodded. His face muscles tight with the memory.

"Which would have meant that I'd missed him."

"Sometimes the sea doesn't give them back," Toby added. Archie nodded. Toby continued, "And needle in a haystack doesn't do it justice."

"I don't think most people realise that a little head bobbing about in a swell is nearly impossible to find."

"Is that why you retired?" asked Toby.

"No, I'd have gone on, but I'd promised Moira a good retirement, and living with a pager wasn't ever easy."

"And you'd never break a promise, would you, Archie?"

"I would try with every fibre of my being to keep it."

"I'm going to make another cup of tea. Would you like

one?"

"Yes, that would be nice. I don't like leaving my post in the Summer. We can make good money at this time of year."

Toby looked up the steps. They hadn't had a single visitor, but Archie had a point. Sometimes they did sell a lot of stuff which all added to the coffers. He walked across to the kitchen. He should really have gone down and asked if anyone else wanted a drink, but he couldn't be bothered taking orders. He was also sure it would involve washing up cups.

Caz had said they should get a dishwasher, which they could put on at the end of every shout. It had been a good idea, but Jim had said it was a waste of money when there was a perfectly good sink. Jim hadn't done a day's washing up in his life. The night before, when Toby had finally got home, there wasn't a single clean plate left. Toby had spent an hour tidying everything up, boiling kettles for hot water because his dad had forgotten to put on the immersion heater. It was like living with a rather disgusting teenager.

"What have you sold this morning?"

Archie had managed a couple of colouring books to a family who really wanted to be down on a beach somewhere.

"I know it's not much, but if the tourists have a good experience, they might make a donation when someone next calls at their door."

"You're a good man, Archie," Toby said.

"None of us are as good as people think we are." Archie looked down at his shoes.

"That's true. If people knew more about me, Genni would certainly never look at me again."

"She's a lovely young woman."

"She's too good for me."

Archie didn't seem to know what to say. Toby would have liked him to have said that it wasn't true, but everyone could see that they didn't match, not really.

"You were married. What was it like?" Archie looked away;

he seemed disconcerted by the question. "I'm sorry, I shouldn't have asked."

Archie shook his head and took a deep breath.

"The thing is, Toby, my marriage wasn't that great. I can see looking back, we weren't terribly honest with each other. We let things slip and slide. She read a lot, I walked and crewed and we never got a chance to sort things out because she died. I'd only been about the place for a month when she keeled over." Toby could see that it was a tough memory, but it must have been years before, because Archie hadn't been on the lifeboat in decades.

"So, do you think I ought to marry Genni? Do you think any couple can be alright? Up front and honest enough to make a go of it?"

"Harriet and Derek seem quite happy."

Toby smiled, because as far as he was aware, that pair weren't married at all. The rumour was that everything would go to the daughter if Derek married again.

A family came in and walked around excitedly. There was a change in atmosphere and one of the small boys began pointing out to sea, hopping from foot to foot. *Rose* was on her way back.

"I'd best go down and help out. Or at least help them keep Dad out of harm's way."

"I hope I haven't put you off marriage. I'm sure it's a good thing, really."

Toby lifted a hand and walked away. He didn't need to see the look on Archie's face to know that Archie wished he'd kept his mouth shut.

Chapter 27

Genni was surprisingly cold. She'd gone out on the Y Boat to help the man and his dog, who'd waved gaily, as if he were meeting friends. He didn't seem one bit ashamed that he'd called them out. She thought he was rather enjoying being the centre of attention. It had made everyone feel grumpy and tense. The dog was a rather silly fox terrier who was terrified. It squashed against its owner's legs and shivered. She'd given it a bowl of water, but it didn't even sniff it. When the man asked for a selfie with her, she just ignored him and went up into the wheelhouse. Knew she wouldn't have dreamt of doing that if Jim had been in charge.

They'd been out for close on an hour. When they began to haul *Rose* back up the ramp, she couldn't see Toby in the boat house, but Jim was there, his foot up on a chair. Genni still wasn't sure what'd happened to his foot, but she knew it had happened at the vicarage. She'd already heard three different versions, but Jim wasn't saying a word.

They tidied up, hosed *Rose* down and when at last they were ready to go, Toby sidled up to her as if he were ashamed of them. For a moment she felt the stupidity of it, the hurt welling up. Everyone knew they were getting married, who did he think he was keeping it from? And they still had to put up with the teasing whatever he did. She squared up to him, he took a step back, she stooped, out of habit really, so that at least for a second or two they were on the same level.

"I've got to take dad up to the house," he said.

"Will you go back to work after?"

"No point. We could get together. I don't want to stay with him."

"Is he managing with his foot and everything?"

"He can. Better than he lets on. And I did wash up last night. Took me an hour."

"What about food?"

"I don't know. He can walk on it, and the shop isn't that far."

"Yes, but he's managing on a crutch, how can he carry stuff?"

"He hardly ever uses the crutch at home." Toby rolled his eyes. "Are you saying I should offer to do some shopping for him?"

Suddenly Genni didn't care one way or the other.

"Please yourself, Toby."

Toby's eyes widened and he took another step back.

"What's the matter with you?"

"I guess I just don't want to get caught between you and your dad."

"You won't. Don't you worry."

He walked over to Jim, just beginning to heave himself to his feet. Genni picked up her bag and headed up the steps taking them two at a time so that at the top her calves were burning, and she could hardly breathe.

Quite a few of the lads were still in the car park, leaning against their cars, chatting. None of them wanted to go back to work, though a few of them could have, quite easily. She couldn't face them and so turned abruptly right onto the coastal path running down into Church Cove. She stopped at the top overlooking the rugged, steep ramp. All the holiday cottages were full, and the tiny beach was dotted with colour. People sitting on blankets, cagoules zipped to their chins, knees up to their chests. It wasn't the right sort of day for sitting on the gritty stones. She made her way down into the lane.

"Hello, Genni." It was Anna. She wore a coat, but as a sop to July she hadn't done it up, she looked as if she was waiting for her to come down off the path. "You've been out, I heard the cars."

"Not a difficult rescue. Some ungrateful man who thought we were there for his entertainment."

"I suppose some people don't realise you're all volunteers."

"He was just a prat."

Genni straightened up; Anna wouldn't mind how tall she was. As if to prove Genni right Anna suddenly smiled.

"I'm walking out to the bench at the end of the promontory. Just there," she said pointing to the other side of the cove. "Come with me."

For a second Genni thought about refusing. Wondered if Toby would be looking for her. Then she thought, why not, this woman at least listens to me, and she'd known Caz, if only for a short while.

"That would be nice. Though I can't stay long."

"I know you've plenty of things to do."

Not really, thought Genni.

There was no one on the Point. The cove below was also emptying. Families finally giving up on the idea of sun, sea and sand. There was sea, but not a lot of either of the other two, rocks and fine shingle only. The clouds were light grey, a fluffy patchwork without a break but for a line of light far out at sea where the sun was breaking through, individual rays like spotlights in a row.

"Even on a day like today it's lovely."

"I'm still a bit cold," Genni replied, putting her hands in her pockets and hunching up.

"Poor Genni. Are you still missing Caz? Sorry, that was entirely stupid. Of course you're still missing her. Not something you can or should switch off. It will take however long it takes."

Genni felt a spike of anger and then it evaporated away to pity.

"I wish I could just switch it off. I wish I could draw a line under that day. Start fresh, begin again."

Anna was silent and Genni wished she would say something. At last Anna spoke.

"What would you change?"

Genni looked around at the woman sitting beside her. Not classically attractive, but there was something about the way she listened. Not that being attractive meant anything. People were entirely wrong if they based their lives on that premise. Anna had pale eyebrows but dark grey eyes that had a way of holding your gaze even when you really wanted to look away.

"I would find out what happened to my dad."

"That sounds like something you could do now?"

"Before it didn't feel important enough, but recently, I realised there is nothing to stop me. I've got an appointment with the records office."

"I asked Tom about unclaimed bodies," Anna said, quietly, "and he said there were more than you think, but the police do keep whatever they found on them, so perhaps if you discovered someone who disappeared on the right day your mum could see if she recognised any of their last effects, like a watch or something." Anna nodded encouragingly. "I could come with you, if you think it would help."

"There's no need. I'll manage, though it could take a while trawling through the old records. The year I'm looking at hasn't been digitised yet."

"Well, let me know what you find out. Having a sense of who you are will make more things fit."

"Who are you? How do you fit?" Genni asked.

"Beloved of God," Anna replied, as if she was asked this question all the time. "I know it sounds corny and a bit weird, but I believe God loves me. That's where I jump from. And the older I get the surer I am of it."

"And the policeman loves you."

"He does. Which is a complication for me, on so many levels, telling Archie for one. But I'm still going to marry him."

Genni thought she ought to feel something about that, but she just felt numb.

"Good. Do you think I should still marry Toby?"

"I think that's something you need to talk over with him,

but I do think Caz's disappearance has shone a light onto all sorts of things you can't let lie now."

"Yes," Genni replied. That was exactly how it felt. How odd that she hadn't seen it like that before. "Caz was like a hand grenade that someone had pulled the pin out of. I was simply waiting for the explosion. She danced on the edge of everything. Made it all sound so simple and straightforward, but it wasn't, not for me."

"Did you two have a row just before she died?"

Genni stopped breathing for a moment and then had to take a large breath to catch up. She couldn't draw enough in. She coughed.

"How did you know?"

"It was in the car park, wasn't it? Simeon heard it. Two women yelling at each other."

"I suppose it was quite public."

"What was it about? And shouldn't you have been in school?"

And for a delicious moment Genni thought she could tell this woman everything. How wonderful it would be to come clean.

"We were doing this Save the Planet Day, so that the whole school was together. We had to take it in turns to have lunch because it was a bit full on. Mine was later than usual, that's all. Caz and I had already arranged to eat our sandwiches together out on the cliffs, even though we were meeting after school to revise, only she started doing her usual. Needling me, asking questions, wanting answers to things I needed time to think about. For once I yelled back."

Anna turned to look out to sea.

She said, "Did you love her?"

"Yes, but not like she loved me. I couldn't give her what she wanted but I found myself making excuses all the time to be with her. I guess she was the sort of person who took a run at life in a way I never had. It was exciting."

Parts of it had been, but Caz had spent a lot of time pointing out all the bits that Genni skated over. Had not wanted to look at. "She hated the fact that I kept my head down. Kept asking and asking, what I wanted? And then when I tried to tell her, she would call me a liar, or told me to dig deeper. What on earth did she see in me? Anyway, she soon found out." Genni felt the tears, deep down. She swallowed and looked up. "I would give anything to start again. Start my life over with a mum who fought for me rather than telling me to not make waves. A boyfriend who thought I was beautiful and worth bragging about. A dad who thought I was worth coming home to."

"What happened after the row?"

"She roared off in her car, but she came back later. I nearly gave up on her that time. Thought she wouldn't come back after a fight like that. But she did. We ended up laughing and joking around. I was so relieved."

"Oh, Genni, don't marry Toby, at least not for the minute. Take a breather, take a moment. There's no hurry. Find out what happened to your dad. He might not simply have left you. And stand tall. You're so lovely, and I know that's not really important, but I think if you were able to see that, you might be able to see other good things about yourself, too."

Genni felt those blessed tears welling up, but she didn't want to cry. She knew feeling this vulnerable was dangerous. Anna couldn't wave a magic wand and make it all go away, but Genni would ring the record office and confirm the appointment. Do a bit of detective work. And perhaps once she got to Falmouth, she'd just keep going and never come back.

"I've got to go. I need to find Toby. I was a bit mean to him earlier."

Anna nodded.

"I'll stay a bit longer. And Genni, come and speak to me, any time you want."

Anna always said things like that. Genni supposed that

being a vicar was more than a job, more than nine to five, at least. Still she couldn't quite get away from the idea that, like Caz, Anna expected more from her than Genni could give.

***

Anna sat for a long time out on the promontory. She was trying to pray but each time she tried, she ended up going over and over the events of the last few months. So much had happened but people were doing things because they were driven by what was going on inside them, what had been done to them. She knew it wasn't her job to change them — Toby, Genni, Jim or even Archie and Simeon, that had to be God. Yet sometimes she felt just like an irritation. Scratching away at the surface of other people's lives, a bit like a rash. Apart from Tom. He'd asked her to marry him. She'd said yes but wasn't sure why she wasn't telling everyone. Not even Harriet. Anna tried to imagine that moment, but she couldn't and yet, telling Genni had seemed the most natural thing in the world.

At the edge of all this, out of the corner of her mind's eye, all she could see was some monstrous figure strangling Caz. Standing behind her and pulling the rope tight. Sometimes it was clearly Jim, for he was a bully, but often it turned into Gerald Denbigh. He was another man who frightened Anna. Standing between them had been stupid, but as with most things she did, she hadn't really thought about it until it was over. She'd been more worried about falling down the steps or what Tom would say, rather than getting thumped.

Gerald was going home for a couple of weeks, but that meant he'd be coming back. Tom had said that by then they'd have to allow him to stay at Caz's house. Denbigh had produced an old text conversation from his daughter about letting him have a key when next they met, something that Tom couldn't ignore. He hadn't liked it, mainly because he didn't trust the man.

Anna realised she was chewing her lip again. She felt so guilty about Jim's foot, felt guilty about seeing him cry and knew that she ought to go and see him. A pastoral visit. Except, what if that simply reminded him of what she'd done? Could he press charges? Make a real fuss? What would the Bishop say? Would she be suspended from her duties? That made Anna shiver, helped by the fact that she'd been sitting too long. The cove was nearly empty of stalwart visitors, towels were hanging over the railings of a couple of the houses and there was the smell of barbecuing. She realised that she was hungry.

"I'm worried about everything, and everyone apart from marrying Tom, which is the one thing I thought would send me into the stratosphere. God, you always manage to turn things upside down and I always get it wrong. But please don't let me annoy anyone so much that they try and push me over a cliff or cause Archie to have another heart attack. And please, help me to find the right moment to tell Archie, Simeon and Harriet about Tom."

Archie had spent a few minutes with her that afternoon, all business-like and well-rehearsed. She'd listened, trying not to look too shocked. There was another layer to him, another level of humanity which had been grinding away for quite a while. His marriage hadn't been all that it should have been, which made him worried for her and Tom. Which made her realise, that that was not the moment to tell him of her engagement. She had wanted to tell Archie not to worry, that she was sure his marriage hadn't been that bad, but he was all pulled out of shape by his memories, and so she was going to treat it seriously. Archie's regrets were deeply rooted, longstanding, and the heart attack had highlighted for him the areas he had kept God clear of. No wonder he was struggling with Simeon, and his faith.

***

Harriet paused with the dishwasher door half open.

"Have you got the fire ready, in the lounge?"

"Yes, but I'll stack a few more logs. He likes to be warm."

Harriet nodded and began to put the jams away.

"I'm glad you asked him. He did come with the others for dinner, but he's not been here since."

"I don't think Simeon just calls in on people," Derek said. "But then, neither do I."

"You've been a bit busy, and Simeon does drop in on Anna and Archie all the time."

"That's true."

"I'm looking forward to seeing Belle," Harriet said.

"So definitely time to go and look for a new pooch?" Derek said, swinging around to look at her. She moved across from the sink and hugged him.

"The house is nearly done, we could at least go and let them know what we're looking for."

Derek began to make coffee.

"I can't see beyond another Dolly. She was such a good dog."

"Perhaps we'll just know, when we see her."

"I guess. I don't want one as old as Belle though. I can't face losing another friend quite so quickly."

"I agree. And a young dog is trainable."

Harriet remembered some of Dolly's less endearing qualities towards the end. She sat down opposite him. She'd thought he would go dashing off to do a bit of painting or rearranging, but she supposed he was right, a lot of it was finally done. Harriet looked around their kitchen. It wasn't large but it suited them, and she was really beginning to get the hang of the space.

"I'd like to try and bake something today."

"Do you have anything in mind?" Derek asked, a little too quickly, which made her giggle, a sound that surprised her.

"What do you have in mind?"

"Now that September is nearly here, I would like one of your sticky apple cakes. It's one of the first things I remember about you."

"It's still only July! What did you first notice?"

"It had been misery upon misery. And then that awful woman kept barging in whenever you appeared, spoiling everything, until one day down at the vicarage I was talking to Anna, and you brought through an apple cake, and we sat and ate it together. I had two pieces and felt full for the first time in months."

"I don't remember that at all."

"You and Anna chatted away as if I wasn't there."

"Oh, Derek, I'm so sorry."

"No, it was wonderful. For a change no one was walking on eggshells around me. I was really grateful. I may even have dropped off for a moment or two."

Harriet nodded slowly. She did vaguely remember an afternoon like that, but it seemed a very long time ago now.

"I'm sorry you had to lose Fiona like that."

"Me too, but it meant I met you and sometimes I feel guilty about how happy that's made me."

"Silly man!" she said. "We are none of us that straightforward that we can step away from our past without baggage. You never have to forget how long you were married to Fiona." She stood up. "Apple cake it is."

***

Simeon rang the bell at precisely ten-thirty, and Harriet led him straight through to the front room, and then dropped down to hug Belle.

"I hope it's not too red for you," she said, looking at the far wall.

"It's fine."

Derek smiled. As Harriet went to fetch the tray, she could hear the two of them already talking about the merits of post-modern architecture. They probably hadn't even bothered with hello.

She had to wait quite a while for a lull in the conversation before she was able to ask Simeon how he was.

"I'm feeling less anxious, but I'm still worried about Archie."

"Is it his health?"

"A little bit, but I also think there's something else, though I feel it's not the right moment to ask him about it. I don't want him to think that every time I see him there will be something he needs to reassure me about."

Derek nodded, as if he knew all about that, which made Harriet wonder for a moment.

"Have you tried talking to Anna?" she said.

"Yes, and I did feel a little easier, but I don't think that I've got to the bottom of it because the anxiety quickly built up again."

"The disappearance hasn't helped," Derek said.

Simeon nodded.

"And I find it quite stressful with all the visitors. With the children off school, there are such a lot of people about."

"Is there anyone in particular?" Harriet asked.

Simeon looked up, a quick glance at her face. She coloured a little. It had been a bit of a leading question.

"Caz's dad is quite frightening."

"I thought he'd gone home for a couple of weeks," Derek said.

"But we don't know when he'll be back exactly. And Jim tried to push Anna, and no one knows what's really happened to Margery Andrews," Harriet added.

"Anna says she thinks Jim slipped," Simeon said. He didn't sound as if he had believed her either. "Anna always takes the blame, but to have got his foot so firmly squashed, he must have been stepping up into the hall. He's a big man, no wonder Anna tried to slam the door."

"She feels really terrible about it," Harriet said.

"He's a bully, just like Mr Denbigh." Simeon sat back. Belle, who was lying at his feet, looked up.

Harriet said, "Do you think either of them had anything to

do with Caz's death? Jim didn't seem to like her very much and Mr Denbigh seems angry all the time."

Simeon replied, "Anna thinks Jim has a problem with women in general." He bent down to pull on one of Belle's ears. Belle settled again.

Harriet continued, "And Caz did seem to be the sort of person who wouldn't let that go. She would know her rights. Perhaps she was threatening to take it higher. Jim wouldn't like his authority questioned."

"I wonder if Tom has looked for a letter or a transcript that Caz may have been compiling," Simeon said.

"He's pretty on it," Derek added, nodding, and poured more coffee. He also had another bit of cake, which made Harriet smile. Simeon refused but she'd cut him a very large piece to begin with.

"Perhaps Tom is simply waiting for Anna to solve it for him. Or you," she said, looking at Simeon. He'd also been quite close to piecing together the last murder.

"Last time the culprits were living with her, and they also kept coming to see me to ask questions."

"Which you were rather good at answering, if I remember rightly," Harriet added, smiling. "How's Georgie?"

"Georgie was well when last we spoke. She will be back next month for a week. She has some term planning to get on with, which she'd like to do down here away from her job in Exeter."

Harriet nodded.

"She does seem to enjoy your walks with Belle."

"I find it easier to talk with her out in the open."

"You've come a long way since you first met her."

"I'm not sure what you mean, because when I first met her was when Archie had his heart attack, so everything became about losing him. It felt like I had gone back to how I used to be. I try to be rational about it, but I'm scared. I do wonder sometimes if I'm able to do what I do only because he's around."

"Just being Archie," Derek said.

"Now you're worried there's something else going on. And he's your best friend. I hate it when Anna and I aren't getting along." Harriet waited for Simeon to reply; instead, he stood up to go.

"This has been nice." Something Harriet knew Anna had told him to say, when he needed to leave.

"Harriet and I are going to the pound to choose a new dog. We need to set a date."

"When are you going? Anna would have to be able to look after Belle."

"Well, let's find out when she's free and take it from there."

Simeon zipped up his coat, not quite to the top, which comforted Harriet a little.

Chapter 28

Jim hobbled to the kitchen. He was going to try driving because then he could go to work and get down to the boat house when he wanted to. Toby didn't always fetch him quickly enough when there was a shout. He thought the boy was being deliberately unhelpful. He'd not seen him for a week or two, though one day he'd arrived home with a large bag of groceries. It was about time, the rent hardly amounted to the cost of the extra electric he used.

He rested his full weight on his damaged foot. It was sore but bore his weight. With the boot they'd given him at hospital, he could get about quite competently, for short periods at least. It was still a little swollen and the doctor had said it would be six weeks before he would be fully recovered, and certainly four or five weeks before he would be able to go out on *Rose*. There were a couple of broken bones on the top of the foot, and he'd wrenched some tendons around the ankle, but it wasn't anything major.

The stupid woman had completely overreacted, particularly sending the copper around to talk to him. Jim had got the distinct impression he was being threatened. He was probably scared that Jim would do her for assault or something. He managed to find a couple of clean cups at the back of the cupboard, though one was badly chipped, so he switched on the kettle and sat down. Just at that moment the bell rang. He heaved himself up. The vicar was standing in the porch, peering through at him.

"What do you want?" he said, yanking the door open, so hard another piece of plaster fell onto the floor.

"I wanted to make sure you had everything you needed."

Jim folded his arms, but then wobbled a little, as his foot took his weight. It was throbbing, but bearable.

"Can I come in? Just for a moment."

He wondered if he could simply refuse. She was standing

back, her hair all around her face from the wind, her chest heaving from just walking up the road. She could certainly do with losing a few pounds. He went back and sat at the table.

Anna made them both a cup of tea. He was going to invite her through to the lounge, but his dinner plate was still on the coffee table from the night before and there might even have been some dirty laundry piled on the floor. He'd expected Toby to come home to tidy up a bit, but he must have stayed over at Genni's again.

The boy's neglect was hard to stomach, particularly as the bruise around his eye had practically disappeared. Jim was at a loss as to what he'd done to upset him now.

"How's the foot?"

"Bloody sore."

"And when will you be able to go out on the lifeboat again?"

He stared at her. It was like she'd simply come here to rub his nose in the misery that she'd caused. For a fleeting second, he wondered if she'd been friends with Margery. That she was secretly enjoying how grubby everything was, how he didn't look as if he were coping. He felt a pit opening up inside him, a hole Margery had left, that he was once again falling into.

"I didn't mean to slam the door."

"What the hell were you thinking?" he snarled.

She muttered something that he couldn't quite hear, then clearing her throat she looked up at him. She looked so timid, he wanted to tell her to get a grip, to stand up for herself.

"I thought you were going to hit me."

"Nonsense. I've never hit a woman in my life."

"But you've hit your son."

"So?"

She stood up.

"I can't stay here," she said. "I'm really sorry I shut the door on your foot, but you can be quite menacing."

"Are you saying I deserved it?"

"No, of course not." She seemed to dry up, her hands were dangling at her sides, useless, just like she was. She stared over his right shoulder, as if looking him in the eye was too hard for her. "I'm trying to say that if you could see how you come across sometimes. That you are so large..."

"You're saying it's my fault," he growled. Didn't she have any idea what he was going through? The sort of mess they were in? *Rose* was going out without him and though his deputy was competent he didn't have Jim's experience. And to accuse him of trying to hit her. He'd never dream of hitting a woman, not unless she truly, truly wound him up beyond reason.

"Let me know if you need anything. We can at least get you some shopping or cook you a meal now that Margery has gone," she squeaked. She began to back away.

"You think I need that sodding woman to live. She wasn't ever a proper mother or wife." He hauled himself to his feet. "Her job was to stand by Toby." He added lamely, "And me." He didn't want this woman's pity. He gripped the edge of the table. "I don't need your help. You're an incomer, a sodding tourist. That's all you are. You don't understand The Lizard. You don't understand what you need to live here. Bugger off, before someone makes you disappear. Us locals are getting rather good at that."

Jim was beyond furious, he wanted to tower over her, to wipe that insipid smile off her face. To be fair, she wasn't smiling anymore. She looked quite scared. Once again, like a switch, all the fight drained out of him, and he was toppling into the pit that bloody Margery had made. If she'd been that unhappy, he might have found the money for the stair carpet, he might have even found a builder who could have redone the kitchen. But it was too late now. It was all too late. He was alone. Alone apart from Toby, and Jim was afraid he might be losing him too. So whatever else that dog-collared-blow-in had said, none of this was Jim's fault. None of it. And as for being a bully, that was arrant nonsense. He looked up to tell her that, but she'd gone, leaving the kitchen door open, a line of light and a frisson of damp air.

He hobbled over to the kitchen sink. The bin was full. Far too full. Toby should have emptied it on his way out that morning. Then Jim remembered Toby hadn't been home. He pulled it towards him and tried to yank the bag out. They'd been jamming more and more rubbish in for days. When he tried to grasp the corners, the plastic ripped under his fingers. His foot was beginning to ache and why should he have to drag the whole thing out to the wheelie bin? Toby should have done it. Jim pushed it away from him, a sharp shove. He watched it teeter and fall backwards so that half the rubbish scattered across the floor. He glared at the tea bags and plastic trays, congealed dinner and sticky packets, turned his back and hopped into the lounge, pulling the door shut behind him. Now Toby would have to do something about it. Toby needed to help out more, now that his mother was gone. And as soon as Jim could drive, he would take the rest of her stuff to the dump. He couldn't bear it cluttering up the place. Not anymore.

***

Anna wondered if she ought to phone Tom to let him know … to let him know she'd wilfully put herself in harm's way again. He'd get angry with her for that, really angry and perhaps worse still, scared for her.

She'd been in all sorts of difficult situations over the years, awkward rather than life threatening, but she'd always seen it as the nature of her job. Now Tom was making her second guess herself. She'd had to go and see Jim. He was part of her responsibility, notwithstanding the door incident — the visit had been her duty. He might have needed something, and the place was a mess. Yes, she'd been scared when he'd lunged towards her, but not quite as scared as just now, when he'd shouted, even though rationally she'd been reasonably safe.

Hobbling was all he could manage, and she'd kept the door at her back the whole time. How long would he weigh so heavy on her conscience, she wondered.

Seeing the shop up the road reminded her that she ought to go and see Jean. Jean was really worried about Margery's disappearance. Several people had told her so. Anna was just hoping that Margery would contact her friend soon, so that at least they could all stop thinking that Jim had bumped her off. Anna closed her eyes. It was so easy to think that he could have killed Caz. Killed her because she was her father's daughter. That Gerald Denbigh had brought her up to know her rights, to lock her windows, to stand up for herself. That she had challenged everyone, even Genni until Genni had begun to question everything too, including Toby's love. Perhaps Caz had niggled Jim until he'd lost it. That felt almost believable, but to contemplate that he'd hurt Margery as well was a step too far.

Anna really wanted to ring Tom, or Harriet. As it was, when she walked past the shop Simeon came out, carrying a shopping bag.

"Hello, Simeon."

"Hello, Anna. Archie is coming round later so I thought I should get some fresh milk."

Anna bent down to stroke Belle, who wagged her tail enthusiastically.

"Anna, would you like to come down to the cafe on the Point? I could buy you a coffee."

She froze, swallowed. What did Simeon need? What had she missed?

"What a lovely idea. It won't be too far for Belle?"

"No, as long as we rest there for more than half-an-hour."

"Is there something you'd like to talk about?" she asked, as they turned around and began to head down the road. "And what about your shopping? You'll have to carry it all the way there and back."

"That's alright. It's not heavy. And no, there isn't anything I'd like to discuss. I wondered if you would like to talk. You were standing stiffly. That sometimes means that you're upset. When I'm upset you often take me into the vicarage kitchen, where you make me coffee and find me something to eat. But if there is something wrong, I think that going into your own kitchen wouldn't be fair, for it's where you take us when we need you."

Anna stopped walking, she turned to stare at Simeon.

"I thought you'd had enough of helping people, after the retreat?"

"You're not just people. You're Anna. And though I'm not always sure how, I sometimes can help people see through to the important bits."

"Come on then, I would love a coffee. I was debating whether I should pop down to talk to Harriet but here you are instead."

They walked briskly along the path next to the road. For the moment the sky above was a washed blue, with clouds, ragged strips high above, dragged by the wind.

"I'm no blow-in," Anna said. The accusation had been rubbing away since Jim had thrown it at her.

"Very few of us come from around here, though."

"Genni does. Her family have lived in Mullion for generations and Toby must have ancestors in our own churchyard."

"No, I wouldn't have thought so. Jim Andrews came here when he was a young man. He got an apprenticeship up at the garage. Saw the advert when he was here on holiday. His family are from Kent. He still has relatives there."

"Simeon, how do you know this stuff?"

"From many different sources. I can't remember how I found out about Mr Andrews's antecedence."

"I bet it was Jean. She's a mine of information."

"She does often tell me things, while she's sorting my

change."

"I think she finds out about people, because she asks and of course she was good friends with Margery. I wonder where she went, and who she went with? Tom says that even the Sandras can't seem to find out who the other man was."

"Oh," Simeon said. It would have been better for all of them to have found out where Margery had run off to, and who with.

When they got to the cafe it was empty. Anna chatted a little with the new boy behind the counter (after all, she had her dog collar on). Eventually, Simeon cleared his throat, and still staring at the floor he asked," What would you like to drink?"

"I would like a cappuccino, please." Anna had to pinch her own fingers to stop herself from laughing at Simeon's manner. He was so serious, so formal. Then she felt a little overwhelmed by his care for her, by what he was trying to do. She swallowed the laughter rather shamefully.

"Would you like a cake or a biscuit to go with it?" Simeon continued.

"No thanks, just the coffee. Shall I go and sit down?"

Simeon nodded. She listened to him carefully telling the young man that he would like a cappuccino and a hot chocolate but that he didn't want anything on the hot chocolate.

"This is such a treat, Simeon."

"Have you forgotten why we're here?"

"No, and yet, yes. I think just the idea of having a coffee with you has made me feel better."

He turned to stare out of the window. Anna tried to think of something to say, and then realised that if she'd been with anyone else, she would have told them all about the visit to Jim and Tom's proposal. Anna would never have called herself patronising, but Simeon seemed to have slipped back into a different category. She began to bite her lip; it was quite sore, and she gently touched it with a fingertip. She really must try to break the habit.

"I'm sorry, Simeon. I don't feel better at all. I would like to tell you a couple of things. Firstly, that Tom and I are engaged." There, she'd said it, though Harriet may never forgive her for telling Simeon first.

Simeon turned back from the view and sat up a little, his eyes for a moment seeking her own.

"That's good, though you don't sound very happy. Are you sure?"

"Oh, Simeon. I am most of the time, but I do have doubts. That's natural isn't it, with such a big decision?"

"What did Harriet say?"

"I haven't told Harriet yet."

"And Archie?"

Anna shook her head, miserably.

"Archie may have doubts, but Harriet will be happy for you. She will probably cry."

Anna was suddenly grateful. Simeon was definitely the right person to have talked to first, or second, if you didn't count Genni. She also knew that he wouldn't say anything, so she had a few more days to work out how she was going to tell Archie.

Simeon asked, "What was the other thing you wanted to talk about?"

This was much easier. She told him how bad she felt about Jim's foot and that she'd decided she ought to go and see how he was managing, particularly as Margery had left him.

"I wouldn't have gone. I find it incomprehensible that you did," Simeon said.

"Thank you, Simeon. Walking up the path was difficult. And I know, deep down, it's not really my fault. What did he think I was going to do, lunging at me like that? I'm half his size."

"I think you were right to be afraid. Not long ago, Toby's face was quite badly bruised. Jean told me that Jim had done it. So even if he hadn't meant to actually hit you, he made you think that he might."

"Yet he genuinely seems to think it was my fault, all my fault. I've made him miss at least two shouts."

"It doesn't matter what he thinks," Simeon said. "You acted instinctively. If he's not aware that his very size, let alone his personality, are a little overwhelming then he's not very perceptive, on any level."

"He makes a good coxswain though and I wouldn't take my car anywhere else for its service."

"But does he make a good leader? I would have thought that if people obey him because they are scared of him, it means the opposite. If Archie asked me to do something, I would do it, because I trust him and I know he cares about me. But if Jim asked me, I would try and find a lot of reasons why I couldn't carry out the order."

Anna shook her head. She wasn't sure.

"Jim does make them practise and practise. That has to be a good thing, surely?"

"Yes, of course."

She began to stir the froth into her coffee, watching the chocolate melt like tiny comets.

"Do you think he could have strangled Caz?" she asked, trying not to remember the last body they'd had to deal with. The state it'd been in when it'd been dragged from the water.

"Strangling is a very difficult way to kill someone," Simeon said, thoughtfully. He spread his fingers out in front of him and Anna wondered again how he knew these things. "Mostly people are partly strangled so that they pass out, and then the perpetrator finishes them off in some other way, because by then they feel they have no choice."

Anna shuddered. She'd got the impression that the body jammed into the crevice was so badly weathered they hadn't been able to find any other injuries, or none that were conclusive. So perhaps, whoever had strangled Caz had been able to finish her off, straightaway.

"They'd have to have been really strong, or angry. Could Genni have done it?"

"Yes, I think so," Simeon replied. "After all, they'd had a screaming match not long before, and Genni seems to be inordinately upset."

"I think she was in love at least with the situation, if not Caz herself. She doesn't seem to have enjoyed any form of friendship before this. It's made me think she is also re-evaluating her relationship with Toby. I think she said yes to marrying him, simply because he asked her."

Simeon looked up again; a moment of eye contact that made Anna realise how tired he looked.

He said, "So Toby might have killed Caz, particularly if he realised what was happening. Jealousy can be very powerful."

"No, that doesn't feel quite right," Anna said, though she knew that would irritate Simeon. "I think deep down Toby's not that bothered. He has this way of looking that makes you feel as if he wishes you would go away and leave him alone."

"How do you do that, Anna? How do you interpret a look, to give you all that information?"

"I have no idea. And, Simeon, most of the time I would say my interpretations are not very accurate." She finished her coffee. "Can I get you another?" she asked. He shook his head. Hesitating for a moment, she asked, "What do you think has happened to Margery? You must have heard the gossip around the village."

"I've heard what Jean thinks."

"But that may be more about the fact that Margery didn't confide in her about her affair, or her plan to go."

"Yes, I can see how that might have made Jean feel, perhaps even a little humiliated. Yet when she described Margery, it didn't sound as if she were the sort of woman to run off with someone without some prior warning."

"What did Jean say?" Anna asked. She looked out of the window, pretending that she wasn't that interested.

"She said Margery was terribly honest. That she wouldn't have been able to carry on behind Jim's back. For example, once, when she found out that Toby had taken something from the shop, she made him return it and he had to write an apology. Another time, she drove all the way back to the supermarket at Helston to pay for some razor blades, which had slipped inside something else, so the cashier had missed them. Jean said there were lots more examples."

Anna wasn't sure those incidents were relevant. A mistake or your son stealing a few sweets was one thing, falling in love, thinking you might have met someone with whom you could be happy for the rest of your life, was entirely different. Simeon bent down to stroke Belle. When he looked up, he said quietly, "unless Margery gets in contact, it may be that like Caz, she's gone missing, too."

"Oh, Simeon, do you really think that?"

"It has to be a possibility." Simeon began to rub along the edge of the table with his knuckles. "A letter is the easiest thing in the world to forge, particularly by someone close to her. Now before you say you must go, is there anything more you'd like to talk about?"

Anna shook her head. Simeon got up to pay the bill. She felt a mixture of guilt and pleasure. It would make Tom laugh to think that Simeon had tried to help her unburden herself, then of course, Tom would want to know what she needed unburdening from. She sighed and went to join Simeon at the door.

Outside they looked South because they couldn't help themselves. The horizon was a line of dark grey cloud, swelling and growing. It billowed towards them so that they wondered if they would make it home without getting wet. Anna began to make her way along the path to the car park. Simeon wouldn't walk up the road under any circumstances. At the steps he suddenly swivelled back to stare at her knees, even glancing up at her face for half a second.

"Anna, please don't go back to see Jim on your own. I feel really anxious just thinking about it."

"Ok," she said. How easy it was to promise that to Simeon, whereas when Tom had tried to get her to agree to something similar, she'd fought back, told him it was her job, told him that there were some things she just had to do. For a moment she was able to see how difficult and mysterious Tom must find her life. How the rules simply didn't seem to apply to her, and how frustrating it must be for him. She shrugged and pulled her coat collar a little higher.

"And congratulations on your engagement. I like Tom."

"Thank you. For listening, too, and for my coffee."

When Simeon turned down his lane, she slipped her phone from her pocket and rang Tom. He didn't pick up, but she left a rambling message about having coffee with Simeon and how much she was looking forward to seeing him later that week. Annoyingly, within a few seconds, he phoned back, demanding to know what was wrong, what had happened and was she alright?

Chapter 29

Toby stared at his front door; his *Dad's* front door. He just couldn't bring himself to go in. He'd been staying over with Genni but that hadn't been a barrel of laughs. Her mother kept appearing and asking if he needed anything. It was like she was watching his every move. He'd thought he would wait until she was asleep and then sneak along to Genni's room, only by the time the woman had stopped clattering about he was too drowsy to be bothered. He had slept deeply and was awakened by his alarm. Neither Genni nor her mum had appeared to see him off to work, but he was used to that. A five-thirty start was too early in anyone's book. His day beyond that had been the usual sort of day. They'd baked trays and trays of bread and pastries, which had been loaded onto lorries, and each time the driver had slammed the door shut, Toby had felt an enormous urge to jump into the cab with him. Anywhere but here.

He just couldn't face the mess. Not the chaos of washing up and dirty clothes but the absence of his mum. He totally understood why she'd gone, but he would never forgive her for not telling him. For not trusting him to have kept it from his dad. Perhaps he *should* do a runner, too. The longer he stayed the worse it was going to get, the more he felt he couldn't breathe. He slammed the car into gear and headed to the village. At the shop he made a handbrake turn past the football field and then almost instinctively he accelerated into Church Cove Lane, as if he were on a shout. He put his foot down, skimmed across the cattle grid and over the field. At the car park, just before the grass bank he skidded into a space. The whole car slewed to one side, the engine over-revving. It choked then died so that all he could hear was the ticking of the metal cooling. He began to cry, dry wracking sobs, because at that speed he would've hit the wall and it would've all been over. He wouldn't have had to make any more stupid decisions.

He wouldn't have to think about his father screaming at his mother, that it was she who was betraying her son. His father twisting reality around to suit him and another stupid row that Toby had run away from. He wished he hadn't, for it would have been the last time he'd have seen his mum.

Someone knocked on the window. He concentrated on the centre of his steering wheel. They knocked again, ever so gently and he knew that in another breath they would try again. He slid it down.

"Toby, are you alright?"

"Yes, I think there might be something wrong with my brakes."

The vicar looked really worried; her eyes large, unblinking.

"You were coming in at such a speed. I didn't think you were going to be able to stop."

He wondered what she was doing there. Out for a walk as there wasn't much else to do.

"I was …" What could he tell her? That he'd just tried to drive into a wall. "I forgot my wallet, left it in my locker."

"Oh, I'm always doing things like that." She sounded relieved. "Shall I come down with you?"

"There's no need," he said, hurriedly. Was she worried about leaving him on his own? Shouldn't she be more worried about being on her own with him? Did anyone know where she was? That boyfriend of hers, for a start. She looked so frail, so colourless.

"I don't mind. It's such an incredible place."

Toby didn't feel she was giving him a choice, and he deeply resented that. It seemed to be happening more and more often. People assumed they knew what was going on in his head and seemed to want to protect him. His mum had done that a lot. He felt he was on a ramp, just like *Rose*, and when she started to slide towards the water, nothing on earth could stop her.

He began to run down the steps, two at a time. He skidded

to a stop at the first platform, hesitated and then jumped across. They were all good at the steps, up and down. Jim made them practise over and over again, timing each of them. There was a table of names up in the kitchen. He was at the top, had been for months. He might be short, but he was fast. Genni was a couple of spaces below; Caz was down the bottom. The only thing she wasn't any good at. The vicar was trying to keep up but was soon way behind. At the door he turned to watch her. She clung to the rail as if she were an old woman. He could easily slip inside, pick up a wadge of leaflets, fold them into his back pocket, like a wallet, and be climbing up past her before she'd even arrived.

Instead, he found himself saying, "Shall I make you a cup of tea? The volunteers often leave some spare milk."

Her face lit up and she nodded vigorously. He wanted to say that he was doing it out of politeness, that it wasn't because he wanted to talk or anything. He punched in the code and led her through the locker room and down into the crew space. There was a large table there.

"Take a seat. Tea?"

"Tea would be great. Thanks, Toby. I'll need it before I attempt those steps again."

"You didn't have to come down, I'd have been fine."

She lifted a finger and touched her lips. He guessed he'd just given himself away. He slumped into a chair.

"I'm going to leave. Dad will manage, Genni will get over it and Mum obviously doesn't care."

"Where will you go?"

"I don't know. I have an aunt in Kent. She was always nice to me. Perhaps she'll put me up while I look for a job."

The vicar nodded. He was a little surprised she hadn't argued with him.

"You should tell Genni, though. If you disappear without an explanation, it will be hard on her, after her dad."

Toby felt a pang of jealousy. Why couldn't it be about him?

For once, just him.

"She's found a John Doe, that fits his description, that died on the right date. A hit and run. There's a watch and a ring that she's hoping her mum might be able to identify. That's a start. She's also going to see if there is any more of his family, her family, anywhere," he said. "She's hoping it will help sort out some of her issues."

"What sort of issues does she have?" the vicar asked, as if she really wanted to know.

Toby thought about it for a moment and then realised he didn't have a clue. Genni hardly ever spoke about how she felt. She normally just smiled and said, "I'm okay. How about you?" No, that wasn't right, that was the old Genni. The new Genni would probably burst into tears. She was soggy and inarticulate when she wasn't silent.

Toby felt the familiar feelings crowding in, the ones he'd lived with for years through school. Of being on the outside looking in, watching a scene playing out that he would never be a part of, that he would never quite understand. Bloody Caz had taunted him for months and it'd made him feel just like this.

"Toby, are you alright?" The vicar was leaning forward in her seat. She was a little shorter than him, which was a relief, even sitting down. She reached across to touch his arm. "Is there anything I can do to help?"

He stood up and moved away. It would be so good to be in control again, to be in charge of what was happening.

"The thing is, no one really understands what it's been like for me. Growing up with dad meant I spent my whole life waiting for the next clout or slap, often I didn't know what for. Nothing ever made sense. I hardly ever worked out what was going on, what I'd done wrong and then when I thought I had, it was shit." He stared at her. Her dark eyes, blinking just like a field mouse. He'd once caught one in their damp kitchen cupboards. His mum had said it was sweet, but Toby knew it was just vermin. He'd said he'd let it go, and he had, in a way. He'd dropped it into the middle of the road. It had scampered a few feet, but two cars had gone by in quick succession, and he'd not bothered to check if it had made it to the other side. There was a tiny dark smudge for weeks that he couldn't look at or go near.

"None of us can know what that was truly like for you, but I also spent years on the outside looking in and Simeon has spent his whole life trying to work out how to be, without getting thumped or chucked into the sea."

"So you're saying, no excuses, just get on with it."

"No, I'm absolutely not saying that. I'm saying there are people around you who will understand. That for some of us, it might be easier than you think. I'm sure Genni feels the same way."

"And we're back to bloody Genni. What is it about her? Is it because she didn't have a dad or that she was the only black girl in the whole school? What if her precious father had turned out to be a lousy father like mine? What if he'd hit her or belittled her, never thought she would amount to anything and told her so, repeatedly? Would you feel sorry for her then?"

"Was that what it was like for you?"

For a second Toby felt ashamed, whining to this stupid woman. His dad would think he was being weak.

"Yes, and not just with Dad. It was like that with everyone. Everyone except Mum, and she was just scared I'd turn out to be like him. She couldn't face that, so she ran away." Toby's voice cracked. He thrust his hands in his pockets and hung his head.

"Toby, I'm so very sorry and I'm sure your mum would have had lots of complex reasons for going."

The vicar had as good as said that he shouldn't think it was always about him! Well, that wasn't news to Toby.

"Perhaps Dad did kill Mum, during one of their stupid rows.

Who knows!" He glared at her until she leaned back but she was looking more thoughtful than scared.

"We found Caz," she replied. Toby was shocked. Had she really just implied that some day they would find his mother's body?

Angrily, he said, "What does that prove except that whoever strangled Caz was not clever enough. It would be easy to hide a body so it was never discovered. Dad would know where all the best places are, any local would." Thinking about his father made Toby feel hot and prickly. He had to get a grip before he said something he would regret. Then he spoke quietly. "Murdering someone can't be something you take in your stride. Perhaps whoever did it was so shocked at what they'd done, they hid her in the crevice to get some thinking time."

"And the longer she wasn't found, the more complacent the person got."

"Or the longer she wasn't found, the more hopeful they were that she would be found."

Anna nodded.

"I understand, Toby. I do."

Jim appeared in the doorway, leaning heavily on his crutch. Behind him, his face a little pink, was Archie.

"What are you doing here?" Toby said to his father.

"I don't need to explain myself to you. What are *you* doing here?"

"I came to get my wallet." Toby folded his arms.

"And then he met me in the car park and we decided a cup of tea and a chat were in order." The vicar smiled, but she was looking worried, and she sounded tense. Archie had moved to stand near her, which meant Toby was no longer responsible for her.

"I'm out of here. You can use the cage to get back up. I'm assuming you used it to get down," he said, addressing his dad.

Toby was almost running by the time he got to the outside door.

Chapter 30

Simeon was supposed to be meeting Archie at the church. He'd said there was something he wanted to tell Simeon but then had texted to say that he would be late. Later, he'd texted again to say that he wasn't sure there'd be time to meet at all. It wasn't like Archie to string him along like that.

Simeon had felt the inevitability of this moment for quite a while. He'd discussed with Georgie a few terrifying options that he was trying not to think about, as to what was wrong with his friend. The first being that Archie was terminally ill. The second that he was moving away, to somewhere more central. The third, that their friendship was over because Archie couldn't cope with Simeon anymore. The latter was not a serious worry, though it was the one he kept coming back to. He'd only made a few friends over the years. Anna, Archie, Derek, and seemingly now Georgie, were those he'd come to rely on.

Anxiety began to build, and Simeon slid out of his pew. He began to walk around the church, his hands thrust deep into his pockets, fingers balled into fists, just in case he began to touch things. The curved metal of the bell, the top of the ends of the pews, the table edge at the back where the tea and coffee were kept. The longing to run his fingers gently over any one of those smooth surfaces was something he hadn't had to battle with for a while. It was no good, on his third circumnavigation his left hand drifted onto the bell. He'd not even noticed reversing back until he could feel the reassuring coolness of the metal. Belle whined and then sort of collapsed as if she knew it was pointless trying to do anything now.

The door opposite swung open until it got stuck in its usual place. Simeon shrunk back into the shadows.

"Very welcoming, I don't think," Toby muttered and shoved the door a little harder so that it screeched again. He turned right and strode down to stand in front of the altar.

"No one else will listen. Will you?" he shouted. "No one else thinks I matter a toss. Do you?" He slumped down into the first row and put his face in his hands. Then laughing he said, "You're not there, are you? Of course not. Just someone else who can't be arsed to stick around." He sat back.

Simeon thought Toby was now swearing quietly under his breath. A string of words hissing into the air. He knew that God wouldn't mind. It was people who thought such things important. Simeon hoped he could make his way across the back of the church before Toby saw him, as he didn't want to engage with him when he was so angry. Both of Simeon's hands were dangling at his sides. He hadn't noticed when he'd stopped touching the bell.

He felt the inevitability of the next moment, the next thought, tying itself around his legs, around his chest. What if Toby, despite having two parents, had never been listened to? What if he felt there was nowhere safe to go and be?

"He's here," Simeon said. He could barely get the words out from between his tightly clenched teeth and his hands were now gripping the pew back so hard he could feel the tendons in his fingers throbbing.

Toby jumped up and peered around. Simeon realised he couldn't be seen. The temptation to drop down and hide was hideously strong, instead he sidestepped the pillar so that Toby would see the movement.

"Who's that?"

"Simeon Tyler." This time his voice worked a little better. He peeled his fingers off the pew and took a couple of paces down the aisle. Everything in him screamed stop. Go back. Make for the door. You know where this might lead. "I'm sorry I startled you, it's just you asked a question." Simeon kept his eyes firmly on Belle's head. She was beside him, moving with him, glued to his leg.

"I didn't mean to swear in church."

"It doesn't matter. God won't mind. God wants us to be

ourselves and if you feel you need to swear to tell him how it is, then go ahead."

"You can't mean that. I bet if I used the 'f' word in front of that vicar lady she would go nuts."

"No, I don't think Anna would. She might have done so a couple of years back, but not now. Even Archie wouldn't be that bothered. Jean, from the shop might, but she'd go to Anna and Anna would put her straight."

Toby turned back to the altar.

"So, you reckon God is here and he's listening to me. So why doesn't he say anything? And why, oh why, is my life so crap?"

"He is listening and he's speaking. He's using me." Simeon had had this conversation before. Why did people find it so difficult to believe that God used other people much more than any sign or wonder? That a miraculous occurrence would most likely be discounted as the work of their imagination. Better by far to have someone tangible speak God's truths to you. To remind you of what he promised. "And I'm not being arrogant, that I'm the voice of God or anything like that, it's just that I'm here, so he will use me to help you."

"Well, it sounds flippin' arrogant to me. How can you help me? I bet you've never had a girlfriend, let alone a fiancée. What do you know of anything?"

Simeon struggled forward another two steps. He really didn't think he could go any closer, but Belle could. He dropped the lead and nudged her with his knee. Toby was still standing, his arms folded, his chin thrust forward, as she pattered around the end of the pew. She went towards him wagging her tail. Toby did what most people did, he dropped to his knees and began to stroke her. After a minute or two she walked back to Simeon to make sure he was alright.

"It's okay, Belle. Go back to Toby."

"You don't have to stay there, I won't bite," Toby said.

"I can't come any closer. I'm sorry. I'm not being rude, I just can't."

"Whatever. So have you always believed in this God of yours?"

"No, only for the last few years. I tried to kill myself and he intervened to help me."

"What did he do?"

"He sent Anna and Archie, Harriet and then Derek and sometimes Jean from the shop and Phil in the pub."

"To do what? And that's a lot of people. You must be very important."

"That's the point, I'm not. I'm really not important at all. I can't look most people in the eye. I get very anxious about a lot of things. If I don't do some actions or jobs in the right order, I have to go and lie under a blanket until I feel better. During the retreat when the man was killed, I talked to a lot of people about a lot of things, but I found it absolutely exhausting and since then I've been hiding."

"So what's the point of your amazing God then? It sounds to me like he hasn't changed anything."

"Oh, he changes everything. I'll never be comfortable talking with strangers or in a place where I can't see the door but I'm talking to you. I want to run away, to grab Belle and get under my blanket and not come out for hours, but I haven't. Not yet anyway."

"Don't stay on my account. Most people will say I'm not worth it."

"You are. God thinks you are, and though it's very hard to say it, so do I."

Toby straightened up from rubbing Belle's ears or at least Simeon guessed that from the fact that he sighed, and Belle came clattering back to him.

"Does this God mind that I'm broken? Worse than my dad, which is saying something. And I'm going to try and walk away from it all, even Genni. I hope I never have to come back."

"Running away is rarely the right thing to do unless you're

being abused in some way. You need to talk to the people who'll listen." Not me, he wanted to say.

"No one ever listens to me but you're right, it was abuse," Toby suddenly shouted.

"I'm listening." Why did he have to say that? He could feel himself being dragged along by the words he was trying not to speak.

"But you're a weirdo. Someone else on the outside."

"Just like you."

Back at school that would have got Simeon a thumping.

"So, I should join your merry band of happy-clappy, Jesus-saves bunch of losers. Spend my time poking my nose into other people's business."

"No one does that, not on purpose."

"Then why did Anna follow me down to the lifeboat station? She wouldn't stay in the car park. I think she thought I was going to top myself."

"If she thought that, then no, she wouldn't have left you on your own. Not for a minute."

"I may have given her cause for concern," Toby said, a little more quietly. "I wondered if I could drive into the bank. Instinct is a powerful thing. At the last minute I found myself braking."

"You feel how you feel, though sometimes it's hard to articulate it. Did Anna come back up with you? Where is she now?" Simeon asked, a sudden shadow darkening the church. It was just the sun going behind a cloud. Simeon had to stay focussed.

"Oh, don't worry. She's alright. My dad turned up with Archie, probably told him he needed a lift, that he had to do some incredibly pointless thing down in the boat house. You wouldn't believe he's been signed off sick. He can't stay away from his precious *Rose* for a minute."

Simeon realised why Archie had put him off earlier.

"Archie is a kind man and would find it hard to refuse your

father."

"Kind he may be, but he's just as screwed up as the rest of us. I asked him for some advice about marriage and he nearly had a heart attack."

Simeon pulled his phone out. He sent a text to Archie and Anna. He hated not knowing why suddenly he was feeling so panicky.

"What's the matter?" Toby asked. Simeon felt as though Toby must be staring at him but didn't dare check.

"Your dad has hardly been himself of late and Anna seems to be the focus of that. He's under suspicion for murdering Caz and possibly your mum. Archie hasn't been well, and your dad gets angry really quickly. He might try and hurt them."

"Keep your hair on. Dad thinks *I* did Caz in and surely the letter from Mum proves he hasn't done anything." Toby's voice tailed off. When next he spoke, it was as if his fists were balled, and his face was red. "He's just a bully. He made it so difficult for Caz, but she kept on fighting back, making notes with dates when he was particularly difficult or particularly mean. One evening we were practising picking up a body from the water and he made her go in three times. It was bloody freezing."

Simeon didn't know what to do now, but he was feeling increasingly anxious.

"It might have been your dad? Caz might have finally pushed him one step too far." Simeon wished he hadn't said it out loud, that he'd kept that thought safely in his head. Toby stood up.

"Nice chat. I've got to go now."

He marched from the church. Simeon ran after him, but where Toby turned right, Simeon turned left. He was in the lifeboat car park within five minutes though he'd had to practically drag Belle the last fifty metres. Neither Archie nor Anna had replied to his text. Archie's car was parked in the far corner. Simeon began to clatter down the steps having tied Belle to the railings at the top. Halfway down he texted Harriet and Derek and asked them to meet him at the winding house. Simeon couldn't see any lights on within the building though as always, the outside light was on. He made it to the bottom, his breath out of control, rasping. The door was locked. He banged on it hard. He banged again and again. Then he went down onto the next level, despite the signs that said he wasn't allowed, and ran around to the front. He couldn't see anyone, or anything. The sea was sliding up and down. It looked almost black under the clouds and the swell seemed much larger than from above. He clambered onto the ramp, immediately afraid that someone would launch *Rose* and knock him into the sea. He'd never been able to walk under her bow on the open days, preferring to stay above her. To the left of the main opening an ordinary looking door was ajar. Simeon hesitated for barely a moment before stepping into the dimness, trying not to look up at the lifeboat, towering above him. Standing just inside he called, shouting for Archie and Anna. His voice echoed and he so wanted to run away. There was no reply. The place felt empty, felt abandoned, but Archie's car was still in the car park and Toby had seen all three of them down here, not that long before.

Simeon made his way back to the cliffside and began to climb up. Very quickly the air he was trying to drag into his lungs felt like straw. His legs were like jelly, and he felt quite faint. Belle pulled at her lead to get to him, but he couldn't do more than pat her head. Derek and Harriet appeared, sauntering across the field. Harriet even looked as if she were laughing at something Derek had said. Why weren't they rushing? Why had they walked? Simeon wanted to scream but he couldn't do more than bend double, resting his hands on his knees.

"Are you alright?" Derek called.

Finally, they were trotting across the car park. Finally, they understood there was some urgency. Simeon pointed.

"It's Archie's car," Harriet said. "Is he alright? Has he had another heart attack? Shall I call an ambulance?"

Derek frowned as Simeon shook his head.

"I'm not sure where he is," he gasped. "I think Anna may be with him, and Toby said that Jim was there too." Simeon finally managed to straighten up. "I've been down, and the boat house is empty but the door on the front, the one that leads out onto the ramp is open. Jim would never leave it like that."

Harriet turned away and began to run up the path towards Beacon Point.

"I'm just going to see if I can see anything from the top," she called over her shoulder.

"I think we should phone Tom. I've sent texts to Archie and Anna and neither have replied," Simeon said.

"They don't always straight away, if they're busy, so what's got you so upset? Just seeing Archie's car wouldn't have freaked you out like this," Derek said, craning his neck to see if he could see Harriet coming back.

"I was in the church and Toby came in. He's going to leave but it was just the way he was saying everything. I wondered if he might know what'd happened to Caz. He said that his dad had thought he'd done it."

"What did he say exactly?"

"Just that his dad had bullied her. Made her work a lot harder than the others."

The gate onto the path crashed shut as Harriet came running back.

"I can see a small boat heading towards the Point, it's hugging the shore. It wasn't that far along, and it did look like Jim at the helm, though he didn't seem to have anyone with him."

"I'm phoning Tom now. I don't know what else to do," Simeon said.

"Why don't you and I go along the path and see if we can see where the boat is going? Keep an eye on it. It's getting dark but we may be able to spot something if we can get above it," Derek said. "Harriet, you stay here with Belle and wait for Tom. Follow us as soon as he gets here."

"It's best," Simeon said, as Harriet began to frown. "He'll listen to you."

"He'll listen to you too, but you know the path as well as anyone, even in the dark."

Chapter 31

Anna woke and retched. Her head felt as if it had been split with an axe and waves of nausea rolled over her. She couldn't work out where she was or why she was so cold. The central heating must have burst a pipe or something or she must have eaten something that had disagreed with her. She'd have to put Tom off; she wouldn't want to see him feeling like this. She opened her eyes. Above her was dark sky, and there was movement all around. She tried to sit up but found that her hands were caught behind her back, her shoulders aching in the unaccustomed position. She tried to roll over, but she seemed to be jammed in the bow of a small dinghy. Groaning, she tried to pull her arms forward but after a while she realised that her wrists were tied with what felt like nylon rope. The edge of her vision was still blurry, and if she strained too hard it spun and heaved. It was very difficult concentrating. She just wanted everything to stay still for a minute, for the side of the boat to stop rising and falling against the clouds. She wanted to be wrapped in a blanket, to drink hot chocolate and to see Tom waiting to haul her to her feet, up onto the ramp.

The ramp! She'd been at the lifeboat station with Jim and Archie. They'd arrived just after Toby had said something that had really worried her. Then he'd left. He'd said goodbye and his father had tried to go after him, but Toby was fast. He'd left him a long way behind. Other things began to come back to her. Archie had kept saying to Jim that they ought to be getting back. Anna had agreed because Tom was on his way to see her, and she didn't want to be late. She'd turned away to climb up the stairs to the locker room and Archie had collapsed. She'd thought he was having another heart attack, but as she dropped down to check on him, she could see blood trickling across his face and even in the shadow of *Rose* she could see he was white and barely breathing. She couldn't remember anything more. It must be Archie she could feel beside her. She stopped trying to undo the rope and tried to find Archie's hands. Because she was facing away from him it was difficult. At last, by stretching until her shoulders were burning, then twisting just a little, feeling her spine dislocating one vertebra at a time, she managed to touch his fingers. They felt warm, so at least he was still alive. She couldn't see anything over the forward bench seat and wondered what to do next.

"Jim," she called but he was either ignoring her, or he simply couldn't hear over the noise of the engine. Jim, it had to be him!

She began to pray. She felt so cold, so sick and was sure that whoever it was, was not taking them somewhere safe and warm. She assumed he was taking them out to sea to drop them over the side. Perhaps that was what he'd done with Margery. Before she could work out where that thought was going, she felt Archie roll a little towards her and she was filled with a flutter of hope. Archie was regaining consciousness and she almost smiled, except then she began to cry. Tom would kill her for getting herself into trouble like this. It was like she'd walked in with her eyes wide open, secretly believing that God would protect her whatever happened. Which of course wasn't what God promised. The swell seemed to increase and for a moment it was as if the boat was hanging in the air, then it crashed down, and Anna felt as though she might have broken a rib. The darkness was sudden, the noise of the outboard filling her head. It was all around them, bouncing off walls that were too close. The sea was no more than the slap of the swell on rocks, an echoey blackness as the engine quieted. They must have come into one of the caves. This was not good.

"Jim," she croaked, again. "Jim, think about this. We can talk it through."

It was Jim's face that appeared above her, leaning close in the dim light of what must have been his phone. He grabbed her coat and hauled her up so that she was sitting. He then pushed her backwards. She thought she was going to fall over the side, into the icy water and she screamed. He slapped her face, hard. Shocked, she shut her mouth.

"I've wanted to do that for such a long time," he said.

Once again, he braced himself and then tipped her up and out, his arms under her legs. With her hands tied behind her back, she couldn't do anything to stop him. Suddenly, she felt rock under her thigh. There was a ledge half a metre wide, so at least she was able to get her feet out of the water. As her eyes adjusted, she heard Jim groan again with the effort of pulling Archie to a sitting position and then, with the same practised movement, he tipped him up and out of the boat, too. She swung round so that her back was towards Archie, trying to grab some part of him. If he regained consciousness, then he might not realise where he was and roll into the sea.

"Archie, Archie, wake up. But slowly. You're on a ledge. A tiny ledge in a cave."

Jim switched off the light.

"Jim, you can't leave us here. No one will know where we are."

He laughed and she realised how stupid that had sounded.

"There's a good high tide that will fill the cave. You won't have to wait long."

"Jim, why are you doing this? And Archie, why hurt Archie?"

Anna leaned away as Jim stood up. He grimaced as his injured foot took his weight, but it didn't give way, and though the boat rocked he stayed upright.

"You know that Toby killed Caz." His voice was flat and calm, only just reaching her over the idling engine.

"I don't know that. How can any of us know that?" she cried, her heart racing, fear roaring up through her. Only she did know. There were the odd knots in the rope left under Caz's body. Tom had mentioned it because he'd got cross with one of his sergeants for wasting her time trying to find out what they were. Tom had thought it didn't matter, so Anna hadn't put it together with what Genni had said. That there were bits of rope all over the lifeboat station, because everyone practised their knots all the time, but that Toby had this slightly odd way of tying the bowline because he was left-handed and had never been able to follow the instructions without getting the last part back to front. It meant it didn't quite sit right and Jim always went nuts when he saw one of his son's attempts. Of course, it wasn't just the knots. Toby had been trying to tell her all afternoon and she'd refused to hear him. Jim was still talking.

"I saw the rope when the policewoman showed us the pictures before she got a bollocking for wasting her time. I knew then."

"But why did he squash her into the crevice on Beacon Point, where she was bound to be found?" Anna asked desperately, hoping to delay him.

"He's not clever. He probably got in a panic and didn't know what to do."

"Jim, he's not a bad boy and he's been in such a mess ever since. He needs help, and so do you."

Archie groaned and moved.

"Archie, stay still, or you'll roll into the sea," she yelled.

The outboard roared back to life, filling the darkness with white churning water. Then the boat was gone. Anna thought she could see a line of grey off to the right where there might be daylight, but even as she stared, it seemed to fade. She tried to find a sharp rock to cut the ropes, there was nothing. In one of the many unsuitable books that she loved to read, there would have been a sharp piece of metal used by smugglers. Archie groaned again.

"Anna?"

"I'm right beside you. Our arms are tied behind our backs. I'm scared you'll topple into the water."

"It's so dark."

"We're in a cave. I've no idea where. I thought Jim was taking us out to sea to drop us overboard."

Archie was silent, probably while he was trying to get his head around everything.

"No, he wouldn't do that," he groaned. "Too easy to get spotted." His voice was no more than a whisper. "Better to stay under the cliffs particularly as there's rarely anyone about at this time of day. I don't feel so good." He sucked in a lungful of air and began to cough.

"Take it steady, Archie. He hit us both. I still feel a little sick and my head is splitting." Archie took some more deep breaths. "Jim said the cave would fill with water on the next high tide." Anna felt another wave of panic. She wanted Archie to contradict him. That really, Jim had been trying to scare her.

"Why has he done this?" Archie almost hissed. He began to cough again and though she knew it would do no good, she edged a little closer, grabbed the end of his jacket and held on.

"He thinks Toby killed Caz and despite everything, he's trying to save him."

"By killing us? I don't understand, Anna, and I'm still not ready to die."

"Nor me. Bloody hell, not yet. Too soon. Please God, we need you." She yelled the last bit into the darkness."

Anna gasped as she felt a splash of icy water. Archie groaned once more.

"Are you alright?" she asked.

"Not really. We're not going to be able to stay on this shelf much longer and once we're in the water we'll drown. If we're going to die, I need forgiveness. For Moira and how I treated her. Will you help me, Anna."

"What can I do?"

"Hear me, that's all."

"Of course. Whatever you need."

He took a deep breath and Anna shivered. She was painfully cold. She wished she could wrap her arms around herself. She wished she could stop her shoulders from burning.

"I was so bloody Navy that I couldn't unbend even when I went home. To survive you had to be on your guard, know what was expected of you, keep your thoughts and feelings to yourself. Moira, I see now, was warm and creative and I gave her nothing. I should have tried to explain, tell her how much I loved her. Stopped being such a cold fish. Why couldn't I just have told her how I felt?"

Anna didn't know what she should say to that. Archie's voice had faded towards the end and now he sounded as though he couldn't catch his breath.

"God forgives you. Of course he does. Invite him into the memories you have of her. He was there, you just need to work out where. We all screw up and wish we'd done things differently. Now Archie, hold on. Please hold on."

"Sorry, Anna. I'm just so tired."

"You're to stay awake. I can't do this without you. I can't do any of this without you." She began to cry again, and it was frustrating because she couldn't wipe away her tears.

"I'm so sorry," Archie mumbled.

"Just don't leave me. That's all I'm worried about."

"Where would I go?" They both tensed as another wave lapped over the ledge.

"Tom was on his way over. He'll know something's wrong."

"But how will he know where we are?"

Anna ignored that. Tom would work it out, he had to.

"He's asked me to marry him. And we're going to do it properly."

The relief was extraordinary, despite being tied up in a cave that was rapidly filling with water. Archie laughed.

"Anna, that's wonderful."

"Is it, Archie? You've never found it easy, our relationship."

"No, and I'm sorry for that. I suppose all the Moira stuff got in the way, and Tom often seems to disconcert you." He stopped, but Anna felt there was more he wanted to say.

"Go on, Archie."

"Okay," he said, quietly, the slapping of the waves punctuating his voice. "Tom doesn't seem to fit with the rest of us."

"I think that's partly our fault. He knows how much you all mean to me, so he'll do what he can to make it work, we need to make space for him." Anna took comfort from talking as if there was a future beyond these words. "Sometimes, I think he's even jealous, envious of us." Another wave, another icy drenching. She gasped, but continued, "I meant what I said, I can't do this, my job, my calling, without you."

"Then God had better do his thing, because we're running out of time."

"We might be able to stay afloat, make our way out of the cave," she said.

"I don't think so."

"I've been trying to rub the ropes on a rock like they do in the films. It doesn't seem to be working. And I think the knot is too swollen for you to undo."

"I could tell you about the pounds per square inch that this particular one can haul just on its own, but it would depress you. And no, I wouldn't stand a chance trying to untie it with my numb fingers."

"I'm getting cold, Archie. I wish I'd told Tom how much I love him."

"It's hard, isn't it?"

"Yes, and perhaps too late."

And yet she found herself trying to fill the cave with words.

"Do you know that when he asked me to marry him, in amongst all this mayhem, I felt quite at peace, which as you know is not my usual starting point."

"Do you think he'll ever come to understand your faith?"

"He wants to try, which is all I can ask. Isn't it all anyone can ask?"

"Yes, yes, it is."

Anna began to shiver, uncontrollably. She wondered how much time had passed. She couldn't see where the entrance must be, even when she stared really hard and now the water was beginning to run over the ledge more times than not.

"Do you think if I tried to help you, you could sit up, Archie? It might give us a bit more time."

***

Tom skidded into the car park. Harriet tried to explain though she wasn't exactly sure what was happening.

Tom said, frowning, "So, Simeon thinks that Jim might have taken Anna and Archie to some cave along the shore." He was taking deep breaths, desperately trying to stay calm. "How long since the boat left?"

"I don't know. Forty minutes? And we didn't see the boat actually leave the ramp. By the time I saw it, I couldn't even be sure there was more than one person aboard, as it was already quite far away."

"Okay, we won't risk it. We'll call the coast guard."

Harriet had tried ringing Anna and Archie, both phones were unobtainable. They jumped when the alarm down below began to wail, bouncing off the rocks and striping the scene orange. Tom was almost sure he could feel the handrail singing with the screeching. Very quickly the first of the crew began to appear. Genni and Toby were the last to come, racing from the car park. Less than five minutes later *Rose* was accelerating down the ramp. Tom was on board with a life jacket and strict orders not to get in the way, but only because he'd used his warrant card and yelled a lot.

Keeping in as close as was safe *Rose* began to make her way along the bottom of the cliff. Near the Point, Genni spotted Derek and Simeon. They were waving Simeon's parka above their heads to catch the dying rays of the sun. Tom would have liked to have seen Simeon's face when Derek suggested that.

He'd never seen him without that coat, hood pulled down, zip done up to his chin or his nose if he was really nervous.

The acting coxswain appeared from the upper wheelhouse.

"Two things, Sir. There's a small boat heading round the Point. It looks like a dinghy. Where Derek and Simeon are pointing, is one of the larger caves. So, do we go after the dinghy, or do we try the cave? If the latter, we'll have to be quick. The tide's on the rise and we've probably not got a lot of time to get the Y Boat in." Tom didn't think there was a choice, and was almost angry when the man added, "and if anyone is in there, and they're further back than the first opening, we've had it."

"We'll get someone else to chase the dinghy. We have to assume that Archie and Anna are in that cave," he said, using the voice he reserved for his constables.

The man nodded. He turned and began to yell instructions. Genni was up front with binoculars, keeping an eye out. Toby was helping get the small boat over the stern. *Rose* was as close as she could get.

Toby appeared beside Tom and said, "Don't worry, we used that cave in an exercise last spring, we know it well."

Two of the crew clambered in and quickly began to make their way over to the cliff, the boat bouncing through the swell. They got quite small, a bright orange patch on the sea that suddenly disappeared. The radio from the wheelhouse crackled and hissed seemingly forever. Tom watched over the side, gripping the handrail. Finally, Genni turned towards him and put her thumbs up and Tom had to hold on tighter to stop himself falling to his knees.

"They've found them," she screamed above the noise of the engine and the wind. She made her way over. "It won't take us a minute to get them out, the issue will be judging the waves. The roof will be a bit close for comfort."

"Is it Anna? Anna Maybury and Archie Wainwright?"

"We don't know for sure, not yet."

Toby sidled a bit closer. He was still peering at the place where Tom assumed the cave to be.

"I tried to run."

Tom had to turn back to face him, but he didn't want to. He didn't want to drag his eyes away from the cliff, not for one second.

"Not now, son. I'll deal with you later."

Toby would have to wait until Tom was sure Anna was alright. There was an ambulance already back in the car park, so there wasn't anything else practical he could do. He'd never felt this way before, he was completely unable to switch on the police officer part of himself. It was frightening, it made him feel brittle, dysfunctional. The Chief Constable would take him apart over these few moments but there wasn't a thing Tom felt able to do. *Rose* rolled and dipped. Finally, he could see the small boat. With each crest it got nearer, until at long last it came alongside. Both Anna and Archie were almost catatonic with cold though Anna reached out an icy hand which Tom grasped and held. This time the crew didn't tell him to get out of the way. Archie didn't look good, and his breathing was a little shallow, his skin grey where it should have been pink.

"Hang in there, Archie," Tom muttered.

"Oh, don't worry about him," one of the crew said cheerfully, "he's old lifeboat! They don't die of hypothermia; they're not allowed to."

"It's in the rules, right at the bottom," someone else called from the stern. They laughed, but the sound was tinny and scared, for though Archie hadn't been on the boat for a long time he was still one of their own, and he really didn't look good. Genni appeared with another blanket to tuck around him. Tom couldn't see Toby anywhere; he hoped his sergeants were on the ball and would stop anyone from leaving.

Once they reached the ramp Genni gently pulled Tom away so they could swing Anna and Archie over the side to the waiting stretchers. She then helped him clamber off so that

Tom could go and stand beside Anna as the cage took them up to the waiting blue lights.

Anna squeezed his hand, and he bent down close to her cold face. She whispered in his ear, "Stay here. Do what you need to do, but I expect to see you later with flowers and chocolate. Lots of chocolate."

"I love you, Reverend Maybury."

"I love you too, DI Edwards."

Chapter 32

"How're you feeling?" Tom asked, holding the flowers in front of her. He looked around the vicarage living room for somewhere to put them.

"They're nice." Anna waved a hand weakly from her makeshift bed on the sofa.

"They wouldn't let me give them to you in hospital. They could probably do with some water."

They did look a little sorry for themselves, in part because Kellow had sat on them earlier, in the car.

"How are you, really?"

"I'm feeling alright. Still a little sick but that'll wear off. Has Harriet gone?"

"Yes, though she did say I wasn't to leave you alone for a second."

Anna smiled. She looked tired, her skin waxy and lined even though Harriet had said that she'd already been drowsing most of the day.

"Has she forgiven you yet?" Tom asked.

"Yes, I think so. She did tell me how silly I was, and that she was surprised it hadn't happened sooner. Did she nag you about a ring?"

"Yes. But to be fair, I had planned to wait until we went away together. Then I would have been prepared, with the ring, champagne and whatever else is required for a well thought out proposal."

"I don't need anything like that."

"Yes, you do. The biggest diamond I can get, I may have to mortgage the vicarage!"

She laughed, and then groaned. She hadn't broken a rib or dislocated her shoulders, but everything would ache for quite a while, and no one could tell her when the headaches would stop.

"Have you sorted it all out?" she asked, trying to sit up a

little straighter.

"Yes, mostly. We don't have to talk about it now."

"I want to. I want to get it out of my head."

"If you're sure." She nodded.

Tom wondered where to start. "We've got Jim and his wife's body was found by the divers, up against the back wall of the cave. It was easy once the tide turned."

Anna shivered. She shifted away and leaned against the far corner of the sofa, the throw tangled around her legs, her head tipped back. He thought she was going to be sick.

"We would've been just above where she was," she whispered.

Tom closed his eyes for a moment, trying not to imagine what would have happened if Anna had gone into the water.

"He did to her what he was attempting to do to you and Archie." In Tom's mind he was trying to reassure her that they'd got their man, but he could see he wasn't helping. Anna had gone rigid and was staring into space. He wanted to wrap his arms around her, but she might not have relaxed into him and then he wouldn't have known what to do.

"Toby killed Caz, and Margery worked it out," Anna said, quietly. "That's why she had to disappear." She shuddered. "Margery was his mum; she would have seen what he was like after Caz's disappearance and she often told Jean how worried she was about Toby and his temper." Anna glanced around, reaching her hand out to him. Tom grasped it tightly. "I bet she told Jim of her concerns, perhaps that she was going to talk to you. He would have lost his temper. He was always bending the situations that he was in, to suit himself so why not this, and I think, deep down, he thought the world of his son. Sadly, his love was of the tough variety. Man up, you'll be better for it etc, so Toby just thought he wasn't good enough.

"It all hinged on Margery's honesty and Toby and Jim's tempers. Jean told everyone that, repeatedly. Margery wouldn't have been able to keep quiet about what her son had done, she would've wanted Toby to do the right thing, to give himself up, to get some help. We should have listened to Jean much earlier; she was the key to this."

Tom shook his head in disbelief. "How do you know all this stuff?"

Anna shrugged. "Jean was really worried about Margery's disappearance. She even asked me to have a word with you about it. She was sure that Margery hadn't just run off, that because she was almost pathologically honest, there was no way she would have had an affair and been able to keep it from Jean. She shared an awful lot with her friend. I would definitely interview her if you want a fuller background."

Anna sat back but kept hold of Tom's hand. "And I should have realised earlier about the significance of Toby's temper. Genni told me she agreed with everything he said so that he wouldn't lose it with her. In that way he was just like his dad. I bet his mum knew straight away that he'd killed Caz."

"Are you going to make excuses for him?"

"No Tom, but Toby did have an awful time. He'd been bullied most of his life by his schoolmates and then by Jim on the boat. That meant Toby was lonely. Had always been lonely. Do you see?" She pulled the throw up over her knees.

Tom nodded. It was one way of looking at it. Of course it wouldn't stand up in court, not by any stretch of the imagination.

"Toby kept telling everyone that no one liked Caz, but he was the one who couldn't stand her. He was the one who felt pushed out by her, and when Genni started to help her with her revision, he would have got very jealous indeed." Anna stopped and sighed. "Any more news about Archie?" The sigh turned into a yawn. Tom was thrown a little by the sharp change in subject.

"They're keeping him in for another night. Are you sure you're okay?"

She nodded vigorously and then put a hand to her

forehead.

"Ok, it does throb a little, but Archie must have been hit harder than me, and he's a lot older."

"You say that, but you still can't be left alone for another forty-eight hours, which means they weren't completely happy about your bump." He reached out and touched her cheek. She leaned into his hand and then shuffled a little closer so he could put his arm around her.

"I've got a lump whereas Archie bled everywhere." She shivered. "It was horrible. Jim must have been so desperate."

"Well, he can't hurt you anymore." Tom held her a little tighter. "When he got to Mullion, he seemed so surprised we were there, but some part of him must have understood it was all over."

"He's not been right since Margery. It was clever of him to put her body in that cave, though. Who would have thought to look? And if she had ever been found then Jim could have said she'd probably fallen in up near the Point. He's an expert on the currents around there and we'd all have believed him."

Tom said, "The divers found all sorts of pots and rope that had been trapped in there over the years, so he knew there was a chance she wouldn't come out again."

"Thank goodness you got to us in time." Again, Anna shivered. Tom knew that processing what had happened would take a while.

"And Jim?" Tom was reluctant to ask what he already knew, but he could see Anna wanted to talk, to get it over and done with.

"I think Jim attacked me because he overheard Toby and I talking. I can see how it might have sounded as if Toby had just confessed, and despite everything, Jim wanted to protect his son. Archie was caught up in it just because he was there.

"It was inevitable that having used the cave to hide Margery so successfully, Jim would try to do the same to us, once he thought we knew. Thank goodness he only knocked us out and didn't finish us off."

Both Toby and Jim were cooperating down at the station. Toby, telling the bare and unlovely truth; Jim a series of stories that were getting more and more far-fetched with each new question. Anna snuggled in closer.

"Toby tried to confess on the lifeboat. I didn't arrest him until you were safe. I think if you'd been hurt or worse, I might have done something I would have regretted."

"No, no you wouldn't have. Not you," she said, into his chest.

He was reassured but felt guilty that he didn't put her straight. Instead, he let her continue.

"To begin with I did wonder if it might be Genni. Gradually, I changed my mind. Nothing specific, I think I just grew to know her better. So, it had to be Toby or his dad. And of course, Caz was always needling Toby about Genni. She didn't think Toby was anywhere near good enough for her friend and she repeatedly told him so. Toby struggled with low self-esteem and a lack of confidence. He was bullied and teased, and he felt on the outside of everything. Caz challenging the one thing he thought he had control over was the last straw."

"Why did he come back? If he'd made a run for it, we might not have caught him."

"That's because he'd thought his mother had left them because she'd met someone else, then when he was with Simeon, he realised Simeon really thought we were in danger from his dad. When the pager went off, what with the adrenalin and urgency, he probably began to think there was a real possibility that his dad had killed his mum. After that I'm not quite sure."

"What about Caz?" Tom asked.

"I think Toby just wanted to see her and Genni together, to confirm his worst fears. So he went down to the station. Only Caz was on her own because Genni had got caught by the headmistress. Caz goaded him for the last time. When she didn't turn up for the next few practices Genni got more and more worried. She didn't put two and two together until a lot later, but she knew something was up for ages before."

Tom nodded. Toby had said as much. Caz even taunted him with the log she'd been keeping of his dad's bullying. Dates with detailed incidents, how she was made to feel. Toby had already warned Jim to be more careful and there was Caz about to blow the whistle, complete with written proof.

Anna suddenly wriggled to the other end of the sofa. She looked at Tom and whispered, "Did she run? Up the steps to the top platform?"

"Yes. How on earth did you know?"

"When Toby and I were walking down together, Toby hesitated there and almost jumped over that part, as if it were too hot to step on. Caz did well to get that far, all the way up from the bottom. He was fast. The fastest. He's been on the top of the crew leader board for months."

"He says he lost it. He'd still got the rope in his hand from practising, and he began to scream at her. She must have got really scared because she went off like a bullet. When he finally caught her, he flipped the rope around her neck and pulled it tight."

Tom held his hand out to her, and Anna caught it again.

"He wouldn't have meant to kill her, and he wouldn't have known what to do next," Anna mused, "that'll be why he took her body and stuffed it into the crevice, at Beacon Point. It's not that far from the top of the steps and he's certainly strong enough to have carried her; she was so petite.

"He told me a couple of times he wasn't good at dealing with things straight away, that he needed time to work stuff out. I thought he was just telling me he felt a bit stupid about Genni and life, but he was really trying to tell me what he'd done." She stiffened for a minute and though Tom couldn't see her face, he knew she'd be looking thoughtful. "As the weeks went by and no one discovered Caz, I expect he thought he'd got away with it or perhaps the whole thing was eating away at him so badly he didn't move her because he hoped she would be found."

Tom patted her arm.

"He did say he hoped she'd be found. And that he hadn't gone there to kill her. He'd arrived early, had been practising the knots with his sea gloves on when Caz turned up. Hence none of his DNA on the rope."

"Good. He's not evil, Tom, and he's been living a rollercoaster of emotions for ages now."

"You're quite good at this, aren't you?"

"Sitting in that cave thinking I might die made me realise it was important to know why I was there! Archie was muddled because of the blow to the head but I was thinking clearly."

Tom suddenly wanted to put his hand across her mouth, to stop her talking. To calmly sit in front of him and speak about dying was too much for him.

"I wish you wouldn't do that," he said, fiercely. "I couldn't manage without you. I just couldn't."

"You could. You'd have your mum and your job."

"But I wouldn't be the best Tom I could be."

He kissed the ends of her fingers. It was time for a change of subject. "Do you think anything is going on with Georgie and our Simeon?" he asked.

"What makes you say that?" she said, stiffening again and he couldn't imagine what expression she had on her face this time.

"Just something you said. That they were writing to each other, and that she's been getting up early to walk Belle with him. It seems an odd thing to do when she normally comes here to crash."

"Only because she wants him to help her with some of the hard questions her young people ask."

Tom leaned far enough to see the frown on Anna's face as she considered this.

"Georgie *has* been driving down more than usual, but don't forget how important Simeon was to her. His view of God and how to have faith is simple, deeply profound, humbling even. If you've lost your way, he's a good place to start on the journey back." Anna was now biting her lip, clearly not quite convinced by her own explanation. Tom found himself inordinately pleased to have thought of something she hadn't.

"Shall I go and talk to Simeon about God?"

Anna giggled.

"Well, it's never going to be me or your mum. Archie would be wonderful too, of course." She sighed. "He'll be alright, won't he?"

"Yes. And you'll all gather around him to make sure it's so."

Tom realised he sounded as if he were a little jealous, which was because he was. Would they ever truly accept him as one of them?

Anna rolled off the sofa and stood up very slowly. The doctor had said she might get dizzy.

"Fancy a cup of tea?" she asked, her face flushed, her eyes bright.

He stood up and kissed her, gently pushing her back down again and went to put the kettle on.

"I've got this, Reverend Maybury."

Acknowledgments

Writing feels like a lonely process until I think of all the people who have helped along the way and who I would like to thank.

Eleanor Wallace, who read this when it was in a very early incarnation. She had not perused any of the earlier books, so her notes were wonderfully pertinent. I would particularly like to thank her for the positive comments. It literally made all the difference in the world.

Kate Yates, so meticulous and so patient with me, and who taught me so much about consistency.

Jutta Mackwell. I don't tell her enough how grateful I am for her ongoing support. Her kindness, the time she spends reading and considering. I hope she knows how much her input means to me.

Bridget Scrannage. A huge thank you, because once again, she had to sort out the timeline, the number of characters, and all my annoying writing ticks. For teaching me so much. For taking the manuscript and making it work. Really work.

Thank you to Ann Peacocke, for putting on the final gloss by checking the final draft.

Tim Evans, Operations Manager at RNLI Headquarters, Poole, who allowed me to ask as many questions as I wanted, from the engineering finesse of the Tamar class to whether they are able to make a cup of tea on board! He was infinitely patient and generous with his time. And I do now know that no Coxswain would drop a member of the crew over the side any more, even in a dry suit. Any other errors are entirely mine alone! Thank you to everyone at The Lizard lifeboat station, for their enthusiasm and kindness.

And finally, Mike. You listen to me working it all out. You watch me swoop and dive through the many stages of self-doubt and self-worth. You never praise unless it's merited, so I value your judgement, particularly as I can argue with you like no other — thank you.

The Reverend Anna Maybury Series

by

Kirsty A. Wilmott

Watching You Fall
Falling Tide
Missing You

Milton Keynes UK
Ingram Content Group UK Ltd.
UKHW010650081023
430140UK00001B/1